PRAISE FOR *THE FIVE*

"One of the best books I've read all year."

—*Literal Addiction*

"A strong series debut. . . . Intense and satisfying sex scenes. . . . Nicely resolved plot tangles and interesting characters bode well for future books."

—*Publishers Weekly*

"I was completely captivated. . . . The pull is magnetic, and you CANNOT put the book down."

—*Paranormal Haven*

"This story drags its characters through the bowels of hell while driving them closer and closer together, making you savor every moment of happiness in all the turmoil."

—*Coffee Time Romance*

"Outstanding. . . . Quinn uses innovative ideas to make her story constantly spellbinding. . . . Filled with blazing passion."

—*Single Titles*

"Creative, unbelievably action-packed, with a really heart-warming romance."

—*Smitten with Reading*

"Quinn never disappoints, as she proves with this brand-new series."

—*The Good, the Bad and the Unread*

"There is only one word to describe this first book in a new series: Amazing!"

—*BTS Book Reviews Magazine*

Also from Erin Quinn and Pocket Books

The Five Deaths of Roxanne Love

Also from Erin Quinn

The Mists of Ireland Series

Haunting Beauty
Haunting Warrior
Haunting Desire
Haunting Embrace

Echoes
Diablo Springs
Web of Smoke

The Three Fates of Ryan Love

Erin Quinn

POCKET BOOKS
New York London Toronto Sydney New Delhi

Pocket Books
A Division of Simon & Schuster, Inc.
1230 Avenue of the Americas
New York, NY 10020

First Pocket Books paperback edition February 2015

Cover design by Min Choi
Cover art by Craig White

Manufactured in the United States of America

10 9 8 7 6 5 4 3 2 1

ISBN 978-1-4767-2749-3
ISBN 978-1-4767-2753-0 (ebook)

To my mother, who's read every word of every book.
Twice. I love you, Mom.

ACKNOWLEDGMENTS

I am so grateful to my amazing editor, Abby Zidle, who pushes (okay, sometimes shoves) me in the right direction and makes me a better writer. Thank you.

Many thanks also go to my longtime agent, Paige Wheeler, who keeps me sane, which is no easy feat.

And from the bottom of my heart, thanks to you, reader, for selecting my books when you have so many wonderful books to choose from. I hope Ryan's story will make you glad you did.

1

Ryan heard the first of the sirens as he turned into the home stretch of his run. He ran most every night after he closed Love's, the bar he owned with his two sisters. The exercise usually cleared his mind, but not tonight. A storm had started brewing as he'd clocked the first mile and the kind of cold that was indigenous to the desert seeped beneath his skin and made old wounds ache. The glowering sky pressed down on him, sinister against the excessive Christmas lights twinkling merrily around every palm tree and the festive banners that snapped in the bitter wind. Instead of clearheaded, Ryan felt chased.

His German shepherd, Brandy, ran at his side, ears up and swiveling. Even she didn't seem to be enjoying the ritual as much as usual.

Glad when Love's came into sight, Ryan slowed his steps and tried to catch his breath. The sirens were closer now and a police car flew past to join more flashing lights about a block down the street. It was after two in the morning, but Mill Avenue near Arizona State University never really slept. Probably drunks out causing trouble. Maybe even the three he'd thrown out of Love's that night. They'd left him with a bruised face and sore ribs.

Watching through the spitting rain, Ryan cut across an alley and into the parking lot behind Love's. That's when he heard the woman scream.

He spun to face the nook between the south wall of Love's and the cinder-block barrier that hid the side door to the kitchen. He peered into the dark recess, sure that's where the sound had come from, but nothing moved. Brandy's ear swiveled as she barked, trying to sniff and see everything at once. She didn't seem able to pinpoint the scream either.

The next scream echoed around him at the same time pressure filled the space behind his ears and made him feel unbalanced. He stumbled back as lightning flashed and a tremendous bolt snapped down right in front of him. When he looked again, a woman sat inside the small, sheltered alcove with her knees pulled up and her arms wrapped around them. Seconds ago, only darkness had waited there. Long, dark hair gleamed under the muted light, spilling over her shoulders and hiding her face. Her skin had an alabaster sheen. There was a lot of it, too. He frowned. She was naked.

With a hand signal for Brandy to sit, Ryan wiped the rain from his face and approached her cautiously. The walls and awning shielded her from the rain, but not the cold. She shivered violently as he crouched down in front of her.

"Hey," he said in a soft voice. "How'd you get here? Are you okay?"

She looked up with wide, clear eyes as blue as a desert sky. Even in the dark the color was vivid and they shimmered with something he couldn't begin to define. Long lashes the same rich shade as her hair framed them and accented their luminescent glow. They tilted at the corners, catlike. The dark wings of her brows drew focus to the shape of her face, the smooth line of her nose, the dusting of freckles that covered it.

He dropped his gaze and saw a raw scrape on her shin, another up high on her thigh. A third marred her shoulder. He thought of the sirens and police he'd heard. Was she involved in whatever had been happening?

"Ryan?" she whispered, chasing that thought right out of his head.

The sound of his name on her lips raised the hairs at the back of his neck, somehow trumping everything else. Like who she was, what she was doing here stark naked in the middle of the night.

"You know me?"

He peered into her face, sure he'd never seen her before.

"You're Ryan," she said with more certainty.

Her gaze shifted to something behind him. Ryan looked over his shoulder to find Brandy right at his heels with perked ears and a wet, wagging tail, watching the woman. The woman stared back at his dog with what Ryan would swear was wonder.

"Who are you?" he asked.

"Sabelle," she replied, still watching his dog.

Brandy got down on her belly, inching closer in the most unthreatening manner a ninety-five-pound German shepherd could manage.

"Where are your clothes, Sybil?"

She shook her head, pulling her gaze from Brandy to look him in the eye. "S'*belle*," she corrected. "Not Sybil."

"S'belle," he pronounced carefully. "Why are you naked?"

A hot flush turned her skin pink a second before she lied. "I don't remember."

She shifted with agitation and Brandy made a sound low in her throat. Not aggressive. Consoling. The dog had managed to army-crawl close enough to put her big fluffy head on the woman's lap. Sabelle's lips parted as she settled her fingers on Brandy's silky black ear.

She shivered and goose bumps rose on her skin. Ryan quickly reached over his head and pulled off his shirt. It was warm from his body, but damp from the rain. It would cover her, though.

"Here, put this on," he said, handing it over.

She accepted it, fingering the soft fabric before she pressed it to her face, smelling it. The action was so surprising that at first all he could think to do was mumble, "Sorry, it's all I have," while hot embarrassment flooded his face.

"It smells like you," she said.

Like it was a good thing.

His mouth opened but no words came out. He lowered his eyes while she pulled the shirt over her head. When he looked back, she was covered, thank God. His shirt was huge on her. The shoulders drooped to her elbows and the long sleeves hid her hands.

She huddled in it, her gaze roaming his face, lingering on the cut over his nose, the puffy skin on his cheek, and his swollen jaw. He almost felt the quicksilver stare on his bare chest and bruised ribs. He must look like a big, ugly thug to her.

She had bruises and scrapes of her own. He could only hope that her wounds had come from something less violent than his had.

"What happened to you? Did someone hurt you?" he asked.

"No," she said with a definitive shake of her head.

"You screamed."

"I didn't expect it to be painful."

"You didn't expect *what* to be painful?"

She flinched at his sharp tone. "Coming here."

He didn't know what to say to that. *Here*—in the parking lot in the middle of the night—wasn't anyplace she should be, but she'd obviously been hurt, was probably in shock. She might not even know where she was. He dug his phone out of his pocket and leaned in so the rain running down his back wouldn't get it wet as he dialed 911.

The storm picked up its pace, hitting the asphalt with such force that raindrops bounced and pooled, pounding the awning overhead with fury. Storms moved fast in Arizona, but this was insane.

"Who are you calling?" she asked.

"The police. They'll—"

She snatched the phone out of his hand and hit the screen repeatedly until the ring cut off.

Ryan's mouth was open again. "Okay, now it's getting weird."

"No police," she said. "What time is it?"

When he didn't answer immediately, she repeated the question sharply.

"I don't know. Two, three in the morning?"

Her eyes rounded and she scrambled to get her feet under her. "We need to go. Now, Ryan."

She stood, long legs protruding from his big shirt. Her hair brushed her shoulders and impatiently she swiped it back. Standing as well, Ryan reached out to steady her as she swayed.

"Easy, girl," he murmured gently. "Slow down. Take a breath. You're safe now. Let's get the police here. They'll get everything worked out."

"No police," she insisted. "They can't help."

"Yeah, well . . ." *Neither could he.* "Can I have my phone back?"

She turned and started out of the shelter.

"Wait," he said. "Sabelle Whoever-You-Are. Wait."

She seemed more alert, more focused, but she'd obviously hit her head. She tucked her arms tight, hands jammed under her pits and head bent as she gingerly picked her way through the glass, gravel, mud, and puddles covering the parking lot, ignoring him until she stepped on something sharp and gasped.

"Hold up. Would you stop?" he said, exasperated. "Let me help you."

He lifted her in his arms and carried her to the back door before she could protest. She wasn't a big woman, but she was lush with all the right curves in all the right places. She felt solid against his chest and soft in ways that played games with his traitorous thoughts and made him glad for the bracing rain. Brandy escorted them like a devoted admirer, her wet nose brushing Sabelle's feet whenever the dog could reach them. Ryan paused before opening the door, half convinced he was making a big mistake. This was the kind of thing you saw on the news where some dumb putz just trying to help ended up accused of wrongdoing.

He jockeyed her weight as he fumbled his keys from his pocket into the lock. Sabelle tightened her arms around him, pressing all those feminine curves closer as Ryan tried valiantly not to notice.

Darkness clustered just inside and obscured the stairs all the way up. The rain boomed against the roof and the cold made plumes of their breath. His skin felt icy.

Except where he held Sabelle. She was like a furnace heating his bare chest.

The door slammed shut behind them as Ryan hit the lights and set Sabelle on her feet again. She continued to hold on to him, staring into his face as if to memorize his features. For all her crazy talk, her eyes looked clear and focused in the dim glow.

Then she twisted away and started up the stairs to his apartment without asking or waiting for an invitation. With a muttered curse, Ryan started to follow, but fingers of disquiet played down his spine, making him pause.

The area under the stairs to his apartment served as storage for cases of beer and other supplies. A door straight ahead made a convenient back entrance to the bar, just as the door behind him was a quick shortcut to the parking lot. Usually the stairwell smelled of cardboard, hops, and old french fries. Familiar, comfortable odors that lingered in most bars. Tonight a whiff of rotten eggs hung over it.

Sabelle was already at his front door, waiting. He'd figured out what smelled after he dealt with her. She tried the knob, found it unlocked, and let herself in before he made it up the stairs. Stunned by her audacity, he picked up his pace. Brandy raced ahead and was beside her as Sabelle padded past the kitchen breakfast bar, trailing fingers over the back of the couch as she took in her surroundings.

His apartment was a loft that stretched over Love's. One room with a wall of windows, it had a spacious, open feel that suited him. Her gaze lingered on the screen sectioning off his bedroom before moving to the clock on the microwave. The digital display read 2:30. He saw her note it with a deep breath and a nod.

"There's still time." She faced him with determination. "I've come with a warning. Your life is in danger."

He might have smiled if she hadn't looked so distressed. "Okay," he said carefully.

She nodded, apparently satisfied with that response. "Good. I'd hoped you'd understand. We need to leave here." She glanced at the clock again. "Quickly."

"And go where?" he said, not understanding at all.

"Away from here. *Here* is where it happens."

Ryan studied her, suddenly weary to the bone. Ever since his brother's bizarre death—*Murder? Suicide?* Ryan doubted he'd ever know the truth—Love's had been a tourist attraction for lunatics. Fanatics who thought that Ryan's twin brother and sister were blessed by the heavens or cursed by demons had always been on the fringe of their lives. Reece and Roxanne had died—and miraculously been revived—more than once. It went with the territory.

Some of the crazies were dangerous, others merely curious. He didn't know which camp Sabelle fell into, but the sooner he got her out of here, the better.

"You don't believe me," Sabelle said with a hint of disappointment in her voice. "I don't know why I'm surprised. It's in your nature to be suspicious. You have trust issues."

Maybe so. But that was his business. "What's this danger I'm supposedly in?" he asked politely.

"Death," she replied almost eagerly. "Yours, I mean."

He let out a deep breath and shook his head. "Listen, Sabelle. I'd like to help you, get you someplace safe. How about back home?" *Or the psych ward you escaped from?*

"I can never go home," she said vehemently.

He lifted his hands, palms out. "Fair enough. But you can't stay here. I just pulled a twelve-hour shift. I'm tired. All I want is a hot shower and bed."

Her eyes widened and she shot another quick glance at the screen that hid his bed. Something darkly erotic flashed across her features. For a moment, he couldn't look away.

"I know you don't believe me," she said, her voice breathy and low, "but this isn't a game or a joke. You can't just take a shower and pretend it will go away. Do you think I would risk so much to warn you if there was nothing to fear?"

"I think you're a confused woman who needs some help."

"I'm not confused. An explosion will decimate this building sometime between now and three a.m. Your apartment will be incinerated. Boom. *Gone.*"

"Between now and three a.m.," he repeated, deadpan.

"Stop it. Stop pretending disbelief you don't feel."

"Oh, I feel it."

Narrowed eyes were the only clue that she'd heard him. She didn't argue, she didn't try to add details to support her claim. Most liars did.

"You'll need the money you have stashed beneath the floorboards in your bedroom," she said with a challenging glance. "Clothes, of course. And Brandy. We'll need her."

"We?"

"I don't know how much time we have, Ryan. I only know that by three it will all be over. For both of us."

She was all-in when it came to this fantasy quest, and her conviction planted a seed of doubt that startled him.

"You are more important than you know, Ryan."

The laugh he'd tried for earlier finally emerged and his doubt waned. The poor woman was definitely delusional.

"I own a pub. Actually, I own about one-fiftieth of a pub. The bank owns the rest. I spend most of my days and nights behind a bar, serving drinks to people who have less of a life than I do. Unless it's critical that the drunks get their next drink, I'm the opposite of important."

With a superior-sounding sniff, she moved behind the Japanese screen and into his bedroom. Dumbfounded, Ryan followed, watching her open his closet. She yanked his backpack off the top shelf and stuffed his favorite jeans, a T-shirt, and a flannel button-down into it.

As she turned, she caught her reflection in the dresser mirror and did a double take. For a moment, she stared at her pale face like she'd expected to see someone else looking back.

He tilted his head to the side, watching her watch herself. She saw the movement and quickly glanced away, but her cheeks pinked up and she avoided looking at him. She began opening his drawers like she had every right.

And instead of throwing her out on her pretty little ass, he watched her, still trying to figure out what to do about her. Wrestle his phone away? Humor her back outside and lock the doors behind her?

The storm boomed so loud it shook the walls. He couldn't throw her out in this.

In his top drawer, she found his briefs, added a pair to the pack, and pulled open the next drawer. She rummaged until she retrieved some basketball shorts and held them up to her hips. When she tugged them on, she gave him an eyeful of long legs and bare behind.

She turned and busted him staring. His gaze snared hers and something darkened in the uncertain blue. Neither one of them looked away.

"Do you have shoes I could borrow?" she asked, her voice husky.

He pointed to the other closet door. It took her a moment to turn around and slide the door open. She eyed his size 14 shoes dubiously before she spotted a pair of flip-flops on the floor and slipped her feet into them.

"Get the money, Ryan."

Crazy with sprinkles on top. That's what this was.

"You planning on robbing me?" he managed to say.

She faced him. "Is that what you think? Are you afraid I'm going to tackle you and steal all your precious belongings?"

She was swimming in his big shirt. The shorts hung down to her knees and the flip-flops looked like snowshoes on her feet. She had the threat potential of a puppy.

Again he wished he could muster a laugh. Instead, "No" emerged in a wooden tone.

"Get your stuff and wait it out on the sidewalk with me, then. If nothing happens by three, you can call your police and wash your hands of me."

She handed him his phone like a gesture of good faith. He took it.

"Or I could do that now and save myself the trouble."

"Yes. You could do that. But we'd both pay the price for your stupidity."

"Did you just call me—"

"You are in *danger*," she said, enunciating each syllable sharply. "You're going to die if you don't trust me. How much clearer can I be? I know you're the kind of man who has to see something to believe it. But why not see it from the outside with me?"

With that, she grabbed his backpack and dropped it at his feet.

He still hadn't moved, but Sabelle didn't wait. She crossed to the front door with a stiff back and an air of determination, ridiculous in her borrowed getup and yet somehow . . . convincing.

"How would you know what kind of man I am?" he asked softly.

The question made her pause. She shot a guarded glance over her shoulder, eyes wide and lips parted. Bravado and hunger stared back at him, a combination so mystifying that it shut his mouth.

So what if she was right? It wouldn't be the strangest thing to have happened in the past month. Hell, in the last week. Even as common sense told him that it was more likely she had someone waiting downstairs to relieve him of the money she'd insisted he pack, he felt himself giving in.

She'd said *beneath the floorboards.* If she already knew where he kept the money, why not just break in and steal it while he'd been out for his run? Why the elaborate naked-and-afraid act?

"I see you thinking," she said. "You're deciding on all the reasons not to trust me. But that's wasting time you don't have. Look at the clock, Ryan." She paused. "*Please.*"

It was the hitch in her voice that unplugged his common sense and pushed him to the edge.

He exhaled a heavy breath. "Let me get a shirt."

The tremulous smile she couldn't hide fast enough called him a fool, but the baby blues sent another coded message he couldn't be sure he was reading right. He ducked behind the screen that divided the rooms and pried up the floorboard by his bed with a long flathead screwdriver he kept in his nightstand drawer just for that purpose. He stuffed the whole hard-earned $10K into his backpack, shrugged on a shirt, and snagged jackets for both of them on his way out. What could it hurt to sit in his truck and wait it out? If nothing else, maybe he'd get to the bottom of her story.

She waited impatiently by the door, watching the clock switch numbers. Brandy sat at her feet, ready to go. According to Sabelle, they had less than fifteen minutes to get out of there before the whole place was incinerated.

"Hurry," she said and stepped onto the landing without a backward glance.

Shaking his head, Ryan clicked his tongue for Brandy to follow and locked the door behind him.

2

Sabelle felt Ryan following her all the way down the stairs. Outside, the storm raged in vengeance and she tried not to pin more importance on it than it deserved. But it was hard. It could be a storm and it could be the Sisters. Knowing what they planned for Ryan, it seemed wise to consider the latter. The storm could be a symptom of their anger.

They would know she was gone by now.

When they reached the bottom of the stairs, Ryan paused, muttering, "Something smells rotten down here."

Sabelle got a whiff of the pungent odor, too, but her sense of smell was something new and the only scent that mattered to her was the warm, masculine one that clung to Ryan's jacket. She pressed her nose into the collar as he took her hand and the lead, turning right toward the pub instead of to the left and the parking lot where he'd found her.

His hand was warm against hers. She felt it from her fingertips to someplace low and deep inside her, a human reaction to his nearness that disconcerted and delighted her. She'd imagined it enough times, but she'd never considered the impact of *feeling*.

They entered the pub from a door behind the bar with Brandy racing ahead. A hundred times she'd seen Ryan's family pub through his eyes, but she'd never seen it through her own. She'd never imagined the *taste* of it. The air was thick and malty, sharp and sour all at once. The graying walls held memories of secrets shared by friends long gone. Framed pictures of Ryan's relatives posing with people she didn't know watched her pass, judging her from their lofty positions.

High up along the front wall, stained glass in brilliant emerald and dusty rose filtered the streetlights and danced pastels over the long, smooth bar. Below them, hazy picture windows looked out on a deserted street where twinkling Christmas lights glimmered from every tree and pole she could see.

"It's smaller than I expected," she murmured.

Ryan gave her a questioning look but she didn't say more. The responsibility of the pub had always seemed such a huge burden for Ryan that she'd expected an echoing chamber instead of a cozy niche. Her steps faltered as she stared at the empty tables and chairs, knowing soon they'd be rubble and ash. Ryan tugged her hand.

"Did you forget we're about to be incinerated?"

Not something to joke about, but he'd figure that out

on his own. Pack on his back, Ryan took a few steps toward the exit and stilled. He sniffed the air again.

"Fuck," he breathed. "That's gas."

His accusing gaze swiveled toward her. The fury of the storm amplified the silence inside the bar as the moment stretched. Hail began to pelt the walls and sidewalk. It battered the roof and bombarded the windows.

Ryan cursed again and moved to the door, Sabelle's fingers firmly clasped in his. She matched his stride, suddenly worried that she'd gotten it wrong and they'd run out of time. He had the key in the lock and the door opened in seconds.

"Keep your head down," he said, shrugging out of the jacket he wore and holding it over them both. "Get closer."

Dutifully, she obeyed, wrapping her arm around his waist to anchor her to his side.

"Brandy, come," he ordered as they stepped onto the sidewalk. Brandy didn't look too keen on the idea, but she scooted out and stayed close.

"Good girl," he praised as the icy wet wind blasted into them.

Ryan didn't take the time to lock this door behind him. Filled with panic, Sabelle held on as they raced across the street, hail hammering them with vengeance. When they reached the shelter of the awning on the other side, Sabelle finally looked up.

Inside, Ryan's pub had seemed small, but outside on the street the world felt endless.

Dark buildings stared vacantly down at the lights twinkling at street level. *Happy Holidays* banners flailed in the frigid onslaught. They passed in front of a bus stop with an advertisement pasted to its back wall showing a hotel nestled in a cove of towering red rocks. Someone had spray-painted black eyeballs over it and signed *Wa Chu* beneath in an elaborate font. She noted it grimly.

Hail bounced against the street like clouded diamonds. Beside her, Ryan stood warm and strong.

This was really happening.

Ryan faced Love's with a look of foreboding on his face that she'd seen before. She knew that as a boy he'd held his finger against the leaking holes his mother's death had caused in the family. He had better methods as a man, but he was still patching the dike with his very soul.

She couldn't stop looking at him. Couldn't keep her thoughts focused on anything but where he stood in relation to her. The rhythm of his breathing. His smell. He was the kind of man people depended on. The kind she hoped she could, too.

He pulled her into a recessed doorway, dug his phone out of his pocket, and punched in some numbers. While he listened, a hot breeze whisked around them, tugging at the hem of her shirt, tousling his hair. It felt so good in the icy cold that Sabelle turned in to its warmth.

A tinny voice answered Ryan's call. "Nine-one-one operator. What's your emergency?"

"There's a gas leak at—"

Lightning snaked from the sky with deadly purpose and struck one of the streetlights directly across from them. It blinded them but Sabelle heard the snap, the sizzle, the *boom* as the light exploded.

"Jesus," Ryan exclaimed, turning to her as a fiery blast pressed against her eardrums, so loud it deafened. "Get down!" Ryan hauled her to the ground with him.

They hit the concrete hard, Ryan beneath her, cushioning her fall before rolling on top of her as a blistering wind seared them. Hot debris shattered windows and impaled the buildings lining both sides of the street. It sucked all of the oxygen away with a shriek. Sabelle screamed—or at least she thought she did. She couldn't hear her own cry over the destruction. It seemed to go on in never-ending waves and yet it was done in seconds, leaving an ominous silence in its wake.

Ryan lifted his head and looked at her. "You all right?"

At least she thought that's what he said. She couldn't hear, but she nodded anyway, not really sure if it was true.

"Brandy," he shouted, already on his feet and pulling Sabelle up with him.

Brandy darted out of a doorway a few feet away, barking madly, wild-eyed.

"It's okay, it's okay," Ryan said, hunkering down so she could smell him. Apparently, the dog needed Ryan's scent as much as Sabelle did.

She stared at the sidewalk, taking short, quick breaths when she wanted one deep one. Her hands shook and her eyes streamed from the smoke. Terror poisoned her bloodstream and blanked her mind. Some distant part of her noticed that the hail had stopped. Was that a good or bad sign? She didn't know.

"Sabelle," Ryan said. She thought it might be the second time. He stepped in front of her and took her face in his warm hands. "You okay? Are you hurt?"

His gaze moved over her and he seemed to find his own answer. He drew her into his arms and gratefully she pressed her face to his throat as her body shook with reaction. He turned them both so he could see the damage to Love's.

Across the street a black cloud of smoke thundered out of the hole where the front doors of Love's used to be. The upstairs was a jagged silhouette outlined in fire. The flames stretched high and swept across the sky with glee.

It had happened. And, against all odds, she'd succeeded. Ryan still lived. Because of her.

"Hey," Ryan said gently. "Look at me."

She hid her fear as she met his gaze. He searched her eyes before murmuring, "Good girl."

Just like he said to the dog. She laughed, pressing her face back into his warmth.

Fire spread from Love's to engulf everything in front of it, turning the banners into sparking bursts of blue flame, and burning through the trees. Two doors down from the decimated pub, another explosion blew out windows and shot sizzling fingers into the sky, where the wind snatched them up and whisked them along.

Without a word, she and Ryan ran away from it. Black smoke thundered after them and more flames jumped from awning to awning. Another explosion rattled windows and jarred the sidewalk. Sparks bounced in the sucking wind and a rain of embers showered her back. She looked over her shoulder to make sure she wasn't on fire and gave a sigh of relief when she didn't see anything smoldering. Brandy ran beside Ryan, head swiveling as she watched for danger.

Sabelle pulled her shirt over her mouth and nose to block out the suffocating smoke, but it stung her eyes and burned her throat. She coughed as it seared her lungs.

Dread made it hard to think. Hard to do anything but hold on while the fire licked its blazing tongue at everything it passed. She clenched her eyes tight, but *not* seeing made it worse.

Ryan turned down an alley that dead-ended at a concrete wall. She could see it ahead, pale blocks that reflected the smoke and fire barreling down on them. He raced toward it with purpose, pulling her along with him.

Sabelle chanced a glance over her shoulder. The smoke bore down on them and it seemed that something moved beneath the surface. It pressed out, stretching like a membrane. Then it was gone, leaving her with the impression of an eyeless face and gnashing teeth.

Once he reached the wall, Ryan braced his back against it and held out his hands for her. "Over the wall, Sabelle. That's it. Climb. Go."

She quickly stepped onto his thigh and he used his hands to lift as she shifted, hefting her weight until her right foot found his solid shoulder and her left swung over. She scraped her bare thighs as she straddled the sharp edge of cinder block.

Ryan scooped Brandy into his arms. She clung to him like a baby. Sabelle reached down and grabbed hold of Brandy's scruff as Ryan heaved her into Sabelle's arms.

"Watch out for cactus on the other side," he warned as he swung up beside her. The fire surged to fill the space he'd just vacated and the building on the corner detonated, sending shrapnel everywhere. She felt the bite of its heat against her cheek, smelled burning hair, roasting flesh. Brandy yelped in pain.

"Go!" Ryan shouted.

She didn't have time to brace or consider. She wrapped her arms around the frightened dog and jumped.

A soft, grassy bed waited on the other side, but she and Brandy came at it fast and flailing. Claws dug into Sabelle's side as the dog pushed off. Brandy spun and got her paws under her, but Sabelle slammed down on her shoulder and rolled.

Her head struck something hard and blinding pain ripped through her. She ended on her back staring up at the startling sky. Ryan hit the ground with more skill but less bounce. She felt the impact of his body crash down. Somewhere in the distance she heard the scream of sirens racing toward them.

Ryan sat up quickly, shook his head to clear it, and looked around to find her. He rolled to his knees and crawled to where she lay, collapsing in the soft winter grass and pulling her up against him. A sharp whistle brought Brandy to his other side. Ryan put an arm around each and held them tight.

They were both breathing heavily, coughing as the smoke they'd inhaled caught in their chests. The fire didn't cross the wall, but the smoke followed them and blotted out the stars. It felt like a message—a show of power. Ryan's hand was warm and comforting against the bare skin at the small of her back. She concentrated on that instead.

They lay like that for a long moment, neither of them saying a word. Finally Ryan turned his head and looked at her.

He had questions and it wouldn't be long before he wanted answers. Sabelle gathered up her scattered wits, ticked off the salient points of her story in her mind, and tried not to get ahead of herself.

Step one, save Ryan Love. Mission accomplished.

Step two, bind him to her. Work in progress.

3

The wall they'd jumped had put them inside the grounds of a resort known for its prime location in downtown Tempe and for its picturesque setting. Even at this hour, lights still glowed brightly around the hotel, and as Ryan stepped from the grassy knoll where he'd landed with Sabelle, he felt like he'd stumbled onto a spotlit stage. Straight ahead, wide glass doors led from the lobby to a horseshoe driveway. This late, there weren't any cars waiting for the bellboys to unload them, but a handful of uniformed employees joined a few other people milling around, peering curiously down the street where the red and blue glow of emergency lights flashed. No one even noticed the two of them crossing the lawn to the street.

Things weren't exploding anymore, and the rain had helped with the spread of fire, but the smoke was thick and acrid. Brandy huddled close as Ryan led Sabelle around the corner and back to the place they'd fled. Neither one of them spoke. Oh, he had a list of questions a mile long for Miss Sabelle Whoever-She-Was, but right now he needed to see the damage to Love's, needed to know if it was as catastrophic as it seemed in that last glance before they'd fled. The storm eased by the moment, leaving a cold drizzle and damp gusts behind.

Drawn by the explosions and sirens, people had already started to gather at the edges of the disaster zone. Police tape gave them clear boundaries, but news and camera crews pushed up against it, wanting to capture any grisly detail they could. The businesses that had bordered Love's were in ruins as well as two across the street. Ryan's second-story loft had been incinerated—just as the woman beside him had predicted—and all but the shell of walls had been blasted away. Ash drifted in the air like dirty snowflakes and the char of his burned future made each breath bitter.

"Brandy," he said as they approached the gathering. "Look small."

Brandy dutifully hung her head and bent her doggy elbows—a trick he'd taught her years ago. She'd never look harmless, but she pulled off pitiful like a champ.

"Good girl."

Her tail wagged nervously.

Ryan was a big man, used to having people get out of his way. But he must have looked every bit as bad as he felt, because he heard murmurs and dismayed exclamations as the small crowd parted for them. When they reached the edge of the police tape, he glanced at Sabelle and caught her wincing.

"You okay?" he asked.

She nodded and reached for his hand, sucking in a soft breath at his touch. Every time they touched, as a matter of fact. As if some sensory overload were going on inside her. God knew she was blowing all his fuses.

He caught the attention of one of the uniformed officers and the man hurried over.

"Sir? Are you okay?" he asked, his worried gaze shifting between Ryan and Sabelle.

Ryan had to clear his throat a couple of times before he could speak. "I own Love's," he said. "We made it out just in time."

Suddenly cameras swung his way and he heard the inevitable babble coming from the news crews. They were torn between asking questions about his sister Roxanne and the explosions that had destroyed his family's pub. The officer motioned him through their barriers and over to a group of officials, saving him from the media's shark-infested waters.

Woodenly, Ryan told the officers what he knew. He'd smelled gas. He'd called 911, but everything started exploding before he could report the issue. They'd run for their lives.

"We've had reports of gas leakages all over Tempe," a tired, scruffy civilian with an official-looking badge around his neck told them. Ryan guessed that he worked for the gas and electric company. "All at the same time. Never seen anything like it. We're lucky that it happened so late. No serious injuries or deaths so far."

Lucky.

Warring emotions gripped Ryan. Thankfulness that no one else had suffered. Relief that there was an explanation for the destruction, which only involved faulty gas lines. And anger, because once again Ryan was left to pick up pieces that he had no hope of ever reassembling. His family had been through so much—too much. He couldn't see a way out of this.

His vision blurred and he lowered his head, rubbing his stinging eyes. Hearing Sabelle in his head telling him she'd come to warn him.

Come from where? How? *Why?*

Beside him, Sabelle's soft touch on his arm tried to offer comfort but only managed to churn his confusion into something worse.

A polite officer with thin blond hair and a square jaw ushered them to an emergency vehicle where two young female EMTs rinsed their eyes, gave them water and blankets, and treated the worst of their injuries until the officer they'd spoken to earlier appeared again.

"Just a couple of questions, Mr. Love," he said. "Any chance you made it out with your ID?"

Ryan had stuffed his wallet in the pack with his money and clothes. Now he carefully pulled it out, knowing that if the officer caught a glimpse of the money stashed in the bottom beneath his clothes, the routine questions wouldn't be so routine anymore. There was no way he'd be able to explain why he'd run from his bar just in the nick of time, yet managed to grab his money.

"Do you have ID, ma'am?" the polite officer asked.

The desperate gleam in Sabelle's eyes spurred Ryan to

speak before he thought. "Her purse was upstairs," he said smoothly. "There wasn't time to get it."

"But you had time to pack?" asked an officer Ryan hadn't noticed. The man stepped into the light and settled a look on the two of them that he probably practiced in front of a mirror. He had dark curly hair and black eyes. Ryan almost smiled. Reece would have called the pair Starsky and Hutch. Ryan could still hear Reece's laughter in his head.

It felt like a lifetime ago.

"We were packing for a little getaway," Ryan said to the cop who looked like Starsky. "I brought the backpack down first. Sabelle was still in the loft getting dressed when I smelled the gas."

He impressed himself with the smooth cadence of the lie at the same time he wondered at the insanity of telling it. But covering for Sabelle seemed less involved than explaining how he'd found her bare naked in the parking lot a few minutes before she'd warned him he was going to die.

Starsky focused on Sabelle and her vagabond outfit. "That's you? You're Sybil?"

"Sabelle," she corrected with a sweet smile.

The officer waited for the rest of it. When Sabelle grew silent, he prompted, "Last name?"

She hid her anxiety well, but all of them caught the desperate glance she gave Ryan.

Ash still sifted down around them and the cold plumed her breath. Ryan forced himself to stay quiet and let her do her own digging. He already felt like he was in too deep.

It didn't take her long. "Snow," she replied. "Sabelle Snow."

Ryan gave a mental groan as Starsky's head came up, his gaze filled with suspicion. Sabelle blinked those guileless eyes at him and finally the officer nodded and wrote *Snow* on his tablet. Reservation glittered in his eyes, but Ryan and Sabelle weren't suspects. They were victims and he had no real reason to question them.

"Address?"

This was the time to cut the tie. To distance himself from Sabelle while he still had the chance. But she'd saved his life. Brandy's, too.

"You're looking at it," Ryan said, taking her hand and pulling her close as he pointed to the disaster zone he used to call home.

Sabelle gave him a furtive, grateful glance. Starsky's gaze moved from the tangle of her hair, over her pretty, dirty face, and down her ample curves in a quick sweep.

"We're lucky to be alive," Ryan said, cutting off any further questions, his voice unsteady enough to bring the point home. "We took what we had in our hands."

"More than lucky," Hutch agreed, staring at the destruction all around them.

"You Loves get lucky a lot," Starsky said, brows raised. "Some of you, four, five times."

Starsky's reference to Ryan's brother and sister and the inexplicable, *miraculous* way the twins had cheated death in the past felt like a jab with a sharp point into a place that was already raw. Reece wasn't cheating death anymore and Roxanne had gone into hiding to avoid the relentless media. It was nothing to joke about.

"That's a good one, Officer," Ryan mocked. "You should tell that at parties."

Hutch laughed and Starsky flushed. He didn't meet Ryan's eyes after that. Hutch told Ryan how to get a copy of the police report for the insurance company and a bunch of other stuff he was too tired to hear. Ryan thanked him, but he already knew they wouldn't get much out of their insurance. Love's carried the bare minimum. It had been that or none at all. Once the debts were paid, there'd be little, if any, left to start over with.

"Where can we reach you if we have other questions?" Starsky asked.

"My sister's house."

Ryan gave him the address of the house his dad had left to the kids and the home phone number there. It hadn't changed since he was a boy and it was the only number he could remember. He'd lost his cell phone in the mad dash for safety and all his contacts with it.

Starsky took Ryan's ID and his notes to his car and Hutch moved on to his next order of business. Ryan and Sabelle remained sitting on the open tailgate of the ambulance, covered by their blankets and numb from shock and cold. Brandy sat at their feet, quietly watching the chaos that went on all around them.

"We are going to Ruby's?" Sabelle asked after a moment.

We. More conflicting emotions followed that word, but he was too tired to break them down and analyze them.

"Was there somewhere else you'd rather go?" he asked. "I can drop you off on the way."

"No," she said quickly, and Ryan felt an inexplicable rush of relief. "I just never thought to meet your sister."

"You know Ruby?"

She nodded, then changed her mind and shook her head.

"Which is it, snowflake?"

She lifted her chin and shrugged. "I've seen pictures."

Starsky chose that moment to return with Ryan's ID. "You're free to go, Mr. Love and Ms. Snow," he said. "I can get an ambulance to take you to the hospital. You should see a doctor."

Ryan shook his head. "I just want a shower and bed."

"Me, too," Sabelle said softly.

Starsky nodded at them both. "You want to talk to reporters before you go?" he asked.

"I'd rather you just stood me against the wall and shot me."

For the first time, the officer smiled. "Where's your vehicle? I'll escort you to it."

Ryan looked to the small lot on the side of Love's where his truck should have been parked. Instead of his battered pickup, a hunk of demolished metal sat beneath a pile of rubble. The sight of it made him want to bawl like a baby.

Starsky had followed his gaze. Now he shook his head. "I take it that was yours?" At Ryan's nod, he said, "Why don't I just drive you to your sister's house?"

4

The officer gave Brandy a suspicious look but allowed her into his backseat without a word. Sabelle sat stiffly next to the wet dog. Ryan took his place on the other side. He seemed calm, but Sabelle knew better. The tension was there in his shoulders, in the way he'd tugged his ear once or twice. His eyes looked tight, dangerous. His mouth hard.

He hadn't asked his questions—yet. She still didn't know how she'd answer them, but so far she'd succeeded against impossible odds. She'd find a way.

"How long has Ruby lived in your dad's old place?" the dark-haired officer asked. Sabelle had noted a name tag pinned to his shirt that read *J. Wiesel*.

Wiesel glanced at Ryan through the rearview mirror as he took his seat behind the wheel. He was a blunt-featured man with a crooked nose and a suspicious nature, but the look he gave Ryan seemed friendly enough now.

Ryan's gaze jerked to his. "How do *you* know my sister?"

"Just seen her on the news." Wiesel paused. "She's got a way about her."

Sabelle felt Ryan's gaze shift to her and she kept her face turned to the window. His reflection in the dark glass looked pensive.

"Most women do."

"I hear that," Wiesel agreed.

She wanted to turn and look at Ryan, see what hidden meaning lurked in his eyes. But she was afraid of what she might reveal herself. She'd always known Ryan had an astute mind, but she'd never imagined he'd make her feel so transparent, like he knew her thoughts.

A slow-burning fuse had lit inside her chest. Panic, some distant part of her, identified it. She'd seen humans cope with it a million times over. It reduced them to action/reaction. It turned their thoughts into fragmented images and ignited their instincts.

She'd just never expected to feel it herself.

"So, she's lived there for a while?" Wiesel tried again. "Your sister?"

"Yeah," Ryan mumbled.

Wiesel still watched him in the rearview mirror, waiting for more. A picture clipped to his visor showed him standing against a breathtaking view of red-stained mountains beside an older version of himself, likely his father. Sabelle squinted at the familiar scenery. She'd seen that red-stained vista too many times not to look for the words she expected to see. Wiesel flipped the visor up and started the car before she spotted them.

"When we decided to sell the house, both my sisters moved in so they could go through everything and clear it out," Ryan said at last, absently stroking Brandy's head. Brandy yawned loudly and lay down between them. "That was three years ago."

"Some people can't let go," Wiesel said.

"Evidently."

Sabelle finally peeked at Ryan from beneath lowered lashes. He slouched against the door, watching her. Shadows hid his expression, but she felt his eyes tracking her every move.

Wiesel gave a halfhearted chuckle and lapsed into silence until they arrived at Ruby's. As the cruiser pulled to the curb, Ryan stared out the window at the stuccoed two-story home sitting beneath the barren branches of a giant tree. He took a breath and slowly stepped out of the car, clicking his tongue for Brandy to follow. Sabelle scooted across the seat and onto the sidewalk beside him while he slung his backpack over his shoulder.

"Thanks for the ride," he said to the officer before closing the car door. Wiesel waved and drove away.

The house where Ryan had grown up looked like her memories of it. Still, it felt surreal to follow him to the front door. To be here at all. With him. Every time he touched her, she felt like he short-circuited her brain. Something else she hadn't expected.

They paused on the front stoop and Sabelle understood the worried light in his eyes as he hesitated. He and Ruby had dealt with a lot in the past few weeks. He didn't know how his sister would take this latest catastrophe.

She touched his arm, drawing his gaze. "There was nothing you could do," she said.

Her soft reassurance tightened his mouth. Without a word, he rang the bell, waited a moment, and knocked. At his feet, Brandy gave a sharp bark. Ryan hushed her and pushed the bell so that it rang continuously.

"Come on, Ruby. Wake up," he said under his breath, leaning his forehead against her door.

A light came on upstairs. Ryan stepped off the porch, looking up at the window. Brandy woofed softly as footfalls came to a stop at the other side of the door.

"Ruby, it's me. Let me in."

The chain rattled and Ruby threw the door open. Ryan's sister stood in the light and Sabelle could only stare. To her, Ryan was the richness of earth and the colors of fall—the thick brown hair, golden skin, and moss-green eyes. In contrast, Ruby was a midnight sky. Dark hair, flashing silver eyes, and skin like a winter moon. Beside her, Sabelle felt pale and drab.

Ruby rubbed her eyes and blurted, "What are you doing here? Why is your face all black? Is that blood? Who is she?" in one continuous stream.

Ryan smiled gently at her, the look in his eye one Sabelle had seen countless times over the years. Ryan loved his siblings like a parent.

"Do you know what time it is?" Ruby demanded as she ushered them through a small foyer that smelled of cinnamon, and into a living room that looked dated even to Sabelle's eyes.

"Yeah, I know."

Ryan's tone stilled his sister and she turned a searching gaze to his face.

"I've got some bad news, Ruby. It couldn't wait."

Ruby's face blanched. "Roxanne?"

"No. Nothing like that. I haven't heard from her. But . . . there was a fire at the pub." He shook his head, staring at a point over Ruby's shoulder. "Love's is gone, Ruby. Burned to the ground."

"Wha . . . *How?*" she breathed.

"Gas leak, I heard, but I'm not sure. Maroonie's is gone, too. Mike's, that new breakfast place . . . everything around it."

Ruby covered her mouth with her hands and stared at him over the tips of her fingers. "What are we going to do?" she asked.

"I don't know," he said with a lift of his shoulder. "I need to eat and sleep before I can figure that out."

"Sure," she said, nodding, her stunned expression telling Sabelle she'd barely processed what he'd said. Full realization of how bad things were wouldn't come until later. "Sure."

Ruby stepped into the kitchen and turned on the light. Ryan went straight to the sink. He washed his face and hands, then moved aside so Sabelle could do the same. When she looked up, Sabelle found him staring at her. Gently, he brushed his thumb around the edges of the burn she'd felt just before they'd climbed that wall. She remembered the eyeless face that had formed in the smoke. Her imagination? Fear, working overtime?

She forced the memory from her mind. Later she

would consider the implications of it. When she was alone and far from Ryan's discerning eyes.

The kitchen had an L-shaped counter with two bar stools waiting at the ready on the short side. A round table and chairs sat in a nook behind the breakfast bar. Ruby sank into one of the chairs and Ryan set some coffee to brew while Sabelle hovered in the background, unsure what she should do now.

"It's decaf," Ruby warned. "I'm out of the regular."

He gave his sister an exasperated look. "Forget to swipe it from Love's?"

Ruby shrugged without apology, turning to give Sabelle a direct stare. "Who are you?" she asked.

Ryan glanced over his shoulder. "Sorry. Ruby, this is Sabelle . . . Snow. Sabelle, my sister Ruby."

Ruby caught his hesitation over Sabelle's last name but obviously didn't know what it meant. Still, it added to the curiosity in her inquisitive gaze.

"Nice to meet you, Sybil," she said.

"*S'belle*," both Ryan and Sabelle corrected at the same time.

Ruby raised her brows in an expression that made her look like Ryan and glanced between them. "How do you know each other?" she asked.

"Long story," Ryan said.

Sabelle fixed her gaze on her sooty feet, saying nothing.

"I'll tell you all about it sometime," Ryan went on. "But do you think we could clean up first? We're both wet and cold. I feel like I'm covered in glass."

Ruby jumped to her feet, pulling her robe tight around her as she said, "Sorry. Yeah, of course. Take showers. I'll wait here for you and then we'll talk."

Sabelle looked up to find Ryan watching her again. He grabbed his pack and left the kitchen. Warily, she followed him.

At the top of the stairs, he turned at the first door on the left and entered a room with a wide bed covered by a dark blue comforter. Pennants hung on the walls and shelves sagged beneath the weight of countless trophies. He gave it all a disparaging look as he dropped his pack on the bed and moved to the closet.

"This was your bedroom when you were growing up?" She remembered to make it a question, but she knew the answer already.

"Dad wouldn't let me throw any of it out. I've never known anyone to hold on to the past like he did." He gave her a fleeting glance. "Guess that's lucky. I've probably got some old clothes in here that'll fit you."

While he rummaged, Sabelle gravitated to a small desk with a picture propped on its surface. In it, a child version of Ryan stood in a bright blue-and-white uniform with a bill cap. His grin revealed a gap where a front tooth should have been. On either side, his mother and father posed with him. His mom looked to be about seven months pregnant, his dad as proud as a father could be. A small Ruby stood in front of her father, a stuffed lion clutched against her heart.

They looked like a typical American family, unaware that in just a few months, their remarkable twin siblings would be born and their whole world would change. A copper penny that had been flattened and punched with a hole at the top dangled off the corner of one of the frames by a key chain. Sabelle stuck her finger through the ring and lifted it, watching the light glance off it as it spun.

"What's this?" she asked.

He glanced at it over his shoulder and shrugged. "Junk. Won it at the fair a hundred years ago."

"It's pretty."

"Keep it."

She tried to hide her amazed delight, but Ryan's surprised laugh made her feel hot and uncomfortable.

"It's a smashed penny, Sabelle. It's not even worth a cent with the hole in it."

She'd overreacted. *Again.*

Her hand closed around the key chain and she bit her lip to keep the smile from coming back. Worth was a matter of opinion.

Ryan pulled a pair of jeans and a shirt from the closet and tossed them on the bed. "Those should work," he said.

He showed Sabelle to the bathroom and turned on the shower for her. "The faucet's temperamental," he explained. "I'm going to shower in the other bathroom. Don't worry about running out of hot water. We've got a big heater, so take your time. I'll meet you in the kitchen when you're done."

She nodded and anxiously watched him walk away. She may have come to save his life, but Ryan was the only thing familiar to her in this world. As he walked down the hall, she had to force herself not to call him back.

She showered quickly—an experience she vowed to savor next time—and dressed in the jeans and shirt Ryan had given her, wincing as her sore muscles protested. It felt very intimate, wearing his clothes . . . feeling the brush of them against her skin. It worried her, how much she liked it. Carefully she tucked the penny key chain into her pocket. It might not have been intended as a gift, but she could pretend.

The bathroom mirror bounced back a steamy reflection of a young woman with dark hair and pale skin. A fringe of black lashes framed blue eyes, making the color seem brilliant. Bangs brushed her brows.

It was hard to evaluate herself, but Ryan couldn't keep his eyes off her. That had to be a good thing. It would certainly make it easier to win him over.

She hurried back to his room and waited for him to return. No way was she up to facing Ruby on her own. Ryan stepped in a few minutes later, stopping abruptly when he saw her perched on his bed. He wore a towel at his hips and nothing else. For a moment Sabelle could only gape. Fully clothed in the trappings of civilization, Ryan Love made her heart stutter and skip, but half naked and dripping wet he took her breath away.

Water made a slow and lazy trail from his wet hair to his shoulders, meandering through the light dusting of hair on his bare chest, down to the point where the towel was cinched. She stared with fascination at the play of light on his flesh, the smooth contours and intriguing slope of muscle and bone. An ugly bruise spread up from his ribs. Nicks and cuts and a few burns marred his arms and shoulders, but it was the trail of brown hair that led from his flat belly to beneath the towel that caught her attention for a long, drawn-out moment.

She jerked her gaze back up to find him watching her with those incredible green eyes. The message she read in them sparked another chain reaction she couldn't control.

He came closer, tossed his dirty clothes on top of the pile she'd made with hers in the corner, and opened his pack. He pulled out the pair of dark blue briefs she'd stuffed in it and faced Sabelle.

"Why don't you have tattoos?" she blurted. "Other men do."

"I'm not other men."

Obviously. "You just seem like the kind of man who would."

"Why is that?"

She shrugged, as if all that bare skin didn't affect her at all. "You like to fight. You seem . . . dangerous," she said, feeling her face heat up.

He snorted. "Guess you got me all figured out, don't you?"

"You think I'm wrong?"

"I wouldn't dare."

She narrowed her eyes at him as she tried to see through the layers of that comment.

"I'm going to need to get dressed," he said.

She nodded.

"Does that mean you want to watch?"

His question sank below her dazed senses and blossomed into something as combustible as the explosions they'd barely escaped. She jumped to her feet only to find herself standing too close to Ryan. He smelled clean and warm and male. She took a deep breath. Very male. Her gaze traveled up to his chin and the intriguing shadow that covered it. She curled her fingers into her palms as she imagined touching it. Tasting it.

"What are you doing, Sabelle?" he asked in that deep, honeyed voice.

Her gaze shifted to his mouth and the full lips that had formed the words. She longed to touch them, too. What would a kiss feel like? She'd imagined it a hundred—a thousand—times. She wanted to know.

Ryan took a deep breath and she remembered he'd asked a question. One she didn't know how to answer. She couldn't tell him what she was doing. She wasn't sure herself.

"I'll wait outside," she muttered instead.

As she walked to the door, she could *feel* his gaze following. It trilled down her spine and stirred the embers that had been glowing inside her since the very first time she'd seen Ryan Love.

She'd only just managed to get herself calm again before he emerged to find her in the hall. Dressed, he was a little easier to resist, but he smelled of soap and fresh air and that uniquely *Ryan* scent she couldn't label but wanted to bottle and wear like cologne. His gaze met hers for a charged moment before he started down the stairs.

In the kitchen, they found Ruby still at the table, sitting with Brandy's nose in her lap, murmuring softly as she stroked the dog. Brandy listened with rapt attention.

"She had glass in her fur," Ruby said. "And a piece in her paw. I got it out."

"Thanks," Ryan replied, moving around the kitchen familiarly. He opened a cupboard and pulled out three mugs. "Coffee?" he asked Sabelle, brows raised.

She'd never had it before, but she nodded. It seemed expected.

"Have a seat," he said.

Sabelle perched on the chair at the table with Ruby on her right and Ryan moving in the kitchen to her left.

"Tell me what happened," Ruby urged in a low voice.

Ryan poured a dark brown brew into each mug, glanced at Sabelle, and added a healthy pour of cream to one cup. "About an hour after you went home, I locked up behind the last customer," he began, delivering their coffee. "Then I took Brandy for our run, like I always do after work."

"Wasn't it raining?"

He shook his head. "The storm didn't blow in until later. It came fast. Never seen anything like it."

"I thought so, too. It was clear when I drove home."

He opened a stainless steel box on the counter and pulled out a loaf of bread. As he talked, he put three pieces in a toaster oven beside it.

"I heard sirens when I was on my way back. I could see them down Mill Avenue, around Apache Road."

"A murder," Ruby told him.

Sabelle kept very quiet. She knew all this. The death had been her ticket from the Beyond to Ryan's world.

"A student out alone. He was stabbed to death."

They both shook their heads in silent mourning for the student neither had known.

"I figured it had to be something bad with that many cops responding." He paused, glancing at Sabelle. "When I got to Love's, I heard a scream. That's how I found her."

Ruby looked startled, then confused. "What do you mean, 'found her'?"

He stopped what he was doing and faced them both. Frowning, Ruby cut her gaze between her brother and his new friend. Sabelle decided now would be a good time to try the coffee. She took a drink and her taste buds sent a battery of reactions to her brain. Bitter. Hot. Creamy. Strangely . . . good. Surprised, she smiled.

Ryan met Ruby's gaze over Sabelle's head and shrugged.

Sabelle could feel the intensity in their interest. She knew it was her turn to talk, to fill in the blanks. But she couldn't tell the truth and she hadn't had time to compose a believable lie—even if she thought she could get away with telling it. She cleared her throat and said, "I was hiding."

Surprise widened Ryan's eyes but he didn't contradict her. When the silence stretched, she tacked on, "I was scared."

"Of what?" Ruby asked. "Did you see the murder? Did you know the boy who was killed?"

"No. But I knew it was happening so I got away."

Not quite a lie. She could see Ryan parsing her words, weighing the true against the false. He was good at it, but she knew he'd never piece together the whole story from what she'd said. In a million years he'd never guess she'd used the reaper coming to claim the boy's soul as public transportation out of the Beyond.

She could scarcely believe it herself.

Ryan made a sound and shook his head before turning away. He stepped through a door with the word *Pantry* etched on the smoky glass inset, and an uncomfortable silence waited for his return. She could feel Ruby watching her, gauging her reactions. Sabelle sat still, trying to look human. She had no idea if she was succeeding or not.

Ryan came out of the pantry with a jar of peanut butter. He already had the lid off and his finger in his mouth.

"She's lying," Ruby said, pulling her gaze from Sabelle and leveling it at her brother.

"I know," Ryan answered calmly.

Sabelle became very interested in her coffee.

"You can sit there looking innocent all you want," Ruby went on. "It won't do you any good."

"I don't know what you mean," Sabelle said, lifting her chin.

"He knows when you're lying," Ruby explained calmly.

Sabelle swallowed hard. "It's the truth. I was scared."

"You still are," Ryan responded, pulling a knife from the drawer.

"Yes."

Ruby was still watching her. Suddenly, her eyes widened and she looked at Ryan. "She reminds me of someone," she said pointedly.

A silent message passed between them. Ryan shook his head. "Not even a little bit."

"How do you know who I'm talking about, then?" Ruby retorted.

"Who do I remind you of?" Sabelle interrupted, confused and curious.

"No one," Ryan answered. Ruby said nothing.

Who were they talking about? Sabelle had only seen one long-term girlfriend in Ryan's life and they'd broken up after college. Ryan had loved that one even after she'd broken his heart.

"Callie?" Sabelle asked.

Ryan's head snapped up at the same time that Ruby's head whipped around.

"No," Ruby said. "The other one."

What other one?

Ryan eyed her suspiciously before switching his focus back to Ruby. "I thought Sabelle might be hurt," he said, deliberately changing the direction of the conversation. "So I took her upstairs. She said I needed to get out or I was going to die." He set down the knife and braced his hands on the counter. Sabelle heard him draw in a deep breath. "She was right."

Ruby leaned forward. "How would you know that?"

"I smelled the gas," Sabelle answered, pleased with the quick thinking.

Ruby just stared at her like she had two heads and neither one of them was working.

"Sabelle convinced me to get out and a couple of minutes later the whole place blew," Ryan said, saving her from answering.

"Oh my God," Ruby said. "You're serious?"

"As a fucking heart attack."

Ryan pulled paper plates from a cabinet, put a piece of peanut butter toast on each one, and brought them to the table. Distractedly, Ruby lifted hers and took a bite. Sabelle thanked him.

He sat across from her and ate. The warm peanut butter dripped and he licked his fingers before washing it down with coffee. He caught her staring again. Instead of the mocking smile she'd come to expect, he blushed. The warm wash of color did strange things to her insides. It made her want to reach over and touch his face, feel the heat beneath her fingers, stroke the shadow of beard on his jaw.

Disconcerted by the power of her desire, she focused on eating. The peanut butter had a rich taste she'd never imagined. It stuck to the roof of her mouth and filled the hollow in her belly. Warmed, it managed to drip on her fingers. She understood why Ryan had to lick them.

"I'm sorry about Love's, Ruby," Ryan said when he'd finished his toast. His voice was low, his words heartfelt.

Ruby shrugged. "You didn't blow it up."

But he still felt responsible. Sabelle knew him enough to have guessed that.

"We're not going to break even with the insurance. You know that, right?"

"We'll sell the house to make up the difference."

Ryan hung his head. "I'm sorry."

"Ry," Ruby said, reaching across the table to touch his hand. "We've been lugging the pub and the house around like a ball and chain for years. We just didn't want to admit it. Dad made us feel like the bar was family. Like if we gave it up we'd be losing our heritage. But it's not true. *We're* our heritage. Love's is just a bar."

"Not anymore. Now it's a pile of ash."

"It always was. I think the life went out of it with Grandpa, if you want the truth. Don't think I don't know about that escape fund you've been padding for months."

Ryan's jaw dropped with surprise. "You know about the money?"

Ruby rolled her eyes. "I have one, too, and now we both have the chance to use it and do something with our lives. The point is, this is a *good* thing. With just the two of us working there now, it was too much. This fire makes walking away easy."

Sabelle waited for Ryan to speak. Ruby's words had upset him. She could see it. But beneath she sensed reluctant relief. Everything Ruby said was true. Sabelle had watched him toil, watched him try to make ends meet, watched him struggle with a burden he'd resented carrying even as he felt compelled to shoulder it.

"You'd give up just like that?" he asked at last.

Ruby nodded. "And so should you. So *would* you if you weren't so stubborn."

"I agree with Ruby," Sabelle offered. The two Love siblings turned their attention on her and she wished she'd kept her opinion to herself, yet she didn't call the words back or look away when Ryan locked eyes with her.

"Why is that?" he asked coldly.

"You haven't been happy there for years," she answered.

"I have too."

"Liar," Ruby said before Sabelle dared.

Ryan looked like he couldn't decide whether to argue or relent. The pub had meant family to him since he was a young boy. Giving up one was like giving up on the other.

Ruby finished her toast and let loose a long, jaw-popping yawn. She stood, rinsed her cup, and put it in the dishwasher before facing her brother.

"You remember I'm leaving for Vegas in the morning, right?"

He frowned, then nodded. "Your friend's wedding."

"I can cancel if you need me to stay and help with things."

"Nah. We'll be dealing with the crap for a long time. Go. Have fun."

"You sure?"

"Go."

"Okay. Lena is picking me up at eight, so I'm going to try to get a few more hours' sleep." She paused. "Ryan . . . This . . . what happened tonight . . . it isn't a failure unless you want it to be." She leaned down and kissed the top of his head. "Love you."

"Me, too."

She smiled, kissed him again, and said, "Get some sleep, Ryan. It won't seem so bad in the morning."

Sabelle didn't think that was true, but she couldn't help liking Ryan's sister for having said it.

At the bottom of the stairs, Ruby paused. "Sabelle?"

Sabelle looked up, surprised and wary.

"Thanks for saving his life. I owe you one."

A bubble of disbelief caught in Sabelle's throat. "You're welcome."

5

Ruby took all the conversation with her, leaving Ryan and his mystery woman alone in the quiet. He leaned against the counter in front of her, watching as Sabelle sipped her coffee. She was so easy on the eyes that he couldn't help but look. Even banged up and smudged around the edges, she was the kind of beautiful that made a man stop everything that didn't involve just *looking*.

Maybe it was the fragile quality about her, the air of vulnerability that pulled at him. Not helpless. Not weak, but a little desperate. She needed help and that spoke to him on a level he couldn't control.

She knew it, too. She was aware of him, aware of her effect on him. She'd sized Ryan up as soon as they'd slowed down long enough for her to catch her breath. He was big, a little angry at the world, at himself, maybe even her . . . but none of that seemed to stop her from getting under his skin. She'd done it quickly, effortlessly. He was intrigued, attracted, and somehow at her mercy—and she'd done it all in a matter of minutes.

So far she'd seemed too busy to capitalize on it, though. She'd entered the house like she'd never walked through a door before, and now that she had, she couldn't wait to do it again. Coffee, conversation, *toast* . . . She partook like it was a once-in-a-lifetime novelty she didn't want to miss. In another woman, it might have seemed disingenuous, but Sabelle came across as so innocent that he had a hard time doubting her sincerity. She was either the best actress alive or . . . Ryan rubbed took a drink of coffee. He didn't know what came after *or*.

His gaze tangled with hers for the hundredth time. She was into him, too. He'd have picked up her signal from across a crowded room, it shone so bright. She made him feel needed . . . protective . . . male in all the primitive ways men weren't supposed to feel anymore. The kind that made a man want to *take* instead of *ask*. Any minute now, he was afraid he might throw her over his shoulder and haul her off to his cave.

She finished the toast he'd made her and sucked a glob of peanut butter off her finger. He didn't even realize how intently he was watching until she looked up and blushed.

They were both doing a lot of that. The air between them felt electric. It sparked with every glance, every chance contact.

"You still hungry?" he asked in a voice that shouldn't have been so low and husky.

She shook her head. "Thank you for the food."

"You're welcome."

He reached over and brushed a crumb from the corner of her mouth, just for the excuse to touch her. Jesus, her lips were soft, her surprised breath so very warm. He made himself sit back again. But that's as far as his control extended. He couldn't stop his thoughts from picking up where he'd left off. Touching, baring . . . tasting. A man could lose himself in the sweet scent of her skin. He wished he could do just that.

But Sabelle wasn't simply a woman who'd wandered into Love's looking for a cocktail and a hookup. She'd come looking for *him*, to *save him*, she'd said. And that's what she'd done. It was the *how* and *why* of it that begged an answer.

Wariness moved across her features as he let the silence stretch. She shifted uncomfortably, opened her mouth as if to speak, and closed it again in silence. Her fidgeting only served to fan the slow-burning fuse inside him.

"You going to tell me?" he asked at last.

"Tell you what?"

"What you're scared of, for starters."

She raised her brows. "You almost died tonight. Isn't that scary enough?"

"From where I was standing, so did you. How'd you know it was going to happen?"

Her gaze slid away, skimming past Ryan until it settled on Brandy, snoozing at her feet. She bent down and stroked the dog's fur. Stalling.

"I got nothing but time, Sabelle."

She snorted softly, the sound disdainful. But when she looked up, he saw apprehension rather than derision on her face.

He crossed his arms and leaned back. “How’d you know what was going to happen tonight?”

“You look very judgmental,” she said. “It makes me feel that you won’t listen to my answer with an open mind.”

He didn’t bother responding to that. He probably did and he probably wouldn’t. She had the cagey, nervous body language of someone who wasn’t good at lying but still felt the need to do it.

“Tell me anyhow.”

At last she lifted her chin and met his eyes. That was her *tell.* The straight-on stare and stubborn chin gave her away every time.

“When you found me tonight,” she said, “I was coming from somewhere else.”

Everyone came from somewhere else, but he wasn’t going to fight over that detail. He had bigger questions in mind. “Why weren’t you wearing any clothes?”

Head bent, she watched her fingers worry the hem of her borrowed shirt. “I was forced to leave without time to prepare,” she murmured at last.

Pretty much the same crock of shit he’d sold to the police earlier. “You needed to prepare to not be naked?” he asked, trying to be gentle while still pinning her down. The answer would determine what came next.

Her lips moved but she changed her mind before she spoke. Ryan knew that *those* words—the ones she’d kept inside—were the ones he needed to hear, but he had no idea how to extricate them from the tension that surrounded her.

"Come on, snowflake," he said softly. "Don't make me pull it out of you. I'm not going to help you if you don't tell me."

"Who says I need your help?" she demanded.

"Snowflake, you are the definition of *needs help*."

The chin came up again, but she wasn't as steady as she pretended, even though she'd tossed the challenge like she had an army behind her to rally to her call.

He tipped his head, snaring her defensive gaze with a sideways glance. "Tell me."

Her eyes grew big. Liquid. So blue he thought he might drown in them if he didn't look away. She lifted her shoulder. "Why would you help me?"

"You saved my life. I'm indebted."

She nodded, accepting the answer at face value. Yet she lowered her lashes, hiding her thoughts. Ryan crouched in front of her chair, weight on the balls of his feet. He used her legs to turn her body so her feet were between his, her knees almost brushing his chest. He left his fingers curled around her calves as he waited her out.

A heavy sigh and then: "I do need help," she said in a low voice. "It's not only your life in danger now."

"Mine isn't in danger anymore," he corrected, still speaking in those careful tones.

"I'm afraid that isn't true. Because of me."

"Does someone want to hurt you, Sabelle?"

The thought of it made his throat tighten and hot anger slide down his spine. Her chin dipped. Was that a nod?

"I'm a fugitive," she said, her voice so soft he wasn't sure he'd heard right. "An escaped prisoner."

Not what he'd expected. Not anything close to it.

"It would be great if you could be a little more specific," he teased, though he wanted to pressure her. "Is a SWAT team going to be busting down my door or did you run away from home?"

"I'm serious."

"So am I."

"I'm not a criminal, if that's what you're asking me. I was targeted and taken."

The conversation had taken a wild turn, and suddenly thoughts of abducted women forced into prostitution and slavery filled his head. Girls kept in dark basements who were sometimes found years later, sometimes never. The ones who emerged as grown women and didn't know where they belonged anymore.

He thought of the bruises on Sabelle's skin, the cuts he'd seen before the explosion. The strangely wondrous look on her face as she sat at his table with Brandy at her feet and clothes on her body.

He took her hands in his, his breath trapped in his chest. A hundred questions shuffled through his head, all too pointed, too horrible to ask.

"What . . . how did you escape?"

"I had help. A friend. She told me how to get away, where to go. She told me to come to you."

Her fingers felt icy. He rubbed them in the warmth of his.

"Why me?" he asked.

"Because you would've died if I hadn't."

"How do you even know me?"

She stared at her hands, clasped in his. Ryan's patience was thin and brittle, but he forced a bland expression. Inside, though, turmoil churned.

"I've always seen you, Ryan," Sabelle murmured. "Since before your brother and sister died. The first time, I mean."

He stood abruptly. He'd moved away before he even realized he'd intended to.

"No," she said quickly. "You don't understand. It's why I'm so valuable."

"What's why?" he demanded, the soothing tones lost in his anger.

He'd known it from the start—that she was like the other lunatics who haunted Love's looking for a glimpse of the infamous twins who'd cheated death so many times. But Reece was dead—the permanent kind of dead—and Roxanne gone, largely because of the stalkers who wouldn't leave her alone. He'd pegged Sabelle as one of *them* in those first few minutes after meeting her. Yet she'd somehow won him over, made him forget.

"I see things, Ryan," she said urgently. "Things that haven't happened yet. Things that are yet to come. Do you understand?"

"Not even a little bit."

"I knew Love's was going to blow up because I'm a seer."

"A seer," he repeated, nonplussed. "You mean you're a psychic?"

"In a way. A powerful one. I was held captive because what I see comes true."

"And you busted out of prison to come save me," he said in tones so cold they made her flinch.

He couldn't help it. He was angry and confused. He wasn't even certain what they were talking about anymore. He'd gone from thinking the worst to absolute bewilderment. What did any of this have to do with him? With his brother and sister? With Love's exploding?

"Do you know what it means to know the future?" she asked, her voice vibrating with her emotion. She pushed out of her chair and came to stand in front of him. "Do you understand the power that can be wielded by knowing what's going to happen tomorrow? Next week? Next *year*?"

Her gaze was steady now; her voice no longer wavered. She stood tall and proud, and so fucking beautiful that he had to look away.

"Do you?" she demanded.

He nodded slowly. "I can guess."

"I see the future," she said again, forcefully, angrily. "And I am never wrong."

"Never?"

She shook her head. All the antsy body language had faded away, but the desperation . . . it was still there, glowing brightly in those baby-blue eyes.

"I came to save you because I knew you would save me."

"Because you saw it?" he said evenly.

"Because I see *you*. I know what kind of man you are. You wouldn't, *couldn't*, turn away a woman in need."

"Don't count on it."

"I *am* counting on it. I've bet my life on it."

The impassioned words echoed in the quiet kitchen and Ryan felt the reverberation down to his soul.

"You saved my life so you could use me?"

She didn't look away, but she wanted to. He could see the shame in her gaze, see the stain of it creep up her throat.

"Yes."

The truth at last.

It was ugly, but the confession had defused his anger.

"I don't like lies," he said.

"I know that."

"You don't know me at all."

Her gaze swept him, head to toe. Fearless, almost insolent. Wisely, she kept whatever she was thinking to herself.

"Where is this place where you were held? Why don't you want me to call the police on them?"

"The police can't help me. I told you that."

"What makes you think *I* can?"

"I won't ask for much. I just need you to take me someplace."

"Where?"

She shrugged uncertainly. "I'm not sure exactly."

"It's going be pretty hard to find it, then."

"I've seen signs," she said. "They appear in my visions when I'm not expecting them. They're always the same, though. Someplace in the north."

"North?" he said with disbelief. "That covers a lot of territory."

"It's a place where the mountains are red and the sky is so blue it doesn't look real. My intuition tells me it's not far from here. I'll know it when I see it."

His brows shot up. "What happens when you get there?"

"I don't know." She looked away. "I only know that I have to go."

Ryan let out a heavy breath and stepped forward. Gently, he took her chin between his thumb and forefinger. "You know how crazy this sounds."

It wasn't a question, but she nodded. "Yes. But you know it's the truth."

He gave a reluctant nod back, though the jury was still out on that one. "So you haven't seen it—what's waiting in the north? Your future peepers don't work in the cold?"

A hint of a smile curled her lips. "No one can see their own future, Ryan. Not even one such as myself."

Such as herself? That could have a host of meanings, which he intended to pursue, but first Ryan asked, "So you don't already know if I'm going to say yes or no? You're just rolling the dice?"

Sabelle sucked in her bottom lip and gave a short, tight head shake. It made him feel better, her uncertainty. The thought of her seeing his decisions before he'd actually made them defied his beliefs and pissed him off at the same time.

"I know that tomorrow's headlines will read 'Three a.m. Wake-Up Call,'" she said. "But I've never known if I'd be here to read them myself."

The answer made sense—or at least something close

to it—but he felt something sift through the air between them. Something she'd left unsaid.

"I still want to know where you escaped from."

"I can't tell you that, Ryan. It would only put you in more danger if you knew."

"Do you think they followed you? Is there a chance they know where you are?" These mysterious "theys" that even the police couldn't stop.

"Not yet."

She looked like a cornered animal, the kind that bared its teeth and fought to the death if it was out of options. The kind that was scared enough to try anything.

They were standing very close, but neither one stepped away. She had secrets, big ones, and everything she'd told him tonight had just been coins tossed in the street. Distractions to keep him from digging at the ugly treasure she had buried somewhere else. But the instincts that had governed Ryan his entire life insisted that she'd told him what she could and it had been the truth. At the end of the day, that was more than most gave.

And Ryan understood secrets. God knew he had enough of those himself and he'd fight to protect them. He couldn't fault her for wanting to do the same. But there was one secret he couldn't let her keep.

"Did they hurt you, snowflake?" he asked carefully. If she answered yes, all bets were off. He'd make her tell him everything. And he'd make them pay.

"Not in the ways you're thinking," she said. "Not physically."

He held her face, looked deeply into her eyes.

"Swear it."

"I swear. No one has ever touched me."

Something sad twisted through those words. He heard the emotion clearly, but couldn't find a way to decode it. Had she been imprisoned by someone she knew? Someone she trusted? Someone who should have touched her with compassion? Love, even?

Her eyes darkened. He suspected that she'd guessed at his thoughts and it hurt her. The answers to his questions would probe a deep wound she wasn't ready to have exposed.

He got that, too. He exhaled softly and rested his forehead against hers. "Okay."

"Okay?"

"I'll help you find 'north,' but only under one condition." He pulled back and watched as wariness moved behind her gaze. "If we can't find your . . . friends or whoever it is you're looking for, you let me get the police involved before we go our separate ways. No asking me to go on another wild-goose chase. No disappearing without a word to do it on your own. Do we have a deal?"

She nodded, displeasure in the tight line of her lips and the lowered lashes that hid her eyes.

"Look at me, snowflake."

She did, her gaze bright with defiance.

"Say it. I want the words."

"We have deal," she said. "Your way. If we don't find them, we go to the police."

He stared at her a moment longer, taking in every nuance of her expression. She wasn't giving anything up, though. As crazy as it sounded, he'd have to take her at her word.

If tonight had just been another night, maybe his answer would have been different. Nothing but ash was left of his old life, though, and a road trip with this intriguing woman held a lot more appeal than dealing with insurance companies and paperwork. Maybe he'd get answers and clear his head at the same time.

"Good enough," he murmured. "We can leave tomorrow."

6

Sabelle was too exhausted to smile. She'd gotten what she wanted. Ryan would take her where she needed to go. He'd let her keep her secrets. For now. She wasn't so naïve that she thought he'd let her keep them forever, though.

He still held her face, his touch so gentle it nearly broke her. How many times had she dreamed of his hands on her? His gaze seemed to see right through her, but he didn't speak, and with relief she watched the tension drain out of him. She wasn't used to such volatile emotions. They were freeing, but they were also frightening. She'd never realized she had so much passion bottled up inside.

At last, he dropped his hands and leaned back against the counter again, all long bones and hard muscle. One leg stretched out in front, the other bent at the knee. White socks covered his feet and soft, worn blue jeans hugged him *everywhere.* Places Sabelle couldn't help but notice. He'd caught her looking several times, but her scalding blushes hadn't been painful enough to keep her from doing it again. She wanted to touch him. She wanted *him* to touch *her*. He'd riled her up with his questions, with his anger, and now she felt like a live wire sparking in a storm, gathering up all of her other confused feelings and electrifying them in the torrent.

The soft rasp of his palms against the shadow of his beard teased her senses. In the Beyond, sensory stimulation was kept to a minimum for oracles. The Sisters didn't want anything distracting them from their visions. Here on earth, everything was stimulating.

"I can't even see straight anymore," Ryan said in a tired voice. "I can't think. Let's get some sleep. We can talk about everything in the morning."

He took their cups to the sink and dumped their paper plates in a blue bin beside the trash, glancing out the window before turning out the light. Only the lamp in the front room kept the darkness at bay.

"The sun will be up soon. Come on."

He clicked his tongue for Brandy, who rolled to her feet with a grunt and lumbered to his side. When Sabelle didn't move, he tacked on: "Unless you want to sleep down here. I can get you some blankets for the couch."

Sabelle looked around. Deep pockets of darkness seeped into the shadows. Textured and scheming. Devious. The thought of staying there alone propelled her to action. Ryan hadn't waited to see if she'd follow, and she hurried to catch up as he climbed the stairs. The look he gave her over his shoulder glittered with dark amusement. It was better than his anger.

Grimly, she followed to the top and down the hall to the room across from his boyhood bedroom. It took a moment before she understood. He meant for her to sleep there. By herself.

She tried to get a grip on her dread before it took hold and owned her, but it moved too fast, tingling painfully through her limbs. She knew humans slept every night, many of them by themselves. It didn't hurt them. But Sabelle wasn't human and she'd never slept, not like they did. Alone. For hours at a time with their eyes closed, their bodies vulnerable.

He let her use the bathroom first. He even produced a pack of new toothbrushes and gave her one.

"Walmart," he muttered darkly.

She had no idea what that meant but thanked him. Afterward, she returned reluctantly to the room across the hall from his. As he passed, Ryan paused at the open door and looked in. At his feet, Brandy gave a huge yawn.

"You okay?" he asked.

"Yes," she said, adding a few desperate nods in case he had doubt.

Still, he hesitated, watching her with those beautiful, jaded eyes. What did he see? Did desire burn inside him as it did within her?

"You sure?" he asked.

She was still nodding. "I'm fine," she said, her voice a little too high. A little too thin. "Unless there are monsters under the bed that I don't know about?"

Her attempt at humor came with sharp teeth that snapped back. She *had* to bring up monsters. Ryan's eyes narrowed.

"I'm just across the hall," he said.

"I know." *But please don't leave me alone.*

He turned without a word, stripping off his shirt as he entered his room and tossing it on the dresser. One hand ready to sweep his door shut and the other popping the top button of his fly, he glanced back and caught her watching him. She didn't look away. His chest was broad, smooth, and browned by the sun, and all that muscle gleamed in the muted light. He was such a big man, tall, heavy with strength. If the Sisters could still play human, they'd be fighting over a prize like Ryan.

A slow smile crinkled the corners of his eyes as he watched her watch him. Sabelle tried to appear unmoved, but Ryan's smile did things to her head, to her body. After their dangerous conversation, it felt like sunshine in the cold.

He left the door open, his pants on, first button undone, yanked the blankets down, and stretched out on top of the bed. Brandy circled in the corner before curling up and closing her eyes.

"Good night," Ryan said and turned out the bedside lamp.

Sabelle crossed the hall to his open door. The light from the other bedroom crept in behind her and softened the darkness that caressed him. She could make out his shape, the golden stretch of his bare chest, the shadow of that intriguing trail of hair at his belly, a restless shift in position. She wished she could memorize the way the light played over the planes of his arms and chest, the taut, flat stomach. After a moment, her eyes adjusted and she could see his face.

"What?" he said without opening his eyes.

"Nothing. It's just . . . I've never slept alone before."

And I'm scared to do it now.

A wave of something close to humiliation closed in on her. The Sisters' oracles had few freedoms and fewer indulgences. Like privacy. Someone had always monitored her sleep.

"There's nothing to it," Ryan said with a yawn. "Just lie down. Close your eyes."

"And after that?"

"Sleep, if you're lucky."

She shifted her feet, fingering the hem of her shirt. "What if you're not lucky?"

His lashes lifted and the smoky green gleamed in the dim light.

Before he could speak, she said, "I know *you* seem to enjoy it. You like to nap." The corners of her mouth tilted at memories of him stretched out on his couch, Brandy curled up at the end, both oblivious to the TV flashing and blaring. "You can sleep through anything."

His eyes narrowed. She *felt* it across the room and knew she'd slipped up, revealed something Ryan wouldn't let go.

"How do you know that?" he asked.

She lifted a shoulder and said as casually as she could, "I must have seen you."

Ryan shifted his weight, coming up on one arm. "Seen me when?"

Her mouth was dry, her throat tight. She didn't know how to backtrack out of it, so she shook her head and plunged on. "It doesn't matter."

"No way, snowflake. When did you see me? Where?"

"Sleeping," she mumbled. "I told you. I see."

Those intelligent eyes watched her, and she knew she hadn't fooled him. She hadn't merely seen him in a vision. She'd watched him, summoned visions of him like a lovesick girl with her first crush. She'd been told that no other oracle could do such a thing, call a vision like humans called their friends, see the world as it was, not as it would be. Peel reality back just to watch the minutiae of day-to-day life. *His* life.

Ryan noted her evasive gaze and busy fingers before she could still them. He was figuring things out—things she'd never intended for him to know.

"You've watched me," he said. Or asked. She couldn't tell.

"Yes," she admitted because she knew lying would only make it worse.

"By that you mean you've had . . . it's been in your . . . ?"

"Visions," she offered helpfully.

Suddenly, a hasty retreat seemed the wisest option. But the room behind her loomed like a nightmare of its own. So big. So empty. So far from Ryan.

"Why would you watch me sleep?"

It was the only time he let down his guard. The only time he looked relaxed. Peaceful. The young man who lived beneath the weight of responsibility emerged then. She could—*had*—watched him sleep for hours.

"I was simply trying to understand," she bluffed. Convincingly, she thought. "You work half the night, prowl the rest of it. It's only in the early hours of the morning that you go to bed."

And so many times, not alone.

He tipped his head, as if listening. For a moment, she feared she'd said it out loud. Quickly, she rushed on.

"For someone like me, someone with the sight, sleep is a time for visions. We're monitored and awakened whenever our brains are active."

"We?"

She bit her tongue. She should stop talking. Now. She had little experience with deception and Ryan was too skilled at seeing it. She was ill equipped on too many levels. She glanced over her shoulder. The empty room behind her seemed cavernous.

"I am one of many seers," she confessed.

"How many?"

"Thirty-three."

He whistled softly. "They're prisoners, too?"

She nodded. "It's my hope that whoever is sending me signs will help me free them."

"What if they don't?"

"That's a bridge to cross when I reach it. I must follow my destiny, my fate. Just as you must follow yours."

He smiled. "I don't believe in fate."

She smiled back. "Fate does not require belief."

Obviously.

He snorted softly. "Fair enough."

They remained as they were, poised with the room

spread out between them, Ryan reclining, his jeans open at the top, the intriguing arrow between hip bones and muscle pulling her gaze down.

"Don't you get tired, not sleeping?" he asked, his voice rough and deep.

Sabelle jerked her gaze up and found him watching her, his eyes filled with male awareness. She could almost taste the tension sparking in the quiet.

"When our bodies require rest, we're sedated," she answered, the words rendered meaningless by that look in his eye. "But that sleep comes without dreams and so it feels . . . counterproductive."

He nodded slowly, taking it all in. Probably seeing right through her.

"Even then someone monitors our breathing, making sure we stay dreamless."

She wished he'd say something, but he only continued to watch her with those knowing eyes. They dared and coaxed, teased and seduced. He was so . . . *manly.* All muscle and bone, hard angles, rough edges.

She glanced around the room with feigned interest, trying to ignore the vulnerable way she felt.

"Sometimes hu—people . . . I mean normal people . . . they sleep together," she said, as if it had just occurred to her. As if she hadn't fantasized about it many times over.

"Sometimes," Ryan agreed in that velvet deep voice. It curled in her stomach and spread like a disease until her whole body felt it, that timbre, that soft rasp.

She cleared her throat and went on. "Couples. Mothers with their children. Siblings . . . friends."

His eyes glittered. "Do you want to sleep with me, Sabelle?" he asked softly.

More than anything.

She shook her head and tried to imitate one of those laughs that said, *Don't be silly*. But the only thing silly in the room was her.

Ryan stilled, his gaze so hot that she felt it against her skin. His voice dark as honey, warm as amber, he said, "Come here."

Quickly, she took a step forward just in case he changed his mind, but paused when she realized how much that hasty movement had given away.

His brows went up in that way of his. The one that dared her to deny what he already knew. It was a hard look, a dangerous, masculine look that burned like a hunger inside her and pulled her to him like a towing line.

"I don't know . . ." she mumbled, and she didn't know what she didn't know. The bold being who'd dared to escape her chains had deserted her, leaving Sabelle exposed and uncertain.

"Suit yourself."

He closed his eyes and adjusted his pillows, as if he didn't care what choice she made. But there was tension in his body, in the cadence of his breath. He was waiting for her. Nervously, she perched on the edge of the bed.

Ryan didn't move or give an indication that he'd felt the dip in the mattress or her presence beside him. Tentatively, she swung her legs up and curled on her side, as far from him as she could, trying to cause as little disturbance as possible. But he'd pinned the covers at the bottom with his legs and she was cold.

Ryan let out a weary breath, rolled over, hooked an arm around her, and pulled her back against his chest, fitting her into the curve of his body. His arm went beneath her pillow, his leg between hers and his hand curled over her ribs. He was warmer than any blanket, so big and strong that she felt safe for the first time in maybe . . . ever.

"Go to sleep, Sabelle. I'll protect you from the monsters under the bed."

His voice was tired, but his words settled deep inside her and she knew they were true. He wouldn't abandon her to this frightening fate that was of her own making. He wouldn't turn out the light when she closed her eyes and disappear into the darkness.

He'd only just met her, certainly didn't trust her, yet he would do his best to keep her from harm.

7

Ryan's room was in the back of the house, his window under the boughs of a giant mesquite that had withstood monsoons, haboobs, and freak hailstorms aplenty. It was a tough, useful native of this desert land. The mesquite and he had been friends all his life. He'd climbed it as a boy, thanked it for not making him mow beneath it in the summer as an adolescent, and praised it for keeping the sun out of his room in the mornings as a teenager. Now the shadow of its branches moved across the wall with the intermittent gusts of wind outside.

It was almost 6:30 a.m., but he couldn't blame the breaking dawn for his wakefulness, because his room was still dark. It was Sabelle, all warm and soft and undeniably female in the bed beside him.

She wasn't asleep, either, and every little twitch she made burned a trail through his senses. He could still see her standing in his doorway, his high school T-shirt taut at her breasts, his jeans clinging to her thighs, tight on her hips. No bra. No underwear, unless she'd borrowed a pair of his. Even the sock feet had turned him on. The socks were too big, baggy at the ankles. Sexy in a way that defied explanation. She looked like some sugar-sweet porn star dressed in too-tight boy's clothes.

He was rock hard inside his jeans and there wasn't a damn thing he could do about it. Well, there was one thing, but the only part of him that thought it was a good idea couldn't be counted on for sound reasoning.

She'd come to use him, but she'd saved his life, too, and even though he knew he'd regret it later, he pulled her closer. His hips to hers, belly to spine, chest to shoulders. The pillow separated her cheek from his arm, but his other one crossed her ribs and came to rest beneath the warm, seductive weight of her breasts. A turn of his palm and he'd be cupping one.

He couldn't help himself. He let the backs of his fingers brush against the underside. It was so soft that it made him groan.

Her hair kept tangling with the shadow of beard he hadn't thought he'd need to shave. Now he wished he had so he could rub his chin against the silky skin at the crook of her neck.

"Are you asleep?" she asked in a soft breath.

The sound of her voice was a welcome distraction. He eased away so she wouldn't feel just how *un*asleep he was.

"Not yet."

"What are you thinking about?"

Touching. Kissing. Fucking. You.

"I'm wondering why I'm not asleep."

"Are you okay?"

She rolled onto her back just as he rose up on his arm to answer. The shift in weight, the dip in the mattress. She kept going, ending up on her side, facing him, her body warm and yielding against his, her hands spread over his ribs. She didn't try to put space between them. Neither did he. He eased down and brought her even closer. His body thought it a good decision. Not enough blood was reaching his brain to contradict it.

Her hair had fallen forward and Ryan skimmed it away from her face, letting his fingers linger at her cheek. She had the softest skin.

She brushed her fingers against his bare chest. He answered the liberty by trailing his hand down her shoulder to the soft slope of her back. She arched like a cat and the languid undulation rippled through his body. Jesus, she felt good. He had one shiny moment of sanity before she did it again. He couldn't remember why he'd thought this a bad idea.

She grew quiet once more, her mouth close to his throat, her breath a heated burst against the hollow. Had she just kissed him? He pressed his nose against the satiny skin of her temple and breathed her in.

"Thank you for letting me stay," she said in a voice so low that every part of him strained to listen.

"Not exactly a hardship, snowflake," he answered gruffly, and his hand slipped back up her spine to the warmth of her nape.

Again her body moved with his touch, a gentle wave against him. He needed to stop this. Nothing from her scream, to the explosion, to her truths and lies, to *this moment here*, said that getting closer was the thing to do. She was one beautiful, soft, scented bundle of trouble from any angle. Getting in deeper with Sabelle would only make her *his* bundle of beautiful, soft, scented trouble. The best decision he could make would be to roll over and go the fuck to sleep.

Her legs moved against his. He pushed one of his between them and her hips flexed forward, the heated center of her hot against his thigh. She made a soft sound that fired his blood and glanced up, her eyes a shimmering silver, her lips parted.

She'd come to him because she thought him a good man who would help her. He tried to remember that, because he didn't feel like such a good man right then. He just felt like a man.

He brushed his lips against hers, once, twice. Her lips clung to his, silky soft and sweetly wet. He eased back so he could see her face. Her eyes were wide, glittering, her lips dark in the pale oval of her face.

"Okay?" he whispered.

"Yes."

Her eyes met his and he was lost for a moment in all the complicated things he saw there.

"Tell me to stop."

"No."

He pressed his nose to her temple, his hands restless on her hips, her back. She was so small, the cage of her ribs delicate beneath the span of his hands. "Then tell me what you want."

She was breathless, her voice unsteady, husky, dark with promise. "You."

The answer should have sent him running, but it hit his senses like a drug. He took her mouth again, this time with less finesse, more of the driving need that had him swollen and heavy, wanting to strip her bare. His hands moved up to the soft weight of her breasts while he kissed her, licked the soft edges of her mouth, let her breath become his. The sound she made went through him like a current, flipping his brain off, switching everything else on.

He shifted and she was beneath him, where he'd wanted her almost from the first instant. He opened his mouth over the pulse that beat behind her ear and her hips bumped his.

He kissed again, easy and slow. There was no reason to rush. Not when she twined her arms around him and tangled her legs with his, not when she moved against him in that soft, fluid way that was driving him mad.

She kissed like it was her first time. Clumsy, clinging. Her teeth bumped his, her tongue darted hesitantly. Sexy in its awkwardness, alluring in its readiness.

"Like this," he said, parting her lips and deepening the kiss.

He held her tight as he brushed his tongue against hers, feeling her shiver, hearing the soft sound she made in her throat. Her hands slipped around to the small of his back as she pressed into him, her mouth hungry, her body fitting the hard angles of his. He kept the kisses slow, deep, wanting to keep kissing her until he'd managed to get every stitch of clothes off her and bury himself deep inside her body.

He couldn't remember ever needing something as much as he needed to be skin to skin with this woman. His hands were under her shirt, palms cupping the soft weight of her breasts, thumbs brushing the hard points of her nipples. He'd been painfully aware that she didn't have a bra since the moment he'd found her. Now he groaned and covered one breast with his mouth, sucking her nipple through the light cotton, feeling the point of no return bearing down on him like a runaway train.

He sat up, straddling her hips as he tugged her shirt up and over her head. He tossed it on the floor and sat back on his heels, looking down at her. She was the color of moonlight, all pearl and shimmer, her skin cool to the eyes, hot to the touch. She was so beautiful it caught him in his chest and squeezed.

Her breasts were full, tight with dark pink nipples that puckered at his stare. He caught them each between finger and thumb, rolling the pebbled tips, tugging gently. She bucked and covered her face with her arms.

Her chest filled when he leaned down and took the tight flesh in his mouth, and a small, strangled cry came from her lips. He licked and sucked and nuzzled until her body throbbed beneath his touch.

"You with me, snowflake?" he muttered, finding her mouth again. Her fingers scraped his scalp as she pushed them through his hair. "Tell me what you want."

"All of it."

Exactly the answer he had hoped to hear and yet . . . something in her voice . . . in the tension he felt in her body . . . He groaned and forced himself to pause. Reluctantly, he lifted his head and looked in her eyes. They were round and wide as she stilled.

"Did I . . . What's wrong?"

She'd been about to ask an entirely different question. One that spoke of inexperience, of a need for reassurance.

"Not a damn thing's wrong," he said, reining himself in, trying to cool his fired blood. "Especially not with you." He kissed her again because he couldn't help it. "But we should probably slow this down a little."

"Why?" she asked in a bewildered voice.

Because I'm an idiot and you don't even know what comes next, do you?

"I've seen . . . you meet new women at your bar and . . . and have sex with them that very night. Why does it suddenly need to be slow with me?"

He stared at her, openmouthed. He could feel the heat rising on her skin. If the light were brighter, he'd be able to see her blush. But she didn't look away or try to hide the defiant desire in her eyes.

There was something else there, too. Something deeper and more complex. The look she gave him could mean so many things.

"Have you ever done this before, Sabelle?" he asked gently.

Her lashes came down, hiding her thoughts, again. "Is there a prerequisite that I don't know about?" she asked coolly.

Except she couldn't quite pull it off. The question had a quaver in it.

Jesus, she was a virgin.

The thought formed with complete certainty. He was already withdrawing as he spoke. "No," he said. "It's just . . . your first time shouldn't be like this."

"Like what?"

"With someone you don't know," he said, wishing he didn't have to. "It should be someone special."

"Was your first time special?"

"I'm a man. It's different."

"How?"

"It just is."

She nodded, unconvinced. "How old do you think I am, Ryan?"

He pushed away and sat back against the headboard, watching her warily. She rolled to her knees and faced him, a bare-breasted goddess with tousled hair and lips red from kissing.

"Twenty-three, twenty-four? Somewhere around there."

"Old enough to know what I want."

She was waiting for him to think that through, but she still hadn't put her shirt back on and she looked like a wet dream come to life. Thinking took a lot more skill than he possessed right then.

"This is my first night with a man, because seers are female. All of us, females."

He frowned.

"It's always been so. Only females are gifted with the sight." She leaned forward, her hair a wild mess, her eyes blazing, breasts heavy and nipples hard. "I want to know what it feels like, Ryan."

"It?"

"You."

She climbed on top of him, straddling his thighs as he'd done hers and leaning down to kiss his belly just above the unfastened top button of his fly. His body jumped to attention as his head fell back, thumping the headboard. All hope for higher thought ceased. Her mouth was wet, her tongue hot against his skin. She nipped at the tender flesh as his cock strained against his jeans, ready and willing, no matter how wrong it was. She kissed him again, a little lower this time and he nearly came right then and there, like it was his first time, too.

He sat up, pulling her with him. Hands on her hips, he tugged her onto the hard length of him and held her face while he kissed her. She rocked against him, creating friction, pressure. He was so hard that it was almost pain. The good kind.

His hands were on her breasts again and all that was soft, warm woman was pressed against him. In total surrender, he rolled her beneath him, pausing just long enough to peel those tight jeans off her long, silky legs.

He stripped them both bare in minutes, caught between the urge to rush, to *take*, and the need to savor, to give. Her eyes shone in the shadows and her lips were swollen. The bruise on her cheek looked dark against her pale skin. Gently he kissed it, then the scratches on her collarbone, the burn on her ribs.

Her scent called to him, to a baser him. One that survived by instinct and obeyed his nature. He couldn't have kept his mouth off her if he'd tried.

"What are you . . . what are . . . oh . . ."

She was pink in the softest places, against his lips, against his tongue. He closed his eyes and lost himself in the way she tasted, the way she quivered. Her feet were flat to the mattress, her hips lifted to his mouth, thighs hot against his ears. She breathed in quick, urgent pants, then not at all while he kissed and licked and nipped.

He slipped his finger inside her, nearly growling at the feel of the tight, wet heat he found. He worked a second in as she bucked and softly cried out. He should have locked the door. Hell, he hadn't even closed it, but the house was silent and he couldn't pull away from her, even for a second. He sealed his lips over her sex and sucked.

Orgasm went through Sabelle like an earthquake. He felt the power of it in the flex of her thighs, the clenching fingers in his hair, the small keening sound she made in her throat. He rode it out with her, so into her that he wanted to do it all over again just to hear the erotic song of her cries, the sensual dance of her body. He made his way up to her mouth, kissing belly and ribs, breasts and chin on the way. He kissed her with her taste on his tongue and her scent in his blood.

Without breaking away, he reached for the nightstand drawer. Two condoms were on the bottom. They'd been in his pocket on the Fourth of July, when they'd closed Love's and held a barbecue in the backyard. Friends and neighbors had joined the celebration, bearing the stifling summer like true native Arizonians. The months before had been lonely and he'd thought maybe he'd get lucky that night. But in the end, he'd gotten drunk instead and passed out in his old room, alone. The condoms had gone into the drawer and had been there ever since.

Sabelle was the first woman he'd been with since . . . April? March? He didn't know and he didn't care.

He stopped kissing her long enough to roll the condom on and take her back in his arms. She locked her ankles at the small of his back and he eased into that silken, wet heat.

"Fuck," he breathed.

He kept his head down so she wouldn't see his eyes rolling back in his head and buried himself by inches, listening for cues in the sounds she made. All good; nothing that sounded like pain or retreat.

She was holding her breath. It came out in a rush against his ear. He was deep inside her, hard and heavy, wanting to thrust, go deeper.

"You okay?" he asked, forcing himself to pull back and take note.

She nodded, her eyes wide. A little dazed.

"You sure?"

She answered with a kiss that made him forget what he'd asked. He braced himself on arms that framed her head, and she shifted, making their fit more complete. He held still for a moment, eyes locked, chest tight, body roaring with lust. She moved beneath him and he rocked once, twice, and then fell into a rhythm of hard, cutting pleasure that spiraled down to her movements, her sounds, her needs.

Sabelle had turned him into a creature of senses, electric nerves, dark hunger. A pulsing shiver went through her, gripping muscles, gripping him.

She came again with a suddenness that clenched him in a hot fist and pushed him beyond the brink. He muffled her scream with a kiss and came hard, climax ripping through his body like a storm. And still the reverberations shuddered through her.

He was breathing heavy, the sound harsh in the silence. Sabelle was, too. His body covered hers and some weak voice of sanity told him he was probably crushing her. He tried to move but she made a sound of protest and held him tighter, arms and legs like ropes binding him to her. At last, he settled for rolling on his side, bringing her with him. He was still aroused, still connected. She was like an addiction, making him crave more even now.

They lay like that, not moving, not speaking until a door closed down the hall and the water was turned on a moment later. Ruby, getting into the shower.

In his arms, Sabelle stiffened, only just realizing the door was open. "Do you think she heard us?" she whispered, like they were high school sweethearts about to be busted by his mom and dad.

"No."

He got up and closed the door, though. The condom went into the trash. He grabbed an old shirt from the dresser to wipe them both clean before tossing it onto the laundry pile and climbing back in bed. Instantly, Sabelle's arms and legs entwined with his.

"You all right?" he asked, still hard, still wanting more

but concerned about the woman whose bare skin was warm against his body.

"I want to do that again," she said, her voice sleepy, her eyes closed.

He laughed. "That's good to know."

But her breathing had already slowed, her arms relaxing as sleep stole her from him. He pressed a kiss to her forehead and followed a second later.

8

Brandy woke Ryan with a soft, apologetic whine. He opened his eyes to find her sitting beside the bed, her nose on the mattress, watching him.

He rubbed his face and instantly, his mind filled. Sabelle. The explosion. The *sex*.

She was still wrapped around him like a clinging vine. He held on to her like he was afraid she'd get away. The clock on the nightstand read 4:11 p.m. They'd slept all day.

Carefully, Ryan eased his arm from beneath Sabelle's head, untangled his legs from hers, and withdrew. She made a soft sound of protest, but when he pulled the covers up, she settled again. She was so beautiful that he almost crawled right back in.

He rubbed his face again. God, what the fuck had he been thinking? She was trouble. Capital *T*. *Virgin* trouble at that.

Well, not anymore.

Fuck.

Even women who knew the ropes expected things from a man. They wanted to know who you were. Who you were going to be for them. They were disappointed when you didn't know. When you didn't want *them* to know.

This one was looking for a hero, and she'd cast Ryan as her knight in armor, come to save her from her evil enemies. But he was no fairy-tale prince even if she looked like Sleeping Beauty.

Yet here she was. In his bed. And like it or not, that pretty much changed everything.

Brandy whined once more.

"Shhhh," he breathed.

He scooped his pants off the floor, grabbed the clean shirt and flannel button-down from his open backpack, and tiptoed toward the door. It was a coward's out, sneaking around with his clothes and his shoes in hand, but she'd want to talk when she opened her pretty eyes.

He glanced back at her. The sheets were white, her hair a rich brown against them. One foot poked from the edge of the covers, pale toes and smooth sole leading to the fine bones of ankle and the soft curve of calf.

He could still taste her. Still hear the soft sounds she'd made in her throat when he'd been buried deep inside her. Still wanted to be inside her now. And there lay the crux of the problem.

He left the door open and padded down the hall. As he passed, family members judged him from framed pictures on the walls. He couldn't look at the smiling faces of his parents, brother, and sisters without thinking of Reece and his blackened remains now buried next to Mom and Dad. He paused in front of the last one—a snapshot from a few years ago of the four kids laughing around the bar at Love's as they toasted St. Patrick. So much had changed.

Dad had done his best raising them alone, but he'd gotten more than any one man could handle. The twins and all of their complications. Ruby, the rebel in the middle, living her own version of the after-school special. Ryan trying to overcompensate and be the child who never needed attention and failing repeatedly. At the end of the day, Ryan and Ruby had put just as many gray hairs on Dad's head as the twins.

Ryan and his old man hadn't seen eye to eye on anything, yet there were days when Ryan looked in the mirror and saw his father staring back. And he missed him. Missed the steady guidance. His unflappable strength. The calm assurance that things would work out.

He stared at his feet, unseeing for a moment until a small movement caught his eye. A scorpion sat less than an inch away from his bare left foot. Ryan jumped back.

It was a tiny one, but he knew from experience that they could be the worst. Scorpions were as much a part of Arizona as the dry heat. Baby scorpions were especially nasty, though, because they hadn't learned to control the flow of venom. The scorpion on the floor was the color of wet sand. It spun to face him, tail curled in the air and ready to sting. It wouldn't kill him if it got him, but it would hurt like a sonofabitch.

Ryan grabbed a picture from the wall and caught the thing with the sharp edge of the frame as it darted forward. He used the corner to grind it down to its flattened, bisected death.

Ryan hated scorpions. He'd take any one of the many spiders or snakes that called Arizona home over the small, stinging scorpion.

When he was seventeen, he'd stumbled over a piece of deadwood hiding a mother and her babies. He'd been stung multiple times and his leg had swollen up like a watermelon. He'd been so sick that his dad had taken him to the ER. And the pain . . . He'd had his nose broken twice, his left arm once, his shoulder dislocated a few times, and torn more ligaments than he could count. Even when they carried him out on a stretcher, he'd gritted his teeth and joked about it. But the pain of the fucking scorpions' poison had made him cry.

Which Reece found hysterical. After that, his brother thought it funny to catch them and leave them in jars by Ryan's bed, in the shower beside the shampoo, on the dash of his car. A very unmanly shudder went through him.

Brandy watched patiently as he flushed the little bastard before following him down the stairs. It was quiet on the first floor, Ruby long gone to Vegas. His sister didn't know how to be quiet . . . or neat. She'd obviously fed Brandy and let her out before she'd gone, or the dog would've woken Ryan long ago. Like a hurricane, Ruby had left the debris of her breakfast and Brandy's behind in the kitchen.

Brandy bolted outside as soon as he opened the front

door. Ryan shrugged into his clothes and shoes in the foyer before following more slowly, shivering in the desert cold. It had dipped below freezing every night this week and the days had barely broken the fifties. Rain kept the air damp and chilly, while the watery sunlight and pushy clouds gave the late afternoon a twilight cast. The street was deserted. No kids. No cars. Not even a dog barked in the distance.

With a jaw-popping yawn, Ryan stretched, wincing at the sting from the burn on his back. The pain reminded him that though the past twelve hours might not feel real, it had all happened.

Love's was gone.

And Princess Buttercup was asleep in his bed.

A black bird soared in the sky. Another landed on the spruce tree in the neighbor's yard. It opened its beak and turned its head. Brandy found the perfect spot to do her business, changed her mind, and began sniffing for a better one while Ryan turned his thoughts to what to do next.

He needed to contact the insurance company, start the paperwork, which would be endless, and do about a dozen other things he didn't want to do. Meaningless steps that would lead to the inevitable closing of a chapter in his life. A chapter he'd expected would last forever. A chapter he didn't know how to end.

For all his adult life and some of his adolescence, he'd been the caretaker of his family and business. Now the business was in ruins, the family scattered or dead, and Ryan didn't know what he would do—what he would be—without them.

One sister thought it best just to walk away. The other sister had headed for the hills with the love of her life—someone Ryan couldn't tolerate for more reasons than he cared to face this morning. He couldn't grasp how so much had changed in such a short time.

A dry rustle made him look to the right. Now there were three black birds in the spruce tree, clinging to a vibrating limb, sitting wing to wing. Their ebony heads swiveled when he moved, the beady eyes tracking him.

Their fixed attention felt eerie in the gloomy light. Thoughtful, hateful. He laughed at himself, the sound hollow and just as unnerving. Disquiet sifted like snow inside him. They were only birds, but still . . . they could be birds in someone else's tree. He picked up a handful of gravel from the drive and chucked a few of the bigger stones in their direction to scare them off. The biggest one opened its beak in a silent taunt. None of them moved. Feeling stupid, he threw another stone. It thunked the trunk below them hard enough that it should have scared all three away, but all they did was cock their heads and snap their beaks.

"Hurry up, Brandy," he told his dog, returning to the porch. "It's cold out here."

Brandy gave him a curious glance and started sniffing faster. He tossed the last stone from hand to hand while he waited.

He glanced at the tree again. The birds hadn't moved. Worse, it looked like a couple more might be up higher, but they were hidden by the thick needles and deep shadows, so he couldn't be sure. He hefted the rock and hurled it at the lower branches. A couple of the birds flapped their wings and levitated in irritation but settled after a moment.

At last, Brandy bounded to the porch with her big doggy smile, but she stopped on the third step and her head went down. Eyeing something behind Ryan, she gave a low, menacing, growl. Ryan spun around and scanned the porch. Dead leaves had congregated in the corners. A few more skittered across the planked surface. Nothing else moved.

A dark gust of wind buffeted the barren oak in the front yard and ruffled the pine. He looked over his shoulder. The birds were gone. Only now, that pricked at his uneasiness instead of expelling it. Brandy's growl grew louder, deeper.

"What's wrong?" he muttered.

His gaze searched the porch, the yard, the disconcertingly silent street. The stillness struck a chord inside him. Weren't the schools shut down for the holidays? Which meant kids should be out playing . . . but he couldn't remember ever seeing it so quiet.

Brandy's engine revved into a snarl.

She stared at the hanging porch swing. It swayed unevenly and the rusty chain squealed in protest. A big raven perched on its back, wings out and feathers spread. It puffed up and glared.

"Get out of here," Ryan snapped and stomped his foot at it.

The bird cocked its head derisively and didn't budge.

Brandy crept to Ryan's side with bent legs, her body low to the ground—a sure sign that she didn't think she could take whatever she sensed. It couldn't be the bird that had her freaked out. Granted, it was huge for a bird, but Brandy wouldn't care about that. He'd seen her charge a coyote before.

"What do you see, girl?"

A ridge of fur stood on end at her shoulders, her lips pulled back in threat, teeth bare and shiny with saliva.

Still the bird watched, swaying back and forth as the chair swung. Brandy's growl drew out, warped by a sudden burst of wind that rattled the branches overhead and stirred the deadfall below.

Something brushed against Ryan's neck. Feather-soft, serpent-quick. He ducked and swiped, spinning at the same time.

A man sat on the swing.

"*Fuck*," Ryan said on a sharp breath. Brandy let loose one hoarse bark but she didn't charge. "Who the hell are you? Where'd you come from?"

The man calmly stood. He wore a light blue dress shirt with a crisp collar and buttoned wrists. His blue jeans had a smart crease—the kind that meant he'd taken the time to iron them—and ended a little short at the ankles. Black socks and loafers finished the outfit. No jacket. No sign that he was cold either. He was tall and whipcord lean, angular in odd ways. At the broad shoulders that lacked meat, at the hips which seemed wide for a man. He had long arms and square hands. Workingman's hands. His chin was hard, his cheekbones edged.

And his eyes were green, just like Ryan's.

"Hello, Son," his father said in that deep tenor that reached out of Ryan's memories and solidified in the gloom.

Except his dad had died years ago.

Ryan's breath came in short bursts, like he'd been running. It steamed in the cold.

"It's good to see you, Son," his dad's imposter went on, tilting his head to the side and giving Ryan an indulgent smile. Ryan had grown up on that smile. He'd spent much of his life pandering to it. Craving it.

In this frosted dusk, it jarred, like the sound of a horn on a tranquil summer day.

Ryan crossed the porch in five angry steps, fists tight. The man who couldn't be his father lifted his hands defensively, but didn't back away. Instead of grabbing the stranger and throwing him off the porch, Ryan just stood there in front of him, numbed by shock, unable to wrench his gaze from the familiar features . . . the salt-and-pepper temples, the tiny white scar that bisected his left brow, the patient look in his green, green eyes.

"I hope I didn't scare you, Son. It wasn't my intention."

"Quit calling me *son*. And if you didn't want to scare me, why are you lurking on my porch? You almost gave my dog a heart attack."

Brandy wasn't growling anymore, but she wouldn't be making friends either. Her fur was still up, her eyes watchful and teeth bared. She scanned the porch, past his dad's look-alike, as if he weren't there.

Ryan narrowed his eyes on the man. "Someone with you?"

"Just me."

Back and forth Brandy's nose went, trying to sniff out

what had her scared. Ryan reached down and stroked the shepherd's head. Brandy flinched and then leaned into him with relief. "It's okay," he said.

Brandy didn't believe it.

"What do you want?" Ryan asked. "Why do you look like my dad?"

"I didn't realize you were so faithless, Ryan," the man said in his father's voice. "Your father's dead. But the spirit never dies, Son. You know that. Your brother knew that."

The tone matched every lecture Ryan had ever received from his dad and wiped him out in a deluge of memory.

Ryan left the reference to Reece alone and focused on what he could see. "You expect me to believe you're my dad's spirit?" he demanded.

"We can play twenty questions if that'll help."

Ryan's jaw set hard. It was exactly the kind of thing his dad would have said.

He heard a sound and glanced over to find the black bird had returned and brought a few of his buddies with him. They lined the railing around the porch, some on the top, some on the second tier. They watched with curious eyes and quick head bobs. Brandy whined.

"I don't have much time," the man said. "It goes without saying that I shouldn't be here at all."

"Don't let me hold you up," Ryan replied, swallowing the feeling of disrespect that was automatic. The man was not his father.

How can you be sure?

The question came from nowhere, filling his head. Confusing him.

The man who was *not* his father strolled to the windows that looked out from the front room. Cupping his hands, he peeked inside.

"Is Sabelle still sleeping?"

The sound of Sabelle's name on this imposter's lips snapped Ryan's attention back.

"How do you know Sabelle?"

The man who couldn't be his dad no matter what he said, no matter that his every movement awoke a memory so deep it hurt, moved to the next window. Ryan watched him, seeing the reflection of the birds in the glass. Their eyes glittered like shiny obsidian balls and the black gloss of their wings looked oiled. Something greedy seemed to fill the air, siphoning off the oxygen. Making it hard to breathe.

The man said, "She's probably faking it. She doesn't know how to sleep."

Listen to your father. He wants to help you.

Ryan's head whipped around. The birds stared back.

"She shouldn't be here, Son."

His dad had always been able to make a simple statement sound like a decree. It vibrated with power, authority. Challenging Ryan's doubts. Demanding respect. Years of obeying that voice goaded him now.

"Neither should you," Ryan answered.

Hurt registered in the man's eyes when he turned, but he looked down before Ryan could understand it.

"I'm too late, aren't I?" he asked. "She's already beguiled you."

"Beguiled?" Ryan gave a derogatory snort. "No."

But the word stuck like a tiny barb in his mind. *Beguiled.* An image flashed in his head. Himself, standing over her as she slept, craving her like an addict craves his next fix. He shook his head. It felt heavy.

The man gave Ryan a disappointed look. "All right. I get it. She's like every stray you ever brought home. You feel protective of her."

Ryan didn't like the comparison but he couldn't think of a feasible argument, not when his thoughts felt so *thick.*

"So what's your plan?" the man asked. He looked more like Ryan's dad with each passing second. Worry pulled his features and softened his eyes—another expression Ryan had seen a million times. One that felt too real to ignore. Too personal to be imitated.

What if he wasn't an imposter?

Yes. Open your eyes. See him for what he is.

"You gotta have a plan, Son," he went on. "You don't even know what she is. Where did she come from?"

Ryan didn't have those answers, but he didn't let on. "You tell me," he said blandly.

The man gave him a condescending shake of his head, a sardonic smile. Ryan's dad, head to toe. But there something important in the expectant silence. It tapped his subconscious and tipped his disquiet over a darker edge. All the moment needed was some creaking chains and screeching ravens.

Oh, wait . . .

Ryan tried to hold out and not be the first to speak. A tense pause like this—it could be read. That's how he knew a lie from the truth. Not the words the liar spoke, but the reticence of the silence in between.

The man gave nothing. His reserve was a cool pond that reflected, but never rippled.

"Okay," Ryan said at last. "I give. Where's she from?"

A thin trace of lightning flickered behind the clouds and the air smelled rainy and sulfurous. Ryan looked at the birds again. The big one spread its wings in victory. What did it think it had won?

"She's from the Beyond, Son," the man said gently. "Surely you've figured that out?"

"The Beyond," Ryan repeated, while inside a montage of Sabelle rolled across his mind. Her naked appearance in the parking lot, the openmouthed wonder, the big-eyed lies.

No. He hadn't fucking figured it out. Not even close.

Suddenly everything made sense in a too-fucked-up-for-words way. He should have known, but Sabelle didn't look like the kind of thing he expected to come from that terrible place.

The Beyond, from what Ryan had gathered the last time it had intruded in his life, was a euphemism for some parallel universe that demons and reapers called home. A few weeks ago, some of those demons had escaped the Beyond and paid the Loves a visit. Ryan's baby brother and sister had been caught up in stopping them and Reece had died trying to send them back where they belonged. Roxanne had survived because of what he'd done. According to her, the *world* had survived because of it. But Ryan was never really able to put that into perspective. The world was a pretty big place.

"I thought the Beyond was supposed to be all sealed up now," Ryan said in a tight voice.

"Parts of it are. But there will always be ways."

"Reece died to keep all the monsters out of our world. Are you saying he died for nothing?"

"I'm saying that there are a lot of monsters in the keep. Some smarter than others."

Ryan stared at him, nonplussed. He wished he could be incredulous, but he couldn't even fake it. Like it or not, the Beyond was real. The things that came out of it were real. He'd lost his brother to the Beyond. Roxanne, too, in a way. Ryan couldn't doubt its existence.

"What kind of monster do you think Sabelle is?"

The man leaned forward, green eyes so intent that Ryan couldn't look away. "Does it matter?"

No. It didn't.

"She's from the Beyond. You know that means she's dangerous. Nothing good ever came from there. But she blinded you and then she let you dip your stick and suddenly you're thinking with the wrong organ. Isn't that right?"

Ryan said nothing, using his silence as a weapon. But the man who might be his father used the same tactic back, watching Ryan as the quiet folded in on itself. After all, he was the one Ryan had learned it from in the first place.

After a moment, the man smiled. "Okay. You don't want to share. Your prerogative. But tell me something. How did she know what was going to happen at Love's?"

There was a trap in that question. Ryan sensed it even if he couldn't see it. "You'd have to ask her," he replied cautiously.

"Because you don't know?"

"Because it's her story to tell."

Cunning moved through the man's eyes. Ryan replayed his last words, looking for the source. He couldn't find it, but his thinking felt sluggish. Too slow to track the nuances of the conversation.

"Her story," the man repeated. "See, that's what worries me, Son. Her *stories*. I think she has a lot of them. Did she tell you she sees the future?"

Ryan nodded before he could stop himself.

"It's a lie."

"You don't know that."

"Think it through, Ryan. She knew about Love's because she made it happen."

"It was a gas leak."

"A leak no one can explain. It's true. Watch the news."

Don't fight. Believe, Ryan. Your father will help.

Ryan eyed the man who wasn't his dad. Could he be right?

"Ask her to tell you what's going to happen tomorrow. She won't be able to, but she won't tell you that. She'll just make you forget you asked." He gave Ryan a sly look. "She's good at that."

In his head, he heard Sabelle say, *No one can know their own future . . .*

Ryan kept his thoughts to himself, but he was remembering last night . . . this morning . . . Sabelle had, indeed, made him forget his questions.

Yeah, as distractions went, that one had done the trick.

Ryan pushed his fingers into his hair, wishing he knew

the way out of this conversation—of this whole encounter. He hated ambiguity. He liked black and white. Straight from the hip. No fancy footwork. His head felt like it was stuffed with cotton. He swayed and braced himself against the railing. The black birds fluttered with annoyance.

"Ah," the man said. "I think you understand."

Ryan wished he'd explain it, then. He didn't understand anything.

"She'll always have a ready answer. If she can't bluff her way out, she'll just tell you she hasn't seen it yet. Visions come when they want to come. Must be very convenient for her. She has a superpower she never has to prove. That would alarm me some, if I were you."

"But you're not me. Are you, *Dad*?"

The man stiffened, the gesture so reflexive, so much a part of Ryan's father's makeup, that Ryan almost blurted an apology for his rudeness. The fog in his head thickened. Why did he feel this way? What did it have to do with this man who was not his father but knew too much to be disregarded?

"So none of this sounds crazy to you, Ryan?"

"Oh, it's crazy," Ryan agreed, his words slurring. He felt drugged, but he hadn't eaten or drunk anything since he'd woken up. There was no way this stranger had dosed him with something without his being aware. There'd been no chance. No method available.

"And crazy doesn't concern you?"

"Things have changed since you've been gone, Da—" Ryan stopped before he said it. "Crazy's the new normal around here."

"But it's got to raise your antenna, a beauty like her, landing in your lap, here to save your life. All by herself. From the *Beyond*?"

Listen to him. Let him help. You can't do it alone.

Ryan narrowed his eyes and focused on what he wanted to say. "Get to the point or get out of here."

"You can't trust the Beyond, Ryan."

"Not all of it."

The man who maybe *could* be his dad stared at him with blazing eyes. "Not any of it. Do you think Roxanne and that abomination she's run off with are in a consensual relationship, Son?"

That one hit hard enough to break through. Roxanne and her *boyfriend*. She'd met him a month or two ago, just as everything had gone south.

While Reece was battling demons—personal and otherwise—a reaper . . . a fucking *reaper* . . . had disguised himself as a man and seduced Ryan's sister. Nothing Ryan had done or said could convince her to leave the bastard. She said the reaper was changed now. That she loved him. It made Ryan sick.

His dad spoke again, voice icy and hard. "Does that make sense to you? Roxanne? Sweet little *Roxanne*? Fucking *a reaper*?"

The profanity made Ryan blink. His dad never cursed. Ever. And God knew, there were many times when he should have. His dad was the kind of man who made up swearwords like *sugar beans* and *dog biscuit* and, if he was really pissed, maybe an occasional *dod gammit*. *Fuck*? Not in his lifetime.

The wrong of that burned. His dad was *dead.* Buried, long ago. It wasn't his lifetime anymore.

Yet, only his dad would share Ryan's biggest fear—that Roxanne hadn't chosen to be with the *man* who kept her from home. The man who wasn't even human.

"You think, when she tells you she's happy, it's Roxanne talking? Your 'lie meter' doesn't work with beings from the Beyond, Son. You can't trust it. You can't trust *her.*" He jabbed a finger toward the house, where Sabelle slept. "She's got your johnson in her hand and she's using it like a damn leash."

Ryan felt like he had at thirteen, when his dad caught him in the backyard with his hand down Tammy Kincaid's pants and the other up her shirt. It had him off balance. There was too much *right* in everything the man did, at odds with the great big *wrongs*—like his being here at all.

"She said she was a prisoner."

His father nodded solemnly. "All the better to play your heartstrings, Son. She's a creature who's gone rogue. A runaway. She'll do whatever she needs to get what she wants. She's using you. She *told* you she's using you. And you agreed to it. That doesn't sound like the Ryan I know."

Ryan was nodding. He stopped and tried again to clear his head. "What does she really want?" he asked without meaning to.

His dad leaned closer, eyes brilliant, blazing. Even the birds watched with interest. "What did she tell you?"

Answer him, answer him, answer him.

Sweat broke out on Ryan's brow as he fought for control of his own mind.

"Come on, Son. I always believed you were the smart one."

"Yeah. I could never figure that out."

"You wouldn't be doubting if you didn't know I was right." He nodded at the house. "She's bewitched you."

The word *bewitched* startled a laugh out of Ryan. It was such an improbable thing, being bewitched. The fog in his head receded just a little. Not enough.

"She thinks she can decide your *fate*, but you don't believe in fate, do you, Son?" said the man . . . imposter . . . father . . . *ghost* . . . ? "You never have."

"People change."

"Not that much. Answer this. Would you be so quick to believe her if she was a man?"

"Maybe."

"I'm your father, Ryan. *My* lie meter is always going to work."

The man who *must be* his father stared at him earnestly. "She's packaged herself just for you. Ryan Love's fantasy woman. Innocent, sexy, helpless, defiant. What did she tell you, Son? She took a big risk in coming. What does she think you can do?"

Find someone she didn't know, someplace in the north. Even in his own head it sounded nuts. And here he was, talking to his dead father in the middle of the afternoon. In front of a bunch of birds that had managed to freak him out.

What was wrong with him?

The birds fluttered on their railing like in a cartoon Ryan had seen when he was a kid. Their beaks opened and their wings ruffled. Birdy applause.

The disappointment in his father's eyes was all too familiar. It nearly sealed the deal. No way that look could be faked so accurately. This had to be his father, in spirit if not in flesh.

"It's going to come down to a choice, Son. She'll pit you against everything you value. Do you understand?"

Not even a little bit.

His father looked up, eyes very green in the pseudo-dusk. It seemed the shadows shifted around him, contorting his features and turning the caring gleam into something that made Ryan want to step back. The impression came from nowhere and vanished as quickly as it had appeared. But it cleared a trail through Ryan's consciousness, a corridor free of the clinging web of confusion and doubt.

Anger flashed in his dad's eyes, there and gone—but not so fast that Ryan didn't see it.

"Open your eyes, Ryan. Look what she's done to your life. You've lost your business—*our family's livelihood*—and your home. She's been here less than twenty-four hours and she's done all that."

Ryan didn't like any of those words. And he fucking hated how they made him feel.

"It wasn't her fault," he managed to say.

"What is *wrong* with you? Sabelle has broken the laws of God and nature alike by being here. If you could see clearly, you'd know that." His brows arched with concern and Ryan *felt* how much he cared. "Son, gods and humans have been dancing together for all of time. It never ends well for the human. She's manipulated you. She's going to keep on doing that. You need an exit plan. I know you're not going to just dump her, no matter what I say. It's not in you. But before you get in deeper, know how you're going to get out."

The birds fluttered some more, hopping and jockeying for a better perch, and Ryan could no longer remember why he was resisting.

"She'll make you think you're in love with her," his dad went on sadly while Ryan fought against a cesspool of doubt and confusion. "Then she'll make you her slave and you won't even know it's happening."

Ryan shook his head angrily.

A lone raven circled against the lavender sky. The others shuffled on the railing and chattered at one another as they watched. Ryan waved his hands at them. "Get out of here!" he shouted. All but the big one took off.

Ryan faced the man who shouldn't be his father. "You're just here to fuck things up," he said thickly.

"Things are already fucked-up enough, Ryan."

The black bird squawked with delight and took off with a noisy flapping of wings. As it soared away, the heavy fog in his head cleared. Relieved, Ryan turned back to the imposter, but he was gone.

Brandy gave a surprised bark and followed Ryan as he searched the yard, going around to the sides, peering over the fence into the backyard. There was no sign of his dad. Unsettled, he scooped the newspaper off the drive and headed back into the house.

On the mat just inside the foyer, he saw a postcard that had been slipped under the door, presumably after Ruby left this morning. He hadn't noticed it when he'd gone outside, but now he bent down and picked it up.

It was a picture of a famous landmark in Sedona, nestled against red rocks and blue sky. A street sign read *Cathedral Rock, Next Exit*. The words *Wa Chu* and two scribbled eyes were spray-painted across the sign. Ryan stared at it for a minute. He'd seen the graffiti before, but he couldn't remember where.

Frowning, he flipped the card over. On the back, someone had written in bold black marker: *SNOW*.

9

The bedroom was dim and quiet when Sabelle woke up. She was naked under the covers and the sheets beside her were cool. She turned her head and looked at the indent in Ryan's pillow and the empty space where he'd lain. The clock on the nightstand read 4:45 p.m. How long ago had he left her?

She stared at the ceiling, wondering what it meant that he'd let her wake up alone. Everything? Nothing at all? She was quickly learning that observing humans had done little to prepare her for acting like one.

So much had happened since last night—this morning. She could scarcely believe it.

But she was here now. She'd survived her escape, the explosion . . . her first sleep . . . her first . . . A shivery sigh escaped as memory of all she and Ryan had done in the pale light of dawn filled her. As longing to do it again wrapped her in silken chains.

She hadn't expected that. She'd imagined his touch, of course. Dreamed of it. But she'd never realized how deeply a kiss, *making love*, could affect someone like her. She'd never thought this experience could change her.

Now she realized how foolish she'd been. Even after she returned to her *rightful* place in the Beyond, she would never be the same oracle who had left.

She breathed deeply; the idea of returning was bitter and hard to swallow. But she wouldn't be going back as she'd left—a slave to the Sisters. She'd be returning as a ruler. Everything she did now was to that end, to follow her destiny.

She'd won Ryan over. He would help her find the ones who could aid her in fulfilling the prophecy. He *had* to help her.

So why had he left her alone in his bed?

The house groaned and creaked as she listened for his voice. Tiny bits of grit peppered the window in a sudden gust. A bird squawked loudly just outside, but she heard nothing else.

Anxious, she found her borrowed clothes, scattered on the floor, and dressed.

A movement caught her eye as she reached the stairway. She looked up and saw a strange, small bug clinging to the ceiling, watching her with black eyes and a curled, vibrating tail. Another like it had wedged itself up in the corner. That one was so pale it almost blended into the shadows. With a shudder, she hurried down the stairs.

The first floor had the still, vacant air that she'd found upstairs, but she heard faint music and followed the sound to a closed door that led to the basement. As she descended, the music grew louder, the beat hard and driving. She knew what she'd find even before she reached the bottom.

The basement had long ago been converted to a recreation room. Carpet covered the floor, and plastered walls attempted to disguise the long rectangular shape and subterranean feel. But small windows up high and level with the ground outside and too-bright artificial lighting only accented the cavelike shadows. One end of the room held a U-shaped sectional—Brandy curled up in its bend—and television, the other end an assortment of free weights, a bench, a mat, and a punching bag that hung from a thick chain and a big hook.

Ryan was stripped to the waist, wearing black gym shorts and nothing else. His hands were gloved, his feet bare, and a whole lot of gleaming skin showed in between. His mussed hair and darkly shadowed jaw gave him an untamed look. Sweat shone on his skin and his face held a hard, distant expression. He hadn't heard her approach—how could he, over the blaring music? His focus was on the bag that he pounded in a steady, punishing rhythm. Sabelle watched for a moment, feeling the anger behind each powerful blow he delivered.

The song ended, and in the hissing quiet before the next one started, he looked up and saw her. For a moment, he only stared, sweeping her from head to toe with a look so masculine, so possessive, that things she didn't have words for melted inside her. Those eyes had seen every inch of her body, those hands had touched her in every intimate place. And his mouth . . . She pulled in a shaky breath.

Ryan glanced away without speaking. Distancing. She'd seen him do it too many times to mistake it now.

The trickles of doubt that had chased her downstairs began to pool inside her. How many times had she watched Ryan take a woman to his bed, only to kiss her good-bye the next morning? The final kind of good-bye. He never pretended it would be more than that, never tried to convince them that he wanted anything long-term or permanent. The women came to him anyway. They took what he gave and left with regretful sighs when it was over. Occasionally one would try to hold on. It never went well for them.

Where did Sabelle fit in that pattern? The exception? Or the rule? What had his thoughts so tied up now? Was he wondering how to get rid of her? She wasn't like his other women, though. When he'd realized how inexperienced she was, he'd backed off so fast, he'd made her head spin. He thought she didn't know the game. He thought she'd cry or cling if he tried to send her on her way with a parting kiss.

He thought wrong. She wouldn't cry. She'd fight to stay. She had a destiny, and whether he liked it or not, Ryan was part of that.

"Good morning," she said, as if she hadn't seen that withdrawal in his eyes.

"Afternoon," he corrected, turning the music down.

Sabelle crossed her arms beneath her breasts, contemplating her next move. That first, unguarded glance he'd given her said he wasn't as cool as he might seem. If he was pulling away, it wasn't because he'd lost interest. The best thing she could do was pretend it didn't bother her. Reverse psychology, humans called it. She hoped she could pull it off.

"What time did you wake up?" she asked casually.

"Maybe a half hour ago." He shrugged. "Brandy had to go outside."

He used his teeth to tighten the Velcro strap at his wrist and went back to punching. Sabelle wandered over to the stand of weights and sat down at the bench. She lifted one in a curl, like she'd seen him do before. She could only guess that Ruby might have been the last to use it, because it wasn't too heavy. Trying her hardest to ignore Ryan, Sabelle brought it up again. Ten, and she could feel her muscles begin to stretch. She switched to the other arm.

"What are you doing?" he asked, his voice darkly impatient.

She hadn't realized that the pause in pummeling the bag had signified his attention being diverted to her. She glanced over her shoulder and surprised another molten look. *Busted*, as his siblings would say. And he knew it.

Hyperaware of him, Sabelle got to her feet and crossed to where he stood by the bag. "I'm just waiting for you to figure out what *you're* doing," she answered sweetly.

The statement hung between them, part challenge, part entreaty. His eyes narrowed, searching for hidden meanings. There were plenty of them to find, but he'd have to do it on his own.

The bag swayed from its hook in the ceiling; the silence stretched uncomfortably. Using his teeth again to pull the straps free, Ryan removed the gloves and tossed them in a bin nearby. Sabelle came closer, putting herself between him and the bag.

"You seem angry," she said. "Why?"

The bag behind her finished a rotation and gently bumped her forward. Ryan was close enough to touch now. He smelled of clean sweat and Ryan, a scent she'd never tire of. One she'd miss when she returned to the Beyond.

He stared down his nose at her, the look icy, arrogant, and definitely pissed off. Something had happened. She didn't know what, but she needed to fix this before it spiraled out of control.

The bag bumped her again and she used it to close the distance between them. The first time had been overwhelming, wonderful, but like standing beneath a waterfall. All at once, everywhere. Sensations she'd wanted to savor had sluiced her senses and drowned her will.

But she understood the basics now. The way a caress could bridge the gap that words would only widen. She touched his chest, dragging her fingers over the taut, slick muscle, the damp heat of his skin, watching the trail she made as she went lower, to the tense ridge of his abdomen and that line of soft hair that intrigued her even more now that she knew where it led.

He caught her hand before she reached the waist of his shorts. Startled, she glanced up to find his face close to hers, eyes locked on her fingers. The moment had teeth and fury, neither of which she understood. But she grasped the outcome if she let it bite. She would never have the chance again.

She leaned forward, up on tiptoes as she caught his mouth with hers. The kiss was clumsy but what she lacked in skill she made up for with determination. She pressed her body to his, trapping their hands between them. Her other arm went around his neck and she held on as she pushed him off balance. He compensated by leaning in just as the bag nudged her again. Triumphant, she licked and nipped at his lips as he'd done hers last night, refusing to let him put space between them, denying his right to *distance*.

"No," he said against her mouth, but his lips had parted and his tongue brushed against hers.

Not the answer she wanted. Her entire body had heated and she refused to accept *no*. She tugged her hand free of his hold and used it to shove the waist of his shorts down. She heard a wincing breath just before the hard length of him popped free and lay tight against his flat belly. She curled her fingers around it before he could stop her. She stroked.

Ryan's head fell forward and he expelled a breath. A hot wave went through her as she eased away far enough to see down the long line of his body to the point where she held him. He was big, thick, hard, and so silky-soft at the same time. She dragged her thumb across the slit at the tip and Ryan caught his breath again. He watched, too, eyes heavy-lidded, lips parted.

She tightened her grip and felt him strain against her palm.

"Like this," he said in a tight voice that fed those fires inside her. He closed his fingers around hers and guided them over the silk-on-steel feel of him. Up and down the hard length, a little tighter, slower. Sabelle made a sound in her throat that echoed throughout her body.

"Jesus," he breathed, taking her face between his hands and kissing her. Slowly, deeply, rougher than he'd been before. She worked his rigid flesh and stirred the embers that willingly burst into flames while he fanned them with white-hot kisses.

Lost in the hunger of it, she shivered as his fingers found the soft, vulnerable dip below her belly and pulled the buttons of her borrowed jeans free with a jerk that released them all the way. Her chest tightened, her nerves stretched. He yanked her pants down to her thighs and slid thick, hot fingers across her swollen sex. She made a sound. High, almost pained.

Her jeans kept her knees together when she wanted to spread them wide, give him access to all of her. She used her free hand to inch them down so she could kick them off. Immediately, Ryan pushed his leg forward and widened her stance, then rewarded her with ruthless, skilled fingers teasing over that piece of her that made her want to beg. She arched into his hand.

She still had her fingers around him, holding that tensile pulse, the hard shape, the indescribable feel. Emotions rushed her in swamping waves. The need to be still and capture this moment. The urge to rush its shores and have it all at once. She knew what came next and yet she had no idea how to get there. How to survive the total surrender it required.

She'd dreamed about Ryan touching her this way, but her imagination had lacked the *desperation* that laced her passion. It felt like she might die if he didn't touch her there, or there . . . anywhere . . . everywhere. The fierce desire inside frightened her and yet she couldn't turn away from it. Denying her own heartbeat seemed easier than denying herself Ryan.

He rested his forehead against hers, their labored breath shared between them. "You want to fuck, Sabelle?"

His voice was raw, his words subterfuge for a more complex question.

He thrust against her hand and slipped another finger inside her. Pressure, friction, demands that thrilled and terrified her.

"Answer me."

He spoke in her ear, the order so dark and graphic it made her moan.

"Yes," she said, a slave to his touch.

"Say it."

"I want to fuck."

Her face flamed as she spoke; her heart raced at her boldness. He pushed her shirt over her breasts and caught one nipple with his teeth, the bite careful and dangerous at the same time. Her head fell back and she moaned again. All the while, his fingers worked her, his mouth taunted, the rough shadow of beard burned and excited her. He was a torch; she was tinder.

She stroked his length from base to tip, squeezing. Maybe too hard, maybe just right. He hissed and thrust into her hand.

Muscles bunched as he lifted her like she weighed nothing. Two steps brought them to the wall. He pressed her back, molding her curves to his hard angles, trapping her between his strong arms. He took her mouth again, possessing it as he did her entire being. His kisses drugged her, destroying her ability to think as her emotions bowed to the onslaught.

Ryan pushed her past her limits into a free fall of sensation with the gruff mutter of words she couldn't quite hear, the rasp of his fingertips, the brush of his lips and slide of his tongue. A burst of hot breath puckered her nipple before the heat of his mouth made her entire body flush as he moved lower. She understood his destination and the total loss of control he would incite.

His beard scraped her thighs an instant before his mouth opened over her sex and his tongue found the point where it seemed all of her nerves came together. He used his hands to keep the soft, damp heat of her splayed as he licked and sucked and kissed while she reveled in the exquisite torture.

Last night—this morning—he'd made love to her. This, right now, was something altogether different. She felt the anger in him, the loss of his usual control. Instead of fear, she reveled in it. *This* was a Ryan no other woman had experienced. The savage man who fought and won but didn't share. The primal male who dominated and branded what he owned. Every touch made it clear that he meant to own her.

That's what this was about.

He didn't know it, but Ryan wasn't pushing her away. He was letting her in.

Sabelle jerked his head back and urged him to rise. Bending to meet him halfway, she kissed him in challenge.

Told him that he might possess her body, but no man—no *human*—would ever own her. In that instant they both saw something meant to be hidden. Sabelle caught her breath, trying to untangle the intricacy of what he'd revealed. She could only hope he was equally confused.

Their eyes locked in a stare that went deep. Naked, trembling, *fierce*, she refused to let him look away. Slowly she let her body slide down his, exchanging places and power. Her mouth opened to the taste of salt on his skin, to the feel of his rippling muscle against her tongue, the scent of aroused male in his prime. She reveled in the feel of all that bunched muscle and golden skin.

His erection was thick and heavy, the skin stretched so tight that the head felt like heated glass. She took him in her mouth like she knew what she was doing and found that perhaps she did. Instinct previously unknown drove her. Using his body as a guide—the sounds he made, the flex of his thighs, and the pump of his hips—she ran her lips over the satiny head and down the ridged shaft. His fingers dug into her hair and he muttered profanities and endearments in the same breath. Commands, praise, urgent instructions that she followed willingly.

She accidently caught him with the edge of her teeth and he hissed but said, "Easy. Do it again."

Filled with power, she did, mimicking what he'd done to her. The flat of her tongue, the swirl of it rising, sucking at the tip, humming at the base. "Fuck," he said again and pulled her up, wrapping her legs around his hips. She kissed him hard, clinging while he took himself in hand, pumped once, and then entered her in a fast and powerful thrust.

The head felt wide, her tissues tender and swollen, but she was wet and ready for him. He stretched her in a rush of heat, took possession of her as he buried himself to the hilt . . . *claimed* her effortlessly with the fury of his lust.

"Say it," he demanded again.

"Fuck me."

The profanity on her lips set them both afire. He drove himself deep, fingers anchored tight on her hips as he held her where he wanted and pounded in and out in a rhythm that matched the beat of her heart. That incredible, overwhelming tension gathered inside her and expanded, replacing thought with feeling, sense with delirium. It tore through her, roaring in her blood, in her ears, building as it crested.

She cried his name when she came, feeling the clench of muscle, the hot, slippery feel of orgasm ripping through her, molding her, changing her. Ryan threw his head back with a shout and inside her his seed spilled hot and eager.

"Christ," he rasped, curling into her, holding her as he shook from the force of it.

She pulled his hair until his head came up and he kissed her. Still hard inside her, but no longer filled with that bewildering fury. He shifted and that small movement was all it took. A second climax rippled through her. Ryan felt it and gave a shaky, masculine laugh before he stole her breath with another kiss. Exhausted, she collapsed against his chest, arms and legs clinging. His fingers skimmed down her spine and slowly he let her feet slip to the floor.

"Come on," he murmured, voice rumbling against her ear.

"Where?"

Instead of answering, he pulled her into a small bathroom barely big enough for his impressive bulk, her, and the sink, toilet, and shower. They would have had to maneuver to shut the door. They didn't bother. As soon as the water had warmed, Ryan pulled her in with him.

"Ryan," she asked, now that his touch had gentled. "What—"

"Later," he answered and lathered his hands, then her body.

Sabelle forgot what she had wanted to say anyway.

10

They didn't speak afterward, but Sabelle knew that the anger she'd felt simmering inside Ryan hadn't been doused, merely banked. He wrapped her in a soft towel, told her to rifle his closet for something to wear and meet him in the kitchen.

Uncertain what she'd face when she rejoined him, Sabelle pilfered a clean jersey with the number 17 on its back and put it on with her borrowed jeans. She stared into her reflection for a long moment, wishing she had a plan, but Ryan wasn't the kind of man you could plan for.

Bind him to you.

That's what Nadia had told her to do when she'd helped Sabelle escape. Sabelle had been more than happy to comply. Being bound to Ryan was the stuff of dreams. Bind him before Aisa, the most powerful and cunning of the Sisters, could turn him away from her.

At the time, it had sounded simple. What a foolish notion. Nothing to do with Ryan could ever be simple.

The television had been tuned to local news when Sabelle entered the front room, but only Brandy was there to watch it. The big dog opened her eyes and watched Sabelle approach. She wagged her tail once in greeting, but didn't bother to get up.

She found Ryan in the kitchen leaning against the counter, wearing faded blue jeans and an undershirt with a soft gray flannel shirt hanging open over it. The color made his eyes look smoky. He'd shaved while she'd been dressing and now her fingers itched to touch the smooth cheeks he'd uncovered.

He gazed at the television through the wide arch that separated the rooms, but he wasn't seeing it. As soon as she walked in, his eyes shifted to her, lingering on her face before it swept down, over her breasts. She needed a bra, but of course Ryan didn't have those in his closet or drawers any more than he had spare panties. His inspection ended at her feet. He stared at the baggy white socks for a long moment that felt mystifyingly charged.

A glass half full of amber liquid sat on the counter in front of him. An open bottle was next to it with big white letters spelling *RESERVOIR* on the front. Without a word he took a drink before pulling a stemmed glass from a cabinet and a bottle of wine from the refrigerator.

"You're in luck," he said. "Ruby always steals the good stuff."

"She steals?"

"From Love's." He shook his head. "I guess I won't have that problem anymore."

Now he had new problems. The silence as he pulled the cork from the bottle said it all. He filled the glass and slid it in front of her.

"It's wine," he said when she stared at it.

"I know it's wine," she shot back, suddenly defensive. Because knowing what it was and knowing it was wine by the smell and taste, the memory of having it before—those were different things.

The glass she lifted felt delicate. So fine, it skinned the wine instead of merely cupping it. Inside, the clear, pale liquid looked crisp and cold. Ryan watched her hold it to the light.

"Like a pro," he said.

Did he mean that in a good way?

A rush of flavor and sensation came with her first taste, quick and resonant, waking taste buds and warming her insides.

"Good stuff?" Ryan asked, his voice deep.

She glanced up and he caught her gaze, searching it in that way of his. The one that stripped her camouflage with unfailing ease.

"Yes."

The breathed word joined in her memory with all the other words he'd liked her to say when he was deep inside her. She knew now that the right ones spoken could turn this moment like a dime. She bit her lip and kept them safe in her very small arsenal for another time.

A few ice cubes clinked in the glass as Ryan took another drink and went back to not watching the television. A newspaper lay faceup beside her wine. The headlines read "3:00 a.m. Wake-Up Call." A picture of the burned-out street where Love's used to be was beneath it.

She looked up to find him watching her again, his eyes almost the same shade as his flannel shirt now. His gaze slid to the headlines. "Just like you said. They can't decide if the explosion was a leak, negligence, or just a freak accident." He paused. "Or sabotage. Seems that's a theory, too."

Had that last been directed at her?

"Are you trying to tell me something?" she said when it seemed he was waiting.

Another searching look she couldn't hold answered her. She wandered to the window and stared out at the yard stretching behind the house. It was unremarkable, but it ended in an open space littered with cactus, spindly desert trees, and stone. The setting sun looked like an explosion through the barren trees, bursting beneath a gloomy, dank sky, swathing the clouds in bruised violet and hot coral. It looked like the sky she'd seen from her bedroom window in the Beyond. Only that view never changed.

In this world, the sky held variances that struck like lightning through the palette of blue, smearing yellow into peach, burning lavender to ash. It was a lovely thing, the sky here. Ever changing. Alive, like the world beneath it. Her sky was a dead façade, frozen in a moment that shouldn't have been captured. As lifeless as the enslaved inhabitants who gazed upon it.

She dropped her gaze to a concrete patio with a wrought-iron table centered in the middle. Positioned directly outside the door, it looked desolate amid the scent of wood smoke and cold, an icon of summer long gone.

She sighed and started to turn away when something long and black darted across the surface of the table. It stopped just short of the edge and raised its tail. Just like the bug she'd seen on the ceiling. She stepped back quickly and bumped into Ryan, who'd moved behind her without her knowing. His hands came up to steady her, but he was staring at the table, too.

"I hate scorpions," he muttered.

"Is that what it is?" she said with a shudder. "I saw two others on the ceiling over the stairs."

Outside, the scorpion held its ninja pose. Watching them back. Reaching over her shoulder, Ryan snapped the blinds shut and started opening drawers until he found the one he'd apparently been looking for. He rifled through a chaos of papers, pens, keys, and other odds and ends, finally extracting a hammer. Grimly, he hefted it and headed out the back door, giving Brandy a sharp "*Stay!*" when she wanted to follow. After a moment, Sabelle heard the hammer bang against the iron table. Hard, loud. Repeatedly. Ryan cursed in between blows with impressive creativity. Finally, there was silence.

A few minutes passed before he returned to the kitchen. He tossed the hammer on the counter and took a drink from his glass. Only then did he look at Sabelle. She could feel his smoldering frustration lurking just beneath the skin. Brandy gave him an assessing look before moving to sit under the table, where she could watch him and stay out of his way at the same time. Sabelle wished she could do the same.

"I had company this afternoon," he said as if in answer to a question. "My old man stopped by for a heart-to-heart."

Her gaze snapped to his. "I thought your father was dead."

"Yeah. Imagine my surprise."

Dread needled her from the inside out as she moved closer.

"I expected you to already know," Ryan said, using his chin to point at the headline she'd predicted so accurately. "You didn't see my dad dropping by in your crystal ball?"

"It wasn't your dad, and I told you, it doesn't work that way. I'm not a security camera watching your front door."

Her answer made his eyes narrow. On any day, Ryan was an imposing man. Size alone would have been enough, but add in the rough edges, the scarred seams . . . all that raw confidence, the kind that came from being the biggest, baddest—and a lot of the time, smartest—man in the room, and it tipped the scales.

Ryan knew how to keep his cool in a fight; he kept it now. Still, she saw the embers burning in those smoky eyes and her dread became something more pervasive and alarming.

He knew.

He crossed his arms over his chest and leaned back against the counter. "Anything you want to tell me, Sabelle?" he asked in flat voice. "And I want you to think carefully about it before you speak."

How? How did he know?

He held her gaze, brows raised. He might have been enjoying her discomfort; he might not even care. She couldn't tell. Yet she knew for certain that all things great disdained what they could make feel small. It was a fact of life no matter who or what you called yourself. She kept her breathing shallow, her fragile calm intact, her cool as fixed as his.

"What did your visitor say?" she asked boldly.

Stormy green eyes held hers. "My *father* wanted to warn me about you. He figured you hadn't been very forthcoming with the truth."

"And you believe him?"

"You got a reason why I shouldn't?"

"You know he wasn't really your father."

"What, with him being dead and all."

Sabelle took another drink of wine, this one for courage. "What *truths* did he tell you?"

"That you're from the Beyond. That you're not human." He shrugged. "Little things."

"You believed that, too?" she asked, anger making hairline cracks in her composed façade. Her own emotions confused her. She wasn't human, and yet it wounded her that he'd be so easily convinced of it.

"I'm listening, Sabelle. Tell me he was lying."

A simple command spoken low, maybe even a little desperately. She wanted to obey. She wanted to keep going as they'd been, with Ryan thinking her simply a woman who needed his help. A woman who needed *him*. It wasn't so far from the truth.

Except she wasn't a woman. Only a female in a strange land with no one to turn to *but* Ryan.

"Do you believe our lives have purpose?" she asked,

staring at the bloodless fingers gripping the stem of her glass.

"Is that a rhetorical question?"

"I don't care for sarcasm, Ryan."

"Yeah? I don't care for lies."

"It's good we avoid them, then."

"Which isn't the same as telling the truth, is it?"

She didn't answer. Instead, she stared back, undaunted. What she was about to share contained no deceptions. She only wished it did.

"Destiny is controlled by the Three Sisters of the Fate, Ryan. It always has been. The Three control the Coven of Oracles. Seers. They use the seers' visions to shape destiny. Yours. The whole world's."

He listened with that implacable expression she was learning to hate. She might have been reading random words from the dictionary for all the reaction he gave.

"They are very powerful. Even gods fear the Sisters of Fate."

"I told you I don't believe in fate," he said.

"And I told you, your belief is unnecessary. It hasn't made a difference so far, in case you hadn't noticed."

Ryan swirled the amber liquid in his glass and drank it, watching her with that silvered stare. Unconvinced. She didn't know why she was surprised.

"Destiny doesn't care if you deny it, Ryan, because it will call you. And if you don't answer, it simply blasts you out of your complacency."

His eyes narrowed. A response at last. "You're pretty quick to pass judgment," he said.

Sabelle blushed. "I didn't mean—"

"I know what you meant," he said. "But you know what? We had a guy in the pub about a month ago, could bend a spoon with his mind."

"That doesn't compare to seeing the future," she answered, bewildered. "It's a parlor trick."

"Can you bend spoons?"

"No," she replied tartly.

"Then I wouldn't be so quick to dismiss it."

She looked away.

"This guy," Ryan went on. "He said he could bend the spoons because he believed that nothing was what it seemed."

"And that makes sense to you?" she scoffed, lifting her chin.

"Like you, for example," he said softly. "You're not what you seem to be. Are you?"

"That depends."

"On?"

"On what I seem to be to you."

"See, that's the problem. I don't know. So why don't you just cut to the chase and tell me? What are you, Sabelle?"

"How many times do you expect me to answer this question? I've told you. I'm an oracle. A powerful seer of the future."

"*What* are you?" he insisted with an angry head shake. "What *are* you? Is that even what you look like? Your face, your body?"

Understanding dawned and with it shame and horror. The demons that had invaded last month and run amok with Ryan's brother and sister had *appropriated* human bodies. They hadn't cared if those bodies were still in use at the time they took them either.

"You think I stole it? You think I've taken possession of someone's body?"

"Wouldn't be the first time something from the Beyond thought it had the right."

It was true, but that didn't make it hurt less.

"I don't know if this is how I look in the Beyond. I've never seen myself there. Mirrors are forbidden in the palace."

"The palace?" he deadpanned.

"The Three control fate. Did you expect them to live in a hovel?"

He shook his head. "You have royalty in the Beyond."

It wasn't a question and his tone made it clear there was no reverence in it either. "As you do in the human world," she answered. "We are of the same maker. Why are you surprised we have common ground?"

"Because what came out of the Beyond before had nothing in common with me."

"Tell me there aren't those in your world bent on hate and violence. Monsters who hurt children and defenseless people."

"They don't take over people's bodies. They don't *possess* people."

"They would if they could. Inability doesn't negate desire."

They glared at one another for a moment. Finally, Ryan shook his head. "Do I want to know why mirrors are forbidden?"

"I couldn't begin to guess what you want, Ryan," she said coolly. "But I'll tell you, anyway. The reason is fear. Mirrors can do more than reflect."

He laughed beneath his breath. Sabelle didn't know what he found funny in that, but she was too proud to ask. His scorn made her feel raw and vulnerable.

"Do any of those sisters have a thing for poisoned apples?" he asked, smiling that cold, unfeeling smile. She was learning to hate that, too.

"Only venomous creatures," she answered.

At the same time, they both turned their heads and looked at the window. Sabelle felt the blood draining from her face as she pictured the black scorpion and what it signified.

"That means it was Aisa," she murmured. "She's cruel and clever. Pretending to be your father was a stroke of genius. That kind of thing is her specialty."

"That kind of thing?"

"Dipping into someone's psyche. Using it to drive him mad with her illusions."

"Nice."

"Were there ravens?" she asked and Ryan's head jerked up, answering. Definitely Aisa. "The ravens used to belong to the demons. Now they're free game. Aisa uses them to see."

Ryan drained his drink, dumped the ice in the sink, and put the glass in the dishwasher. He didn't face her again. That was fine. What she had to say would be easier if she didn't have to watch his reactions.

She looked down, fingers numb against the wineglass. "You want to know what I am, Ryan?" she said, her words coming from a well of fury, pain, and humiliation. "I'm Aisa's slave. Her runaway slave."

He didn't speak for a long time but she knew that he'd turned. She wanted to look up, see what moved through his eyes, even though she knew it would disappoint her. Sympathy would feel like acid. Dispassion, salt in an open wound. Anger could be directed at anything. None would make it less real.

"If you're a slave," he said at last, "why hasn't she come to drag you back? She knows you're here."

"The Sisters cannot travel between worlds."

"But their slaves can?"

She lifted a shoulder. "Evidently. I didn't know it until it actually worked, though. I made the decision half expecting it to be my last." Still, she refused to look at him. "The Sisters don't have to be here to exert their power. They use illusion and manipulation to make others do their bidding. If you turned me over to her, I'm sure there'd be a generous reward."

"What kind of reward?"

Finally, she raised her chin and stared him down, needing to show him he hadn't hurt her. Her defiance backfired when he caught her eyes and held her gaze prisoner.

"Aisa is the most powerful of the Sisters and I am the most gifted of the seers. I'm sure the reward would be substantial."

"I think you've got a bit of a God complex, snowflake."

"Call it what you will."

"How would I turn you over to her if she can't come collect you?"

"Do you really expect me to tell you?"

"Do you really think I'd do it?" Ryan asked.

"I don't know what you'll do, Ryan. I'm entirely at your mercy."

His laugh sounded bitter. "If you say so."

"What else did Aisa tell you?" Sabelle asked. "No, let me guess. She said I'd seduced the sense out of you. That I'd stolen your will to resist with my overwhelming sexual prowess. Is that about right?"

Ryan moved suddenly, pushing away from the counter, graceful and predatory at the same time. He prowled to where she stood and backed her into the corner of the counter's L. One hand went on either side of her hips, boxing her in, bringing his eyes level with hers.

"*Beguiled* was the word used."

It was Sabelle's turn to laugh, but her eyes burned and a fist tightened around her heart.

"Beguiled," she mocked. "No female has ever beguiled you."

He reached out and tucked her hair behind her ear, letting the backs of his fingers skim her jaw. The gesture was so tender that Sabelle searched for the hidden threat.

"I didn't wear a condom," he said softly. "Downstairs."

It took her a moment to make sense of those words before the vivid memory played in her mind. She could feel him, even now, hot and thick inside her, hear her name on his lips, the tension in his body, the hot thrust of his release. She lowered her lashes.

"You know how many times that's happened, Sabelle?"

She shook her head, but she could guess. He was a careful man and his partners were always temporary.

"Never," he confirmed. "Not even once." His fingers curled gently around the column of her throat. He was so close that she could smell the soap on his skin, the faint scent of aftershave on his face. Beneath it was the delicious smell that was all his own, more intoxicating than the wine.

He went on, his voice making her shiver, making her yearn. "I went downstairs so pissed off I could hardly see. I swore I'd never touch you again."

He waited. She said nothing.

"It took you a minute to change my mind. One touch and I quit thinking. I was so into you, the condom never even occurred to me until the damage was done."

Damage.

She forced herself not to flinch.

"Which is the one you're mad about?" she asked. "Is it that you forgot? Or that you forgot with *me*? Maybe you're worried that you'll catch something from my inhuman being."

She could feel his stare burning into the top of her head, but she didn't look up. She couldn't. He'd see how hurt she was and that would be a mistake.

Ryan made a frustrated sound, his warm breath fanning her temple. "Why'd you make me back you into a corner to get the truth, Sabelle? You should have told me yourself."

There was no sarcasm, no emotion whatsoever in his words, but Sabelle felt it all the same. The burn of accusation, the sting of disappointment.

"You wouldn't have helped someone from the Beyond. Not after all it's taken from you. And like you said, I'm the definition of 'needs help.' "

She chanced a glance up. His jaw hardened.

"I don't help women I can't trust."

She couldn't stop the flinch this time and that made her angry. It gave her false courage.

"You don't trust at all, Ryan. Not ever."

He raised his brows in a speaking look. *Because people lied to him.*

"So what did you think, snowflake? You were just going to bat those baby blues at me and I'd never figure things out?" he asked. "You had it right—I've given all I plan to give to the Beyond. My brother is dead because of it. Nothing that comes out of there can be trusted. My father told me that, too. If it was your sister—"

"Not *my* sister. Don't make that mistake again. It was Aisa. Just a tactic in her manipulation playbook to win you over. It worked like a charm, apparently. It was probably exactly what you wanted to hear. I know you bolted out of bed this morning. You couldn't get away fast enough. Your *dead father* told you I'm some kind of sorceress who's turned you into my love slave, and you probably hit your knees in gratitude for the explanation. You can't keep your hands off me and you want it to be my fault. A trick. A *spell.* You can't walk away if you can't stop touching me, can you? And that chafes. That goes against the grain, having to deal with a woman *after.*"

"You don't know shit about me, Sabelle."

"I know enough. I've seen enough."

She snapped her mouth shut. She shouldn't have said that.

Ryan's eyes turned glacial. "Just how long were you up there watching me?"

"The Beyond is not *up there*," she shot back angrily. "It's not up or down. It's everywhere and everything."

"Yeah, well, my tiny human brain can't really grasp how someone who looks like you can come from everywhere."

"You don't like the way I look?" she taunted.

He answered with a wolf's smile. "Oh, I like. That was the plan, right? Dope me up with that killer body. Make me your boy toy. Someone you can control."

"I didn't realize that was an option."

"How long, Sabelle?"

"For as long as I needed to. No more, no less."

"Days? Months? Years? Throw me a bone."

"You ask me questions and mock my answers."

"Tell me the truth and we can skip that part. How long were you watching me?"

"You have an astounding ego. Have you ever heard that before?"

"Only from women who stalk me."

"It wasn't like that, but bravo on the deflection."

Disbelief glinted in his eyes. "Watching me doesn't make you an authority on who I am."

"No, but it's not rocket science, is it?"

Her face felt cold and numb, but she raised her gaze and gave him a derisive smile. "What part do I have wrong? You didn't bolt as soon as you could this morning?"

"Survival instinct."

"Women expect things, don't they, Ryan? They want intimacy. They want a piece of you to hold on to. But you don't like to share. As soon as you let someone get close, you become defensive and hurt them until they leave you."

He made a disdainful sound. His jaw was tight, his eyes hard. "Unlike you, I don't live in a fairy tale. I'm not looking for happily ever after."

"Who was Ruby talking about last night?"

Ryan frowned. "No one."

"Someone I reminded her of. Someone you were with long enough to introduce to your sister."

"No one important. She came into Love's. Ruby was there. No big deal. I hardly knew the girl."

"I wonder if she'd describe it the same way."

"I'm not having this conversation."

"Is that what it is? A conversation?"

Bristling silence filled in all the spaces around them, thick with challenge. She could almost feel that pacing fury inside him pause, eyeing her with distrust, with emotion so explosive it finally silenced her.

He caught her wrist when she tried to walk away from him and she looked up, into eyes that churned with turmoil. No doubt he saw the same in her eyes. Sabelle shook with the power of her own conflicted feelings, but she pushed through them. It was her turn to rule the corner of the ring.

He was too big to move, so she leaned into him, her fingers slipping beneath his undershirt, up to his chest.

"Say no to me, Ryan. Say you don't want me to touch you."

She trailed her fingers over his rigid abdomen and up to his muscled chest. Soft hair brushed her palms as she pushed his shirt higher. Without speaking, he watched her press her open mouth over his nipple, but he couldn't hide the beat of his heart as it raced beneath her hands. His breath came in a harsh burst as his hands slid over her hips to her buttocks. He gripped her tight and pulled her against him.

"Tell me you don't think of me on my knees, like I was downstairs." She went on tiptoe, arms winding around his neck, fingers in his hair. She tugged his head down so she could whisper in his ear. "Sucking you."

Reaction went through his body, his arms flexed, bringing her closer to his hardness, molding her soft curves to granite muscle. It gratified her. If she was going to be accused of seduction, she damned well wanted to know what it felt like. But before she could gloat, he caught her mouth in a kiss so slow, so deep, that she forgot what she'd hoped to accomplish when she began touching him.

Slowly, he teased her lips until they parted and her tongue found his. He stroked and teased until she sank into the kiss, into him. She was lost in the taste and feel of Ryan. Her body bent back, bowed to the curve of his as he leaned down, trying to bring all of her against all of him.

She moaned softly and he lifted her off her feet, still kissing her like he would never tire of it. Somehow the refrigerator was behind her, the cool surface the opposite of Ryan's heat. She wrapped her legs around his hips as he leaned them both into it.

She'd started something she didn't know how to stop. Didn't want to stop. The stakes were too high, though. She might be a passing distraction for him, but for Sabelle this was *real.* As real as anything she'd ever hoped to experience. She'd spent her whole life looking in from the outside. To be here, now, with Ryan Love drugging her with his kisses . . . If she wasn't careful she'd lose sight of any goal but making him do it again.

They'd begun in anger. Vengeance, even, on both of their parts. Now this thing between them became something on its own. A flash fire out of control.

With one hand, Ryan caught both of hers and pinned them over her head. His other hand slipped under her shirt to her breast. He rubbed, fingers strumming the puckered nipple, sending zings of sensation through her body.

He muttered something she was too far gone to hear or understand and then his hand slipped down the front of her pants. She was tender there; he was oh, so gentle. His lips coaxed sighs, his fingers moans. He made her come in a matter of minutes, capturing the cry that ripped from her throat with that sinful mouth and velvet tongue. Savoring it as she slowly melted into him. Only then did he ease his hold. Her legs felt unsteady when her feet touched the floor again. He'd scrambled what few wits she had left.

The look he gave her was all male, as hard as his body, as hot as his touch.

"No," he said over his shoulder as he left the kitchen.

She stared at him blankly, trying to weed through the turmoil of her emotion and grasp what that meant. When she did, her disbelief struck her silent. She'd thought the fire burned inside them both, that it had reduced Ryan to the same searing need it had her. Now she realized Ryan had never lost control.

She lifted her chin and tugged down her shirt, shamed and furious at the same time. "Feel better?" she demanded. "Feel like a man now that you're walking away? That's your favorite part, isn't it? Being the one who does the walking."

He paused and turned. The cool smirk she expected to see was nowhere to be found. Instead, he looked as confused and off balance as Sabelle felt. His face was hard, his expression tense. His erection strained against his jeans. She stared at it pointedly.

"No," he answered again. "But I'll survive."

She didn't even know what they were talking about anymore.

"Where are you going?" she demanded as he started up the stairs.

"Why don't you ask your crystal ball?"

"It's temperamental where you're concerned."

"Then I guess you'll just have to play it the human way. Wait and see."

11

Ryan climbed the stairs like he wasn't rock hard and shook up. He entered his old bedroom, where he'd slept with Sabelle just a few hours ago, trying to convince himself that he was in the right. But as he stared at the mussed covers, all he could think of was that Sabelle had looked like an angel when he'd left there and just now she'd looked like sin. His cock throbbed; his body felt like it did just before a fight. Stretched, antsy, ready for excitement and pain.

He yanked his backpack off the floor in the corner and tossed it on the bed with more force than necessary. The money was stuffed at the bottom. He dug down, pulled ten bills from one of the stacks, and stuffed it in his wallet. The rest he zipped back up in the pack. He almost made it out of the room without facing himself in the mirror. Almost. But he couldn't stand the cowardice of avoiding it.

In many ways, it felt like last night had happened to someone else and Ryan had only been a spectator to the explosion, the fires, the destruction of his life. But the last couple of hours? Up front and center, balls deep for the whole show.

He felt like someone had punched through his chest and ripped off all the scabs that covered his heart, scabs he'd mistakenly thought didn't even exist. Now he was bleeding out from a thousand bitter little wounds.

Whoever—whatever—had shown up on his porch today started the torture. The landslide of memories, of unresolved feelings that he'd just as soon forget. Sabelle had brought it all home. She'd lied to him and he hadn't had a clue about it. Sure, he'd thought she had secrets. But the Beyond? Not being human? Those weren't private matters she didn't want to air. Those were lies.

She wasn't an abducted woman who needed him to help her find safety. She was a runaway slave from a fucked-up place that shouldn't even exist. She thought she shaped the fate of the world, for Christ's sake. But fate was nothing more than the excuse people gave when they couldn't own up to their own mistakes. Ryan wasn't that guy. He knew how to man up to his own mistakes. He just hadn't expected her to put a spotlight on how many he'd been making.

From the huge pieces of himself he'd given to keep the family business afloat and the family together, to holding everyone back from their own dreams, even when he'd heard the voice of reason coming from inside, telling him to let it go—he'd lugged the past into a future where it didn't belong, where *he* didn't belong. Afraid that letting go would equal giving up.

Sabelle would probably say that was destiny, trying to change his course. Fate rebelling when he didn't comply.

He called it being too hardheaded to see reason.

He turned away from the mirror and left the room. On the way downstairs, he remembered to look up and scan the ceiling for the scorpions Sabelle said she'd spotted, but didn't see them. Still, one was too many. Two, an infestation. Aisa might like venomous creatures, but Orkin knew how to kill them. He'd have the exterminator come out as soon as he got back from Sedona.

Where he'd be leaving Sabelle behind. Where he would happily say good-bye to her smart, lying mouth, he corrected himself. The sooner, the better. So why did he fucking hate the idea?

Back in the kitchen, he found Sabelle turned away from the door, sipping her wine and lost in thought. The sun had gone down and she stood in shadow, a pale beam of moonlight with dark hair, winged brows, and lips a dusky rose. She stared into space, probably wondering how she'd been so off about his character. She'd come for a hero. She made him wish he could be one.

Which is the one you're mad about? Is it that you forgot? Or that you forgot with me?

Neither. He was mad at himself. Every second he spent with her tied them tighter, and like a dog on a short leash, he'd snapped. Downstairs. In the kitchen. She hadn't deserved it. She was scared, on the run, and he'd turned on her instead of helping. Why? Because of where she came from? That tasted too much like bigotry to swallow.

"Sabelle," he said softly.

She blinked and looked at him over her shoulder, eyes guarded. He didn't know what he meant to say until the words came out.

"I'm sorry."

She'd gotten under his skin and he didn't even know how it had happened. In what felt like a handful of moments, she'd turned his life inside out and he no longer understood his own actions and reactions. But he knew right from wrong.

He lifted his shoulders in a lost shrug. "I was wrong. I shouldn't have touched you. Not like that."

He looked into her eyes, needing to see what she was thinking. She stared back, saying nothing. Giving him no clues.

"I'm an asshole."

At last, she nodded. "Sometimes."

The response startled a smile from him. He hadn't expected her to agree. Not out loud, anyway.

"Are you going to keep being one now?" she asked.

The smile vanished. "Not if I can help it."

"Good."

He moved closer, holding her gaze. Waiting.

For forgiveness, he realized. It was a startling revelation. She'd lied to him, but it was Ryan who needed absolution. Since when did he care about that kind of thing?

"I'm sorry, too," Sabelle murmured, and a tight feeling

eased in his chest. "I should have told you the truth and let you make your own decisions."

"I wouldn't have listened. You were right."

She opened up a little, turning her shoulders, leaning her hip against the counter, but he lost her gaze in the shuffle. She fixed it on her wine. She'd poured more while he'd been upstairs. Now she took a deep drink and spoke again.

"You don't have to worry," she said in a low voice that shook just a little. "About the condom. I'm not human. Not a woman."

"I could argue that."

"You'd lose. I may be female, but you can't make me pregnant. And I don't have diseases." Her cheeks flushed. "Before you, I was unsullied."

He tilted his head and bent his knees, bringing his face level with hers so he could see her expression, but she kept her chin down, the stain of her blush his only clue.

"I'm afraid you're not unsullied anymore." When her eyes came up, he smiled. "I'm pretty sure I sullied every last inch of you, snowflake."

A small, shy smile answered and relief spread through him like pain. He'd been afraid. That she'd leave. That she wouldn't. That he'd care. That he shouldn't.

"Not quite every inch," she said, so softly he almost missed it. The tip of her left ear poked out of her hair. It was so red, her skin looked translucent.

"Who said we're finished?" he asked.

Lightning fast, clouded blue, she met his gaze but couldn't hold it.

He smoothed the surface of the counter with both hands and bent to give it an appraising look. "This feels pretty sturdy."

She laughed at him and suddenly the whole fucked-up mess didn't seem so bad. He moved closer still and touched her brow with his fingertips, slipping them down the silky line of her cheek.

She was the kind of beautiful that brought men to their knees. Swearing he wouldn't be one of them, Ryan leaned in and caught her bottom lips with his, then the upper, and then he covered her mouth and kissed her like he wanted to. He didn't touch her anywhere else, though. Just his mouth against hers. She sighed when he lifted his head and she came up on her toes to keep from letting the kiss go. He stared into her face, the pearl of her skin, the long lashes making lacy shadows against her cheeks. Her eyes opened slowly and she stole his ability to breathe.

"You are very beautiful, Sabelle," he said in a husky voice. "I don't care where you come from or what you think you are. You're beautiful."

She smiled into his eyes and Ryan felt another scab ripped off his stupid, bleeding heart.

He cleared his throat and moved away. "Are we good?" he asked, when he shouldn't.

"We're good," she answered softly.

"Are you ready to go?"

Go. With her. Take her, with him. So many variances, supports, nuts and bolts required to hold it together. If he did this thing, took her north where she was determined to go, he would only be getting in that much deeper.

It never ends well for the human, Son. She's manipulated you. She's going to keep on doing that.

Sabelle was watching him. Evidently, she had some experience with that. He didn't like knowing she'd seen him unaware. It made him feel like she knew his thoughts now.

He stepped back, covering the sudden withdrawal with action. Earlier he'd tossed the hammer on the counter. Now he picked it up and stuffed it back into the crap drawer where Ruby stuffed everything else. He had to shift things around to get it back in and he caught sight of a shiny corner of blue sky and red rocks peeking from the clutter.

Ryan pinched the edge of the picture between first and middle finger and fished out a postcard of Sedona on a glorious spring day. There was an exit sign in this one, too, this time for Oak Creek Canyon. Two scribbled eyes with the spray-painted words *Wa Chu.*

Suddenly Ryan remembered the bus stop across from Love's. That's where he'd seen the graffiti before. He flipped the postcard over. No address or postmark. Just one word in bold black marker: *Boom.*

He strode to the counter where the newspaper was spread. He hadn't told Sabelle about the other card he'd found on the doormat. He couldn't say if that had been intentional or if he'd legitimately forgotten. Like the condom.

Sabelle was watching him with a frown. He slid the postcard he held across the counter in front of her and pulled the other one out from under the paper. Silently she scrutinized first one, then the other, her brow puckered as she frowned. Maybe she was seeing signs within the signs. He didn't know.

"I meant to tell you sooner about that one. Someone slipped it under the door while we were asleep. I don't know how long the other one's been in that drawer."

She nodded woodenly, her face pale and her eyes huge.

"You look a little freaked out, snowflake. You said you'd been seeing signs. Like this?"

She shook her head. Stopped. Nodded. "But I wasn't sure until . . ."

"You weren't sure?" he said, his tone sharper than he'd meant. "You said it was risky coming . . . You did that on a hunch?"

"It was more than that but . . . The mind is a powerful thing, Ryan. It can show you what you want, even if it's not real."

Intrigued by the wistful tone and evasive eyes, Ryan said, "What did *you* want?"

She looked sad but she smiled through it. The kind of brave, brittle smile that usually meant something hurt. She met his gaze, not saying a word. Yet, those eyes spoke plenty. Ryan really wished he understood what they said.

"Have your changed your mind?" she asked.

"A couple hundred times. About what exactly?"

She tapped the postcards. "About taking me."

He stared at the blue skies and red rocks, the disturbing graffiti. No, he hadn't changed his mind about that. But everything else? Like he said, a couple hundred times.

"I'll take you," he said solemnly. Her fingers stilled and her head bent with relief. "But no more lies."

Her emphatic nod was meant to reassure him, but he wanted words and he wasn't going to budge until he got them.

"Say it, snowflake," he murmured, and of course in his head, the echoing memory of her hot whisper, *Fuck me*, unfurled like rolled silk.

"No more lies," she promised. "Can we still go today?"

Her hair brushed the back of his hands, soft and warm as heated satin.

"We'll leave just as soon as you tell me why we're really going."

She shook her head, and beneath his fingertips, her pulse pounded an erratic tempo. The caginess was back, too. She stared at his chin as she chose the words she'd share.

"Whoever sent those postcards, whoever's been sending me signs, was powerful enough to communicate with me in the Beyond." She picked up one of the cards. "'Boom,'" she read. "They knew about the explosion, before it happened. I have to believe that means they, too, are seers." She lifted the other card. "'Snow,'" she read. "That must mean me."

"I know."

"Whoever they are, they can *see*, yet the Sisters don't know they exist."

"How can you be sure?"

"Because they'd be dead. The Three are very jealous of their power. They would never tolerate rogue seers here on earth. Either they'd have brought them to the Beyond and enslaved them already or they'd have destroyed them."

"What do these *earth seers* want with you, snowflake?"

"I don't know. I swear, it's the truth."

"See, that's what bothers me. Not too many things know you're here, and so far none of them has been good. If something's calling you, I wouldn't be so sure answering is the right decision. They could be worse than what you came from."

She finally looked him in the eye again. "What choice do I have but to find out? Aisa knows where I am. She will see me returned or dead. Nothing else would be an option for her. As long as I'm here, I'm a danger to you. I'm going north because it's my only hope, my only chance to get away from them."

He shook his head. "Something doesn't feel right about this."

Her gaze slipped away and she went back to staring at the postcards.

"You feel it, too," he said grimly.

"I don't know what I feel. It's been almost forty-eight hours since I've had a vision. It's like having one of my senses turned off. I feel lost without it. The only thing I know is that I was called here for a reason. *I* have a destiny, just like you, Ryan." She gave him a tremulous smile. "I never thought I would. Seers are mediums, not catalysts. But here I am and I have to follow through to the end. I hope you can understand that. I *have* to do this, and this . . . my destiny . . ." She settled her finger on the postcards again. "My destiny is leading me here."

They both stared at the images on the cards. In his head, Ryan heard his dad speaking again. *What are you thinking, Son? Try using the big head for a change.*

But Ryan had heard the ring of truth in her words and he couldn't say no to her any more than he could to himself.

"All right, then. Let's get this show on the road."

12

The car they took had belonged to Ryan's brother, Reece. They found it parked in the garage, next to Ruby's red SUV. It was an older model that Sabelle didn't recognize but it had a long hood that promised a big engine. Steel gray with clean lines, it had two doors and *Charger R/T* on the grill. Ryan held the door for Brandy, tossed the few things they'd packed in the backseat with the dog, and got in behind the wheel. Sabelle slipped in on the other side. He met her gaze in the dim light.

"Buckle up, snowflake."

The car roared like a beast when he started it and the tires barked when he pulled out and stopped to watch the big garage door swing down. The moment felt final.

It wasn't late, but the winter chill hushed everything. Christmas lights sparkled merrily, but against the barren trees, prickly cactus, and towering palms, they seemed as garish as the inflated reindeer and giant Santas anchored in yards or on rooftops. The gloom that seeped in with the cold seemed to mock the gay decorations and flaunt the feeling of threat that lurked in the flickering shadows.

Sabelle anxiously watched the street disappear behind her. She hadn't lied to Ryan. She had no idea what waited at the end of the *Wa Chu* signs. Though she hadn't mentioned it—which wasn't the same as lying, she assured herself—for all she knew, it could be a trap. Her choices were limited, though. Staying in one place with Ryan would only bring captivity on the heels of disaster. This way, the Sisters might let Ryan live. Now that she was here, Sabelle realized what a mistake coming to Ryan had been. She should've been strong enough to stay away.

She should tell him that, but she lacked the courage. Instead she sat silently while he navigated through the traffic on the highway.

"We need to stop and pick up a few things before we go," he said as he took an exit not far from his house. "We both need clothes and I want to get some supplies."

He stopped in a crowded parking lot in front of a brightly lit building he called a superstore. He said it carried everything from toiletries to cell phones. Leaving the windows cracked, Ryan told Brandy to wait in the car. The dog look offended, but she obeyed, settling on the backseat with a grunt that spoke her displeasure.

"It's not the mall," he said to Sabelle when he took her hand. "But I didn't think you'd want to take the time for that. Not at this time of year, anyway."

She agreed. She felt the ticking clock inside her, counting down to a future she didn't know. Ryan's human way, *wait and see,* was not as easy as it looked. How did any of them survive not knowing what waited around the corner? Sure, they had guidance from the Sisters, but not on a one-to-one level. The Sisters cared about things like war, presidents and kings, catastrophes and power plays.

Ryan had always had Sabelle to guide him, of course. She'd done her best to help him over the years, though he'd resisted most of her efforts. He was stubborn that way. He liked to make his own mistakes. She couldn't fathom why.

Inside, he pointed toward a section of the store packed with racks of clothes and shoppers. "Pick out enough for a few days at least," he said. "Make sure to get stuff that's warm. We'll probably see snow up north. I'll meet you back here, okay?"

She nodded like shopping for clothes didn't make her feel skittish, like being alone in this crowded place didn't terrify her. He was gone before she could think of a way to stop him. She tamped down the surge of panic and bravely joined the pack of shoppers riffling the racks.

Now that they were away from his house, she didn't feel so hunted. The Sisters would track them, but if they stayed on the move, it would be harder. No doubt they were working the other seers around-the-clock, trying to compensate for Sabelle's absence. Trying to find her in the vast web of humanity.

Sabelle glanced around the busy store, wondering if any of the seers had sighted her yet. What would they think of her being here, now? Passing for human. Would it awake a yearning in them as watching Ryan had awakened one in Sabelle? Or would they judge her, disparage her for wanting to be something she was not?

Thoughts heavy, Sabelle sorted through soft sweaters and fuzzy fleece, long-sleeved tops with bright weaves and beaded patterns, mimicking the actions of the other shoppers who pulled items out to inspect before tossing them in their carts or returning them to the racks.

The store carried pants in every shade and cut: skinny, boot, low-rise, high-waisted. She had no idea which ones she should choose and she felt shallow for caring so much. She lost track of time as she moved through the racks, frustrated by her ignorance when it came to something as basic as dressing herself. Every item she touched came with the question . . . *Would Ryan like it?*

She stood holding a pink-and-white-striped sweater with a plunging neck and its twin in pale blue, wondering how other women—real women—made such decisions.

"The blue matches your eyes," Ryan said behind her.

She hadn't realized he was there. Instantly, her body went on alert, tingling with excitement at his presence. She glanced back and met his gaze.

"It does?"

He nodded. "You almost done?"

"I think so."

He had his hands full and dumped everything in their cart. He eyed the two pairs of jeans—one low-rise, one skinny—and blue sweater she'd thrown in—not because Ryan thought it matched her eyes, but because it was soft and looked warm—and shook his head.

He walked to another rack and riffled it for a pair of

yoga pants and some dove-gray sweatpants. Both went in the cart along with two thick hoodies, one lavender, one teal. On top of it all, he threw in a powder-blue jacket with big buttons and a round collar. Did it match her eyes, too?

"I think that's enough," she said, looking at it all, worried that she wouldn't be here long enough to wear it all. Ryan didn't know that, though. He thought once she reached Sedona, she planned to stay with her messengers.

With a dark look he pushed the cart across the aisle where bras, undies, and nightclothes hung in every shape and size. Sabelle followed, eyeing all the satin and lace. She'd seen the way he looked at her breasts, the way he tried *not* to look at her breasts but couldn't seem to help himself. She loved that look.

She knew it was wrong, feeling so excited over lingerie when her future was so nebulous. But she couldn't help it. She had this one chance to live, to try new things, to pretend that she was just like everyone else.

She touched the silky slips and ornate gowns as she passed them, a little breathless knowing that Ryan followed quietly behind her.

Even underthings had countless options and varied styles. She didn't even know what size she'd wear, let alone which of the many shapes would be the best. Full or demi? What was the difference between support and push-up? And what was a thong? She picked out a white bra that looked to be more lace than anything else, but Ryan stopped her with a smile and a shake of his head before she put it in the cart.

"What?" she asked.

His gaze dropped to her breasts and lingered for just a moment. Just long enough to make them feel tight and tingly.

"No way you're an A, snowflake." He reached for one with a C on the little plastic hanger. "Try that."

She took it from his hands, pleased and embarrassed and flushed to the core.

He watched with interest while she selected panties from a host of bins arranged in a circle, and she could feel the heat of his gaze as she sorted through the different styles. She found some to match the bra and blushed as she imagined how it would feel when he peeled them off her.

And he would.

He nodded at a door with the words *Dressing Room* and told her he'd wait while she made sure everything fit. "If you want to wear it out, you can. Just give me the tags."

Sabelle scooped up all of her items and went into one of the small rooms. She started with the bra and panties. White-laced and so lovely that she stood in front of the mirror admiring herself for a long time.

Ryan couldn't keep his hands off her in his hand-me-downs. What would he think if saw this? She pictured his dark head bent over her body, mouth hot on her breasts, sucking softly through the cotton of her shirt. The memory was enough to make her sway.

Conscious of Ryan just outside the door waiting, she quickly tried on everything else. The sweaters hugged her curves, enhanced by the wonderful bra. The jeans fit like a dream, soft and comfortable. Even the coat made her spin so she could see it from all angles. Ryan had sized her up with an eye for detail that whispered, *My hands have been here, and here.*

She transferred the penny key chain Ryan had given her to the pocket of her new jeans, gave herself one last look in the mirror, and emerged, overly conscious of how her new blue sweater matched her eyes and how her new bra hugged her breasts. When she met his hooded gaze, she knew that *he* knew what she'd been thinking.

He winked and desire blossomed low inside her.

She dropped her choices into the cart and looked up. It seemed she'd exchanged one set of chains for another. She'd become a slave to Ryan's eyes. He was watching her, as she'd known he would be. His gaze moved to her mouth. Her lips softened in response and her breathing slowed as she waited. But Ryan didn't shift, didn't lower his head and kiss her even though every cell in her body begged for it.

Finally, he tucked her hair behind her ear, leaned in, and whispered, "You need shoes."

Confused, agitated—*frustrated*—Sabelle watched him walk away.

Her irritation vanished when she saw the shoe department. It was hard to maintain self-control as she walked down the aisles of footwear. Ryan led her past the high heels and strappy sandals without slowing long enough for her to look, though, and didn't stop until they stood in front of a wall of sneakers in dozens of colors and patterns. She managed to pick quickly, but it was hard. She wished that one day she could return to this place of treasures and take her time.

"I think that's it," he said, checking the list he'd made. "Anything else you can think of?"

She shook her head and he led her toward the front of the store and the registers, walking ahead of her, tall body bent, elbows and forearms resting on the cart's handles as he pushed it in front of them.

"Ryan," she said hesitantly. "I need to tell you something."

He glanced back. "That's a confession voice."

She shouldn't be surprised. Ryan seemed able to see right through her.

"I can hear one of those a mile off," he said. "It's the hush to it. Like saying it softly will make whatever you have to say better."

"Is that how you always know what I'm thinking? You can tell by my voice?"

"I know what you're thinking?" he asked with a crooked smile—the one that made her voice breathy and her breasts heavy.

"It feels like it sometimes."

He gave a soft snort.

"Why is that funny?"

"Because I don't have a clue what you're thinking, snowflake. You're a mystery to me."

She gave him a veiled glance, expecting to see mockery. Instead he looked uncomfortable, as if he'd just revealed something he hadn't intended.

"What do you want to confess, Sabelle?" he murmured.

She pulled her gaze from his and tried to even her tone, but she knew he'd hear the many layers hidden inside her admission, and even if he only guessed half of them, he'd still figure out more than she wanted him to know. Yet she owed him the truth, on this at least.

"You asked me how long—"

Something darted across the floor and disappeared beneath a rack. It had been small, the size of a fingernail, perhaps. It had moved so fast she wasn't absolutely certain she'd even seen it.

Ryan gave her a curious look. "You okay?"

"I thought I saw something." She shook her head. Whatever it was, it was gone now. Ryan kept walking. Gladly, Sabelle moved on, too.

Side by side, they navigated the busy shoppers pushing their carts through the aisles. Sabelle took a deep breath and went on.

"I've been watching you since you were a boy."

His startled glance made her stomach plunge. He hated that he'd had an unknown voyeur. She'd known he would. Her limited time in his world had taught her why.

"I understand now how that must make you feel. In the palace, privacy doesn't exist. Before I came here, I don't think I truly knew what it meant. But everything is so *real* in your world. Everything I feel is so complex that I barely understand it myself." She swallowed hard. "I wasn't trying to invade your privacy, though. I swear it. I only wanted to . . . I mean, I've been guiding you. When you'd let me, anyway."

"Guiding me?" His voice was mellow, but his eyes had a sharp gleam.

"Most seers . . . all seers but me, actually. They can

only view the future through their visions. I'm able to follow it. I'm able to picture what, *who*, I want to see and call a vision of it. Like changing a channel on the television. Once I do that, I can . . ." Her words felt thick, her throat tight.

"You can what?" he asked warily.

"Influence."

"Influence," he repeated softly.

His smile struck a chill deep inside Sabelle. She didn't trust that smile.

"You think you've been doing that to me?" he asked. "*Influencing* what I do? The choices I make?"

There was no mistaking the skepticism in his tone, though his smile remained friendly. She shouldn't have broached this topic.

She nodded. "You rarely listen, but I've tried."

"When?" he demanded. "Specifically."

He pushed the cart into an empty aisle that held paintbrushes, hammers, and other tools. Apparently not high-priority items for holiday shoppers.

Taking her shoulders between his hands, he looked into her face. She had to tip her head back to meet his gaze, but for once she was more concerned about what she'd seen in his eyes than what he might find in hers.

"You wanted to have your sister's new boyfriend arrested," she said, remembering his frustration when Roxanne had told him that she was in love with Santo Castillo, a man who'd once been a reaper from the Beyond—Sabelle didn't know what he was now. "It was me who made you reconsider."

Hesitate was closer to the truth, but that's all it had taken, really. Once Ryan slowed down enough to think, he'd gone through the pros and cons, losses and benefits. It had seemed pretty obvious even to Ryan when he finished but Sabelle had nudged him, made him really think about what he planned to do.

"It was me, whispering in your ear. Reminding you that Roxanne is every bit as stubborn as you are. She wouldn't have ever forgiven you for your decision. I could see that future. You would have lost a piece of yourself as well as your sister."

Ryan's eyes narrowed and the smile disappeared. She could see his mind working, analyzing turning points in his life.

She'd been watching Ryan since the first time his younger brother and sister had appeared in a vision. He'd fascinated her then; he fascinated her now. The moment Nadia told her Ryan would die because the Sisters wanted it so, she knew she would do whatever it took to stop it.

"I had to come in person. I have to believe this is what I'm destined to do."

She took a deep breath, feeling so transparent that it hurt. But she'd started down this path and now she needed to see it through.

"When you found me in the parking lot," she said, "you asked me why I screamed."

He nodded, something new in his expression. Suspicion, most likely.

"I screamed because it was painful. It felt like I'd been ripped in two. It felt that way because that's what happened." She sucked in another breath, knowing her explanation probably confused him more. She tried to be clearer. "I told you no one can see their own future and that's the truth, but not all of it. I can't see anyone's future now. My mind's eye is blind and I don't know what's supposed to happen next, what's supposed to happen to anyone. I feel . . . crippled without it."

He studied her for a moment before slowly straightening and stepping close, invading her personal space without touching her. She wished he would. She *needed* his touch. She flattened her palms against his chest and tilted her head back to face whatever he intended to say.

He held her gaze and her fingers curled into his shirt. She came up on her toes as his hands slid over her hips. His kiss came with teeth that caught her lip in a tender nip. A shivery sigh escaped her.

"You're not crippled, snowflake," he said gently. "You might be limping for a while, but you'll figure things out. You're strong. You're brave." He kissed her again, this time just lips, soft against hers. "Have a little faith."

"That's not so easy when I know what we're running from."

"And here I thought we were running *to* something."

"We are, at the same time."

He smiled and rested his forehead against hers. "Guess we better get a running start, then."

"But what if we're running in the wrong direction?" she asked, voicing the fear she'd been afraid to acknowledge from the start. With her mind's eye blinded, how could she be certain about anything?

"We'll find out faster."

His answer surprised a laugh from her.

"Does this feel like the wrong direction, Sabelle?" he asked in a suddenly solemn voice.

"No." How could it when she was here? With Ryan. Every bit as fascinated as she'd been from afar. For all her fear, some secret part of her felt relief, too. She didn't want to know how or when she would have to say good-bye to him. If she couldn't see it, she could cling to the possibility that it wouldn't happen, no matter how foolish it was.

At the register, Sabelle watched as Ryan unloaded her clothes and shoes, an assortment of toiletries, a new cell phone, jeans for him, shirts to go with them, and a pack of men's briefs in blue, red, and black. The bras and undies came next and Ryan slid her a hot look that she felt to her toes. His eyes were like a forest in shadow and Sabelle wanted to whisper, *Wait until you see them on.*

As the machine beeped with each scan, a commotion started by the doors. The cashier looked over his shoulder as he hit the total button. Something had happened at the front of the store. Employees and an ancient security guard rushed to the section between the entrance and the snack bar.

"Must be a shoplifter," the cashier mumbled.

But a bad feeling suddenly coalesced inside Sabelle. She turned a worried look to Ryan just as he took his change.

"We need to get out of here," she said softly. "Now."

He nodded, loaded up the bags, and started for the door. Sabelle grabbed the last one. As she lifted it, a small, lethal-looking scorpion raced up the side. She gasped and dropped the bag and a dozen more scuttled out from inside. They made an arc from the end of the checkout counter in a miniature, terrifying blockade.

The cashier jumped, bumping the register, and more scorpions rushed out. Shouting profanities, he hit the switch to make his light blink. "Manager, register six," he yelled into his phone.

Ryan grabbed Sabelle's arm and took a step back, but the scorpions swarmed behind them, surrounding them completely while up ahead at the doors, people began to scream.

13

Ryan pulled Sabelle close, trying to calm down and not let the bugs freak him out. But it was hard. He could see them everywhere now. Climbing the walls, perched on the ceiling, scurrying across the walkways. People screamed throughout the store, pushing and shoving to escape, but there was no place to go where scorpions didn't already wait. Ryan had no idea where they'd all come from.

A clearing in the crowd spread at the front doors. From where Ryan stood he could see that the sliding-glass exits quivered with the jostling, stinging creatures. No one dared try to go through them.

Centered in the growing circle of terrified people stood a boy with dark skin, hair shaved short, and a Phoenix Suns sweatshirt. A woman who must be his mom hovered nearby clutching a younger version of the kid by one hand

and holding a baby girl with a pink bow in her hair with the other. The woman was sobbing.

The boy shuffled awkwardly in the middle of the impromptu stage, his eyes enormous and his mouth open, but silent. His arms and legs seemed to be at weird angles, striking a bizarre memory in Ryan of an old GI Joe doll Reece had had once upon a time. Each joint moved on a ball and a determined kid could make them all rotate backward. That's what the boy looked like, disjointed, at odds. His arms were twisted so his palms were out, his fingers spread and cocked at the knuckles. He wobbled from one foot to another, ankles turned funny, knees knocking. He made a one-eighty and stopped, facing Ryan and Sabelle.

Ryan could have called it. This was about the Beyond and the sister who wanted Sabelle back.

The kid's mother kept sobbing his name over and over, leaning in toward her son, but two men held her back.

"Cardell, come here, baby. Cardell, brush them off," she cried.

Cardell's eyes looked like pools of oil in an ivory pond. Even from a distance, Ryan could see the horror inside them. The kind that sealed the throat and paralyzed the mind. The kid was shaking with tremors that racked him at intervals as the scorpions scuttled across the floor, pushing the crowd farther back as they swarmed at Cardell's feet and covered his shoes. He didn't dance and stomp them. He didn't scream when they raced up his legs. The boy made a choking sound and a dark stain spread at the crotch of his jeans.

"*Cardell*," his mother moaned.

The terror came off him in waves, but it didn't seem like he was even aware of the venomous bugs. No, what scared Cardell was coming from the inside.

Ryan took Sabelle's hand and together they stepped closer to the edge of the crowd pulsing around the kid. Cardell's desperate gaze tracked them.

"Cardell," Ryan said, his voice sharp, hoping to jar the kid out of his catatonic state.

Ryan took another step forward and the scorpions skittered around him. He had to battle his phobia before he could move. It shamed him, but some things went deep. His revulsion and the memory of their stings had left a scar that he couldn't pretend didn't exist. And they were fucking everywhere.

"People," the boy shouted suddenly, silencing everyone. "Die. People will die."

Cardell's mother gasped and the crowd backed up even more. The kid sucked in air through labored breaths. Ryan found himself breathing deeply, as if his efforts would aid the boy. He stopped a few inches shy of the border the scorpions had made around Cardell. The ancient security guard told him to stay back, but it was obvious the old guy didn't plan to interfere.

Muttering a curse beneath his breath, Ryan dropped Sabelle's hand and stepped forward. The scorpions charged aggressively, their threat no less for their size—that many of them might even kill him. He jumped back quickly and they halted just shy of his shoes.

Tears spilled over Cardell's thick lashes and streamed down his face. He was shaking his head, his lips moving over a word he couldn't vocalize. He didn't need to. Ryan saw it.

Help.

"How?" Ryan asked softly. "How can I help?"

Cardell stared into his eyes. "Give. Her," he shouted, veins sticking out on his neck. "Give, give, give."

Ryan tried to move forward again. Two big striped scorpions came from nowhere and raced up Cardell's pant leg with incredible speed. They reached the rounded collar of his sweatshirt and slowed. Almost daintily, they inched onto his brown skin and struck their ninja poses on his jugular.

Something seemed to be moving on the back of each one. It took less than a second for Ryan to figure it out. Babies.

Ryan froze mid-step, hands in the air as if a weapon had been aimed. Cardell's breathing escalated, harsh and heavy and filled with all the fear that his eyes couldn't contain.

"Lying," he rasped. "Evil."

He raised a hand that was covered with squirming black, brown, and tan scorpions. So far it didn't look like they were stinging him, but the very sight made a cold sweat break out over Ryan's skin.

The kid pointed at Sabelle. "Lying. Tricking. Don't. Trust."

Spittle flew from his mouth and dribbled down his chin.

"Lying. Lying. Don't trust, Son. Lying. Go. Give. GIVEHERUP."

White foam appeared at the corners of Cardell's lips. Had he been stung? The boy's eyes rolled back in his head. He keeled to the right and Ryan rushed up to catch him, forcing himself past his fear to reach the boy.

As his hands slipped beneath the Cardell's arms, the scorpions dropped from their perch at his throat and hit the ground with a soft plop. They pushed their way to Ryan, inching up to the soles of his shoes, crawling over one another in their haste, scaly bodies writhing with pincers and stingers raised. They looked prehistoric. They looked deadly.

Ryan could hear Sabelle whispering his name as he watched the scorpions move down the kid's body, over the creases and bulges of his sweatshirt. He felt the dry scrape of their legs as they clambered over his fingers where he gripped Cardell. He braced for the stings that didn't come.

In a chaotic, revolting exodus, they scuttled to the floor. Like a wave churning with black sand and brown grit, they rippled through the screaming crowd, finding the seams where the floors and walls met, climbing up and disappearing into the panels of the ceiling, beneath the checkout counters, under the industrial carpet. In a matter of seconds, they were gone. Every last one of them.

Ryan had Cardell in his arms. He could feel the boy's muscles releasing the crackling tension that had held him.

"Water," he barked at the guard.

The old guy ran to the snack bar while Cardell's mother rushed up and took her child from Ryan, babbling "Thank you, thank you" as she held him.

Ryan waited long enough to see Cardell's eyes open

and hear him say "What happened?" before he stood and found Sabelle waiting behind him. He grabbed her hand, scooped their bags out of their abandoned cart, and pushed out the sliding doors before anyone had time to react and wonder why he'd been involved. With each step he took, he pictured the scorpions in the walls and ceiling, ready to drop down on them as they passed through the threshold.

Other people in the crowd were of the same mind and stormed the exit in a frenzy. Ryan pulled Sabelle in front of him and kept her there as he quickly steered her toward the car. She was shaking. So was he.

Brandy's loud and angry bark met them as they drew close. He opened the door, let her smell him, calmed her down before he closed her in again while he threw their purchases in the trunk.

They hadn't spoken. He didn't know what to say and Sabelle looked like she was in shock. "Get in the car," he said.

She turned those baby blues on him. "No. I can't keep putting you in danger. I thought you'd—"

"Get in the fucking car, Sabelle," he said. "Or I'll throw you in myself."

Her mouth snapped shut, but before she could move, a horn blared. A split second later another joined in. Suddenly car alarms began to wail and bleat from every vehicle in the lot. The customers who'd escaped the store were behind the wheels now, but they obviously hadn't triggered the alarms. He could see stunned faces through the windows as they tried to shut the alarms off. Ryan scanned the lot, watching as the vehicles on the move began careening out of control. One slammed into another, and like dominos, others followed until the sound of cars crashing echoed through the lot. Sabelle turned in place, gaping at the chain reaction of the accidents.

A minivan with a window decal of a happy family in graduated shapes and sizes slammed into an SUV right behind them. Ryan moved quickly, grabbing Sabelle's arms and pulling her back. The minivan's doors sprang open. The driver jumped out and ran away like he was being chased while the minivan kept moving forward, stalling directly behind the Challenger, blocking it. Parked cars on both sides and one in front effectively trapped them in the lot.

"Get in the car," he told Sabelle again. "I'm going to move the van and then we're getting the hell out of here."

She nodded, but before he'd taken a step, the radio switched on inside the minivan and loud, bouncy music blared out. It sounded like chipmunks singing Christmas carols. Suddenly the dial spun and hissing static reached out, louder than the horns and the crashes. Ryan didn't know how that was possible, but he didn't take time to reason it out. He stepped up to the open door.

The minivan had a full theater system inside with viewing screens embedded in the backs of both front seats. The displays lit up and more sibilant static joined the radio. The dial spun again, zipping through voices and melodies with such volume and speed they became ear-rupturing white noise. The cacophony was overwhelming, and the need to escape rode Ryan like a desert wind.

Ryan climbed into the driver's seat, turned the key,

and the sounds stopped. He cranked the wheel and moved the van to one side just as a police car zoomed in with lights flashing and siren screaming. The cruiser came to a screeching stop in the space Ryan had just cleared of the minivan and a uniformed officer leapt out like he was in hot pursuit. Ryan cut his eyes to Sabelle. She hadn't listened—why was he surprised? She still stood outside the car, watching with rounded eyes.

All around them, car lights blinked and radios blasted while frightened people dashed back and forth, seeking safety in a world gone crazy.

A low, deep growl rumbled across the disaster zone of a parking lot, coming from nowhere and everywhere at once. Shadows sprang through the wreckage, looming here, scampering low there. Inside the car, Brandy went ape-shit and raced from window to window, barking ferociously.

"What are you doing here?"

The deep voice spun both Ryan and Sabelle around. In the pandemonium, they'd forgotten about the police officer. He stood in the crisscrossed high beams of a pickup truck at an angle on his right and a Toyota Corolla on the left. It was the same cop who'd driven them home after the explosion at Love's. His name was Wiesel, Ryan remembered, and he'd smiled when he waved good-bye. He wasn't smiling now. His eyes were narrowed and he held his gun in his hand. From inside the Toyota, a woman screamed and the threatening growl took on a satisfied tone. Two cars down, someone else shrieked in terror, and suddenly it seemed that everyone was screaming. Ryan was covered in cold sweat. What now?

"What's going on here?" Wiesel snapped. "What have you done?"

Ryan didn't understand the man's anger, but he didn't need to understand it to know that nothing happening here, now, was of the real world. The question was: How far did this insanity stretch? How the hell were they going to get out of it?

Carefully, Ryan eased closer to Sabelle, wishing she'd get in the fucking car. Wiesel watched him, his expression a mask of icy rage. His face was blotched, his eyes wild. The screaming went on and on, but Wiesel didn't seem to hear it. His entire focus was on the two of them.

Ryan had his hands in the air and said, "No need for the gun. We're just in the wrong place at the wrong time. We're not the problem here."

"I said don't move!" Wiesel shouted.

He hadn't said it. Nor had Ryan moved. Neither had Sabelle.

"That's your last warning," Wiesel yelled, as if Ryan and Sabelle had tried to flee instead of remaining stone-still. "Stop or I'll shoot!"

He raised the gun, swiveled until it was aimed at Sabelle's head, and pulled the trigger. It happened so fast that the shot rang out before Ryan realized he'd fired. Instinct moved him as his mind scrambled to keep up. He hurled himself at her, shoving her out of the way just as the bullet sped past. It grazed her cheek and slammed through the rear window of an SUV in the next row over.

Instantly, Wiesel aimed again but Ryan didn't give him the chance to shoot. Bent low, he charged, ramming the cop back into the parked police car and slamming his wrist against the edge of the open door until the gun flew from his fingers. It bounced across the hood and onto the asphalt.

Ryan shouted at Sabelle, "Get in the fucking car!"

He didn't have a chance to see if she'd obeyed. Wiesel was on him in a fury. Ryan might be bigger and stronger than Wiesel, but the other man had the crazed strength of a lunatic. He fought with determination and excessive violence, gouging at Ryan's eyes, biting. He made claws with his fingers and went for the groin.

Ryan had been fighting most of his life, though. He knew how to move and how to use his weight and size to bring an opponent down. He managed to pin Wiesel against the cruiser, then he started pounding. He slammed punches into Wiesel's face and ribs, aiming for kidneys and the vulnerable belly. He landed at least a dozen blows that should have put the other man's lights out, but Wiesel didn't seem to feel any of it. Ryan leaned in and hammered his face, alternating punches and keeping them hard and fast. Wiesel managed to get his head forward and sank his teeth into one of Ryan's pectorals.

The pain shot through him. Ryan punched harder, but Wiesel didn't let go. Christ, he was going to bite a hunk of flesh right out of him. He staggered back, Wiesel coming with him, still latched on. A movement came from the corner of Ryan's eye, and a second later Sabelle had the gun that Wiesel had dropped. She pressed it to the other man's head. The cop's eyes widened and his jaw went slack—just for a second. Ryan jerked away, grabbed the pistol out of Sabelle's hand, and brought the butt hard against Wiesel's temple. It took a second direct hit but finally Wiesel's knees buckled.

Ryan caught him under the arms before he hit the blacktop. The cop's eyes had rolled back, leaving slits of white gleaming between his lashes and a stain of blood around his mouth. Ryan managed to muscle the man into the backseat of his cruiser so he didn't get run over by the lunacy of the evacuation happening all around them just as, overhead, a helicopter turned on its spotlight.

Knowing how this would look if caught on film, out of context, Ryan shut the cruiser's door and pulled Sabelle to their car. Brandy's bark was frantic when he yanked open the door and shoved Sabelle in. Before closing it, he leaned down, fury and fear pulsing in his blood.

"Next time I tell you to get in the fucking car, you do it."

She nodded.

He slammed the door and got in on the other side. It took maneuvering to get the car out of the parking spot. He skipped the clogged exit and went over the embankment and onto the street with squealing tires. The Challenger fishtailed and then he was speeding away from the wreckage.

With a grim look at the woman beside him, Ryan floored it.

14

They left the city lights behind and accelerated onto the highway, watching as flashing emergency vehicles flew past, moving in the opposite direction. Beside Ryan, Sabelle sat quietly. He didn't have a lot to say either. His heart had finally started to slow, but his knuckles burned and the bite on his chest throbbed like a sonofabitch. A circle of blood had filled in a ring on his shirt.

Everything that had happened played in his head, sharp-edged memories that sliced through him as they rotated from one to another. The scorpions. The kid. The parking lot. Wiesel firing his gun.

The cop had nearly killed Sabelle. A split second either way, and she'd be dead.

Sabelle had warned him that these sisters of hers—*Not my sisters!* he could hear her say angrily in his head—could twist a man into whatever they wanted him to be. He'd heard her. He'd even believed her. Seeing it, though . . . She'd said the mean one—Aisa—could drive someone to suicide without breaking a sweat. After looking into Wiesel's eyes, Ryan had no doubt. The cop had wanted him dead. Wiesel had been an asshole the other night, but not homicidal. Yet he'd pulled the trigger without hesitation. He'd aimed to kill. He'd *wanted* to kill.

Beside him, Sabelle sat stiffly, her face so pale that in the glow of the dashboard lights, she looked blue.

"Do you believe in fate yet?" she asked in a low, hurt voice. Her hand shook as she tucked a strand of hair behind her ear. "Do you think I've exaggerated the power of the Sisters? Do you still believe I have a God complex to go with my delusions of grandeur? This was just a demonstration, Ryan. The Three have been searching for us. They'll keep doing it. They'll keep finding us."

He'd worked that out on his own. As much as he hated it, he knew she spoke the truth.

She covered her face with her hands and shook her head. "I was wrong to come here. You can't help me. I'm just going to get you killed."

Probably true as well, but if she didn't have Ryan, she wouldn't survive either.

"Hey," he said. "Don't get all hopeless on me. I'm tougher than I look."

"You're human, Ryan. You'll never be enough to defeat them."

That truth was the hardest to take, so he chose not to believe it. "Have a little faith," he said.

He didn't take his eyes off the road, but felt her gaze

on his face. She was looking for answers, wondering what she should place her faith in, no doubt. A higher power? God's ability to strike out evil? Or Ryan, and the unspoken declaration that weighted his voice.

He didn't know what she might see in his face and he refused to look away from the road and meet her searching gaze. He wasn't ready to think about—let alone *talk about*—what he was feeling.

"You're tougher than you look, too, snowflake," he said softly. "Don't forget that."

"Tough?" she repeated with a bitter laugh.

"You busted out of prison, ran headlong into danger, and saved my ass. From where I'm sitting, tough as nails, baby."

She didn't smile, but he'd made her think.

He went on: "Maybe when we find these messengers of yours up north, they'll know how to fly under the radar. Maybe they're runaways, too."

"Not possible. No one's ever escaped."

He laughed. "You did."

She shifted and stared at her clenched hands resting in her lap. Her tension seemed to spike without cause. It snagged Ryan's attention and brought him back to the sinkhole of questions he had about Sabelle and how she'd come to be here, with him. Landing on that mystery only sucked him down to a bigger one. Why had she been permitted to stay? Why were either of them still alive?

The sisters could have turned their swarm of scorpions on Ryan and Sabelle and dosed them with lethal amounts of venom or crashed one of those out-of-control vehicles into them . . . or given Wiesel better aim. With the kind of power they had, the three of them could create a million deadly scenarios.

Yet here Ryan and Sabelle sat, alive and well and headed north.

"Tell me how you got away, Sabelle," he said.

"Why?"

"Because something's off. Too much of this"—he lifted a hand and waved it—"it doesn't make sense."

"Are you seriously trying to rationalize what just happened?" she said hotly. "You want it to make *sense*? We're talking about the Sisters of Fate, Ryan. We're talking about the Beyond. You'll never fit either one into something you can call *sense*."

He let out a heavy breath. "They could have killed us at least five times—and that's just tonight. I get why this Aisa doesn't want to do that where you're concerned. But me? That should be a no-brainer. I'm your wheels. Take me out of the equation and you're stranded."

The night lights and billboards flashed by as she considered what he'd said. Every time he saw red rocks, he felt chased. Which was the opposite of what was happening, wasn't it? They were following clues toward an end, not being herded toward it.

Unless it was all another illusion. Christ, he didn't know what to believe anymore.

Sabelle looked back at her hands. She worried them in her lap, thinking. She had so much going on in that head of hers that he could practically feel the steam from the effort. Overriding it all was fear, though. She liked to accuse him of not trusting. He was man enough to say she had good cause. His reserve had served him well in the past. No man was an island and all that, but a strong man stood a better chance if he stood far enough out that no one else could catch him by surprise and bring him down.

Sabelle was another matter, on every level. She'd latched onto him and somehow become his responsibility. Somehow become his to take care of. At least until he saw her to a safe harbor. If he was going to protect her until that point, though, he needed answers.

"Why are you afraid to tell me how you got here? You think I'll use it against you?"

The dip in his voice surprised him. Hell, who was he fooling? The whole avalanche of emotion that had begun when Sabelle crashed into his life surprised him.

"It's not that," she mumbled. "I just know you won't like what I have to say."

He shifted. Odds were good that she was right. Still, he needed to know, and obviously she needed to know it wouldn't make a difference. "Doesn't matter what you tell me, snowflake. I'm all in. We'll see this through together."

She slid her gaze across the darkened car, doubt as prevalent as the hissing tires and snaking road. "Do you mean that?" she asked.

Feeling heavy with the weight of it, Ryan reached over and took her hand. "Can't promise armor, but we've got some horsepower under the hood. I'll get you where you need to go."

She didn't smile. "And after that?"

"Now you're wanting me to see the future?"

A small smile curled her lips. "No. I just . . ." She took a deep breath and left the thought unfinished.

That was a good thing, he told himself. They'd moved into dangerous territory. He already felt chin deep in quicksand. He'd been sinking inch by inch since she'd turned those big, wondrous eyes on him. Any deeper and he didn't know how he'd get out.

And Ryan *always* knew how to get out.

"There are only so many things that can move between the Beyond and your world Ryan. Without . . . help, I mean," she said softly.

Help could be a lot of things, most of them ugly.

"Angels can, of course," she went on before he could dwell on it. "But demons, as you know, need a method. A doorway of some kind."

That's why they'd been so interested in Reece. He'd been one big revolving door for them. It still made Ryan's brain lock up when he thought of it, how they'd used his brother. How they'd killed him.

"There are guardians who are bred to patrol the borders and slip in and out undetected. It's said the guardians can even pass for human, but they're kept in isolation, away from the rest of us. No one even knows where."

And Sabelle was a slave in a palace. The Beyond was as difficult for Ryan to conceive of as dragons and unicorns.

"That leaves reapers," she continued so softly he almost didn't hear. "Reapers are intended to move back and forth. It's their purpose."

She gave him a wary look from beneath her lashes. Ryan felt the anxious flick of it but didn't turn his head.

There was no way he could hide his feelings. Reapers were a sore spot with him.

"There are some reapers who enjoy death more than they should. They're like drug addicts, always craving the next soul. They steal souls instead of ferrying them to their next destination. If they're caught, they're punished and only allowed the scraps and leftovers."

"What does that mean?" he asked in cold voice. He couldn't help it.

"When a natural death comes, a reaper is beckoned to take the soul. Condemned reapers are never beckoned. They live like vultures, watching their brethren and following, hoping they'll find a way to get there first."

"Jesus."

"The Sisters have gathered the damned and made a pact with them. These reapers do their bidding and the Sisters let them know when the seers predict the coming of a catastrophe. A feast of souls. They're always hungry."

"Why would the sisters do that?"

At Sabelle's curious glance, he explained, "You told me the three of them can't come here in person. What do they care about souls and outlawed reapers?"

Understanding lowered Sabelle's eyes. "The condemned spy for the Sisters."

"If they have seers telling them what's coming, why would they need spies?"

Sabelle grew quiet as she considered his question. He didn't know if she was editing her response or simply searching for the way to explain.

"Seers are like spotlights, randomly searching in the

dark. We see pieces of the future with brilliant clarity, and yet what's on the fringes is hazy, and past the border of that light . . . it's indiscernible. The world is immense. We can never see it all."

"What about the sisters? What do they see?"

It made sense to him that if the seers were spotlights, these powerful beings would be like small suns.

Sabelle shook her head. "The Three Sisters can't see the future. They can only control it."

"I'm lost."

"That's why they enslave the seers. I have no way of knowing for certain, but I believe at one time the Sisters could see the future but they lost their sight. Now they rely on us to tell them what's coming so they can change it or encourage it or fan it into chaos."

"Just for the hell of it?"

"Sometimes."

"You're saying there's no master plan? They're just playing a game without rules?"

"I don't think it was always that way, but now . . . yes."

Ryan swallowed hard. It made him sick to think of the world she described. He couldn't understand how something as sweet and caring as Sabelle had come out of it. It made him doubt her, no matter how he tried to fight it.

"I am kept secluded from the other seers because of my power. Aisa would never say it, but she's worried I'll taint the visions of the others somehow."

"Still lost."

"Sometimes our searchlights find the same thing, sometimes we see the same thing differently. Those visions are the most accurate because they come with perspective. Different views of the same future. My beam is so strong that the glare would wipe out the others."

He reached over, pulled her hand into his lap, and smoothed the long, fine-boned fingers over his thigh, keeping her anchored as her voice wavered. Now that he had her talking, she was giving up details she hadn't offered before. He wanted her to keep going.

"The palace where we live is huge. I've only seen parts of it. I don't know if that's because I'm isolated or if all seers have the same restrictions."

"So you never talk to any of them?"

"Only Nadia. She's a slave, too. A servant who brings me food, washes my clothes, keeps my environment clean."

"A slave's slave?" he asked.

"Even tasks like caring for myself are considered too much of a distraction. My purpose is to see. I think they only allow me breaks in between because they must."

She paused and Ryan felt the straining silence. She wanted to say something else.

"What do you do in those breaks?"

"Eat. Sleep. Bathe . . . Watch you."

He pulled his gaze from the road and looked at her, but Sabelle had turned her face away and so he was left with the smooth curve of cheek and a dark fall of hair as his only guide.

"Why me?"

He'd been asking that a lot. He desperately wanted an answer.

"My 'spotlight' found you when your twin brother and

sister were born. But it wasn't until they began dying and coming back that I learned how to call you." She took a deep breath.

Ryan listened, trying to place her words into a frame of reference. While he'd been going about his life, managing the bar, trying to keep his family together, walking his dog, Sabelle had been trapped in her own head, forced to use voyeurism as a means of escape. It troubled him, thinking of her seeking him out, spending her only free time watching him. He couldn't imagine how lonely she must have been.

"It's not like Google, having visions. You can't simply enter your search criteria and click *go*. What we see is random. Except for me. I can search. I can find."

"Anything?"

She shrugged. "I suppose, but in order to find something, you have to know what you're looking for. And you have to want to find it."

And she'd wanted to find him.

"I never told anyone I could do it, though. It's a dangerous power and I was afraid Aisa would find a way to use it against me."

"How?"

"If they knew what I could do, they'd force me to focus on important people. Like your president, like rulers all over the world. Imagine the havoc they could wreak knowing every political move and countermove of the future."

He nodded, dreadful understanding filling him. With that kind of knowledge, these terrible three could destroy the world as Ryan knew it.

"Have you ever tried to call a vision of anyone else?" he asked.

"Yes."

"Did it work?"

"Yes."

"Don't overwhelm me with the details."

He glanced over and caught a small smile.

"I practiced on others and I was able to bring them into focus, but the only vision I ever wanted to call was you." Her voice grew very soft. "With you, I learned how to create order. How to bring sequence into the vision."

"You mean you could call these visions chronologically?"

"Yes. I could pick up where I left off. It made me feel like I was part of it. Like I knew you. Like you knew I was there." She gave a small laugh. "Like you called me, too."

Ryan's skin felt tight. Once again the conversation had taken a turn, and he felt strangely stripped by it. His thoughts tumbled back through the years, making him wonder if he *had* felt her. He remembered times when he'd been alone with his problems and he'd bounced them out, needing guidance but too stubborn to ask for it. Had she heard?

It was such an invasion of privacy, what she was telling him. He should be pissed off, but what moved beneath his breastbone wasn't anger.

"I marked the passing years by you. How you changed, how you didn't. In the Beyond, we don't count time the way you do. Where I live, the sky is painted with perpetual sunset. Enough to light the way, but not enough to keep us awake. With no dawn to follow, there's no way to track the days or tally years. It's all one continuous flow with no way to measure it."

"Is that why you asked me how old I thought you were?"

She nodded. "I wasn't quite sure what your answer would be."

She pulled in a trembling breath and squared her shoulders. Ryan noted the signs and prepared for another confession he probably wouldn't like.

"I wasn't altogether truthful when I told you that I saw the explosion that destroyed Love's, Ryan. It wasn't me. Nadia heard the Sisters planning the destruction and she told me about it."

"Does Nadia know what you can do?"

"No," Sabelle said quickly. "I've never told anyone before. But she probably guessed that I was . . . interested in you."

An intriguing silence followed and Ryan wanted to probe it, but they'd already gone places he thought best avoided. Deeper would only put him in the borderlands of reckoning and emotion. Sabelle might be from another world, she might not think herself a woman, but Ryan knew enough about females to recognize what was happening. If he allowed it, they'd be toeing a line of confessions, declarations of feeling. Not anywhere close to a place Ryan wanted to be.

"After Nadia told me you were going to die, I searched and searched, but I could never see it. I didn't believe it. Then I saw the headlines—just a flash, but I knew it was true."

"I still don't understand why they'd want to kill me."

"Because of me, Ryan. Once I started calling your visions intentionally, my mind stayed fixed. Most of my visions focused on you. I knew better than to report them, so I lied. My productivity dropped. Aisa was not pleased. Somehow she figured out what was going on and she planned for your death. The explosion was sabotage, arranged by Aisa."

He thought of Love's, turned to rubble and ash, all because some bitch from the Beyond didn't want her slave distracted.

"Nadia bribed a reaper to help me escape. I've never been so scared in my life as I was moving through the darkness with him. It hurt, like nothing I could imagine. I entered your world as naked and vulnerable as an infant. I couldn't even believe I'd survived it."

Ryan exhaled and the hand still gripping the wheel clenched, but he said nothing and tried to disguise the way his insides tightened at the thought of Sabelle trusting a reaper with her life. Letting one touch her soul with its dark, corrupted fingers.

"I didn't have time to plan or prepare. I never really thought it was possible. But watching you had taught me how meaningless my existence was. How warped the Sisters had become. They use our searchlights to mine the unfolding drama of civilization, and when they can fan a flame and change the course of the world, they do. When they can bring disaster, they rush in for the thrill of it. The Sisters don't care about the Ryans or Rubys or Reeces in the world. They care about presidents and overlords. Wars.

Mass murder. These are the things that make history books, that shape the past, present, and future."

Sabelle looked out the window and shook her head.

"I was willing to risk death if that's what I needed to do to save you. You'd become *my* searchlight, in some strange way. I knew you'd help me. Now I see that making that decision was as wrong as all of Aisa's twisted manipulations. Because of me, you're on the run, too."

That was a lot of baggage she'd just loaded in the trunk and Ryan didn't know how to respond. Was she waiting for him to give something back? Did she want him to share now?

"Do you know where your sister and her reaper are?" she asked, catching him off guard.

He looked away from the road long enough to give her a surprised glance. "Why do you want to know that?"

"I just wondered. I was curious, I guess. When he was allowed to stay . . . I never understood."

Ryan almost laughed. "That makes two of us. Roxanne tried to explain it to me. She said he'd passed for human or something like that. I guess there was a test. I don't know. She even brought him to Reece's funeral."

Ryan still hadn't forgiven her for that.

"What's he like?" Sabelle asked.

Ryan shrugged, remembering the big, dark man with the sardonic smile and razor-sharp eyes. The body might be human, but those eyes . . . Ryan hadn't liked him on sight. Still, it had been a shock to learn that Santo Castillo, his little sister's new boyfriend, wasn't even human. Roxanne had explained how he'd managed to fool the reaper police, or whoever they were, and stay on earth. The whole time, Ryan had felt like he was trapped in a nightmare. He hadn't been able to accept it. Still couldn't understand how his sister had become so entwined with the reaper that she refused to leave him.

He slid a glance at Sabelle. Well, maybe he understood a little bit.

"I don't want to talk about Roxanne with you," Ryan said.

Instantly, Sabelle's eyes shuttered and the fragile link of *sharing* that had joined them broke. She tugged her hand away and folded it in her lap. Ryan realized too late just how sharp his voice had sounded and how Sabelle had interpreted his tone. He'd shut her down when he'd only meant to push her around a curve and onto another topic. It wasn't that he didn't want to talk about it with Sabelle specifically, though in his haste to nip the subject at the bud, that's what he'd said. He just couldn't go there. Not after his *father's* visit and accusations. Not yet, maybe not ever.

"Sabelle, I didn't mean that the way it came out."

"Don't," she said. "I get it."

"It's not that I don't trust you with it," he pushed. Her head turned and her gaze was steady on his face. He pulled his eyes from the road once more and met it. "I just don't talk about Roxanne. What's going on with her is her business and she's got enough people talking about her already."

"How convenient for you," Sabelle said flatly.

"Meaning?"

"Do you understand what I just told you? I told you how I came to be here. I just gave you the secret to how to give me back. I trust you not to do it. But you? You can't share anything that's important to you. Call it what you want, Ryan, but you're so good at not letting people in that you don't even know you're doing it anymore."

The tires hummed against the blacktop in the silence that followed and Ryan let it stretch. Maybe she was right. With a shake of her head, she went back to looking out the window, ignoring him. Brandy's head popped up from the back and the big dog wedged her upper body between the seats, a position that couldn't be comfortable, and whined. Sabelle stroked her and Brandy sighed with contentment.

Ryan let a few miles pass before he spoke. "With me, *in* isn't such a great place, snowflake."

"Do you have a stockpile of convenient excuses for your lack of trust?"

"You're going to psychoanalyze me now? You're probably qualified, what with all the hours of clinical observation you've put in."

"You know what I see, Ryan? I see a big, strong man with all the right parts in all the right places. Women get near you and they lose their minds. They know you're the real deal inside out, and they want to be a part of it. They want to wake up to your scent, hear your voice say their name, feel your body next to theirs."

Her voice wavered and the longing in it struck a note in Ryan that made him want to pull over and drag her across the console and into his lap. He hadn't had sex in a car since college, and he'd been about five inches shorter and fifty pounds lighter back then. But Sabelle was just the kind of motivation to make a man achieve the impossible.

Sabelle went on before he could act on the impulse. The longing in her voice vanished. Bitter truth replaced it.

"They flock to you, don't they? A different woman every night if you want. They don't realize that's all you'll ever want."

"You looking to become something permanent, Sabelle?" he asked, his voice steady, his emotions in turmoil.

She laughed. "If I was?"

"I guess I'd need to know how that was going to work."

"Nice bluff, Ryan. You know how it works. Faith. You're quick to point out how I lack it, but when was the last time you took a leap of faith?"

Something reared up inside him, a great beast of desire to prove her wrong. To show her that he was more than the man who said hello and good-bye while giving nothing in between. But proof was a flipping coin that only she could catch and this woman had no place in his life.

She was transient, as fleeting as a summer storm. Only a fool would think she'd be a keeper.

She shook her head. "Didn't think I'd call you on it, did you?"

"I could say the same to you."

"Really? I've been watching you for years. That's no passing thing."

"You're in the trenches now. The view has changed a bit."

"Not so much."

His heart thumped hard and heavy in his chest. One word could change everything.

Stay.

He wanted to say it and that scared the hell out of him.

"Don't worry, Ryan," she chided. "There's no hook. Even if you wanted me, Aisa would never allow it. After tomorrow, I won't be your problem anymore."

"I never said you were."

"That's the point, isn't it? You never say."

Ryan stared at her profile, wishing she'd look at him. Wishing he had the words she wanted. Maybe he did. Maybe it was for the best that he kept them inside. Maybe he was just trying to convince himself that this leap of faith wouldn't destroy everything he considered himself to be.

15

Sabelle held her breath, wanting to see his face, needing to hide her own. They'd wandered close to a razor's edge that had appeared out of nowhere, leading to a drop into a vast unknown.

"Got me all figured out, don't you?" Ryan said, his voice a deep rumble in the tight space.

She heard frustration in the question, but she sensed it was directed at himself, and a desperate kind of hope filled her no matter how she tried to stop it.

"Am I wrong?"

Please, tell me I'm wrong.

The silence siphoned the air from the hissing quiet, leaving her light-headed and afraid. Why was she doing this? She couldn't stay. Aisa would hunt her down and destroy her before she allowed it, and the only way *out* was the one Sabelle had planned all along. Destroy Aisa and take her place. Only Sabelle would bring justice to the fates. She would guide with hope and benevolence.

Ryan didn't fit into that future. Knowing this didn't stop the yearning or the need to hear Ryan say he wanted to, though.

She turned her face and stared out the window so he wouldn't see her confusion or dismay. One word and he could crumble all the carefully constructed rationalizations she'd built.

Stay.

The blacktop and lighted advertisements blurred as they sped past. She should break the silence before it became unsurmountable. But there was safety in the unsaid. She was fast learning that every time she peeled back a layer of Ryan, he managed to do the same to her.

Still, it seemed cowardly to hide. She'd risked *everything* to come here. Cowering behind her dread now was unacceptable. Fate stretched out like the road ahead. Hers, his. Lit only so far, it might change in the next second. It might twist after the next bend and spin them both in another direction. More than anything, she wished she could see *their* future, wished she had some way of knowing if her blindness was caused by the tangle of their lives or simply by geography. Maybe her gifts didn't work in Ryan's world.

"I'd be a poor stalker indeed if I didn't understand you after all this time," she said, finding that within her hurt was anger. "You'll be relieved when I'm out of your life."

"Will I?"

"Do you deny it?"

"Would it do any good?"

"No. You'd only be doing it to be contrary and we'd both know it. Even before . . . when I tried to guide you from the Beyond, you never listened to me. If I nudged you to the right, you'd go left. If I whispered yes, you'd say no."

"Maybe I didn't like being pushed."

"I never pushed."

"You're pushing now."

Was that what this was? Not Ryan waking up and realizing that he needed her, but Sabelle backing him into a corner, trying to take what he would never give? She curled her fingers into her palms, refusing to let him see how shredded she felt by that perception.

It was time to change the subject, steer clear of this vicious cyclone. She knew exactly what to say to distract him. Of course she did.

"I won't push anymore, Ryan. I won't ask about your sister or her—I won't tell you they were fated to be together. I won't tell you how long it will last."

He glanced at her in surprise. "Fated? Is that true?" he asked with heartbreaking predictability.

She wanted to cry.

"You don't believe in fate," she reminded him woodenly.

"I don't believe in angels either, yet here you are."

At least he hadn't called her a demon.

"I need to know something," he went on. "Before we go another mile. Did you know about my brother and sister? Did you see what was going to happen to them when you were pulling strings and playing with my fate?"

His words offended her to her core. She never *played*. She never *pulled strings*. She guided. She did the best she could. He didn't appreciate it. Not then, not now.

She cleared her throat and said calmly, "I saw them, but I didn't know what the vision meant. They were pet projects for the Sisters."

"Which means?"

"Even if I'd fully understood what waited in their future, even if I could have guided you with that knowledge, there was nothing you could've done, Ryan. That's what you're asking me, isn't it? Not if I could have changed things. You're asking if *you* could have."

He cast her another look. In his eyes she saw the veneer of rage, but beneath it glimmered a vulnerable light. A need for reassurance. She felt her anger die as quickly as it had flared.

"You couldn't have altered the course of their fate. It wasn't yours to change."

The uncertainty she saw in his face cut deep. He didn't know whether or not he could trust Sabelle. She felt the pain of that to her core. She'd devoted every moment of her limited freedom to him, wishing that she wasn't invisible to him. But now that he could see her, he couldn't—or wouldn't—see deep enough to know her. She should be grateful for that. He saw too much already.

Twenty interminable minutes passed before she tried speaking again.

"God created the Beyond before He created earth," she said when the silence grew too long again. "Did you know that?"

"Before last month, I'd never even heard of the Beyond," he answered.

"It's true. He populated it with all manner of creation, wishing to make His world diverse and unique in every way. What He didn't plan for was jealousy. Vanity. He never imagined those with horns would envy those with wings. Or those with cunning would use it to destroy those who were good."

"Everybody wants what they can't have."

She nodded. She was living proof of that. "Each time unrest and violence broke out, He would try to fix it."

"By creating something better."

It wasn't a question, but she answered anyway. "In the beginning, He made us all immortal, but it didn't take Him long to see the error in that. It's why our world is separate from yours. By the time He realized He needed to start over with *only* creatures that could be destroyed, there were already too many of us to control. Eliminating the few of us that were capable of death wouldn't have made a dent in the problem. So He settled for containment."

"What about you?"

"Can I be killed?"

He looked away from the road and caught her gaze. She didn't understand what she saw there. Maybe she'd never understand the moving depths and shifting shades of Ryan's eyes.

"Can you?"

"Yes. I'm disposable, just like you. Does that make you happy?"

He laughed. "Not even a little bit. What about the sisters?"

"I don't know. They're goddesses."

"Self-proclaimed, no doubt."

He turned back to the road, leaving her to overthink what he might have meant by that. The flashing scenery offered no clues, and at last she continued. "The lesser demons—the ones your sister and brother faced—they were the first to find ways out. They'd have gotten away with their escape, too, if they hadn't killed anybody. But of course that went against their nature."

"Of course," Ryan muttered.

"No human death goes unnoted in the Beyond. There are battalions of light keepers cataloging deaths, looking for anomalies. Humans can rip themselves to shreds and bomb themselves off the planet and no one in the Beyond cares. But a human death caused by a demon—that sets off alarms throughout the Beyond."

"Then how were they going to get away with killing me?" he asked.

"The Sisters aren't demons," she said stonily.

"You sure about that?"

"They haven't been banished to the underworld. Not yet, anyway. Which is not to say that what they've been doing is right. They are too clever to be caught breaking the laws of the Beyond, though. They work through others and cover their tracks. You've seen how they manipulate. Convincing someone to turn on the gas was child's play. As a seer, I'm an accomplice to their crimes. As a slave, I'm theirs to blame if they're ever caught. My visions are their looking glass. My *only* purpose is to spy."

Spy on the people she longed to be.

"Things have been pretty screwed up for you," he said softly.

The statement slipped beneath her guard and struck something deep and fragile. "I didn't know any different," she said.

"Yes you did. You knew me, and I'm all about friends and family."

A warm inner circle that she could only see from the outer rim.

"What was it like for you when you were seeing me? I mean, was it like watching TV or was it like being here?" he asked.

"I wasn't in some glass bubble hovering up above," she said, imagining that's how he pictured it. "I was right beside you. Always. You just couldn't see me."

You still can't.

"I've watched you make wrong choices," she said, once again luring him away from a topic that had become too volatile. "I've watched you long to change them."

"What wrong choices are those?" he asked on cue.

"To take care of your family and sacrifice your dreams."

"Who said I sacrificed?"

"Of course you did."

"Because I know *I've* never said it."

"You've thought it."

"I thought it a lot. But if I'd *felt* it I wouldn't have stuck around."

"You always knew you'd end up taking over for your dad."

"So? Love's has been in the family for generations and I'm the oldest."

"But I've never felt like you were happy."

"Maybe that's because I had someone pushing me in the opposite direction I wanted to go in. Ever think of that? Ever wonder if your *guidance* might have felt like doubt? And doubt's like poison no matter who you are."

His words were so cruel that she stared at him in stunned silence.

"I wasn't pushing you," she said in a voice like stone. "I was trying to *help* you."

Ryan exhaled and rubbed the shadow of his jaw. Sabelle sat stiffly beside him, furious and hurt, then hurt and furious. A sign up ahead told her that Sedona was only fifteen miles more. Suddenly it was too close. Sedona marked the end of her time with Ryan.

"You hated the responsibility," she said carefully. "It's no secret that you were unhappy there. You wished your father had sold Love's. You wanted to leave it all behind."

His glare was meant to discourage her. Sabelle chose to ignore it.

"Yet when Ruby said she was glad that Love's was gone, her words wounded you. I saw it."

Ryan said nothing. The smart thing to do would be to let it go.

"Is it because of your father?" she asked softly. "Is that why you're so . . . conflicted?"

"My father's dead."

"Not in your heart he's not."

Ryan glanced her way and she felt something within him give, crack . . . crumble. She knew then just how right she was. In his heart, Ryan's dad lived on, larger-than-life. Driven, mostly misguided, leading Ryan to a destination he resented to this day. Using the image of Ryan's father had been both conniving and brilliant on Aisa's part.

"Maybe," he said.

He didn't want to talk about himself and she could see that he liked discussing his father even less. But to move on, he had to let go. It was a simple fact of human nature that even someone who'd only observed life knew to be true, and as much as he'd hurt her, Sabelle couldn't leave it alone to fester.

"You loved him," she said.

"He was my dad," Ryan replied with a stony expression.

"That's not an answer."

"You're suddenly Oprah?"

She paused, proceeding with care. "Your feelings for him . . . it's why Aisa used his image. She's a master at identifying weaknesses and exploiting them."

He didn't look away from the road as he spoke to her from the muted darkness. "I know you're trying to help, but I don't want to talk about my dad either."

"It hurts too much," she said knowingly.

"It fucking pisses me off," he corrected. "I loved my dad, but there were times . . ." He hesitated, searching for a way to describe the complexity of their relationship. "He had tunnel vision. He only saw what made sense to him."

"You don't think you made sense to him?"

"Not a single minute of my life."

"I think you're wrong. What I saw of him seemed likable. Charming. A lot like you."

Ryan flashed a bitter smile at her. "You think I'm charming?"

"You have your moments."

"Everything looks a little different from the outside, I guess," he said.

It was a cold reminder that he felt as warmly about the Beyond as the Sisters did about humans. No matter what they'd shared, Sabelle was not part of his inner circle. Not human. Not someone he trusted or cared about. Not someone he'd mourn when she was gone. She'd always be on the outside when it came to Ryan.

She quit talking and turned away. Minutes passed before she felt Ryan's gaze on her again. She ignored him.

"I said something," he murmured at last. "Before, too."

She shook her head, horrified by the lump that seemed lodged in her throat. Afraid if it moved it would release the burning tears that pressed against her eyes. She was going to cry. How had that happened?

"Yes, I did," he said. "What was it?"

She squared her shoulders, the way she'd seen Ryan do a hundred times over. She'd just never grasped what it said, that small gesture.

Ryan glanced at the road and back again, his stare direct and burning. She saw it from her periphery but didn't face it. His body heat reached her across the short distance that separated them. He covered her hand with his again. She didn't push him away but she still didn't look at him.

"It's because I said you're on the outside."

"Of course I'm on the outside. I don't belong in your world."

Ryan squeezed her fingers gently. "You feel like you belong."

Her breath caught, stung. "Don't laugh at me."

"I'm not laughing."

"You're playing a game," she said. "I may not grasp the finer points of it, but I know when I'm entertaining you."

She couldn't help it. She glanced at him. His eyes were solemn as he split his attention between the road and Sabelle, seeing everything she wanted to hide.

"You didn't just come here to right a wrong or to save me, did you?" he asked, the question so perceptive that it filled her with fear. "You came looking for something for yourself."

The observation hit a bull's-eye inside her. How she hid it, she'd never know.

She held her breath as danger signs flashed in her head. It took more composure than she thought she possessed to respond. He was right, of course. She'd come looking for a life she had no business wanting.

"You're wrong, but it doesn't matter. You've done what you said you would. You brought me here. Once we find who I'm looking for, you can leave me and be on your way. I'll make sure I don't intrude in your life again."

Minutes passed in brittle silence before finally Ryan mumbled a soft curse. "You think I'm just going to drop you off and drive away?"

"You'll have fulfilled your promise. I don't think it would be wise to go home, though. Maybe you should think about taking a trip somewhere, keep moving—"

"Dammit, Sabelle. Stop. Just stop."

She crossed her arms and went back to looking out the window. Ryan sighed heavily. "We're almost to Sedona. I think we need to get out of the car, stretch our legs." He gave her a searching glance. "Cool down. Get something to eat."

As if in answer her stomach gave a long, loud growl. She nodded in concession. Cooling down seemed a good idea. Ryan had started a flame inside her from the first touch. If she didn't find a way to bank it, she would turn to ash.

16

They came upon the red rocks like a mirage they'd chased across a desert. The brilliant moonlight muted the vibrant colors she'd seen in the pictures, but night added a beauty of its own. Graduated shades and midnight silhouettes layered depth over the black-and-white world, and the shifting shadows gave it movement and life. Sabelle stared out the window, transfixed. Nothing in the Beyond could compare to this. She tried to absorb every detail and nuance, but she knew memory would never come close to the vista her eyes beheld.

"There's a little place up ahead we can get some grub," Ryan said.

They were the first words spoken in miles and they had a tone of truce that sounded sincere, but Sabelle felt too vulnerable to answer it.

"You hungry?" he asked.

"I'm always hungry," she muttered.

Brandy raised her head and gave a soft woof.

"I'll bring you something, too," Ryan told her indulgently.

They exited the highway and drove for some time before finally slowing at a stop sign. An overhead light illuminated the interior of the car, throwing his features into stark relief. He still had bruising on his face and cuts from the explosions, layered now with fresh ones from his fight with Officer Wiesel. His hair took on a mahogany glow in the dark and his eyes look liked jewels. The first shadow of a beard covered his jaw and strain tightened his expression.

She'd never seen a more beautiful man.

Ryan pulled into the parking lot of the Red Rock Café, stopped the car, and got out, clicking his tongue for Brandy. Sabelle got out, too, stiff from her rigid posture and anger. The dog bounded from the backseat and Ryan walked her over to a grassy patch that bordered the parking lot so she could do her business. When they returned, he told Brandy to be good and he'd bring her something. Brandy climbed into the seat Ryan had vacated and rested a paw on the steering wheel as if to say, *Go ahead, Dad. I got it covered.*

He cracked the window, shut the door, and hit a button on his fob to make them lock. Then he faced Sabelle, his expression dark, still pensive. She felt exposed standing beneath the overhead lights, her emotions churning and raw.

He prowled closer, his gaze moving over her face, then down to the swell of her breasts, the curve of her waist and flare of her hips. It felt as if he touched her. It made her wish he would.

Without a word, he reached for the open sides of her coat and pulled her to him. His kiss stole her breath, but Sabelle didn't need to breathe. She only needed the feel of his hard body standing between her and the aching loneliness that would be her life again once she returned to the Beyond.

He parted her lips with sensuous skill and kissed her like it was the most important thing he could do. For her, it was. Her hands rested on his hips, fingers curling into his belt loops as she tried to pull him closer. He was hard, masculine in every way, and she wanted him. Desperately. But he'd hurt her, and she couldn't pretend otherwise.

"I'm sorry," he said at last. "I'm still figuring out what to do with you."

He wouldn't have to figure it out. She'd be gone soon.

As if he'd heard, his next kiss was punishing, but Sabelle met it gladly. Her arms went around his neck and she came up on tiptoe. She kissed him with all the longing locked deep inside her, wanting him to feel it, too. Passion raged through her, so fierce it singed her nerves and sharpened her wits. Need so endless that she thought she might die of it followed in its wake. Her days were numbered and he kept pushing away only to tow her back. Perhaps it was vain or selfish, but she wanted him to be sorry when she was gone. She wanted him to think about this moment and wonder what he should have done differently. She wanted him to *miss* her.

His hands were in her hair now, his kisses a drug that chased her thoughts away. She forgot everything but the feel of him. Where they were, where they were going . . . why. His hot breath mixed with hers, as dark as midnight, as fresh as dawn. He licked her bottom lip and caught it gently between his teeth.

"I want to take that new bra off," he said against her mouth.

"I'd be disappointed if you didn't."

His laugh held surprise and hot desire. But in his eyes, she saw conflict. He wanted her as urgently as she wanted him; he didn't want to want her at all.

He held her there, his eyes locked with hers. A million messages passed between them in the current of that exchange. She understood only one. This thing between them would not die willingly.

Silently, he turned her palm against his and led her inside. A lone waitress wiping a table inside the café looked up when they entered, eyeing Ryan's bruised face and broad shoulders with interest. Her gaze flicked to Sabelle with an assessing gleam and lingered on her cheek before moving back to Ryan, where it stayed.

"You closing up?" he asked.

"In a few. Jeff hasn't turned off the fryers yet and we still need to clean up. We can make you the special easy enough."

"Sold." Ryan held up two fingers and flashed his smile before they took a seat. A television was in the corner above a booth. He pointed at it. "Mind if I turn on the news?"

She laughed. "You can try but it hasn't worked in about four months. Owner keeps saying he's going to get a new one but hasn't bothered yet."

"Well, how about a couple cups of coffee, then, if it's not any trouble?"

"That I can do," the waitress said. "I'll make some fresh."

Another smile from Ryan had the waitress scurrying to do his bidding. Sabelle didn't blame her. She'd been struck dumb by it before herself.

"What's the special?" Sabelle asked when the waitress was gone.

"Does it matter? They're serving and we're hungry."

When the waitress brought their coffee, Ryan cajoled an order of scrambled eggs out of her for Brandy and the last piece of pumpkin pie she said was in the fridge.

A few minutes later she returned with two plates of something savory and covered in gravy, the slice of pie, and a to-go box with Brandy's eggs.

"I put a couple pieces of bacon in, too," she said, blushing to her roots at Ryan's deep "Thank you" before she disappeared into the kitchen.

Ryan dug into his food and so did Sabelle. Whatever was beneath the gravy tasted amazing. Crunchy, hot, and filled with flavor. She didn't bother asking him to identify it. She didn't really care as long as it warmed her belly and gave her lagging energy a boost. Ryan cleared his plate and sat back. Sabelle finished hers a few bites later and did the same.

"They put something in that gravy," he said, running his finger along the edge of his plate and tasting it. "I can't tell if it's chili powder or cayenne pepper. It's good. Did you like it?"

She looked at her empty plate. "No."

He laughed and the deep rumble filled her with pleasure. Just like that, the strain eased behind her breastbone and the hurt faded. Sabelle was happy to pretend their argument had been nothing more than a lovers' quarrel. Pretend the next stop for them wasn't one that ended in good-bye. Pretend she was a real woman and Ryan the man who'd stolen her heart.

Well, there wasn't a lot of pretend in the last. That part was painfully true.

He reached for the pie, cut a bite with the edge of his fork, and held it in front of her.

"I'm going to explode if I eat any more."

"But this is pumpkin pie," he said. "Homemade."

"How do you know?"

"Look at the crust. Better yet, taste it."

"You like to feed me, don't you?" she said, her voice all soft and husky.

"I do."

"Why?"

His smile had a wicked slant and his eyes spoke of things she wanted, even when they confused and scared her.

"You gonna try it?" he asked, reaching across the table so the fork was near her lips.

"Sometimes it feels like you're talking about two things at once," she said, looking at him. "I'm never sure which one I'm answering."

"Which one do you want to answer?"

The one that made him touch her again.

It was safer to open her mouth than respond to that loaded question. Ryan slid his fork in. Her lips closed around it and slowly he pulled it out. The moment was charged, sexual. He watched her with so much intensity that she felt it in places he couldn't even see. He took the next bite, his lips on the same fork, her gaze fixed on his mouth. Another bite for her, alternating until the pie was finished. Her pants felt tight and her stomach so full it would be hard to move. And yet beneath her skin she felt hot and empty, needing something more than food to satisfy her. The air between them was so dense she struggled to breathe it in.

He pushed the plate away and leaned back. Sabelle felt a compulsive urge to fill the silence.

"Can I ask you something?"

"You don't usually ask first," he said, wrapping his hands around his coffee cup. "Makes me think I should say no."

"Why did you refuse to cook at Love's? I always assumed you hated it."

"Was there anywhere you didn't stalk me?"

"You seemed to enjoy cooking—when you allowed yourself to do it, that is," she went on, ignoring him. "But never at Love's."

His jaw tightened and she knew she'd hit another nerve, but he gave a casual shrug and took a drink from his mug. Still the tension radiated off him, and for a moment she regretted that she'd destroyed the easy camaraderie they'd shared. But she'd always wondered. When he was younger, his father had made him work in the kitchen, but as soon as he could, Ryan had moved to the bar and never gone back. His brother, Reece, had become the cook after that. Reece had hated every second he'd spent there and made no secret of it.

Ryan put his finger on the bowl of his spoon and spun it. A moment ago she'd wished those perceptive eyes would look another way; now she longed to see what lurked in their depths.

"There was never time," he said finally.

"Someone I know would call that a big fat lie."

That drew a startled glance, but she couldn't read what she saw in his eyes before he looked away again.

"My dad used to say the only way to have spice in your life was to cook with it," he told her. "And then he refused to change anything on the menu so we could. We just kept serving up the same bland slop. I couldn't stand it."

"After he died, you could have changed it."

He pushed the spoon away and leaned back against the booth. From squared shoulders to hard jaw, resentment still held him in its grip.

"Why do you care?" he asked.

"You're the only one who can ask questions? I'm just trying to understand you."

"I'm not that complicated."

That made her smile and his hooded gaze shifted to her mouth. She fought the urge to lick her lips for as long as she could but it was inevitable, that small gesture that revealed so much. She felt him focus on it, stoking her longing with his beautiful eyes.

She forced herself to look away. "Ryan Love," she said softly. "You're the most complicated man I've ever known."

"According to you, I'm the only man."

"The only one I've known in the flesh."

His gaze sharpened and her heart raced over that word. *Flesh*. So base. So descriptive. She cleared her throat and glanced out the window at the parking lot.

"I never changed the menu because my dad taught me that if it ain't broke, don't fix it," he said after a long moment.

"But you thought it *was* broken. Otherwise you would have been happier."

"Matter of opinion. Customers never complained."

Since when had Ryan Love based his opinions on those of others?

"Changing it would have made it mine," he said at last, reluctance in his tone. "It would have felt like giving up on my dream of ever getting out. Now it feels stupid. A fucked-up passive-aggressive stand that only made me miserable."

He made a disgusted sound and shook his head. "My dad was such an obsessive guy. He hated change."

"And change is all you ever wanted," she said softly.

"Funny how the harder we try to be different, the more we're the same."

He was silent for a long time and then, softly, as if he really didn't want to speak the words but couldn't hold them back, he said, "After the first time the twins almost died—did die for a little while—my dad drilled into me how important they were. I was supposed to be watching them the day they drowned, but I was a teenager and there were a lot of girls around." He shook his head. "When they pulled their bodies out of the lake and I thought they were dead, I wanted to die, too. Afterward, when they got the twins breathing again, it felt like a second chance. I promised myself I'd never be so careless again with someone I loved."

He wadded up his paper napkin and tossed it on the table. Sabelle stayed quiet, letting him work through his thoughts.

"Dad told me I needed to step up and be a man. He was ashamed of me. *I* was ashamed of me, but it killed me seeing it in his eyes. Only time I ever did. But there's no mistaking it."

She nodded.

"You saw it, too?"

She knew she shouldn't nod again, but she couldn't lie. Not just because he'd sense it, but because he deserved the truth.

"That was the first time I was able to summon a vision of you. I'd been thinking of you so hard and there you were." Beautiful, golden skinned, face soft with youth but filled with the promise of the man he'd become. "The twins were playing in the water, but you weren't paying attention to them. You were . . . distracted."

Ryan nodded. "The girl in the purple bikini."

Sabelle still remembered the flare of jealousy as she'd watched him watch her. "The bikini distracted you." What was inside it fascinated him. "I knew the twins had gone out too deep and I . . . *pushed.* I shoved my warning at you, trying to get you to look away. But I'd never done such a thing before. I didn't know how."

Ryan's gaze narrowed. She had his attention now.

"I felt it," he murmured, his tone mystified. "Like a voice in my head. I just heard it too late."

She blinked, certain she'd misunderstood. "You heard me?"

"Not just then either. Other times, too. I didn't know what I was feeling, but . . ."

She held her breath, waiting for what he would say.

"I felt you." He smiled, the smoldering light in his eyes again, traveling over her face, lingering on her throat, dropping to her breasts. "I just didn't know you were . . . you."

That look made her feel alive. Jittery. Hungry. He knew it, of course. He noticed the way she caught her breath, curled her fingers tight, and avoided his eyes. He noticed everything.

Trying to hide how much what he'd said meant to her, she tucked a strand of hair behind her ear and forced herself to look up.

"You want to hear something crazy?" he said at last, and the look he gave her was filled with turmoil. "It's like ever since I heard you scream, I feel like I've been flying blind, making all the wrong decisions."

"What do you mean?"

He frowned, searching for his words. "After my dad died, it was just me trying to raise Reece and Roxanne. You know that? Ruby helped, but she was young, too."

Sabelle nodded. She remembered, but she had no idea how this related to what went on inside his head now.

"You don't get through being responsible for three kids without learning how to make decisions. Without trusting your instincts. But since you . . ."

Her mouth was dry, her heart fast. He looked up again and his eyes glittered. He leaned in.

"These past couple days . . . I've been lost, reacting without thinking it through. I thought it was because so much was going on. You. The explosion. My dad showing up on the porch . . ." He took a deep breath. "Now I . . . I see I'm not just turned around, I'm drifting."

Within his eyes she saw the real question. A plea he was too much of a man to speak.

"You're dealing with something that defies explanation, Ryan. You can't decide on a course of action when what you're fighting changes all the rules. It's not that you don't know what to do. It's that everything you do can be used against you."

"I get that, but . . . it's something more. It's me. It's you."

Me . . . you . . . but not us. She craved that word like she did food. She waited, unsure where he'd take it from there. Afraid there'd been blame. "What are you saying?"

"Maybe it wasn't you who made me doubt," he murmured, holding her gaze. "Maybe it was me."

She lifted her chin, searching his eyes for the truth. Wanting it to be there so desperately she could hardly breathe.

"Maybe I didn't always do what you wanted me to, Sabelle. But that doesn't mean I wasn't listening. I'm still listening, but you're not there anymore."

It sounded like he was saying he missed her. Like they'd shared unity, if not worlds. That he'd depended on her guidance. Her partnership in his life.

Her gaze shifted to his lips, wanting him to utter more words like those. "Your instincts have always been good, Ryan. That's all you."

"But you believed in me."

"I still do. I trust you with my life."

An almost-smile curved his lips. "Last year, there was this guy," he said, voice a velvet rumble in the quiet café. "He walked across the Grand Canyon on a tightrope. I watched every step on TV and I thought, what would make someone do that? Something so irreversible, so reckless. There was no net. Nothing between him and a plunge to death but his belief that he'd make it to the other side."

She understood what he was saying. She felt it deep inside her. The thrill of it. The danger. The absolute stupidity of taking the risk and letting herself become more involved with him, of believing the other side existed and could be reached.

"Sometimes I feel like I've known you my whole life," he said.

"The human soul doesn't measure in time," she answered.

He gave her that *Ryan* look. The one that said, *What new bullshit is this?*

She said, "People find each other because they were meant to be together. I see it all the time."

"Because you make it happen?"

"Because it was meant to be."

She searched his face but couldn't read his thoughts. Instead she probed, seeking the answer to all things Ryan. Knowing that in a thousand human lifetimes, she'd never really understand him. She didn't care. Every piece of him she uncovered was like a gem she could hold in her hand and cherish, even if it was the last thing she did.

Ryan stood, nodded toward the restroom, and said he'd be right back. Sabelle sat in the quiet, waiting, when a low hissing noise snaked through the deserted café, making her look up. The television in the corner had turned on and the screen flashed white static. Frowning, she stared at it, noticing the dangling cord that wasn't even plugged into the outlet. Suddenly the static crackled and images flashed across the screen. A news desk appeared, with two serious newscasters staring out from the television.

"The Tempe family, famous for their extraordinary near-death experiences, is in the news again," the clean-cut African American anchorman said, leveling an intense stare at the camera. "First their pub, Love's, was destroyed in an explosion that rocked Mill Avenue around three this morning."

The perky blonde sitting next to him leaned forward and asked, "Have they isolated the cause of—"

Her voice was abruptly silenced, yet Sabelle could still see her lips moving. For a moment the picture stayed that way, and some hopeful part of her brain tried to explain what she saw right up until the moment when the image changed.

The camera swung to the right and focused on a beautiful dark-haired woman with tilted, cold eyes and a serene expression who had calmly entered the studio. Familiar, hated—feared—Aisa, the most vicious of the Sisters, moved to the broadcast desk and perched gracefully on one of the tall high-backed chairs behind it. On either side of her, the two anchors spoke to the cameras with earnest expressions on their faces and silenced words on their lips. Aisa sat between them, unnoticed, focused only on Sabelle. She stared with a look that made Sabelle's blood run cold.

Aisa smiled placidly as images of destruction flashed in the upper-right corner of the screen and the anchors detailed the devastation on Mill Avenue caused by an unexplained gas leak.

Still Aisa said nothing, but her steady, malevolent stare made Sabelle break into a cold sweat. Her muscles began to ache with the effort to hide the treacherous tremble in her hands, her knees, her constricted lungs. Aisa couldn't cross over to the human world. Not physically, not *really*. But Sabelle was not so foolish as to think that made her safe. The powerful Sister was insidious. She couldn't collect Sabelle herself, but she would use other means. Deadly ones.

Aisa leaned forward on her chair as a new picture took the place of the smoldering street where Love's had been.

Like the footage that had been shown before, there was smoke, but as the camera panned out, Sabelle understood that the scene had changed. From the thick black cloud, a woman emerged. She'd been badly beaten, her face battered and broken, her arms and legs bruised and bloody. Still, Sabelle recognized her. Nadia—her friend.

"No," Sabelle breathed.

Nadia looked terrified. Tears streamed down her face. Her chest rose and fell with labored breaths. Sabelle couldn't look away, but she knew what was coming, and not because she'd seen it in a vision.

"There is only one way to free an oracle," Aisa said in her dry, clipped tones, drawing Sabelle's attention from the unfolding horror. "One for every day you defy me. A reaper is on the way for your lover. I expect you to make use of his services and return with him."

The television screen went black, but the sound continued. Meaty, bloody, violent. There were screams and there were pleas. Until the end, when there was only silence.

17

Ryan opened the car door and let Brandy out to inhale her eggs and bacon. He could feel Sabelle watching him from the front seat of the car and he was rattled by the realizations he'd made tonight. She'd been guiding him and he'd been fighting her for most of his life. At the same time, he'd come to depend on her. She was a sounding board he hadn't even known he'd been using.

He gave Brandy water from his bottle and let her visit the grassy patch again before silently climbing behind the wheel and turning north once more. The itchy feeling that had been under his skin since leaving Tempe was worse now that they'd neared the red rocks of Sedona. It felt as if their destination had sunk tenterhooks into his flesh and towed him inescapably closer to a point that couldn't possibly end well.

The silence between the two of them had become as thick and textured as the night outside their windows. He guessed she'd been doing some thinking, too. She was deep in thought now and as still as a marble statue.

They'd only gone a handful of miles when suddenly she snapped out of it. "Wait," she exclaimed. "Slow down."

Ryan glanced in his rearview mirror to make sure no one was behind him before slowing the car. The road was dark. Budget cuts had doused every other streetlight and they were caught between the glowing orbs. The fat moon lent a hand but there was too much night to battle. He almost passed the road that veered off to the right before his high beams picked it out and illuminated it.

"Here. Turn right here," Sabelle said.

He'd known she was going to say it but it still filled him with dread as he cranked the wheel. The prickly feeling at his nape grew.

"Where are we going, Sabelle?"

She shook her head, but she sat at the edge of her seat, the safety belt trying to hold her back as she leaned forward.

Trees lined the road, some scraggly and brown, cooked by summer heat or frozen by the winter chill. Hard to tell in the glancing beams of his headlights as they drove through. The pitted surface made Ryan wince as he maneuvered the low carriage of Reece's car over it. They'd gone about a mile without a sign of life when Ryan caught the first glimpse of them. Two men stood in the middle of the road, just past the curve, holding high-powered lanterns. Waiting.

"I don't like the look of this," he said, slowing the car as they rounded the bend.

Sabelle asked, "Who are they?"

"Got me. This is your show."

He stopped about a hundred feet in front of them and got out. Far enough away that the two men would have to sprout wings and fly to reach them before Ryan and Sabelle could scramble back inside the car. Close enough to hear what they had to say.

The high beams threw the two men into the spotlight and kept Ryan and Sabelle in shadow. Aware of Sabelle getting out on the other side, Ryan clicked his tongue for Brandy and crossed in front of the hood to meet her. His dog padded at their feet, her head high, tail straight as they approached. Alert, ready for trouble. She gave the two men a warning bark that filled Ryan with pride. When roused, a German shepherd can radiate menace. He was never more thankful to have her at his side.

The older of the two men was in his fifties, had steely hair, fair skin, and deep lines on his face. His buzz cut said military. The hard look in his eyes said commander. Dressed in dusty blue jeans, cowboy boots, and a denim shirt that looked like it had been washed a thousand times, he might be masquerading as a hired hand, but Ryan wasn't fooled.

He leveled a stare at the three of them that was as cold as the night and alive with a hard glint of cunning. Even from a hundred feet, Ryan could feel the man taking in every detail of his appearance, assessing his threat potential and evaluating options should it come down to a fight. The old guy looked tough, hard with muscle that hadn't withered with age and with the kind of readiness that said he wouldn't hesitate to use deadly force. Not for a second.

In contrast, the man next to him had a cool, sophisticated air. Late thirties, maybe early forties. Tall and trim with polished black skin, he made Ryan think of a *GQ* ad. The kind that juxtaposed expensive city clothes against the rough-and-ready West. The commander looked like he'd been working since sunrise; GQ had probably spent the morning deliberating between blue socks or black. Or so it might seem. Ryan truly doubted that either carefully constructed image was real.

The commander held a baseball bat. GQ had a smile. Ryan knew which one he'd take at face value.

He grabbed Sabelle's hand when she would have approached and pulled her back. "Stay behind me."

"Why?"

"If the old man starts swinging, I stand a better chance of walking away."

"State your business," the commander said in a low, hard voice.

"Joel," GQ reprimanded. Still wearing the easy smile, the tall man took a step forward and held out a hand.

"I'm Elijah Douglas," he said. "This is my partner, Joel Kesher."

Ryan stayed where he was, ignoring the hand. Brandy revved her engine and flashed her canines for good measure. GQ's smile faltered. Behind him, he felt Sabelle shift restlessly.

"You're Ryan Love," Elijah said.

Ryan didn't know why he was surprised to hear his name. He'd known the minute they turned down this dirt road that what they'd find at the end would be every bit as strange as Sabelle's appearance in his life. Still, it shook him. Made him feel like he lived in a cage and everyone who walked by had the need to rattle it.

"Wa Chu," Sabelle said under her breath.

Yeah, Ryan had figured that out, too.

The commander gave Sabelle a hard look. "You've made a mess of things," he said.

"Joel," Elijah admonished. "Take it down a notch."

Surprisingly, Joel nodded, and the bat he'd held clenched at the ready eased to his side. He kept a tight grip on it, though. The stretched knuckles said it all.

"What's your name, honey?" Elijah asked.

"You don't need to know her name. We're not here to make friends," Ryan answered, wondering why they'd known his and not hers.

"Ah. So you're just passing through?" Elijah asked with a pointed look over his shoulder at the barren stretch of dirt behind him. "Or did you come because you felt like you should?"

"We got your invitations," Ryan acknowledged.

Joel made a strangled sound. Elijah shot him a look that had a lot to say. Unfortunately, Ryan didn't speak the language.

"I'm glad to hear it. I'd like to hear more, as a matter of fact," Elijah told Ryan. "But this isn't the place for that conversation. Not in the open."

"Why not?" Ryan said, irked by this cat-and-mouse game.

"Because that's the way it needs to be," Joel said coldly.

The bat moved up a few inches. Elijah reached over

and pushed it down. He angled his body so Ryan and Sabelle wouldn't see his face and said something to the older man in a low voice. Joel responded in kind, tension radiating off him in waves. Elijah rested a hand against the side of the other man's neck and touched his forehead to Joel's.

Ryan glanced at Sabelle, who watched with wide eyes and parted lips. After a moment, Joel relaxed, gave a small nod, and Elijah stepped back. Ryan realigned his opinions of the two. He'd thought Joel was the force to reckon with. Apparently he had it wrong.

"Come with us," Joel finally said, lifting his lantern in his other hand.

"I don't think so," Ryan retorted.

"Told you he'd say that," Joel muttered to Elijah as he turned his back and started walking toward a path that wove its way through the dense woods. He didn't wait for a response or even look back to see if anyone followed.

Elijah watched him go with a shake of his head, but there was an amused look on his face when he turned back to Ryan and Sabelle.

"We have a rental house about a quarter mile down the road," he said. "You can't miss it."

"We can if we try."

Elijah smiled. "Did you come all this way just to turn around and go home? Or did you come for answers?"

Sabelle squeezed his hand, her expression excited and eager. Here at last was what she'd been looking for. The *X* that marked the spot where her questions converged.

"You're going to want to hear what we have to say, Ryan." Elijah cast his dark eyes on Sabelle. "About her."

He paused for effect. "And about a certain twisted Sister who's decided you're expendable."

Ryan felt cold all over. He gave Sabelle an uneasy glance and caught a look of dismay on her face. He'd known all along that she had secrets, but some messed-up part of him wanted to hear them from Sabelle, not these two strangers he already didn't trust. But answers about the Sisters who made Sabelle tremble, he'd take any way he could get.

Elijah tossed him a key ring and Ryan caught it automatically.

"I know you're thinking you must be insane to even consider following two strangers into the woods. But tell me something, Ryan. Has anything in your life been sane since she came into it?"

Ryan hated to admit that he had a point. "Adding another level of crazy isn't going to make things right," he said.

"But wouldn't it be nice to have your questions answered?"

"Why should I believe anything you tell me?"

"Because I've walked in your shoes. Because on a clear day, I can see the future. Because you need our help, whether you want to believe it or not."

With a knowing look, Elijah turned and followed Joel into the forest. Over his shoulder he called, "We've got a full kitchen and cold beer already stocked in the fridge. Amstel Light, Ryan. And a fresh bottle of Reservoir Rye."

Ryan's favorite.

"I only drink with people I like," Ryan said.

Elijah turned and walked backward. "You're going to want to rethink that."

Ryan cursed under his breath. Brandy made a high, whining sound and Sabelle cast him a worried glance. The layers of darkness rushed the edges of their headlights as Elijah disappeared and a gust of wind came from nowhere, whisking through tree limbs, turning the forest into a symphony of creaks and commotion. Instincts older than caves told Ryan shelter—any shelter—needed to be found. Now.

"A drink, Ryan," Elijah's disembodied voice carried back as his lantern bobbed in the distance. "Hear us out. Be on your way if you don't like what we have to say."

Ryan looked at Sabelle. "What do you think?"

He saw wariness in her eyes, but she said, "I don't think we can afford to turn our backs on someone who might help us."

She was right. They'd answered the invitation. He'd turned when she'd said *Here*, and driven down a dark road with no idea what waited for them. It seemed ridiculous to turn around now just because Joel had rubbed him the wrong way.

But it wasn't just that. Ryan realized a part of him was afraid of the answers the two men would give. About Sabelle, who'd somehow become important to him in the span of a couple of days. More than important. Vital.

Besotted.

"You get ten minutes to convince me," Ryan said loud enough to be heard. "After that, we're gone."

"It'll only take five." The light quit bobbing. Elijah was standing still now. Not far away, but still obscured by the gloom. "This path cuts straight through. I'll be there before you are. The road passes our house on the left. Once you see it, keep going for a bit. The road snakes back on itself before straightening out again. The cabin's on the right."

With that he was gone. Ryan watched the light disappear, hating that itchy feeling telling him he'd just been jobbed. Behind the wheel, he hesitated.

"You think they mean us harm?" Sabelle asked before he started the engine.

Ryan didn't know how to answer that. He couldn't shake the bad feeling that they'd been baited, but he was wound too tight to base decisions on his gut. Years of fighting had taught him to trust the doubt as much as the instinct. "They knew my name, but they didn't know *yours*. That doesn't strike you as odd?"

She lifted a shoulder. "Who am I to say what's odd?"

They followed Elijah's directions past the large A-frame on the left and through the loops of the winding road to the smaller cabin he'd told them about in a secluded cove just beyond it. The cabin was all lit up inside but both men waited on the wide porch in front of it.

Split rails and river rock worked in tandem to make the dwelling solid while blending it with the rustic surroundings. Pine and oak trees circled it like a snow-dusted posse. A high-wattage light gave the gravel drive a bright glow and the moon had finally lifted its head above the treetops. Lurid dark pooled in the distance and slid through the forest like a toxic mist held at bay by illumination.

Ryan parked, opened his door, and took a deep breath

of wintry air. Sabelle stepped from the car on the other side, cheeks pink and her breath pluming in front of her.

He'd never seen a more beautiful woman.

He wanted to pull her tight against him and protect her. He wanted to run away from her—as far and fast as he could. And he wanted it all at the same time. She'd rung his bell and he wasn't sure he'd ever be the same again.

Brandy bounded out with an excited, apprehensive bark at the looming forest. Fur up, she patrolled the edge with diligence.

"You coming in or what?" Joel growled as he thrust open the front door of the cabin.

Ryan debated it for a moment, but he and Sabelle were navigating the treacherous waters of the Beyond and these two might offer them a boat—or at least a paddle. For all the strangeness of their appearance, Ryan didn't get the same hair-raising vibe off them that he had from the visitor that looked like his dad. He didn't see cunning in their eyes either. Just determination and, where Joel was concerned, hostility. If it was a fight the man wanted, Ryan was more than ready. Hitting something might release the ball of tension in his gut.

"I see what you're thinking," Joel said when Ryan stepped through the door. "I may have some miles on me, but I can take anything you want to dish out."

"Whatever helps you sleep at night."

Joel laughed.

"Do you two need a moment to beat your chests?" Elijah asked mildly. "Maybe whip out your dicks and measure them?"

"Nah," Ryan said. "We're good."

"Glad to hear it."

Joel gave Ryan a smile filled with everything but warmth and Ryan sent it back. Man talk for truce. He could feel Sabelle's confusion as the tension ebbed but couldn't have explained it to her even if he'd had the chance.

In the kitchen, Elijah pulled two bottles of beer from the fridge and handed them to Joel, then opened a bottle of sauvignon blanc. Ryan glanced at the label. You could tell a lot about a person by the labels they flaunted . . . or didn't. Elijah poured a good white without the pretentious price tag.

Sabelle would like it.

He rolled his eyes at himself for caring.

Ryan took the beer that Joel handed him and the small rocks glass that came next. At the bottom, a healthy splash of whiskey floated without ice. A good swallow but not a full shot. He relaxed a little. If Joel had meant to loosen Ryan's tongue and dull his reflexes, the glass would have held more. Ryan had poured spirits for a living for too long not to recognize that.

"As nice as all this is," Ryan said, taking a drink of the beer, "let's get to it. How do you know who I am?"

What I drink? And what does it have to do with this woman who's under my skin?

"Elijah saw you coming," Joel said gruffly.

"Obviously."

"He's been seeing it for about a month now."

"How?" Sabelle demanded.

Joel raised his brows. "Same way you do, I expect."

"But he's male."

"Really? How did I miss that?" Joel slid Elijah an amused look that made the other man blush.

"Seers don't have to be female, " Elijah said gently.

"You're wrong. The Sisters—"

"Lie."

That was Joel, his tone hard as steel.

Elijah pulled up a chair and sat at the table beside Joel. He rested an arm over the back of the other man's chair and stretched out his legs. "Now that you're here, will you tell us your name?"

Instead of answering, Sabelle turned troubled eyes to Ryan, waiting for his cue. He felt the strength of her trust in that small gesture. They'd followed *her* instincts to get here, but she was relying on his to get them out safely.

He held a chair for her and hooked another beside it, sitting close enough that their thighs touched. Close enough that he could settle his free hand on her knee. At the click of his tongue, Brandy gave up her snuffling exploration and flopped at their feet.

"Her name's Sabelle," Ryan answered at last. "How come you didn't know it already?"

Elijah shrugged. "It's a good question. Wish I could answer."

"S'belle," Joel said slowly, pronouncing it correctly on the first try. Sabelle stiffened at the look he leveled at her.

"Why don't you like me?" she asked Joel bluntly, taking a careful drink of her wine.

The cool sweet drink hit her tongue, distracting her from the aggressive question. Her lashes fluttered. Ryan watched her expression change with the same fascination he felt each time she showed pleasure. Sabelle was living, breathing sensuality. Every single thing she did made him feel tight and antsy. Territorial. *Possessive.* He forced himself to look away and found the other two men watching *him* with a look of concern.

Joel shifted his narrowed eyes to Sabelle. "I don't like what you've done."

"What do you think she's done?" Ryan asked coolly.

"She knows what I'm talking about," Joel said. "Isn't that right? Pulled out all the stops, didn't you?"

"You promised me you wouldn't do this, Joel," Elijah interrupted.

Joel scowled at his friend, but he shut his mouth and leaned back in his chair.

"What's he talking about?" Ryan asked Elijah, but he was looking at Sabelle. She didn't look up.

Joel leveled a challenging stare across the table and Sabelle paled. "Ask her why she's here," he taunted.

"I know why she's here," Ryan shot back.

"You sure about that?"

Elijah turned on Joel in wordless warning and Joel fell silent.

Ryan shifted his gaze to Sabelle's downturned face, foreboding coiling inside him. The moment of reckoning had been coming since she'd opened her pretty mouth and lied the first time. Yet now that it was here, Ryan wanted to slow the clock. The gnawing anticipation holding the room hostage didn't bode well for any of them.

"I can't help you if I don't know what's going on, snowflake," he murmured.

At last the blue eyes came up. "You won't want to help me when you do."

He shook his head once. "Maybe. Maybe not."

She searched his eyes and he tried to show her that she didn't need to be afraid. He hated being lied to, but that didn't mean he couldn't understand why sometimes lies felt like the only way out. If Sabelle had lied, the reason was probably born of fear. He'd had a taste of the tactics Aisa used. He couldn't blame Sabelle for being afraid.

"She's here to steal the crown," Joel blurted, disregarding Elijah's disapproval. Ryan frowned, wrenching his gaze from Sabelle and narrowing it on the older man.

"What does that mean?" Ryan demanded. He felt dense and pissed off at the same time. Joel had pricked his last nerve, and fair or not, Ryan wanted to reach across the table and plant his fist in the older man's face.

"Give yourself a minute," Joel said. "You'll figure it out."

"You're an asshole, you know that?"

"He knows," Elijah said.

But Joel was right. It took less than a minute for Ryan to start piecing it together. *Steal the crown* couldn't have too many meanings. Sabelle was a slave; Aisa, her master. Sabelle had made it clear that she wanted to help free the other slaves left behind—that's why she'd been so desperate to answer the call she'd felt from the north. But *steal the crown* implied overthrowing the queen and taking her place . . . going *back* . . . didn't it? He wished she'd look at him, but she remained stonily silent, her head bent, eyes fixed on her fingers.

"She thinks it's her birthright."

Joel again, ever helpful. Ryan shot him a glare. "Next word out of your mouth is going to come with teeth."

Joel grinned. "Think you're pissed off now? Ask her how she plans to do it."

"Joel," Elijah said sharply.

"He's got a right to know. You hear me, sweetheart? That's why I don't like you. He's got a right to know."

"I mean it, Joel—"

"Know what?" Ryan demanded.

"Hell," Joel shouted. "She's got you so spun up you couldn't find your dick with both hands and a hard-on. It's what they do. They get in your pants and then they fuck with your head. Both of them."

The bitter words came like a hard punch to the solar plexus. The imposter who'd pretended to be his dad had chosen a different way, but he'd said the same thing.

She blinded you and then she let you dip your stick and suddenly you're thinking with the wrong organ. Isn't that right?

Sabelle had called the dad-imposter a liar. An illusion from Aisa, the master of the mind fuck. Now doubt crept in with the mists of betrayal. What if Ryan had it all backwards?

He wanted to laugh. God knew, he wanted to laugh.

"She *selected* you," Joel said, leaning into the hot tension. "If it takes yanking your chain to make you see, so be it."

Ryan looked at Sabelle again, his jaw tight, his heart racing. "Say something."

"He's twisting things around," she muttered.

"Which things?"

"Yes, I chose you, but not for the reason he thinks."

Ryan could feel Joel simmering like hot butter in a skillet, hissing as it melted, turning black at the edges as it burned. Elijah put a restraining hand over Joel's but the older man wouldn't be able to keep it in—whatever *it* was.

Ryan stood and pulled Sabelle to her feet. Whatever was coming, he wanted to hear it from Sabelle, in her words.

"The bedroom is right around the corner," Elijah offered with obvious relief. "You're right. You should have this conversation in private. We'll wait."

"Lucky us," Ryan said as he led Sabelle from the kitchen.

18

Ryan switched on the lamp and watched Sabelle move away from him, still silent. Still a mystery he wanted to believe could be solved. She eyed the bed, but didn't sit, looking everywhere but at him. He opted to keep standing, too, and leaned against the door, letting the silence stretch, wishing just once she wouldn't make him drag each word out of her.

"Talk," he demanded at last, unable to temper his frustration.

Angry because of it. Angry that he had to demand at all. Most of all, angry that Joel was right. She had him in fucking knots. She'd slipped beneath his guard and laid him open from balls to brain. He'd had warnings from inside, from out, from the fucking Beyond, and still he'd let it happen. He'd let her in. And now she was going to make him pay for it.

"I was going to tell you," she said in a low voice. "I *should* have told you before . . . this." Her hands fluttered in front of her, bracketing the distance that now separated them. "I just didn't get the chance." She shoved her betraying hands into her pockets and shook her head. "No, that's not true. I had chances. I just . . ."

She stared at him, her eyes begging him to understand. He might have been swayed if he had even an inkling of what was coming. Instead he crossed his arms without a word and waited.

"I—I've been *watching* my whole life, Ryan. Outside, looking in, just like you said. Then I saw you and now I'm here. You're here." She shuffled her feet. "I'm not watching anymore. It's happening *to* me, not because of me or in spite of me." She flashed him a shaky smile that didn't stand a chance. He didn't even pretend to return it. "I knew when I told you . . . you wouldn't turn me away. But whatever this . . ." Her hand moved between them again, this time a fragile sail in the winds of storm. "Whatever it is . . . I wouldn't have that anymore."

"You always planned to go back," he said flatly.

"Yes."

"Not just to help the others get free."

"No."

"Why? Why go through the trouble to escape in the first place? Why drag me here? What the fuck is that guy talking about?"

Her shoulders hunched and her arms crossed defensively. "There's a prophecy," she began.

"Enough of the bullshit, Sabelle," he barked. "I don't

give a fuck about prophecies of the Beyond. I want to know about *you*. I want to know what *you're* doing *here*."

With me. To me.

Her chin came up and her jaw set. If not for those liquid eyes, she'd have pulled off the tough-as-nails look she gave him.

"I'm trying to tell you, but you're going to have to listen to hear it."

"I'm all ears, snowflake."

"The prophecy foretells the end of the Sisters' reign. It goes like this: 'The owned will become the owner, the fruit the poison.' "

"You can't be serious."

"It means that one of their own will bring them down."

Ryan cursed softly. This was like a bad movie. Except for the fist clenched around his heart.

"How do you figure that?"

"I am an oracle," she said in a steady tone. "I see."

"And you think it's you? Is that it? You're the one who's going to bring them down?"

"I'm the most gifted of all the seers. Of course it's me."

"What are you doing *here*, then? Why pull me into it?" She turned away and it took everything he had to keep from grabbing her shoulders and forcing her to face him again. "Why, Sabelle?"

"I needed you to get me here," she said in a low voice.

"One-Eight-Hundred-Taxicab. You didn't need me. You could have fucked a ride out of anybody."

She flinched, but his cruelty did the trick. She turned to him.

"Does that make you feel better, hurting me?"

"Little bit."

"I needed you," she said angrily.

Past tense. He heard it. He hated it. Right that second, he hated her almost as much as he hated himself for being such an idiot.

She's using you. She told *you she's using you. And you agreed to it.*

Thanks, Dad.

"I needed you," she went on, unaware of the waves of self-loathing washing through him. "Just as I need them."

Them being Joel and Elijah. But they didn't seem to be rallying to her cause.

"You think they're going to help you kill Aisa? That's your big play, huh? What then? You're going to be the new master of all those slaves?"

She looked so horrified that for a moment his certainty wavered and hope glimmered like a distant star.

"My rule would never include slaves," she said proudly.

And there it was, a truth so bald it shone. He hadn't admitted it to himself yet, but he'd been dreaming of a future that had a place for them both. She'd been dreaming of scepters and thrones, manipulating him into willingness so she could use him to get there.

"How are you going to handle this coup of yours?" Ryan asked. "Did you come here to draw your sisters out?"

"They're not my Sis—"

"What about the rest of us? What are we? Bait?"

"No," she gasped. "I didn't have a grand plan. Yes, I'd been thinking about it. There's injustice—with the Sisters, with how they treat the seers. With how they treat the *world*, Ryan. No one could live knowing about it and not want it changed. But my plans were fantasies. Dreams. I had no idea how to get there. I didn't even know how to get *here.* When Nadia told me you were going to die, I acted. She told me how and I came. Once I was here, I realized I had a chance to do something."

Ryan wanted to believe it, which only seeded his doubt.

"Believe what you want," she said quietly. "But it's the truth."

"So what now?" he asked, and it felt as if the words had been coated in gunpowder. "You said the sisters couldn't follow you here. So how are you planning on getting close enough to do the deed? How can you . . ."

The words trailed off like a dirt road into a perfect storm, churning, gritty, blurred where it met the horizon. Then suddenly everything was clear. Ryan braced against the door as realization rained down on him. He couldn't believe he'd missed it before.

She'd told him she'd hitched a ride with a reaper to get to this world. It didn't take much to guess she'd need to find another reaper to ferry her back.

She selected *you.*

Not because he'd pulled her by the heartstrings and made her yearn to be in the same space with him. Not because she felt compelled to save his life. She'd chosen him because his sister had a fast pass to a reaper. She'd chosen him because she'd known—after all those years of watching, guiding, *pushing*—she'd known that all it would take to spin Ryan into chaos was the destruction of the glue that held his life together. Love's, his family's center. And once that was gone, he'd be adrift. Easy prey. The sisters hadn't blown Love's up. Sabelle had.

Do you know where your sister and her reaper are?

She'd asked on the way here, couching the question beneath a longing that had damn near broken his heart. Fuck. He was such a dumbass.

"You think I'm going to hook you up with my sister's boyfriend, don't you? That's what this is all about. You think those two"—he jabbed his thumb over his shoulder—"can help you win and you turned me into your fucking errand boy so you could have access to Roxanne and her reaper."

Sabelle shook her head, but her expression said it all.

Ryan pushed away from the door and stalked closer. He knew touching her would be the wrong decision, but he couldn't seem to help himself. He brushed the back of his knuckles against her jaw and tilted her face.

What he saw in her eyes shattered something inside him, something that had been too fragile to survive all along. Rage and pain bubbled up and spilled over. He turned away, needing to vent the steam or be poached by his own ire. Cursing, he slammed his fist into the wall, once, twice. Drywall caved in and turned to dust. It didn't change the facts, but his seared knuckles gained him an iota of focus. Without looking back, he yanked open the door and strode out.

"Where are you going?" she asked.

Ryan didn't bother to answer.

19

Ryan had taken Sabelle into the bedroom holding her hand. Coming out, she walked alone. She wasn't surprised. She didn't even blame him. She'd been living a lie since she came. It didn't matter to Ryan that she wished it had been true—that she could stay and live as a human. That making love to him had been worth dying for, if that's what waited around the bend.

She deserved the anger that shimmered around all that muscle. She deserved the hurt that nested beneath her breastbone. The one that felt like her heart breaking. She hadn't trusted him with the truth about what she intended, and now, because of her omission, he thought everything she'd told him was a lie.

Ryan went straight to the kitchen and took a fresh beer from the fridge. Joel poured another whiskey, setting it in front of him with a quick pat on his shoulder, a gesture of commiseration that startled them all. Sabelle's glass was still full, but the wine had grown warm. She felt Ryan's gaze on her face as she sipped it and grimaced. Without asking, he took the glass, dumped it, and poured her a fresh one. No one spoke. Sabelle wished it would stay that way.

"Why don't we all take a step back," Elijah said in his ever-reasonable voice.

"I got a better idea," Ryan said. "Why don't the two of you tell me what any of this has to do with you? Why did you call her? Signal her? Whatever the hell you did. How do you know about us? About *her*?"

"Fair enough," Elijah said.

From the look on his face, Ryan didn't care if it was fair or not. He wanted answers and he obviously didn't want them from Sabelle.

Calmly Elijah pulled a bag of frozen peas from the freezer and handed it to Ryan. "You might need that fist later for something worse than walls."

Scowling, Ryan accepted it and placed the bag over his raw knuckles. Joel took a long draw from his beer and chased it with the whiskey. Something glittered in his eyes that Sabelle recognized. Intuition rushed her, planting the idea before she had time to doubt.

"You're from the Beyond," she breathed, staring at him in astonishment. She didn't know why she was so surprised, but she hadn't expected it.

Ryan's head snapped up, eyes hard and narrowed.

"That's why you know so much," Sabelle went on, sure she was right. "That's why you're so hostile."

"I'm *hostile* because you used this man like you had the *right.*"

Sabelle flinched but she shot back, "I saved his life. I risked my life to do it."

Joel shifted his glare to Ryan. "From the look on his face, I'd say that's not good enough. You only helped him to help yourself."

Suddenly furious, Sabelle leaned forward. "You don't know anything about me or why I—"

"Did you blow up Love's?"

Ryan's question was spoken so softly, his voice so deep, that it took her a moment to parse the melodic words into meaning.

"What?" she said as the breath went out of her. Then the full impact of the accusation hit her. "Is that . . . You think I'm capable of that? You think I would do such a horrible thing?"

"You think you're bad enough to take over the *fate of the world*. Who knows what else you can do."

"No," she said angrily. "I didn't blow up Love's. If you think I would, then you don't know me at all."

"There's the rub," he said with a bitter laugh. "I guess I *don't* know you at all."

Her heart was breaking but she didn't look away. She held his gaze, chin up, pride and hurt and fury right there for him to see.

"You may not have lit the fuse, but what happened at Love's happened because of you," Joel butted in.

"Or because of you," she said pointedly. "And now you're afraid the Sisters will come looking for me and find you."

Joel gave a mean chuckle. "That ship has sailed already, hasn't it, sweetheart? Aisa knows where you are, doesn't she?"

Sabelle's mouth snapped shut. Ryan looked ready to start hitting things again and Joel seemed a likely choice. Instead, he moved to her side, strong, solid, and so distant that he might have been on the other side of the universe.

"That true?" he asked. "You've seen her here?"

Reluctantly, Sabelle nodded. "In the café, when you left to use the restroom. She threatened me. She said she'd kill a seer every hour until I returned. I'm pretty sure she murdered my friend."

Her voice hitched and a burning lump of emotion lodged in her throat. She blinked back tears, knowing they'd be scorned by these three men who didn't trust her.

"You didn't think that was something you should share?" Ryan asked. "We were having such a moment."

His sarcasm whipped her. She could feel his disappointment, his stewing resentment, his sense of betrayal. Her *should have* list had already grown long, but she added one more item to it because he was right. She should have told him that, too. She hadn't because she'd been afraid. Afraid that repeating Aisa's threat would make it come true. Afraid that Ryan would turn back when she was so close to her destination. Joel took another drink from his beer, exchanging a look with Elijah.

"You have something to add?" Ryan asked. "Spit it out. I'm out of patience."

"Only that Aisa's lying," Elijah said.

"About?"

"Killing seers. She can't. She didn't."

Sabelle shook her head. "I know what I saw."

"You saw what Aisa wanted you to see."

"She had Nadia with her and she'd been tortured."

"Who's Nadia?" Joel asked.

"Who are *you*?" Sabelle countered, feeling like a cornered animal. "*What* are you? You're not human."

"No more than you are," Joel agreed.

The room grew very quiet. Elijah took his seat beside Joel and put his hand on Joel's leg in silent support.

"Are you from the Beyond or not?" Ryan demanded.

Elijah answered. "I was born in San Diego, Joel was born in Denver. He isn't from the Beyond and Aisa may not have tracked Sabelle to this cabin yet, but she will eventually. It was always her plan."

Ryan's eyes became glacial. Sabelle felt their frosty burn as he turned her way. Sabelle felt light-headed. She braced herself against a chair.

"What do you mean? There was *no plan*. I made the decision to come here in a split second. Aisa didn't even know."

"Aisa sent you," Joel said. "To find us."

"I'm here with you because *you called me*," she cried, feeling like she was talking in circles that would never make sense. "And what possible reason could Aisa have for sending me? I'm a valuable possession she'd never risk losing if she could help it."

Joel bit his lower lip and shook his head. "We're talking about Aisa. She'll have many reasons."

"Like?"

"We pose a threat she wants to nip in the bud and she knew her little seer would lead her to our doorstep."

Sabelle laughed coldly. "You could never be a threat to Aisa."

Joel said nothing, but his confidence shook Sabelle's.

"She couldn't have known," Sabelle insisted. "I didn't even know until I was on the way."

Elijah's expression held pity, not malice. "How did you escape, Sabelle? No seer has ever made it out of the Beyond alive before."

Sabelle's mouth was dry and the room felt suddenly hot. She sipped the cold wine, tasting nothing but her own fear.

"If you think Aisa sent her, why would you call her here?" Ryan asked, suspicion thick in his voice. "That doesn't make sense."

"Sabelle was destined to come here no matter what we did," Elijah answered. "Joel and I simply tried to control the circumstances. We wanted to bring her under our terms. Sabelle isn't the only one who wants to see Aisa brought down. We've been waiting for the chance for a long time."

"How do you even know about Aisa or the Beyond if you're not part of it?" Ryan demanded. Sabelle nodded. It was a good question, one she wanted answered as well.

Elijah raised his brows at Joel. The older man made a disgruntled sound and splashed more whiskey in his glass. He held the bottle out, but Ryan shook his head. "Suit yourself," Joel muttered. He drank, wiped his mouth with the back of his hand, and scowled at Sabelle.

"Do you know why the Sisters can't cross over from the Beyond, but you can?" he asked.

Sabelle narrowed her eyes, trying to figure out where he was going with that question and how it might trip her up in its winding path. He wanted to make her the enemy and she had made it very easy for him to paint her in a villainous light.

Warily, she answered, "The Sisters are goddesses. I always assumed that was the reason."

"It is, in a way. Was a time when they made themselves frequent guests here, though. They liked to go native, mix with the simple folk. Do what they do best."

"Change the fate of humans?" she asked.

"Well, they certainly did that enough, but that's not what I'm talking about. They came for a bit of action."

Sabelle wasn't following and she felt this must be an important point. Ryan reached for the whiskey and poured some in his glass, hesitated, and poured some more.

"Fornication, sweetheart," Joel went on. "They liked the sex and they discovered it had benefits."

Sabelle's face grew hot. She could feel Ryan watching her but she didn't look at him, couldn't look at him.

"Do you know what benefits I'm talking about?" Joel asked slyly.

She shook her head, sensing the trap, but unable to make out the trip line. "Love?" she asked tentatively.

Joel laughed. For the first time, it didn't sound mean. "The Sisters wouldn't know love if it bit off their noses. They came wanting something they could take to the bank. Something that had worth in the Beyond."

Elijah was watching her, too. She felt like a butterfly spread wide on a pin board.

Joel went on. "The Three have been around for longer than we can conceive. One of the perks of being a goddess, I guess. The trouble is, they started running out of juice. They'd seen so many years, so much of the past and present, so much future, that they couldn't keep it straight anymore. They couldn't tell visions of the future from memories of the past. They couldn't determine fate because they didn't have a clue what it should be."

Sabelle frowned, turning each word and fitting it into a picture that had begun forming in her head so long ago that filling it in had become second nature.

"As you can imagine, it was a problem, the Sisters of Fate not being able to tell yesterday from tomorrow. Their power hinges on their accuracy. If they can't prove their worth . . . well, the Beyond has little use for burned-out goddesses."

Sabelle knew the truth of that. The Sisters constantly worried that their power had been compromised. At one time, even the gods feared them. Sabelle didn't know for a fact, but she suspected that fear was no more.

"It infuriates them when our visions are filled with everyday people," she murmured. "They don't care if a push here or there could save the lives of hundreds—unless one of those hundreds is destined to be a king."

Joel nodded. "You can see their problem. If they couldn't see the future, they didn't have a future to worry about. So they came up with a contingency plan. They decided on a little road trip to earth."

"Get to the point," Ryan said.

"The Sisters got themselves knocked up."

Confused, Sabelle looked at Ryan. "Knocked up?"

"Pregnant," he clarified.

She hadn't thought his eyes could look colder, but the word frosted them green and hardened them. She knew why. She'd told him she couldn't get pregnant. She'd believed it to be true, but now Ryan thought it another lie in the long list she'd told.

She shook her head, but she couldn't dispute any of this when she didn't know the truth herself. Besides, something else was coming. Something big. Something she didn't have time to brace for.

"They mated with humans," Elijah said softly. "And created seers of their own blood."

Joel added in steely voice, "Three little goddess babies. Seers who weren't corrupted by all that had happened in the past."

Sabelle's knees wobbled and her vision blurred. Ryan took her glass and guided her to a chair. Once she'd sat, he gave the wine back and Joel went on.

"The kiddies weren't as skilled as their mommas and the Sisters realized they'd need more to make up the difference. Quantity to compensate for quality. So they came back and did it again. And again. It wasn't hard finding men to mate with them. What human male can resist a goddess?"

Ryan stiffened, drank. Said nothing. Sabelle was too stunned to speak. Stunned and bewildered. What had happened to these children? Sabelle had never seen them. If they truly existed, they'd been hidden away.

"The poor besotted men they'd chosen didn't know what hit them until the Sisters were gone and the humans were left ruined. What mere woman could compare to a *goddess*, after all? Babies were born. The girls were kept in the Beyond. The boys rejected and put to death."

"Because the boys were ungifted?" Sabelle asked, her voice cracking with the horror of it.

Joel shrugged. "It was all picture-perfect for the Sisters until they got caught. Fornicating with the chosen ones is generally frowned upon in the Beyond," he said with a grim smile. "Murdering little half-human baby boys . . . well, that was a crime that had to be punished. The Sisters were forbidden to ever return."

"That's it?" Ryan said with disgust. "That was their punishment?"

"Fucked-up, isn't it?" Joel answered.

"What about the girl babies they let live?" Ryan asked. "What happened to them after the sisters were caught?"

"No one really knew what to do with them. Sending them back to the human world might tip off the Big Guy, clue him in to what his depraved creations had been up to in the Beyond. The decision was made to let the Sisters keep their spawn and the whole incident was considered closed. No one cared what happened to the babies after that."

He paused and the tight silence that rushed in brought Sabelle's eyes up.

"No one even noticed when the Sisters made them slaves," he finished softly.

It was so obviously the point to his story, yet Sabelle hadn't seen it coming. The blood drained from her face as the wine soured in her belly. "Their children? Slaves?" she repeated, because she needed to say the word, to apply it. "Are you . . . You're saying . . ."

"Eleven slaves apiece, so they'd have equal power," Joel continued.

Sabelle stood, her heart suddenly a hammer in her chest, her mouth so dry she could hardly speak.

"Their *children*?" she said again, still not believing it. "You're lying."

"Wish I was," Joel said solemnly.

Waves of disoriented memories crashed over her. She couldn't recall a childhood . . . a mother. She opened her mind, searching for one single recollection of being touched by love . . . being held by a parent. There was nothing.

"You're wrong," she said, her voice so hard it rang. "I wasn't born. I was created, just as the Sisters were. I'm not human—half-human. I'm not . . ."

"Eleven apiece," Joel continued, unwavering, uncaring that things inside Sabelle were crumbling. "Thirty-three seers searching the world for events that the Sisters could twist and turn and make into something they shouldn't be. Balanced chaos. Until the children began to die. One by one, until all that was left was you, Sabelle. The last child. The last seer."

Sabelle felt as if her head had been stuffed full of cotton and now it muffled what she heard, making it incomprehensible. Ryan was watching her, but she couldn't fathom her own thoughts, let alone whatever mystery gleamed in his eyes. "That's not true," she said. "You're wrong. Aisa's not my . . ."

"Mother?"

Sabelle shook her head. "No. She's not. We aren't . . . Seers were created, like the stars, like the . . ."

The pity in Elijah's eyes stopped her denials. She saw truth within his sympathy. Horrified, she lowered her gaze, trying to keep the stinging tears from coming.

"When was the last time you saw one of the others?" Joel asked.

"I only see Nadia. She's also a slave but not a seer. She's my friend."

Joel and Elijah were silent for a moment, and Sabelle felt more of that distressing compassion in the quiet. Ryan's head was bent and his focus on the circles he drew in the condensation ring his beer bottle made, but he listened closely. She could feel his attention.

At last Joel spoke again and his voice sounded almost kind. That frightened her as much as anything he'd said so far.

"Whoever Nadia is, she's not your friend, Sabelle. There's no such thing in the Beyond."

The tears she'd managed to hold back burned her eyes, but she felt stripped to the bone and shedding them now would destroy what was left of her. Fortunately, Joel didn't make her respond. He continued his calm narrative, firing darts at her soul with each unbearable word.

"We think it must have been a disease that wiped out everyone. Something you and Aisa were immune to, but not the other seers . . . not even Aisa's sisters, Moira and Nona, survived it."

"That's impossible."

"Is it? Have you ever seen the Sisters together?"

She hated admitting that she hadn't. "Not in a very long time, but that's not unusual. I'm a slave. I see other slaves. I mean, I used to before my power became so strong that they had to isolate me to keep it from corrupting the visions of the others. Only Nadia could be around me after that."

The explanation had made perfect sense when Nadia explained it to her. Now humiliation seared the edges of her composure and nudged her into the hot flame of despair. The more Joel and Elijah said, the less she believed her own view of her world. She wasn't just a slave. She was a fool.

"How did you escape, Sabelle?" Elijah asked again.

"Nadia helped me. She summoned the reaper who carried me from the Beyond."

"How?" Joel asked.

"I don't know. There wasn't time to ask."

The three men exchanged glances and Sabelle felt that, once again, they'd all heard something she'd missed.

"You said it yourself," Ryan murmured reluctantly. He leaned forward, resting his arms on the table. "Aisa is the master of illusion."

Like bits of glass falling to a marble floor, she heard the shivering sound of understanding. She stared into the distance, trying to see through the tangle of her thoughts to what these men had discerned already. "You think Nadia is Aisa's creation? An illusion?"

Joel shrugged. Elijah folded his hands together and nodded. Sabelle moved away, giving them her back. She wrapped her arms around herself, her pain so deep it had no beginning, no end.

"That doesn't explain who *you* are," Ryan said, and Sabelle couldn't help but look over her shoulder, desperate to understand what he thought of all this. His face was turned, though, as he spoke to Joel. Sabelle remembered that's how all this had begun. She'd asked that question and Joel had led them through a labyrinth of twisted nightmares instead of answering.

Joel looked up with eyes that seemed a thousand years old. "You can't guess? I'm one of the boys—one of the ungifted sons Aisa left for dead. Imagine her displeasure when she realized I'd survived. She's been trying to kill me ever since. But seers—we get these feelings when bad things are coming. Turns out we're not so easy to kill."

20

Sabelle could see herself standing in the kitchen as if she were no longer part of her body. She could feel Ryan's silent perusal as he waited for her reactions. Yet she was in some other place where Joel's words echoed on.

He'd said so much. Lies. Truths. She had no way of untangling the knotted mess. Was Aisa her mother? Did she share blood with the most terrifying being she could imagine?

Or was Joel a consummate liar with an agenda of his own? How did he know any of this? Could he truly be—

Her thoughts stuttered as a realization she'd been too blinded by shock to see suddenly snapped into focus.

"If you're . . ." she began, disbelief thick in her voice. "If Aisa is your . . ."

Joel's eyes were clouded as he met her stare. "That makes us blood," he finished. "I'm your little brother, Sabelle."

A hundred conflicting emotions rained down, cold

sleet that made her shake from the inside out. Brother. Family. Human—half of him. Half of her. What did that mean? She wanted it to be true with a desperation she could barely contain. Yet some piece of her had already stamped it false and moved on.

"How can you be her little brother?" Ryan asked carefully. "You've got at least twenty years on her."

"The mileage takes its toll down here," Joel replied. "My guess is that she'll start to age if she stays."

If she stays. The idea floated like fairy lights in a world made of cotton candy and dreams.

"You still look dubious, Ryan," Elijah said. "You don't believe him?"

"Sabelle says she wasn't born, Joel says they share a mother. I don't know that I believe either one of them."

Sabelle swallowed hard.

"How'd you see us coming? Sabelle said no one can see their own future."

Joel grimaced. "Well, what do you know. You got more than rocks in your head."

Ryan stared back, nonplussed. Waiting for his answer.

"Wasn't me who saw it," Joel said grudgingly. "It was him. Elijah's wired a little different than a seer. He doesn't have the burden of being half-monster. He's all human, right down to the dreams. Only thing is, they tend to come true."

Together, Sabelle and Ryan looked at Elijah for confirmation. Elijah said, "I dreamed of Joel my whole life. I knew exactly who and what he was before I ever met him."

"He was waiting for me. Just like we were waiting for you."

Sabelle's chest tightened. She fought to keep her voice steady and asked, "What about you, Joel? Did you know he would be waiting? Could *you* see *him*?"

"Are you asking because you can't see anything anymore?" Elijah asked in that kind and coaxing voice she was afraid to trust.

Warily, she nodded. "Since coming here, my mind's eye is blind."

"You don't know how to open it yet," Elijah said. "You probably don't even know how to have a proper dream."

She looked at Joel. "Is that how you see? In dreams?"

"I could if I wanted to, which I don't. I trust Elijah to tell me what I need to know. I live *now*. That's all I care to see." He shrugged. "We all have powers. Every last person on earth. Doesn't mean we all have to use them."

With an irritated look at Joel, Elijah leaned forward. "Sabelle, what Joel is saying is that you don't have to be from the Beyond to be gifted. Your view of the world may have changed when you became part of it, but that piece of you that helped you guide, that made you what you are . . . it's still there. You just have to figure out how to tap into it."

Sabelle looked at Ryan, wishing he'd say something, but he'd grown so distant, she wasn't even certain he was still listening.

"Listen," Elijah said. "We've given you a lot of information. You're safe here—as safe as you'll be anywhere, I guess. Sedona is a special place and this property is sacred. Mystics have been settling on this soil for centuries and for a reason. It's not just beautiful, it's filled with pockets of such intense energy they make your skin crawl. Vortexes, they call them. It creates a blanket that keeps us hidden. Aisa may know she's close, but now that you're here, it'll take her some time to find you."

"What makes you so sure?" Ryan demanded.

"No one's tried to kill me lately, that's what," Joel muttered.

"And when it's time to come out of hiding?" Ryan asked.

"We figure out a way to cheat fate," Joel answered. "We bring Aisa down."

Ryan laughed under his breath. "As easy as that, huh? What about her?" He pointed at Sabelle.

"What about her?" Joel countered, as if she weren't in the room.

"The owned becomes the owner. Does that mean you're going to support her when she becomes the owner?"

"Are you?" Joel shot back.

The three men stared at one another, no one answering, and Sabelle felt the burn of rejection stain her face. She wanted to say something cutting. If Aisa was her mother, she should be able to think of a retort that would put them all in their place.

But all she managed was to draw herself up and huddle in her broken pride. Not a single tear spilled. Not a whimper escaped. They'd wounded her today, these three men she'd thought were her allies, but she didn't let it show.

"Why don't we cross that bridge when we reach it," Elijah said softly.

Of all of them, she suspected he was the one who knew how close to the edge Sabelle stood.

"It's too late to save the world tonight."

21

The cabin should have seemed bigger, less two occupants. Instead it shrank down to the small space she and Ryan shared. Sabelle watched him warily, unsure what came next. Wanting to bring back the warmth she craved. Everything had changed, though, and she saw the truth like a light through a tunnel.

Ryan thought she'd lied to him, tricked him, *fornicated* with him like her mother to steal his seed and begin stocking her own stable of seers. She had no credibility, no way to convince him otherwise.

He turned away from her.

"I'm going to grab our bags from the car," he said, which was so much better than *I'm going to leave you here*.

Still, Sabelle moved to the window and watched him, unconvinced that he'd return until the front door opened, letting in a gust of cold air, a frisky dog, and Ryan. He carried their bags to the bedroom and returned as silent and pensive as he'd been most of the night.

In the kitchen, he poured himself another drink but left it on the counter as he stood staring out the window over the sink.

After a moment, he turned. "Why don't you try to get some sleep?" he said over his shoulder, his voice low. "I need to think."

She knew she should do as he asked. Go to sleep, do some thinking of her own. But she couldn't bear the thought of putting a closed door between them. It was time to admit that more than her relationship with Ryan had changed. *She* had changed. She'd come with a clear goal. She'd felt a sense of purpose.

She'd wanted to save Ryan . . . and then she'd wanted to save humanity. She'd thought humans needed her help, poor misguided creatures. How arrogant she'd been. The only help they needed was to get way from Aisa. Sabelle would do everything in her power to make that happen. Afterward, though . . .

It was her duty to return, to carry on the important task of guiding fate for the beings God loved most, but each moment she spent with his beloved creations, with Ryan Love, she found her will to leave diminished. Joel's revelation that she might *belong* here, that she was half-human, glimmered like diamonds in a wall of slate.

"I don't want to go to bed," she said, lifting her chin, trying to look bold. "Not alone."

He glanced at her over his shoulder, his eyes a stormy

sea. Tension bunched his thick shoulders and broad back. She waited, willing him to turn around.

"I'm too tired to talk anymore, Sabelle. Even if I wasn't, I don't know what I'd say to you."

"I don't want to talk."

A deep breath stuttered out—laughter, disbelief. Rage. She heard it all in the tight burst of air.

"I'm not Aisa. Maybe what they said is true. Maybe she's my mother. Maybe they're both full of shit."

Another glance over his shoulder. This one less frigid cold, more stormy sky.

"It doesn't matter if it's true or not," she went on. "I'm not my mother and you're not your father."

At last he turned and leaned a hip against the counter. He watched her, his expression inscrutable.

"Your dad turned into someone you didn't like much when your mother died. You felt betrayed."

"And you're a poor little goddess who wants to play human before she goes home."

The arrow flew true. She felt it deep in her heart. Defensive and hurt, she lifted her chin.

Ryan went on: "I don't know what you want me to say. You've had me off balance since the first time I laid eyes on you. It hasn't even been a week, Sabelle."

"But you've known me for years."

"*You've* known *me.* Not the other way around."

"You sensed me. You said you felt me there." He didn't deny it, but his doubt shouted at her. She swallowed hard. "Before I came here, I didn't know what it meant to feel. To ache and want and *need.* I didn't understand how it could consume me. I care more about what you're going to say next than I do about Aisa hunting me down and forcing me back. You're worried that I've somehow *enslaved* you with all my otherworldly powers. Well, I'm worried about the same thing, Ryan."

He hung his head for a moment and shook it. "Stop. Just *stop.*"

"I can't do that. I might not have another chance."

"To what?"

"To be with you," she said softly.

Ryan took a deep breath. "Everything's coming at me like bullets, Sabelle. I don't know which ones can kill me and which ones are just going to hurt a lot." A small, bitter laugh followed. "I need to get out of the line of fire."

"No you don't. You're just looking for ways to put distance between us."

He shrugged. "It's the smart thing to do."

"When was the first time you thought I'd be more trouble than I was worth? Five minutes after meeting me?"

"You mean while my livelihood was being blown to hell and I was running for my life?"

"You call *me* pushy, but that's all *you* do. You push and you push until no one's left around you."

"I'm pushing you somewhere you don't want to go?"

"Yes. Away."

"How can you say that? I woke up today holding you so fucking tight, it was like I was afraid I'd lose you while I slept. What's it going to be like tomorrow? Or the next day? Or the one when you leave?"

He cursed, shook his head again, and looked away.

"You've been lying to me since we met. That should be enough for me, but I'm still here and I can't figure out why. My head is saying get the fuck out, but the rest of me . . . I can't seem to make it to the door."

"Quit looking for reasons to say no to me, Ryan."

"Then tell me how this conversation is going to play tomorrow. What's it going to be when you don't need my help anymore?"

And in that statement lurked all the worries that made Ryan Love the man he was. The kind of man who stood in the eye of a storm and dared it to do its worse. He was a boy watching his mother die and his father mourn for the rest of his days. He was a teenager watching his brother and sister die again and again, only to mystify the world by opening their eyes after it should've been over. A grown man toiling to hold on to something he loved and hated with equal passion. Holding on for all he was worth.

Losing it all anyway.

Sabelle moved closer, defying the invisible boundaries meant to keep her afar. "You're not the only one who's all mixed up inside, Ryan. Cards on the table, like you said. This. Here—now. This was my one chance to try everything I'd longed for. With you. And you're right. I thought I could just pop in, sample the human world, then leave with my souvenirs and my heart intact." She laughed. "Things just didn't work out that way, though, did they?"

He watched her intently, so wary it broke her heart.

"I don't know what's going to happen tomorrow. I can't tell you where either of us will be. I can only say what

I hope. I want to be here, Ryan, figuring this all out. Who we are. What we are to each other. If Joel is my brother, then I'm half-human. I want to know that part of me. I want *you* to know that part of me. I want to be with you. I don't need to see the future to know that."

Her words fell like snow. Soft as breath, melting as they touched. She saw Ryan react to each tiny flake. The darkening of the green in his eyes, the softening of his lips.

"I came because I couldn't let you die. I swear it. Nothing else was as important as that. But I want to stay because leaving you would be worse than dying."

His shoulders had been bunched tight. Now his arms dropped to his sides. He tilted his head back and stared at the ceiling for a long moment while Sabelle waited, breathless, for him to come to terms with the truth or throw it all away.

The night chill still clung to his skin, as cold and fresh as an icy wave. But beneath it was flesh, blood, muscle, and bone. Warmth. All the things that made this big man the stunning creation he was. Sabelle took deliberate steps forward, wanting him to know she meant them.

She could touch him now. Easily.

The hand that reached up shook, but her fingers brushed his hair back from his brow, smoothed it against his temple. His eyes tracked the movement, his thoughts as hidden as the shadows.

"Will you let me in?" she asked, her voice wavering. "Take a leap of faith, with me? I don't want to be outside anymore."

His head moved, a half shake of denial, but he didn't say no, so she took another step. Measured. Needy. Chin up, eyes steady.

He looked away, his color high, his chin low.

"I don't know if I can," he said at last.

"I'm no expert," she returned. "But I think you just say yes. Simple as that."

He exhaled through his nose in a breath of laughter. "Nothing's simple where you're concerned."

She raised her brows. "Ditto."

His eyes held a golden glow that seduced her as she came up on tiptoes and took his face between her palms.

In the beginning, Sabelle had come in desperation, thinking in terms of *now* and *maybe* and *if*. But Ryan had forged a bond stronger than those of fate when he'd touched her, and she no longer knew what she was or where she fit. Except here, next to him.

A pulse beat between them, low and steady. Ryan's eyes had the hot glitter of desire, but he didn't move. Sabelle tried not to either, but her body canted forward. She pulled his head down and his hands curved around her hips, his grip knowing, masculine, filled with promise he still refused to make.

She was having trouble breathing. Thinking. She wanted to pull his shirt up so she could press her hands to the flat muscled abdomen, open her mouth over the ridges there and feel his warm skin against her lips, her tongue. But she wanted his mouth first, the taste of what he felt. She needed to know if his emotions were as strong as hers.

She pressed her mouth to his, capturing his bottom lip

and sucking softly, as he'd taught her to do. She nipped it with her teeth, licked it, and moved to the upper. He held her against him, his hips hard at her belly, muscles flexing as he opened his mouth to hers. His tongue tasted of warm whiskey that fired her senses and made her drunk with the power of her need.

He might not give her the words, but his kiss was demanding, owning. His big hands slipped down to her bottom, cupping, squeezing, holding her still while he stole her soul. She sacrificed it to him willingly, knowing he'd care for it—probably better than she could.

The hands moved again, up over the soft denim until he reached the bare skin above the waist. She sucked in a breath and let it out in a rush as they slipped under her sweater and to her new bra. He made a sound as he touched the silk. In the next instant, he peeled her sweater over her head. His breath stopped as he stared at her and she looked down, seeing the soft light against the swell of her breasts held by the bits of flowered satin. His big hands covered them, hot and possessive. "God, I love that store," he muttered hoarsely.

He pulled the cups down beneath her breasts and palmed her sensitive flesh, thumbs over her nipples, teasing them into hard points that ached for more.

A sense of power settled over her, diluted by the vulnerability of her position. Exposed, aching to have something only he could give. She shoved the hem of his shirt up and he obliged by tugging it over his head and throwing it on the floor with hers. Her fingers moved over the alluring ridges of muscle, watching them contract at her touch, feeling the answering clench inside of her. His chest was broad, solid as oak, and smooth in the golden light.

He leaned back and stared into her eyes and she rocked gracelessly against him, her body arching in instinct. Her heart acting out of survival. He cupped her face and held her while he kissed her, fitting his lips to hers, sucking them softly, the tip of his tongue teasing. Finally he parted her lips with his tongue and deepened the kiss until Sabelle fell into a sexual haze she never wanted to leave.

She'd reached a point of no return. Emotionally. Physically. A place of stark decision that culminated in this act. It would mean more this time than it had the times before when they'd come together. She knew him now. As a man, not an image. She knew that he feared wanting to hold on as much as she feared being let go.

She traced the mesmerizing trail down his belly and tugged open the top button of his jeans. The others followed in quick succession. Beneath, he wore dark blue briefs that swelled with the length of him. She pushed the elastic down and curled her fingers around him and stroked. Ryan's chest lifted with a deep breath that hissed as he sucked it in and his belly tightened. She did it again. He cursed and kissed her again.

Pulling her hands away, he lifted her and she wrapped her legs around his waist as he carried her to the bedroom and lowered her onto the bed, settling his weight over her body. His mouth on hers was possessive and slow, demanding and hot, and her lips clung, yielding to the pleasure.

Leaning back on his knees, he pulled off her jeans and panties at the same time. In an instant, he'd stripped, too, and shifted until his hips slid between her thighs, his mouth on her breasts, his fingers finding the places she wanted him to touch. But it felt important that this time she take control in some way.

She rolled, using her body to push him back against the cool sheets, and then she kissed her way down, loving every hard angle that made up the flesh and bone of Ryan Love. She slid to her knees at the edge of the bed, his knees bent on either side of her, his feet flat on the floor. He sat up and looked down at her as she spread her hands over his bare thighs.

He smelled of soap and Ryan and she pressed her nose into the silken skin of his belly before she took him in her mouth. The sound he made sent a liquid wave of heat through her. He tasted salty and male as she ran her tongue over the length of him, circled the ridge beneath the head, sucked as he'd done to her. Ryan's hands were in her hair, his gaze so hot that it made her bold.

She didn't really know what to do, so she tuned in to the sound of his breath as it rasped, the feel of his body as it moved, the gentle pressure of his hands as she brought him to the very edge.

"Wait," he breathed, trying to pull back.

Sabelle had waited long enough. She didn't let him go until she had all of him.

He cried her name. She would remember that forever.

She looked up from where she knelt at his feet and Ryan leaned down and kissed her like nothing would ever drive them apart. Her arms went around his neck and he pulled her up to the bed and turned her beneath him. He held his weight on his arms, his fingers cupping her head as he stared into her eyes. Then he pressed his lips against her throat, her shoulder, behind her ears, against her mouth as his fingers slipped down low. His touch was rough but not careless as it slid against her wetness and circled, building the tension in her until she moaned with the power of it. She pushed against his fingers and came with a cry.

"Jesus," he muttered.

He held her gaze as he entered her with a hard thrust that set the pace for his sensuous assault. The part of her that could still think realized he hadn't stopped to sheath himself. Not because he'd forgotten—she saw that in his eyes—and hers filled with tears over what that meant, the trust and forgiveness that he hadn't voiced but showed her with this gift.

He knew that she didn't want his baby to enslave, to boost her power. But the thought of his child inside her made her heart swell with love. Did he know that, too?

He met her eyes. "We'll ride this out together," he said softly. "Whatever comes next. Together."

She tightened around him, his body a piston hitting all the right places with all the right pressure. Orgasm ripped through her again, a flash of hot lightning, the roll of thunder echoing through every cell in her body. His climax powered through them both, a hard, hot burst of feeling and sensation that wiped her mind and forged her into something new.

Ryan rolled over, pulling her on top of him, still deep inside, already hard again. She straddled his hips, bending to kiss him. She couldn't seem to stop. She could have done it for hours, for days, and he answered her need with his tongue, teasing the roof of her mouth, her lips, her heart. He moved inside her, insatiable as she. Every thrust spoke of some deep desire to possess her, as if anything less would push her away.

She'd wanted this man forever and now here he was, inside her, changing everything she'd considered herself to be. She was no longer on the outside looking in. Now she was the center of a life she'd never expected to have.

"Don't let me go," she whispered against his mouth.

"Don't you fucking try to leave," he answered.

His hands slid around, cupped her behind as he lifted her a few inches, then let her come down at her own speed—slowly burying him to the hilt in her heat. He lifted again and this time he thrust as she came down, driving himself into her with a dark, erotic purpose.

His steady rhythm touched her tender flesh and she wanted him all over again. He brought his chest to hers, shifting his angle, finding a spot within her, triggering a rush of liquid fire that made him curse in her ear. His breath was hot, his words hotter.

The feeling inside became an echo, doubling back and growing as it settled in her womb. Then he reached between their bodies and touched her just so, just there. She cried out, her voice tight in her throat, her breath strangling the sound as both tried to emerge at once. A second later Ryan thrust hard and held, deep inside her, so hot that she clenched around him and simply surrendered.

22

The sound of Sabelle's voice woke Ryan up. They lay nestled together under the thick down comforter, his body curled around her from behind, his arms holding tight. Possessive even in sleep. Morning light spilled through the open curtains in the kitchen, but here it was cool and dim.

His thoughts traveled back over the night before. Joel. Elijah. Sabelle . . .

He believed her. If that made him a horse's ass, so be it. But he'd seen too much good inside her to assign devious ploys and murderous intentions to her. And he'd told her in the most basic human way he'd known how. No holding back, no barriers. She'd understood what it took for him to give; she'd understood the rules that came with it.

Their fates were bound now.

He smiled wryly.

She'd probably say they always had been.

Beside him, Sabelle shifted restlessly. She murmured again. It sounded like she said, "I'll kill him," or "Until then." With Sabelle, either one was an option.

He eased up on his elbow, looking down at her. Her beauty had always taken his breath away, even from the first moment when he'd found her huddled against the side of Love's, proclaiming herself his savior. Now that he knew what she was, the effect should have waned. Hers was an otherworldly glamor that mere humans could only aspire to and therefore it should seem fake to him, now that he knew.

Maybe it was because his little brother and sister had been called ugly names like *half human* that kept Ryan from harboring prejudice now. Maybe it went deeper. Ryan had wiped both Reece's and Roxanne's tears over the cruelty. It had always been a mystery why the twins had defied death so many times. For all Ryan knew, there was a reason why a reaper had fallen in love with Roxanne and the demons had come to claim Reece. A reason that might be flowing in his own veins, too.

Ryan never claimed to be in touch with his feelings or aware of those deeper currents that flowed through him, but last night Sabelle had cracked a shell he'd protectively denied his entire life. She'd exposed a fear that ran so deep it owned him. Now, he felt a little raw, a bit vulnerable, and a whole lot relieved. Harboring something so detrimental had been like carrying an anchor that kept him moored to a past he'd never really understood.

When he looked in the mirror, he saw a big, tough guy

who'd take on anyone who dared to challenge him. Sabelle skipped the reflection and looked straight to his soul and saw that kid who was scared to death of being left behind. Jesus, how had he never known that about himself?

Gently, he brushed a lock of silky hair from her fine brow and let his thumb trace the line of her elegant nose. Goddess. He believed it. But what was she doing with a troll like him?

She frowned in her sleep and her legs thrashed beneath the covers. A soft whimper broke from her lips.

"Sabelle," he said softly.

"Don't wake her."

The voice came from the open door of the bedroom. Ryan's head whipped around, his body already tensing for a fight. Brandy yipped in the corner where she'd slept and jumped to her feet.

A woman stood just inside the room, dressed in gray wool trousers and a pale pink sweater. Japanese, by the shape of her face and eyes. In her fifties, by the fine lines that mapped her features. Her black hair fell in a curled mess to her shoulders, shot with silver and white, somehow managing to look styled for all the waving mess. She smiled and it had such genuine warmth that Ryan almost answered it with a smile of his own.

Brandy growled and scanned the room just like she'd done before on the porch. She was looking right through the woman without seeing her. Ryan blinked and suddenly realized who she must be.

He'd expected Aisa to come with designer heels and bloodred lipstick to match her dagger claws, or perhaps glittering gowns with a bejeweled beehive. This woman was petite, with sensible shoes and a scrubbed, wholesome face. Still, he didn't doubt her identity. The air around her crackled with something he couldn't identify but sure as hell didn't like.

"She's having a vision," Aisa said. "It's dangerous to wake her now."

He glanced at Sabelle. Her face was flushed, her mouth drawn in a tight line. He didn't know whether to believe Aisa or not.

"I suppose introductions would be redundant," she said. "You know who I am. I know who you are. The only thing we're not clear on is motives."

"I'm pretty clear on that," Ryan spoke at last.

"Your opinions come from misinformation, though."

"I've seen some of your handiwork firsthand. Explosions. Scorpions. I know all I need to know."

She stood very still, never looking away from him. "I was trying to warn you."

"I've been hearing that a lot lately. Consider me warned."

"Then why are you still here? Why are you trusting *her*?"

"Maybe because she doesn't pretend to be my dead dad."

"I didn't have a choice."

"There's always a choice."

"You trusted your father. There aren't too many people you can say that about, and I thought if my warning came from him, you'd listen."

Ryan said nothing. Beside him, Sabelle tossed her head and muttered again. Aisa took a step closer. Brandy jumped on the bed—something she never did. Still searching the room for the threat she couldn't see, she moved to the end and lay down, nose resting on Sabelle's foot, canines flashing soundlessly.

"I thought about coming as your brother," Aisa went on, frowning at the dog. "But I didn't think he'd be as effective."

Before his eyes, she changed, morphing into something unrecognizable before solidifying again. His brother, Reece, stood in her place. Dressed in blue jeans and an ancient Eagles T-shirt, he looked like he had the last time Ryan had seen him, a few days before he died. Fair and beach-bum beautiful, Reece had carried the same height and bulk that Ryan did, but had a few less scars to show for it.

With Reece, the scars had always been on the inside.

"Would you have listened to me?" Aisa asked in Reece's voice.

"No," Ryan said, but it took some effort.

She transformed back into the Japanese soccer mom and smiled again. "I'm coming to you now in my true self. No glamour to blind you, no lies to distract you."

As if she'd plucked the thoughts right out of his head.

"I've done what I can to help you, Ryan. Now it's up to you to help yourself. They've told you their sad little tales. They've said I'm evil. I'm here to destroy humanity. The pictures they've painted of me don't fit the image, though, do they?"

"Who's to say?" Ryan answered. "You could be anything."

Her laugh had a happy, tinkling sound that unsettled him. He managed to keep his expression bland.

"You're smarter than you look, Ryan Love."

"I have my moments."

"How about I give you something no one else ever can or will."

"How about you get the hell out of my bedroom."

He was tired of looking up at her, but he was naked beneath the covers. Deciding he didn't give a damn, he climbed out of bed. She didn't turn away or blush. In fact, she eyed him like he was dessert. He grabbed his pants and pulled them on. Aisa sighed. In the bed, Sabelle's legs scissored, then stilled. Brandy positioned herself across Sabelle's legs.

"Sabelle was called here because she and your two new friends have a plan. You, luscious Ryan, are the critical element to that plan. Through you, they hope to return to the Beyond and destroy me."

Nothing he didn't know already. "I don't have a problem with that."

"But you will. I know you don't believe in fate. You don't understand its purpose in your world. But I have guided humanity since its conception. I have cared for it like a mother. Our holy Creator made me your guardian."

"Just you? What about your sisters?"

"They probably told you I killed them."

They hadn't, but he asked, "Did you?"

"No. Did they also accuse me of killing my own children?"

"Let me guess. It's a vicious rumor?"

"They wouldn't have fared well here. Sons of the gods rarely do."

"Joel seems pretty well-adjusted."

"Does he? Perhaps to you. After all, you share a common denominator."

Ryan frowned. "Meaning?"

"Tell me, how do you explain your youngest brother and sister? The deaths. The revivals."

"I don't explain them," he said coldly. "Especially not to you."

"Really? You've never wondered? What makes them so special? Are you special, too? Tell me you're not curious about your origins."

Sabelle moaned and kicked her feet again. He heard his name on her lips. Clearly. Sweat dampened the skin at her temples and made tiny wisps of her hair cling.

"What would you give for answers, Ryan?"

He looked back at Aisa. "From you? Nothing. I don't want your answers or explanations or anything else you might be peddling."

"I wouldn't be so certain of that. I don't think you fully grasp what it means to control fate, to wield the power I have. What would you say if I told you I could give you your brother back?"

"I'd say go fuck yourself. In fact, I'll say it anyway."

"So fierce." She laughed, the sound young and carefree and as engaging as tinfoil on fillings. She moved closer and Ryan sidestepped, putting himself between her and Sabelle. Brandy growled and bared her teeth again.

Ryan watched Aisa. Her hair gleamed like black silk

and he realized he no longer saw the streaks of silver and white. Even her face looked younger. He glanced at Sabelle. A frown puckered the skin between her brows and her face was so pale it looked gray.

"What are you doing to her?"

"Nothing."

"Bullshit. You're taking something from her. Draining her. I can see it."

Aisa raised her hands. "It's not me, Ryan. It's *here*. She won't survive if she stays. This is what I'm trying to tell you. Joel never left, but Sabelle is a delicate flower that needs proper tending. You want to keep her. I do understand. Human men always want what they can't have. It's a failing that has fascinated and disarmed me over the centuries."

Her dark gaze made a lazy trail over his bare chest down to his groin, where it lingered boldly before returning to his face. He knew she wanted a reaction, maybe a blush or a show of anger.

He smiled mockingly. "Must get pretty lonely up there with no one to scratch your itch."

Aisa's eyes grew hard.

"You're dead wrong when it comes to Sabelle," he went on. "She's no daisy, and your kind of special care is the last thing she needs."

"What about you, Ryan? What do you need? You've tried to care for your family, but you just keep failing again and again. Poor, poor Reece. I saw his sacrifice."

Her voice was low, steady. It punched through Ryan's defenses effortlessly and demolished any sense of victory.

"I still see his suffering," she said. "Even now."

"There's no *now* where my brother is concerned," Ryan said, leaning forward, blatantly using his size to menace the petite woman. "Reece is dead."

Aisa's gaze never wavered. "Is he? Humans are more than flesh and bone, Ryan."

She spoke softly, succinctly, knowing that each word was a spike tearing through him, ripping open fears he'd pretended didn't exist.

"The soul is not a corporeal thing. You're a smart man. You should know that."

Obviously, he wasn't smart enough. He asked the next question when he knew he he'd been led to it. He couldn't help it. He couldn't keep quiet, not about Reece. "You're saying his soul is stuck somewhere, suffering?"

"Yes."

"What's happening to him?"

"Don't ask me, Ryan," she murmured, as if she cared. "Not when you already know the answer."

Her response hurt him in ways he could barely fathom. He'd never understood Reece, but that didn't mean he hadn't loved his little brother. The image that filled his head made him want to shout. Hit something. He clenched his fists.

"And your sister Roxanne has promised herself to the bringer of death," Aisa went on relentlessly. "How do you live with yourself, knowing you let that happen?"

"Shut the fuck up."

"Do you just pretend it's not true the same way you pretend that Reece died a normal death and is now with his maker? Your denials trap Reece in a place so horrible you can't imagine."

"How?" Ryan asked hoarsely when he knew he shouldn't.

"Admit what it is, ask for my help, and I can save him."

Ryan forced himself to stand his ground. "I know what it is. Bullshit."

"So stoic. So certain. Fate is mine to change. Just as I can whisper in the ear of a distracted driver, make him turn right instead of left, make him plow into the happy young woman stepping out of the movie theater, I can bargain with the demons who hold your brother's soul. They're torturing him, you know. I think sometimes before you fall asleep, you hear his screams."

She was right. He heard them. He felt responsible for them. Reece's death had left an open wound in their fractured family that would never heal. He'd tried to comfort himself with the knowledge that at least Reece was finally at peace.

But on late nights when the quiet was thick and his mood dark, he couldn't escape the screams or the certainty that he *had* failed his brother somehow.

He swallowed hard and shook his head. "Jesus, you're good."

An impish smile flashed so quickly, he almost missed it.

"I'm not playing a game, Ryan. I'm not lying. I can free Reece. I can make sure Ruby comes home safely from her trip to Las Vegas and Roxanne leaves her reaper behind. All those things you want."

For the low, low price of one soft, scented woman who slept so trustingly in his bed.

Aisa didn't make him say it. She didn't pretend it was something else. Instead she waited with motherly patience for him to cave. Ryan had made a lot of mistakes in his life. Maybe he was making one now.

"Sabelle belongs to me," Aisa pressed. "I'm her mother."

"You're her slaver."

"What young girl doesn't think her mother is trying to control her? If your mother had lived long enough, Ruby and Roxanne would have felt the same. Parents hold on. It's what we do."

Everything she said sounded so reasonable. But she'd played him before, with his father. He understood how cunning she could be.

"Sabelle makes her own choices."

"Between you and me?"

"About what she wants."

"And you, Ryan? Are you making those choices, too? I'm offering you your family. Not just Reece, but Ruby. Roxanne. Your dog. Dogs get run over all the time."

"You can't see what's going to happen without Sabelle."

"Not quite the truth and not quite relevant. I don't have to *see* to know you'll have to go home eventually. All of you. Ruby from Vegas. Roxanne for the funerals.

She paused to let that sink in. It took everything he had not to blurt, *What funerals?*

"You won't be around to watch over your little seer, because the grief and guilt will be the end of you. Give Sabelle back, problem avoided."

"Veto."

Aisa let out a frustrated breath. "There's no reasoning with you, is there?"

"If you're so all-powerful, why can't you just take her?" Ryan asked. "Why are you wasting your breath talking to me?"

"As a show of trust, I'll answer that question."

Yeah. He could tell she was all about the trust. She might look like she was teed up to drive the carpool, but he'd seen her scare the piss out of a kid with scorpions. There was nothing benign about Aisa.

"I'm listening."

"Sabelle has to agree to come back."

"Come again?"

"She must consent."

Ryan blinked. *She had to consent?* The significance of that washed through him, making him smile with relief. She had to *consent*. "I'll tell you right now, that's not happening. Not now, not later. She's not going back."

"Are you her new master?"

"I'm her new muscle."

Aisa ran her gaze over him again, a slow, insolent trail that he matched with an insulting look of his own.

"Impressive," she said, unimpressed. "It will do her no good, though. I'll kill her before I let you keep her."

"I don't see it that way."

"You're known for your insight?"

"The way I hear it, seers aren't so easy to kill."

Aisa tilted her head, amused. "She'll *beg* to come back, Ryan."

She said it so simply and with such firm confidence

that Ryan almost faltered. "You don't know her as well as you think," he said.

"Clearly, one of us is misinformed. Maybe I'm not speaking plainly enough. Once I start killing your loved ones, Ryan, Sabelle will come running home. She won't be able to stand it. She's sensitive that way. But by then you'll have lost everyone, including the one you're trying to save."

"Get the fuck out of my sight."

"Get the fuck away from my seer and open your eyes. *I* am not your enemy, Ryan. I didn't come bearing lies. I've told you the truth as best I could. It may not be the truth you want, but Sabelle belongs to me."

"Sabelle belongs to Sabelle."

She shook her head.

"Why did you send her here in the first place?" he demanded.

"Send her? Why would I do that?"

"Because you both knew I'd help her and you wanted her to lead you to Joel."

"Joel is male," she said scornfully.

"I'm sure he'll be touched you noticed."

"I have no use for males. They're as inept at divination as they are at following orders. If I wanted him, I would have taken him years ago."

"Someone I know would call that a big fat lie."

Aisa scowled.

"Joel tells a slightly different version. You couldn't kill him and you sure as hell won't get his consent. Until Sabelle found him, you didn't even know where he was."

Aisa laughed that tinkling, jarring laugh. Living proof that humor couldn't be faked by someone who didn't understand what it meant.

"Let me guess," she said. "The *vortexes* have kept him hidden while I've search high and low for him. Even you don't believe that. While I applaud your sense of intrigue, you're wrong. I want Sabelle and only Sabelle. I didn't send her here. You've spent enough time in her company to see how helpless she can be. She'd walk into oncoming traffic before she realized she could be hit."

"She's smarter than you think."

"And naïve, not to mention a wee bit unbalanced. It's a side effect of seeing. It's why my sisters and I had to give it up."

"It's like you believe your own bullshit."

Aisa's features hardened. "I've played nicely up until now, but I need my seer. Give her back."

"She's not mine to give."

"That's not what she thinks. She imagines herself in love with you. She thinks you're going to save her. Make her a mommy. *Love* her. That's really not your game, is it? Love. Permanence." Aisa gave him the once-over again. Slow and hungry. "She has good taste, I'll give her that. Now it's time for her adventure to be over. Send her home while you still can."

He shook his head.

"Are you willing to sacrifice everything you love to keep her safe? You know the officer who drove you home the other night? The one who tried to shoot Sabelle in the parking lot? I think I'll send him to pick up Ruby when it's time to identify the bodies. I think he has a thing for her. Perhaps not a good thing. He struck me as a little passive-aggressive. Do you think he looks like Ted Bundy?"

"Fuck off."

"Think about it, Ryan. How much is Sabelle worth? You hardly know her."

From outside, the sound of two car doors slamming one after another broke the morning hush. A moment later heavy footsteps climbed the porch stairs. Ryan glanced past Aisa to the front door and saw Joel through the small cut-out window centered there. Brandy jumped to her feet and barked sharply and Sabelle sat straight up in bed with a frightened cry.

"Ask her to come home. She'll do it for you."

Aisa stepped into the shadow between the door and the wall and was gone in a blink.

23

Brandy's bark pulled Sabelle from a horrible nightmare. It had been vivid, like a vision. Aisa was there, of course. Ryan, too. The terrible dream had unfolded in choppy sequences. There'd been gushing rain, freezing cold . . . a moment of decision and a choice Sabelle never wanted to make . . . Ryan's life for her freedom. She'd been poised on the cusp of the decision when she'd awakened.

Ryan was the first thing she saw when she opened her eyes, and she cried in relief, scrambling across the bed and throwing herself into his arms as someone pounded on the front door. Ryan called, "Just a minute," and held her close, murmuring "Shhhhh" in her ear, rubbing her back as she trembled. She cried, big hot tears that streamed down her face and onto his bare chest.

"You had a nightmare, honey," he told her. "It's okay, you're safe."

For now, maybe. But Aisa wouldn't give up.

Brandy whined and circled at Ryan's feet. Leaning away, Ryan took Sabelle's face in his hands. "You okay?"

Another knock and Brandy raced from the room to the door, barking loudly. "Put some clothes on," Ryan said, giving her one last kiss before releasing her. "Joel and Elijah are here."

She dressed quickly, finger-combed her hair into a ponytail, and made it to the kitchen just as Joel and Elijah took seats around the table. The three were quiet when she entered, but it was obvious from the tension that they all had a lot to say.

Elijah led with "The woods are full of ravens. They've been gathering all morning."

Ryan shot Sabelle a look. "Sabelle told me the ravens used to be on the demons' payroll. Now they work for Aisa."

"It's true," she said when all eyes turned her way. "They spy for whoever will feed their twisted hungers. Aisa is more than happy to do that."

"Well, ain't that dandy," Joel said with a sound of disgust. "Looks like we need a plan."

Sabelle agreed. She wondered how long the birds had been out there. What had they seen and heard? What could they do? Sabelle had no idea, but the black birds were universally feared in the Beyond. It was rumored they could slip into a person's thoughts and compel them. That made them the perfect accomplices for the master of illusion.

"I dreamed last night," Elijah said softly.

"So did I," Sabelle admitted.

"What was your dream?" Joel asked gruffly. "He won't tell me his."

Sabelle lifted a shoulder. She didn't want to speak of it either. "Mine was filled with Aisa's threats. It was just a nightmare."

"Except Aisa can back up her threats," Elijah said.

"I know."

Joel looked like he might press for more information, but the sound of a car's engine and the hard spray of grit peppering the wheel wells of a vehicle cut through the thick silence.

Ryan strode to the kitchen window and looked out. "Anyone you know drive a black SUV?" he asked, glancing back at Joel.

Both Joel and Elijah shook their heads but came to stand beside him and look, too. Anxiously, Sabelle approached, but she couldn't see past them. Without a word, Ryan tugged her over so she could stand in front of him. The feel of his strong chest at her back brought instant comfort. He pressed a kiss to the side of her head, and for a moment, she could almost believe there was a way out of this. Then memories of her nightmare and Aisa's threats quickly chased her well-being away.

Outside, the sky rode low to the treetops. Thick clouds churned, sooty black and ashy gray. It hadn't started raining yet, but the smell of damp cold hung in the air and frost crackled the edges of the window.

The approaching vehicle winked through the trees as it followed the switchback road to the cabin, the rumble of its engine big in the silvery quiet, the spray of gravel rattling loudly. As the SUV drew closer, an endless burst of black wings exploded from the surrounding forest.

Startled, Sabelle gasped and Ryan's hands gripped her shoulders as hundreds of ravens darkened the already glowering sky, circled overhead, and then soared into the distance with raucous, angry cries.

The SUV stopped behind the dusty white truck Joel and Elijah must have driven and the doors opened. A woman with shoulder-length hair and a slender body stepped out, speaking across the hood to the man who climbed out on the other side. She had her face turned away, but behind her, Sabelle felt Ryan stiffen with recognition. She looked closer and guessed who the woman must be.

Surprised, she shifted her gaze to the man with her. Like Ryan, he was tall and built for strength. He had light brown skin and endlessly black eyes she could see even from the distance. He met Sabelle's gaze through the window. Her mouth went dry.

She wouldn't need to be introduced to him, either.

Roxanne Love and her reaper had arrived.

Ryan was already out the door by the time Sabelle put it together, Brandy charging at his feet with a big doggy smile and waving tail. The dog skirted the reaper but leapt up to put her paws on Roxanne's chest and lick at her face.

Ryan pulled the adoring dog back and in the next second Roxanne caught him in a hug. He kissed his sister's forehead and held her, completely ignoring the man at her side. His rudeness startled Sabelle—treating a reaper poorly was never wise—but the tall, dark-haired man seemed to find Ryan's insolence amusing. He stood a step behind, gaze alert and scanning while Brandy raced around their feet, determined to knock someone over in her enthusiastic efforts to welcome Roxanne.

Sabelle looked to the sky warily. Ravens didn't just *go away*. But not even a black feather floated down from the trees.

"Where did the birds go?" Sabelle asked.

It was the reaper who surprised her by answering, "They're afraid of Roxanne."

Afraid of Roxanne? Sabelle looked at Ryan's sister with new respect.

"Why?"

"You'd have to ask them."

That mystifying answer left her speechless.

"What are you doing here?" Ryan asked his sister.

Roxanne pulled away and glared at him. "I saw the damn news, Ryan. You couldn't call and tell me what had happened? What the hell is that?"

"I lost my phone and—"

"You lost your *phone*, not your head. Ruby has my number—who I *did* talk to because she remembered to call. What are you doing up here anyway?"

"What are *you* doing here?"

"We live here. You'd know that if you ever called."

"I meant *here*. This morning."

Hands on her hips, Roxanne glared at him. "Oh, so you do remember that I live in this town. But it never occurred to you to get in touch? Come over and say hi?"

"Are you going to keep yelling at me?"

Roxanne sniffed. "Maybe. I'm mad at you."

"Well, get in line. I've got worse things than you pissed off at me."

That seemed to take some of the stiffness from her posture. She gave the trees a baleful glare. "Who else have you been pissing off?"

He smiled grimly. "Some bitch who doesn't like to share. How'd you find me?"

"The birds," she said.

"You follow them around?"

"Only when they come in hundreds. In my experience, that's always bad." With no further explanation, Roxanne turned to Sabelle. "Hi. I'm Ryan's sister, Roxanne."

"I'm Sabelle. Hi."

Roxanne waited for her to say more, but Sabelle wasn't sure who she was to Ryan. She wasn't quite certain who she was to herself.

Like Ruby, Roxanne had a direct stare and a friendly smile. There was no judgment in it, but she was brimming with curiosity, especially when Ryan touched the small of Sabelle's back and pulled her closer. Roxanne gave Ryan a look that made him blush.

"This is Joel and Elijah," Ryan said, indicating the other two, who'd been watching the reunion with interest. "They own this place. This is my sister Roxanne and her—"

"Santo," the reaper interrupted, shaking hands with both men. He turned to Ryan and said in a deep voice, "Good to see you, too."

Ryan's handshake was no more reserved than Santo's, but Roxanne watched them both with narrowed eyes, obviously just waiting for one to slight the other. The reaper didn't seem bothered by the tension, but Ryan did. Neither man seemed to care if the other approved of or liked him, but neither one of them wanted to upset Roxanne.

"Let's go inside," Ryan said with another glance at the sky.

They moved toward the steps, Ryan and Joel bringing up the rear. As Joel drew even to Ryan, Sabelle heard him mumble, "You sure about that guy?"

"Not even a little bit," Ryan answered.

Sabelle didn't blame Ryan. Santo was cloaked in an air of menace that was hard to miss. It seemed incongruous that the reaper held hands with Roxanne as they walked. As boyfriends went, Santo was unique in every way.

Six adults and one excited German shepherd made the cabin feel packed, but they shuffled around until they all fit in the tiny kitchen. Santo took the seat next to Roxanne, but he eyed Sabelle and Joel with distrust.

"You've been busy," he said to Ryan in that deep, dark voice. "Entertaining seers in your kitchen and ravens in your yard. I'm surprised."

Roxanne's head snapped up. "What are you talking about?" She looked from Sabelle to Joel to Elijah. "What's a seer?" Her head swiveled to Ryan and back to Santo as understanding widened her eyes. "They're from the Beyond?"

"*I'm* from the Beyond," Sabelle said before Santo answered for her. "Joel is from—"

"Denver."

"Seriously?" Roxanne said.

Roxanne turned that stare on Sabelle again. "And who are you to Ryan? His girlfriend?" She faced her brother before Sabelle could respond, even if she'd known how. "Your girlfriend's from the Beyond and you're giving me shit about Santo?"

"I'm not giving you shit."

"What do you call it, then? I'm in love with him, Ryan, and I don't care who knows it."

"You've made that known."

"So you're going to punish me for it while you diddle around with her?"

"I'm not diddling and I'm not punishing you. It's just taking some getting used to. You may not have noticed, but it's been a little chaotic lately."

Roxanne snapped her mouth shut and looked away. "What do you want?" she asked Sabelle.

"She's here for me," Ryan answered.

The reaper cast Roxanne a sideways glance. "That sounds familiar."

Before the conversation derailed completely, Ryan explained that Sabelle had warned him about Love's and convinced him to bring her here, where she hoped Joel and Elijah would have answers about how to stop Aisa from destroying life as they knew it. Joel interjected when he could until they'd pieced together the shell of the story. Roxanne and Santo listened quietly.

It sounded unbelievable, even to Sabelle, but the pair took it all in stride.

"We aren't safe here anymore," Ryan told them. "If we ever were. We need to move on."

He held Sabelle's gaze for a moment and she balked at what she saw there. "Aisa was here?" she breathed.

"This morning."

"Here?" Roxanne repeated, mystified. "Why didn't she just take Sabelle, then?"

"Aisa needs consent," Santo said, meeting Sabelle's eyes across the table.

Shocked, Sabelle's stared back.

"You didn't know?" Ryan asked. Sabelle shook her head, wondering how *he* knew, but the conversation moved on before she could gather her wits and ask.

"Aisa can't take her unless she agrees?" Roxanne said. "Well, that makes it easy, doesn't it?"

"Aisa doesn't care if it's *willing* consent or coerced," Santo clarified. "She doesn't care how she gets it."

Suddenly Sabelle understood what she'd felt in Ryan's taut silence. "What did Aisa tell you?" she whispered.

Ryan's jaw clenched. "Nothing I believed."

"She threatened your sisters, didn't she?" Joel asked.

"Among other things."

Ryan was watching her again. She was afraid to look up. She didn't know what he'd see in her eyes. She didn't know what she'd see in his.

Santo leaned forward. "She threated Roxanne?"

A chill went through Sabelle at the reaper's tone. Ryan locked gazes with him.

"Does it matter?" Ryan asked. "If she could do more than threaten, we wouldn't be talking about it."

"We're missing something," Elijah murmured. "Aisa is after more than getting Sabelle back."

"I still think she's after you," Ryan said to Joel.

"What good would I do her? She left me for dead when I was born and then tried to make me dead when I dared to survive."

He had a point, yet Sabelle agreed that Aisa wanted something more than just Sabelle's willing return. She thought back over the time since she'd broken free from the Beyond. Before that, when Nadia—who might not even exist, according to Joel—had shown her how to escape.

"Has anyone ever seen this woman?" Roxanne wanted to know. "What's she look like?"

"She's beautiful," Sabelle said. "Eternally young and perfectly flawless."

"Japanese," Elijah added. "And very beautiful. Not so young, though. I've only seen her in dreams, but she has gray hair and enough wrinkles to make her look about sixty. Around there. Not bad when you consider how old she must really be."

Wrinkled? Gray? *Aisa?*

"She was waiting when I woke up," Ryan said, staring into the distance. "And when I first saw her I thought the same. Older. Graying and wrinkled. But the longer she was there, the younger she looked." He turned to Sabelle and touched her cheek. "I may be wrong, but I definitely had the feeling that you were giving her a charge. She was taking something from you."

Santo stood and paced away. "How do you know about their history?" he asked Joel when he reached the window. Sabelle had wondered the same thing, but last night the revelations had been too fast and devastating for her to stop and ask.

"My dad told me some of it. Aisa stayed with him while she was pregnant. He thought she was a little crazy—a lot crazy—but he didn't care. He'd have loved her if she'd had two heads and one eye. She told him her family had been wiped out by disease and she feared for their child. When I was born, I wasn't breathing. To hear my dad tell it, she disappeared right out of his arms. She was long gone by the time the doctors got my heart beating."

Joel rubbed the bridge of his nose. "My dad was always going on about her beauty, how she was an angel from heaven. I didn't believe anything he said until I met Elijah."

They all looked at the other man, who sat calmly listening.

"Elijah can see the past and the future," Joel finished with a nod. "His dreams go both ways."

Santo glanced at the black man with interest. "What are you?"

"I beg your pardon?" Elijah asked.

"Dr. Death wants to know if you're human," Joel said. "The answer is yes. Gifted. Cursed. Human. Take your pick."

Santo liked this answer. He smiled and his stern, cruel features transformed. Sabelle had a glimpse of what Roxanne probably saw when she looked at this intriguing man.

"I'm with Joel," Ryan said after a moment. "This isn't just about Sabelle. Aisa planned this down to the last detail. Blowing up Love's. Pretending to be Sabelle's friend so she could give her a warning and show her how to escape. Why bother if the only thing she wanted was to get her back?"

"What else could she be after?" Santo asked.

"I thought it was Joel, too," Elijah said. "Because of the prophecy."

"There's a prophecy?" Roxanne said. "What is this? Some kind of twisted fairy tale? Is she going to show up with a poisoned apple next?"

Sabelle almost smiled. Ryan had said nearly the same thing.

"I must be missing something," Ryan's sister went on. "You two are seers and he's a psychic, but nobody knows what's going to happen next?"

"It's not pay-per-view," Ryan answered, surprising them all. "She can't see her own future, Joel doesn't want to see it even if he could, and Elijah . . ."

"What I see has to be interpreted," Elijah said. "As all dreams do. Sometimes it's clear. Sometimes it's clear as mud."

"But you've seen something," Roxanne insisted.

"Yes," he admitted grimly. When Roxanne opened her mouth again, he held up a hand. "Until I understand it, though, I won't be commenting."

"Why not? Maybe we can help you," she said.

Elijah's dark skin had a gray cast. Joel leaned closer and gently squeezed his hand, murmuring something that the rest couldn't hear before leveling a look at Roxanne.

"Quit badgering him," he said.

Roxanne sat back, chagrined. "Sorry."

Elijah shook his head. "It's me who's sorry. I know it's frustrating, but I have to trust my instincts and they tell me I don't have a clear enough picture to discuss it. The only thing I know for sure is that there *is* a poison apple—metaphorically, anyway. And we need to find it before she does."

"So you've seen that part?" Roxanne blurted.

Beside her, Santo smiled. "She's like a dog with a bone. It's not in her genetic makeup to simply let go of something once she has her teeth in it."

He said it like it was a good thing. Sabelle peeked at Ryan from the corner of her eye and caught him grinning in agreement.

"I haven't seen anything that I am sure about," Elijah said, leaning back in his chair, discomfort in his expression.

Joel watched him closely. "That's what you dreamed about this morning, isn't it?"

"Yes," Elijah answered, "but there are too many ways to interpret what I saw and none of them made sense. I couldn't see it through to the end."

He grew quiet, but Sabelle sensed what he was trying to avoid saying.

"Because you might be dead when it happens," Santo filled in calmly.

"Because I might be dead."

Joel turned on him. "Are you fucking kidding me?" he said in a low, angry voice. "When were you going to tell me?"

"When I knew for sure."

"When would that be? When you're six feet under?"

"Or when I was sure," Elijah said tightly. "At this point, I don't trust anything I see."

Joel's face was pale except for the two red flags over his sharp cheekbones.

Santo leaned back in his chair and turned those black eyes on Sabelle.

"You escaped with a reaper?"

She nodded.

"Your plan to get back includes another reaper?"

Warily, she nodded again.

"Me?"

"If you'll help me."

"Oh, hell no," Roxanne interrupted. "I'm sorry, Sabelle. You seem like a very nice woman—being—whatever you are, but Santo and I have fought the Beyond already. He's earned the right to stay here. He's not for hire."

"Do you know how to kill her?" Santo asked Joel.

"Pretty sure."

"That doesn't inspire confidence."

Elijah shrugged. "It's the best we can do."

"Does anyone but me think this is a poorly constructed plan?" Santo asked.

Ryan laughed and Sabelle heard all the complex emotions that hid behind the mirth. So did his sister.

"Believe it or not, I'm on your side on this one. Before anyone goes anywhere, we need to know what she's really after and how to stop her. For good."

"I agree," Sabelle said.

"Me, too," Elijah offered.

Joel gestured with his hand. "Yeah." He looked at Santo. "Can you still do it?"

"By *it*, do you mean move between the Beyond and this world?" Santo asked coolly.

"Yep, that's what I mean."

"Reapers were created for that purpose."

"The way I hear it, you're not a reaper anymore."

Santo's smile made Sabelle shiver. "Now I am something other." His black gaze moved from one face to another. "A distinction it seems we can all claim."

Joel laughed. "You're a funny guy."

"Don't encourage him," Roxanne muttered.

"But can you still do it?" Ryan insisted.

"Like riding a bike," Santo answered.

"You can't honestly be considering this," Roxanne exclaimed. "Any of you. This crazy lady is trapped in the Beyond. You all agree she can't get out."

"She can do a lot of damage from there, *angelita*," Santo said.

"Going back into the Beyond can do a lot of damage to *you*, Santo."

"You'd rather I let your brother fight this battle on his own?"

All eyes turned to Ryan. He still leaned against the counter, watching the conversation like it was a spectator sport. He didn't answer so Sabelle spoke up.

"It's not Ryan's fight," Sabelle said. "It's mine."

"And you believe he'll let you fight it alone?" Santo asked.

Ryan shot Santo a surprised look, as once again, the two men seemed to see eye to eye.

"He's right. Besides, it's not just your fight, Sabelle. Not anymore. She made it mine, too, when she threatened my family. When she threatened *you*. When she blew up Love's. She wants a fight. I'm ready to bring it."

Sabelle's vision blurred. "You should walk away from this, Ryan. Go home before she takes that away from you, too."

Ryan pushed away from the counter and knelt down in front of her, his weight balanced on the balls of his feet. He put his big, warm hands over hers and waited until she met his gaze.

"It's our fight now, snowflake. I'm not going home without you."

Her tears breached her lashes and spilled down her cheeks. Ryan brushed them away and pressed a kiss to her forehead. Roxanne looked on with her mouth open and Sabelle laughed as Santo leaned over and used his finger to push her jaw up and close it.

"We need to make a game plan," Elijah said. "Not here, though. I can feel her in the air now. We need to go someplace new. She'll be sending more than birds next."

No one questioned the certainty in his voice. Sabelle sensed it, too, that hard, tainted feel of Aisa hovering like a spider from a sticky, silken thread.

"You can follow us to our place," Santo said, and Roxanne's tremulous smile told them all how much his offer to let these strangers and her brother into their home meant to her. "It's about ten miles east. We'll go as a caravan. Keep up."

24

Sabelle sat in the passenger seat, watching the brilliant reds and greens of sandstone and pine zip past. Brandy sat right behind her, ears perked as she fogged up her window, occasionally smearing it with her wet nose. She and Ryan drove behind Joel and Elijah. Roxanne and Santo had the lead in their black SUV.

Civilization seemed to be a million miles away as the road twisted through red-stained sandstone spires rising up over uneven ground and sudden ravines. A coyote dashed across a clearing with something limp and furry dangling from its mouth. A lone bird with an impressive wingspan glided beneath the low ceiling of thundering clouds. Ryan had both hands on the wheel as he fought the buffeting wind to keep the vehicle on the road. Rain looked to be a certainty.

"What is *that*?" Sabelle asked softly, looking across

the rugged landscape to where a cloud of swirling red and brown seemed to be building ahead on a plateau.

"Dust devil," Ryan answered. "Welcome to Arizona."

Lightning split the churning atmosphere in huge strikes followed by thunder that shook the ground. The rain came all at once and in sheets, mixing with the thick ocher silt that coated the windows and obscured their vision.

Their low-slung car hit a patch of slick mud and skidded sideways. Ryan fought the momentum, tapping the brakes and gripping the wheel, but this vehicle had been built for racetracks, not rough terrain. It nearly slammed into a rising ridge before he got it back to the road. The wipers smeared mud on the windshield, but Sabelle could make out the white pickup fishtailing in front of them. There was no place to pull over so Ryan shifted down to a crawl while the storm rocked them like a rowboat on an ocean.

Lightning struck just ahead, followed a split second later by another, inches from Sabelle's door.

At the same time, the sound of sirens shrieked from behind. Sabelle turned to see flashing blue and red lights racing toward them. When she faced forward again, she saw more police cars in the distance, coming from the other direction.

Grimly, Ryan squinted at them. "That can't be good. Ten bucks says Aisa sent them."

Sabelle agreed. Aisa seemed to get some twisted satisfaction from using law enforcement to do her bidding.

Ryan peered out the streaked windows as the vehicles drew closer, his head on a swivel as he tried to see everything at once. Sabelle did the same. On a ridge up to their right, lightning struck a tree and it burst into smoldering flames, tumbling from the cliffside and into the road, missing Roxanne and Santo by inches, but making both Joel and Ryan swerve, braking and turning as the two vehicles spun out of control. They came to a stop straddling the lanes. The sirens still screamed as they closed in, the rain still pounded against the roof and sides of the car, but it was a different sound that cut through the rest and made Sabelle look around in alarm.

The fallen tree had left a muddy gash in the ridge and now water gushed out of it with rising power and ferocity. The banks disintegrated under the onslaught and suddenly a wall of water burst from the side of the mountain, tearing up trees and slamming into rocks as it hurtled toward them.

Ryan reached for Sabelle as it plowed into the car, propelling them off the road, over the side, and into a ravine. It happened so fast that Sabelle barely had the chance to scream before they were careening nose first into a chasm that seemed never-ending. Brandy barked wildly, crouched on the floor behind their seats.

Something caught the car's undercarriage as they plunged, slowing their descent but not halting it. Through the window, she saw the white pickup leapfrog over them and roll a few times before it bounced into the gully, landing on its roof with a loud *boom.* The roar of the floodwaters swallowed all other sounds. Ryan's car hit the ground so hard that they left their seats and crashed forward into tightened seat belts and the punch of air bags before it settled awkwardly on its wheels.

Sabelle couldn't move, couldn't catch her breath. Ryan reached for her, winced at the jerk of the belt, and fumbled to get out of it. He was breathing heavily, hands clumsy. At last he was free and cupping her face.

"Are you hurt?"

"No."

"You sure?" he asked, but his voice sounded thick, his words slurred. He shook his head and blinked his eyes. Blood trickled at his temple.

"Ryan, you're bleeding."

She reached for him but he was already turning away. Brandy popped up from the floor, favoring one leg but otherwise unharmed. Ryan ran a gentle hand over her paw. She didn't yelp when he touched it. He murmured a few words to calm her down.

Mud coated the glass completely, turning the interior of the car into a cave. She couldn't see out. Brandy gave her a nervous look and whined. The car had stalled and the windows wouldn't roll down, so Ryan cracked his door, looked out, and quickly closed it again.

"We're caught half on the bank, half in a gully filled with water. We need to get out on your side while we can."

Sabelle nodded, but in truth she was afraid to get out. It had felt like they'd plunged for an eternity. Another world might be waiting outside.

"Come on. It'll be okay."

The door opened upward at an angle and Sabelle struggled to keep it open while she climbed up and out. She made it and then held the door so Brandy could crawl out, too.

"Do you see the pickup?" Ryan asked.

Sabelle looked around and shook her head.

The car creaked ominously as Ryan wedged his weight around the steering wheel and maneuvered over the seats.

River water rushed across the banks of the gully. In the time it took Ryan to get out, it had risen past the tires. Still, the rain fell in huge, cold sluices, freezing them to the bone. Ryan balanced on the car and jumped to the embankment. Braced, he helped Sabelle across. Brandy had a slight limp but leapt on her own and landed gracefully.

Ryan turned in a circle, scanning for the truck. He cupped his hands to his mouth and yelled, "Joel!" An instant later he pointed at the white bed of the pickup poking from behind another downed tree that dammed the racing floodwaters in the ravine. The truck was flipped on its roof and filling fast.

Slipping and sliding, Ryan hurried over. Inside the truck's cab, the two men hung by their seat belts, trapped in the cab. Joel was conscious but wedged in by the door, seat, and steering wheel. Elijah's eyes were closed, his face bloody.

"I can't reach my seat belt," Joel said, helplessly trapped.

Ryan eased around the hood of the truck while Brandy stood on the bank and barked. Sabelle didn't know how she could help, but followed closely, ready all the same. Inside the cab, water poured through the broken windows and doorjambs. It was almost up to Joel's head.

Ryan tried the door but it wouldn't open.

"Joel, I'm going to have to get you out from Elijah's side."

"Do it. Help him first."

The current was manic now and harder to fight as they circled back to the passenger side. Ryan tried that door, managed to get it to unlatch, but it only opened enough to let water in. Cursing, filled with desperation, they worked to clear the debris as the water rose so quickly it was up to Elijah's forehead before they succeeded.

Ryan reached in, used his shoulder as a brace, and unfastened both of their seat belts. He caught Elijah and pulled him out. Joel clawed his way after them and helped Ryan heave Elijah onto the embankment. Sabelle scrambled up, hooked Elijah under the arms, and dragged him back from the edge while Ryan and Joel climbed through the mud to join her.

Exhausted, they collapsed beside Elijah's prone body. Joel went up on his knees and pressed his ear to Elijah's chest.

"He's still breathing, but it sounds bad. Something's gurgling. Jesus, what happened?"

Ryan tilted his head back and stared at the washed-out road above them, tracking the path of the landslide down to the gully. The damage had taken out the road as far as they could see. On either side of the gulch, police cars lined up—three on either side. Roxanne and Santo stood among them.

"They're probably calling in for help right now," Ryan said, pointing.

It didn't look like they were calling for help, though. It looked like a fight was going on. Roxanne was waving her arms. One of the officers seemed to be standing aggressively close. Joel's focus centered on Elijah, but Ryan noticed the discourse above, too. He met Sabelle's gaze with a taut expression.

The rain finally eased from a torrent to a downpour, but the water still surged in the gully. It breached the makeshift dam made by the truck and downed tree and jetted over the undercarriage, churning up whitecaps and debris as it rushed by. Sabelle felt to her bones that something greater than a storm had them in its eye.

"He said there was a flood in his dream," Joel muttered. "He wouldn't tell me anything else. Dammit, he knew something was going to happen and he didn't tell me." Joel's eyes were red and the tough-guy exterior crumbled beneath his worry. "Where the hell is that ambulance?"

"Do you have a cell phone?" Ryan asked.

"Somewhere in the truck."

Which was now completely underwater. Ryan tried to wipe the mud from his face but only succeeded in adding more. "I'm going to try to get close enough that they can hear me. Make sure they know we have injuries."

"Make sure they know? We just dropped into a fucking ravine. Of course they know," Joel shouted. He took a deep breath. "I'm sorry. Please. Tell the morons to get us help."

Ryan nodded and stood, pulling Sabelle to her feet. They moved as close as they could, but it was still too far away. The argument going on up there had escalated and no one seemed particularly interested in the people trapped at the bottom. They both tried shouting but no one heard them.

Frustrated, Ryan returned to Joel and Elijah, holding on to one another as they slipped in the muck.

Suddenly, Ryan stopped, turned Sabelle around, and took her chilled face in his hands. He stared at her for a moment, his gaze moving over her hair, her brow, her lips. He kissed her quickly and fiercely, the feel of his lips unexpected and more welcome than any reassurances he might have spoken. She didn't question his timing or motives. She simply sank into it and let his taste and touch soothe her.

When he pulled back, it seemed he had things to say. Things she desperately wanted to hear. After a moment, he shrugged. "When this is over . . ."

"Yes."

To whatever it was.

His eyes smiled into hers as he took her hand again and returned to Joel.

At the older man's questioning look, Ryan shook his head. "We couldn't hear them, they couldn't hear us."

Joel cursed beneath his breath as Ryan surveyed their options. The force of the water had moved asphalt, cracked the road's surface, and twisted the safety barriers as they powered through. It barreled down the narrow chute of the ravine, churning up debris and carrying it like spoils. Even if they found a way across it, they'd never manage to scale the steep incline to the damaged street where the police lights flashed red and blue.

Ryan turned to look in the other direction. Sabelle followed his gaze and saw a thick mist bubbling out of the earth, cloaking the ravine, obscuring them from the ridge and the road. In a blink, it became fog so thick that it seemed to pin them down.

Brandy's ears swiveled, her head hung low. She didn't make a sound, though, and that alarmed Sabelle as much as agitated barking would have. Suddenly it seemed very dark. Too dark for the time of day. Lightning spidered across the clouds and thunder boomed to the north, yet they stood in a pocket of vacuous quiet.

The skin at Sabelle's nape prickled and she spun to find a woman standing just behind them, dressed in a simple gown of pale blue fabric. A servant's uniform. Ryan turned quickly and Joel looked up, his eyes narrowed with suspicion. He angled his body over Elijah's while Brandy bared her teeth and growled.

"Nadia," Sabelle said.

Nadia smiled and opened her arms in greeting. The gesture was so wanted, so familiar that Sabelle nearly answered it. But the eyes stopped her impulse. Nadia's eyes had always been a warm and faded blue. Now their color was more vibrant and a lot colder. By degrees, Nadia's features began to blur and the familiar, loved face of her friend vanished.

If Sabelle had doubted Joel's theory that Nadia was simply Aisa's illusion, she doubted no more.

A petite Japanese woman with a vicious smile stood in Nadia's place. The baggy blue jeans and worn Arizona sweatshirt wasn't the woman's usual style, but Sabelle would recognize Aisa no matter how she appeared. Aisa had a timeless beauty that would never fade, but Ryan and Elijah hadn't been mistaken. She'd aged and withered drastically since Sabelle had last seen her. The change in her was all the more shocking given that she presented herself in illusion. Why did she appear as an old woman instead of her usual youthful beauty?

Sabelle knew better than to ask, just as she knew not to meet Aisa's eyes. She'd been Aisa's slave for her entire life. A simple look from the woman—*her mother*—could bring Sabelle to her knees.

A raven cawed and circled overhead. More joined it, skimming the low clouds, centering their flight above the humans and Aisa, avoiding the higher ground where Roxanne and her reaper waited.

Aisa turned her chilling stare to Ryan.

"Resilient as ever, Mr. Love."

"You sound disappointed," Ryan replied, eyeing the birds distrustfully. "I'm hurt."

"A nice, clean car crash would have made things easier."

"Easy's not really my style. You know what they say: Go big or go home."

"In this case, I pick go home. You to yours. You can take that one with you." She gave Elijah a dismissive glance. "He's defective anyway. I'll keep the others."

"Defective because he's only human?"

"See, we do understand each other."

"Not quite. You're not keeping anyone. Not Sabelle, not Joel or Elijah. Not my family. Got it?"

Aisa stretched her lips. Sabelle supposed she meant to smile. "What about the reaper? Am I permitted access to him?"

"Wrestle that alligator on your own, lady."

"I appreciate your stand, Ryan. I truly do. But I'm not known for my patience and the wants and whims of humans . . . I really don't give a shit about those."

"Sounds like a personal problem. Maybe it has something to do with all that gray hair and wrinkles. You should moisturize. Hydrate."

Aisa narrowed her eyes. "You *are* as dumb as you look."

"I get that sometimes."

"I'm sure you do." Aisa locked eyes with Ryan and stared deeply. Ryan's hand tightened around Sabelle's and his muscles tensed. Sabelle knew he was weighing odds, looking for weaknesses, calculating how fast he could move. What damage he could do to Aisa; what damage she would do to Sabelle, Joel, and Elijah. The answers were clear. None and total.

Aisa didn't let him look away and the birds spiraled down, down, until Sabelle could feel the brush of their feathers, smell the musty stench of their bodies.

Aisa said, "Sadly, you're missing the point here, Ryan. The simple fact is, I can take . . . I can *keep* whoever I want."

She paused, and her satisfied expression alerted Sabelle a second before she noticed that Ryan's face had gone blank, his eyes distant and unseeing. Was Aisa whispering in his mind?

"What are you doing to him?" Sabelle demanded.

"Whatever I want," Aisa answered coldly.

Ryan didn't even blink. Sabelle squeezed his hand, tugged. "Ryan," she shouted, pulling harder.

The birds shrieked and fluttered as they landed on the ground all around them. Fear rose up like a sickening wave inside her. Sabelle could feel the emotions raging beneath Ryan's lax expression, emotions Aisa had trapped inside.

Still kneeling in the mud, Joel cut his eyes back and forth, splitting his attention between the unfolding drama and Elijah's labored breathing.

Aisa leaned close and spoke in Ryan's ear. "Reece says hey, by the way. I'm afraid his new digs aren't quite up to par, but he's a stubborn one, your brother. He'll have a thousand lifetimes to regret his decisions . . . and yours. You could've upgraded his standard of living so easily."

Ryan was breathing fast. Aisa had hit her mark. Satisfied, she turned her attention to Sabelle.

Sabelle held herself very still, trying to hide the panic that cramped her muscles and made her shake, trying to think of some way to intercept, intercede, but she was so afraid and Aisa . . . Aisa was so powerful that even in illusion she made Sabelle want to cower.

"Sabelle's a mouse, Ryan. You won't even miss her when she's gone. Let her go."

Sabelle thought he shook his head, but she couldn't be sure. She didn't understand what Aisa had done to him, but she guessed that whatever it was, she could have done it at any time. Joel thought Aisa had a plan from the start and Sabelle had to agree. Aisa had allowed Ryan to feel that he had free will so he would bring Sabelle to Joel and Elijah. She still had no idea why Aisa wanted that, though.

"Let Sabelle go, Ryan. She's mine."

The coaxing tone, the dark words . . . Sabelle's horror blossomed into terror.

Aisa switched her attention to where Joel knelt on the ground. Elijah lay across his lap, unmoving. "That doesn't look good," Aisa said. "One can only hope the ambulance gets here soon. It would be a shame if they got lost or the police . . ." She paused and looked up at the ridge where the police cars waited with their flashing lights. "Or if the police thought you'd done something wrong. You might resemble killers on the loose."

Sabelle swallowed hard and forced herself to meet Aisa's eyes. Her knees shook, her throat felt hot and swollen, but she kept her shoulders squared and her gaze steady.

"Defiance isn't a good look for you, seer," Aisa warned, and Sabelle struggled not to cringe.

Aisa stroked Ryan's cheek, never looking away from Sabelle.

"It's time for your little snowflake to come home, Ryan."

Ryan made a tortured sound, but still he didn't move, didn't speak.

"Joel should come with her. Tell them to give me their consent and I won't send deranged policemen to rape and murder your sisters. I won't urge a drunken doctor to perform massive surgery on Elijah's wounds. I won't kill everyone you've ever cared about."

A big, fat raven flapped its wings and perched on Ryan's shoulder just as a sound from up above echoed down at them. An instant later, a bullet plowed up the mud and dirt near Joel.

Sabelle jumped, staring in shock at the point of impact. Joel shouted, pulling Elijah closer. Ryan didn't even flinch.

"I love it when a plan comes together, don't you?" Aisa

said. Another gun went off. The bullet whizzed over Sabelle's head and snapped the tether of dread that held her prisoner. Ryan had tried so many times to protect his loved ones. She wouldn't stand by and watch him fail now. *She* would protect *him.*

"You can't just *take* us," Sabelle said angrily.

Aisa's eyes widened in surprise. "I don't intend to. That was yesterday. Today I expect you to beg for the privilege."

Two more guns went off, their sharp claps overlapping as they traveled down. The first bullet slammed into a low, flat boulder near Brandy and sent shards of granite flying. A jagged piece hit the dog and made her yelp. The other bullet caught Elijah in the shoulder. His body jerked and blood pooled around the wound instantly.

"Send her back, Ryan."

Aisa was toying with them, delighting in their fear, their wounds. She'd whittle away chunks of Sabelle's friends, of the man she'd come to love—had probably always loved—until she finally got what she wanted.

With the clarity of a vision, Sabelle saw the truth. She could never win against Aisa. She'd been a fool to even think it possible. Now she had two choices. Watch Aisa torture to death the people she cared about or sacrifice herself.

The next bullet caught Elijah in the gut and Sabelle heard the message. Aisa had run out of patience with her game. She'd escalated from playful to deadly and the next shot would be for keeps.

Still Ryan said nothing. He stared sightlessly, entrapped by whatever Aisa spun in his head.

"Fuck," Joel shouted, trying to cover Elijah with his body. His face was red, splattered in blood and mud. He looked like he wanted to charge Aisa, but he didn't want to leave Elijah unprotected. Another shot embedded itself in Elijah's thigh. Blood gushed from both wounds as Joel tried futilely to stanch the flow.

"The next one has Ryan's name on it," Aisa warned.

"No," Sabelle said.

The bullet seemed to come before she heard the shot. It grazed Ryan's arm, tearing through his shirt and leaving a red trail in its wake, more threat than wound. Sabelle knew that Aisa wouldn't kill Ryan right away—he was her bargaining chip. Still, it terrified her how Ryan didn't even jerk with pain.

"That was close," Aisa said, smiling sweetly at Sabelle. "Beg and I'll make it stop."

"You fucking bitch—" Joel yelled as the next shot cut through Ryan's shoulder and out the other side.

"I beg you," Sabelle cried, watching in horror as blood spread. "I beg, I'm begging. Take me. Please—"

Ryan made a sound—muffled but agonized—and Sabelle took a step forward, hoping. His eyes met hers and in them she saw his rage and confusion. Panic added darkness, fear made them wide.

Aisa hadn't released her hold, but he fought her power. "I'm sorry," Sabelle sobbed. "I'm sorry."

She screamed as the next bullet slammed into the ground so close to Elijah's head that mud sprayed his face.

"Beg," Aisa said again, her voice soft, her command immense.

Her cold eyes were on Joel this time. Joel stared back at her with revulsion and loathing, but he gave her what she wanted.

"Yes," Joel said.

"I didn't hear you."

"Fucking yes. Whatever you want. Just stop hurting him."

The gunfire ceased so abruptly that Sabelle's ears rang. She could hear a woman screaming, "Stop shooting, you idiots. That's my brother," in the sudden quiet.

Roxanne desperately trying to stop the inevitable. And that's what this was, Sabelle realized sadly. She should have known. She should have been smarter. She, who thought it her duty, her *calling* to guide the fate of humans.

"No," Ryan gasped, his voice rough and hoarse, as if inside he'd been screaming all along. A new emotion joined the turmoil in his eyes—pain. "No," he whispered again. "Take it back. Dammit, take it back."

But it was too late. Aisa had her consent.

Aisa slipped something around her neck. Sabelle jerked and looked down at the necklace Aisa had put on her. Its twin now circled Joel's neck, too. Some sane, rational part of her knew the necklace was an illusion, but Sabelle could feel the chill of the chain against her skin, the weight of it around her neck. She reached for it, trying to tear it off, but it slipped and slid through her grasp like a writhing snake.

Suddenly, Sabelle realized what it was . . . what it meant.

"No," she breathed.

Copper, like the penny key chain Ryan had given her, it looked like an ordinary necklace, with dainty links on a shiny bright chain. A clear crystal with a red stain at its center dangled at the end of it, blunt-edged and heavy. Copper had powerful qualities, crystal held its own mysticism and blood . . . *Aisa's* blood . . . Sabelle shuddered.

It appeared to be a delicate piece of jewelry in this world, but in the Beyond, it would be solid and unbreakable, like Aisa herself. That's how she worked. Understated, terrifying.

The necklace was a manacle that would shackle her forever.

Sabelle had been a slave her entire life, but she'd never worn a collar. Aisa hadn't needed to use such tactics. Her seers had feared her wrath. When betrayed, she was vicious. Never lethal to her seers, but so cruel. So very cruel.

Sabelle knew the only way out of this collar was for Aisa to remove it, but she clawed anyway. Futilely, desperately, while Ryan fought the prison Aisa had erected in his mind. Sweat beaded on his brow and blood saturated his clothes, but he never looked away from Sabelle.

He managed to raise his hand, fingers trembling with the effort. He brushed her chest as he tried to reach for the necklace. Sabelle caught his fingers with hers and held them to her heart. The chain around her neck felt like it weighed pounds instead of ounces and it grew heavier by the second.

"I'm sorry, Ryan," Sabelle said. "Please forgive me."

Aisa allowed her that moment, but only because she knew how sweet it would feel when the reaper ripped Sabelle away. The darkness rolled in like a storm, clouded mist so black that it lacked depth but not texture. She felt the presence within, recognized the cold taste of death, the needy grasp of the reaper.

Aisa looked at Ryan. "You'll be seeing me again," she said coldly. She vanished first, and Ryan's body suddenly went slack as her hold released.

Sabelle's gaze snapped up, knowing it would happen suddenly. "Good—"

Ryan's shouted "*No!*" rebounded off the fogbank as all the feeling left Sabelle's body. A great pressure built behind her ears, hot and fierce. Ryan called her name. His hands were on her shoulders, trying to hold on to her. He begged her to look at him. To stay with him.

Stay. She'd longed for that word from him for so long, but now that he'd given it, she had no choice in the matter.

She fought to keep her physical form even when she knew she'd fail. The reaper who'd brought her had been gentle. The one who took her now used sharp talons to yank her out of Ryan's world. She heard the ripping of her heart.

Then she heard nothing but her own screams.

25

Like magic, the ambulance arrived soon after the gunshots ended. Up on the road, it looked like mass confusion, with Roxanne shouting at the cops who'd tried to kill Ryan and Elijah and the bewildered officers trying to understand what had just happened and why they'd been compelled to shoot the innocent victims below. Ryan waited what seemed an eternity for the emergency medics as they lowered their equipment and carefully followed, navigating the treacherous gully with caution. He sat in the cold mud next to Elijah, putting pressure on the worst of the wounds. It's what they did on TV. He hoped it was the right thing to do in real life.

He couldn't believe what had just happened. Aisa had been in his head, squeezing his brain, blinding him. Crippling him. He knew now that she'd had that power all along—all those moments when he'd thought *he* was in control.

It had been a game for her, a psychotic round of chess, and she'd manipulated him expertly, planting seeds of doubt. Making him think the decisions he made were his own. Driving them like cattle to this ravine, where she could pick them off like targets at an arcade.

She'd taken Sabelle. And he'd stood there helplessly. He'd let her do it.

His shoulder throbbed. He had no idea how serious the gunshot was. Though it didn't matter when his heart felt like it had been ripped out and stomped to pulp.

Sabelle had begged him to let her in and he'd held her at a distance, even when he'd been buried deep inside her body. He'd given her everything but the part of him she'd needed most.

You've known me for years.

She was right. He had, yet he'd denied it. No one fell in love in a matter of days and fate wasn't real. That had been his mantra. So he'd withheld his love and acceptance when she'd given hers so fully.

And now she was gone, in a place where he couldn't follow.

Filled with the hollow ache of her loss, Ryan stared at the mud and blood swirling in a puddle beside him and something glinted from its surface. Frowning, he shifted and pulled it from the muck. The smashed penny he'd given Sabelle came free of the sucking sludge.

The key chain had broken off, leaving only the penny with a hole at the top. He wiped the mud off it with his shirt and held it tight in his palm, remembering her delight when he'd told her she could keep it. He'd forgotten about the stupid key chain but she had kept it like a treasure. His eyes stung and a deep tremor went through him.

The news crews arrived as Elijah was hauled up on a gurney. He looked gray beneath his dark skin and he lay so still that he might have been dead already.

Elijah roused briefly when they transferred him from the rescue stretcher to the bed. While the EMTs hooked him to an IV, Ryan took Elijah's hand and spoke to him in a low voice.

"Joel must really love you, Elijah, so you better hang on. He'll kick my ass if you die while he's gone."

Elijah's eyes stayed closed, but Ryan heard a rattling chuckle go through his chest. "Is he coming back?" he asked.

"If I have anything to do with it."

He opened his eyes. They were bloodshot and unfocused. The medics had given him something for pain but they weren't talking about his chances. The shot to his gut had them worried. They were moving fast, readying him for the ride.

"Is *she* coming back?" he asked.

"Sabelle's coming back."

"I believe you."

For some reason, that made him feel better.

"Mr. Love? We need to go," one of the medics said.

Ryan got to his feet, bent so he didn't bang his head on the ambulance roof. He put his palm against Elijah's forehead and smoothed his brow. "I'll see you soon. Hang in there, buddy."

Elijah's eyes were already closing, but he fought it and mumbled, "It was always you, Ryan."

"What was always me?"

The other man moved his lips but he slipped back into unconsciousness before he could speak.

The reaper and Roxanne lived in a small A-frame located deep in the heart of Oak Creek Canyon. Tiny and remote, it had an open floor plan that backed into the side of a mountain, leaving only the front exposed to the elements. It made the interior dark, but solar tubes and lamps alleviated the cavelike atmosphere, and the security it offered brightened everything else.

Roxanne brought Ryan a change of clothes and showed him to the bathroom. He took a quick shower to clean off the mud and blood and clear his mind. The wound on his arm hurt like hell, but his resolve didn't require reviving. When he joined Roxanne in the compact kitchen area, he felt hyperaware and ready to go, the kind of adrenaline charge that came after shock. He was too wound up to sit down, so he leaned against the far wall and accepted the glass that the reaper handed him.

"Thank you," Ryan said, sniffing it. Wild Turkey. Santo was a bourbon drinker. Ryan took a drink anyway, letting it run down his throat. The alcohol hit his stomach and sparked the burning embers to flame.

The reaper said, "Tell me what you saw before Aisa took them."

Roxanne had been moving about the kitchen, putting water on to boil for something. Ryan hoped it wasn't food. Even if his sister could cook worth a damn—which she couldn't—Ryan couldn't eat.

"Aisa was in our bedroom when I woke up this morning," Ryan told them. "She threatened me. She said she'd do exactly what she did—make Sabelle beg. She swore she didn't need Joel, though. I don't know if she took him just to piss me off or if that was her plan all along. I should have said something. Maybe if I'd warned Sabelle . . . I was afraid telling her would scare her off. She was already heaping responsibility for this whole fucking mess on her shoulders. If she'd known about Aisa's threats, that would have been it for her."

Ryan swallowed hard. His eyes still burned and it felt like he had a boulder lodged in his throat. He kept seeing everything in instant replay. Aisa. The shots. Elijah. Sabelle.

He wanted to shout at his memory of himself for not doing anything to stop it—even when he knew he'd been as much a prisoner as Sabelle was now.

"At first Sabelle stood her ground," he went on. "She didn't beg, but then the shooting started and Aisa had me all locked up. All I could do was watch."

Sabelle had consented in order to save him and his family. She hadn't even thought twice about it. As soon as she'd seen it coming, she'd bowed her head and accepted it.

He couldn't just go on as if she'd never been a part of him. He couldn't leave her to a fate she didn't deserve, whether he believed in fate or not. She'd come here for him. All the other reasons took a backseat to that one. She'd come for him and he hadn't kept her safe.

"After the shooting started?" the reaper prompted.

"Sabelle saw how it was. Aisa would have happily killed me and Elijah, and if Sabelle still held out, she said she'd start on Ruby. On you, Roxanne. She even asked about Santo."

The reaper narrowed his eyes.

Ryan went on: "Aisa wanted Sabelle to beg, so Sabelle begged."

"And Joel."

Ryan hung his head, remembering the anguish in the older man's voice as he'd surrendered. "She didn't give him a choice. Elijah is in bad shape. There was so much blood . . . As soon as Joel gave in, she came up with these necklaces. I don't know where she got them."

"Describe them," the reaper demanded.

Ryan looked up. "Why?"

"Because it might be important."

"They were just necklaces with a crystal or piece of glass hanging on it."

"What color was the chain?"

Ryan's mouth opened. He shook his head, trying to picture them. After a moment he said, "Copper." He stuffed his hand in his pocket and pulled out the smashed penny. "Same color as this."

The reaper stared at it for a long moment. "Was there blood in the crystal?"

"I don't know if it was blood, but something dark, inky-looking in the center."

"What do you think, Santo?" Roxanne asked.

"I'm not sure. Copper is an old metal—maybe the oldest of all metals. It has ties to blood. The gods thought it had protective qualities. They thought it would keep them from disease."

"So?"

"So, everything Aisa does, she does for a reason. She's shackled Sabelle and Joel with copper—not steel, which is stronger, but copper. If we want to help them, we should know why."

"Help them?" Roxanne said. "How can we help them?"

"The original plan involved going to the Beyond," he said calmly.

"Which we unanimously agreed was a crap plan."

The reaper stared at Ryan thoughtfully. "I may have a better one, Ryan."

"Let's hear it, because I got nothing."

"It's risky. Before you say yes, you need to consider that."

"He's not going to say yes," Roxanne said in a tight voice.

"*Angelita*, look at him," Santo murmured. "He already has."

The reaper's unemotional tone grated on Ryan's already torn emotions, but his shadowed expression wasn't filled with mockery. Ryan would swear he saw compassion there. For Ryan. For Sabelle. The comforting touch he gave Ryan's sister held all the warmth his words lacked. He really cared about her. He really cared about what had happened to them all. He and Ryan might not see eye to eye, but this reaper wasn't as unfeeling as he liked to let on.

"Your boyfriend's right. It doesn't matter what the plan is, Roxy," Ryan said. "I'm in."

"You're going to get yourself killed."

"If that's what it takes. All I know is, one way or another, Sabelle is coming home. I told Elijah Joel would, too. I meant it."

It might be pointless, hopeless, probably futile. But something in the reaper's eyes gave Ryan hope. He looked like a man with an idea that might work, and Sabelle and Joel were at the mercy of a being who had no conscience. If it took a fight to the death to get them out, so be it. He'd told Aisa he was Sabelle's new muscle. It was time to flex.

"She'll scramble your brains just like she did today," Roxanne insisted in a pained voice. "They were *shooting at you* and they didn't even know why. She made them do that and I watched it happen."

Roxanne looked close to tears. When she was little, those tears had made him want to do anything to dry them. But there was nothing he could say this time to make it all better. Aisa could kill him. She could kill all of them.

"But can she bend spoons?" he said with a tired laugh.

"What do spoons have to do with anything?" Roxanne demanded.

Ryan shook his head. "When Aisa's down here, she has to work through other people. Even when she's up there, she has to manipulate others. She can't pull the trigger herself."

She could only control through illusion.

Both Roxanne and her reaper looked at him blankly.

"Never mind. It was a joke and not a very good one. It doesn't matter anyway. I'm not leaving Sabelle. She risked her life to save mine. My life isn't going to be worth anything to me if I don't do the same for her."

"If you die, she'll have done it all for nothing," Roxanne said flatly. "Can't you see that?"

"No. I can only see the look on her face before she vanished. I can't live if that's my last memory of her."

He took a deep breath and slowly let it out. He looked at the reaper—Santo, Ryan corrected himself. If the guy was going help him, Ryan ought to at least call him by name. "So. What's your plan?"

Santo met his gaze and shrugged. "We go in after them."

"Can you really do that?" Ryan asked, knuckles on the table, body leaning forward. "You can take me?"

He hadn't believed it when they'd discussed it earlier. The weak plan hadn't held water and so he'd discarded any hope of it. Now he desperately needed an answer.

Santo nodded and more hope swelled in Ryan's chest.

Roxanne threw her hands in the air. "Do you have any idea how insane this sounds? Ryan, I know you're hurting. I know you want to help Sabelle and Joel. But you're a human being talking about going to a place where humans don't belong."

"You've done it."

"I'm different."

"Maybe you are, maybe you're not. We've got the same blood in our veins. Maybe I haven't been there because I have better survival skills."

"Well, this isn't one of them."

"*Angelita*," Santo interrupted softly. "You know he's not going to walk away without a fight."

"But this is a fight there's no way to win."

"I don't accept that," Ryan said. "Do you think Aisa's just going to leave us alone now that she has what she came for, Roxy?"

Ryan's question caught her off guard. She didn't answer.

"I pissed her off when I tried to keep Sabelle from her. As soon as she's sure everything has settled down back at slave central, she'll be at the door and she won't be knocking."

Roxanne's brow puckered in a frown. She shook her head, but she couldn't argue with a truth so blatant.

Ryan looked at the reaper. "I'm all in. What do we do next?"

26

As Sabelle had imagined, in the Beyond, the chain around her neck looked nothing like a necklace. Now the copper links were thick and forged like steel. They rested heavily against her collarbone, cold and burning at the same time. The crystal dangled like a dog tag. The drop of blood winked at her when she moved.

When she'd escaped to save Ryan, she arrived in the human world naked. Coming back was no different and every bit as painful. Aisa didn't give her or Joel clothes as Ryan had. Instead she locked them in a storage room off the kitchen. It was the closest to a cell they had in the palace. The doors here didn't even have locks. Such a thing had never been needed. Fear kept them caged well enough.

Sabelle and Joel huddled against the walls, not looking at each other.

"Ryan thought she wanted me all along," Joel said. "I didn't believe him."

"I was too arrogant to think she wanted anything but me."

"Don't beat yourself up. You couldn't have known."

Sabelle almost smiled. "We're seers, Joel. Of course we could have."

He snorted. "It's our own fate, remember?"

She had her knees pulled up, ankles crossed, using her limbs to cover as much of her naked body as she could. They were quiet for a little while, then Sabelle asked, "What did you think I would be able to do?"

It took Joel a minute to follow. "You mean, when we called you?"

Sabelle nodded.

"I didn't have a clue. But Elijah, he was sure you had some mojo."

"And he thought I'd be able to destroy her?"

Joel leaned his head against the wall. "He never came right out and said it, but he worried about Aisa tracking me down and squashing me like a bug so goddamn much that I just wanted to get you there and get it over with. One way or another, he needed to know if you could."

"You didn't worry?"

Joel shrugged. "I was against calling you. I sure as hell didn't think we should leave invitations. Elijah wouldn't have it any other way. He'd seen some of it in his dreams. Not all, but enough to convince him he was *interpreting* things right. He may not look like such a badass, but when he gets something in his head, he's a force to reckon with."

Joel's voice broke. He cleared his throat, looked away. "If she thinks I'm going to be seeing the future for her, she's going to be disappointed," he said after a moment.

Sabelle fingered the chain at her neck. "Ryan was right. Aisa was pretending to be Nadia all along. She made me think I had a friend, someone to trust. Nadia told me to escape. She did that so I would lead her to you. She wouldn't have risked it if she wasn't sure what she'd find."

Joel let out a deep breath. "I wish I knew how Elijah is doing."

"He's strong. He'll make it."

Sabelle hoped it was true. She wished she knew how Ryan was holding up. He'd feel responsible. She could still hear his voice, the agony as he shouted "*No! Stay*." Finally, when it was too late, he'd asked her to stay.

The door opened and Aisa strode in. She wore a big tank top with a sports bra beneath, tight shorts, and athletic shoes. Her curly mass of hair had been pulled up in a clip on top of her head. When Aisa had appeared in the ravine, Sabelle had been stunned by the haggard face and graying hair. She'd assumed it was part of Aisa's illusion, displayed for reasons Sabelle couldn't know. She'd expected the return to the Beyond to bring back the beautiful, perfect woman Aisa had always been.

The exercise clothes accented the slack skin at her arms, her knees, her neck. The hair still had a dull gray sheen and a map of decades covered her face.

Aisa tossed a robe at each of them. Gratefully, Sabelle covered her nudity and stood. Joel shrugged into the other one and did the same.

"Come with me."

Aisa led them through a door into a great dining hall. A long table was set with platters of meat, bowls of fruit, crystal dishes of breads and pastries. Sabelle had been hungry the whole time she'd been in the human world. Now her stomach soured at the thought of eating.

"Nourish yourselves. Eat," Aisa ordered.

"Nah," Joel said. "I'd just as soon get this over fast."

"Fast?" Aisa strode closer. She put her hand against the side of Joel's throat and brushed her thumb against his jaw. "This will never be over."

The words almost made Sabelle cry. Only knowing that Ryan would want her to be strong helped her keep the tears at bay. She let her eyes close for a moment and thought about him. What would he do? What would he say? Ryan wouldn't waste time on sorrow or fear. He'd start poking the dragon.

"Why are we here, Aisa?" she demanded. In her effort to sound assertive she came across downright aggressive. Aisa looked up in outrage.

"Did you just address me by name? Do you know what that is around your neck, seer?"

"Chains," Sabelle answered insolently. "I'm no stranger to them. You've had me chained my entire life."

"You lived in luxury."

"I lived in slavery."

Aisa shrugged. "Same thing."

"You may have forced my hand to get me here," Sabelle said coolly. "But some things you can't force. You can't see what I see. You can't make me share what I see."

"I can. I will. I always have."

Joel came to stand beside Sabelle, his presence fortifying. "You got us here, we're all dressed up in your fancy robes. What do you want now?"

Aisa gifted them with her terrible smile. The one that quelled gods and demons alike. It usually made one seer tremble. Sabelle lifted her chin and stared Aisa down.

Amused, Aisa said, "Around your neck is a chain of copper. Egyptians were the first to use it. Did you know that? It's a blood metal."

"Whoopee," Joel said.

"Inside that crystal is a drop of my blood. Put the two together and you are bound to me for as long as I keep you alive."

She turned and Sabelle noticed that her hair looked darker, more lustrous. The change had occurred in a matter of minutes. Ryan had been right.

"I don't care about your visions, Sabelle. I wouldn't care if you were both blind." She gave Sabelle a dismissive glance. "You were never that good anyway."

"I am the best," Sabelle said.

"Because Nadia told you so?"

Realization brought an instant flush of shame. She'd been so gullible, so foolish.

"And you," Aisa said to Joel. "Men can't see what's right in front of them. Why would I trust your visions of the future?"

"So why the fuck are we here wearing your copper blood shackles?"

"In the olden days—"

"I don't give a shit about the olden days, you bitch."

Aisa turned on him, her hand at his throat again, pressing him into the wall as if he were a child. "Do not defy me, little man, or I will reach out and snuff the one you love like a candle."

"I wish to hear," Sabelle interrupted before Aisa felt compelled to prove it. "What about the olden days?"

Aisa shifted her narrowed eyes between the two of them. Deciding Sabelle's request was sincere, she stepped away from Joel.

"Goddesses were worshipped in that time. Sacrifices were made to them, power was given through their love. Now humans think they're better than that. They think they control their own destiny."

Sabelle reached for Joel's hand when he made a sound of disgust. She squeezed it. *Let her finish.* They would never know how to escape if they didn't understand why they'd been captured. She was sure of it.

"Bringing the children here was brilliant. Moira's idea. Nona was against it until we saw how wonderfully it worked. The children worshipped us. You used to squeal with excitement when you saw me."

"Why don't I remember that?"

"Memory can be an unreliable thing."

"Yours or mine?" Sabelle said coolly. "My money would be on yours being the faulty part of the equation."

Aisa's eyes narrowed. "Careful, little snowflake. I can melt you into nothing."

"I don't think that would be as much a problem for me

as it would be for you, seeing how you went to so much trouble to bring me back."

"Such a sharp tongue. Perhaps you're safe for now. But not for always."

Joel harrumphed. "Safe. Like all the other little kiddies."

Aisa's scowled at him. "It was a great tragedy when the filthy human disease went through them."

Her eyes looked solemn and for once there was no mockery in her tone. "I'm not surprised those memories are gone. You know the power of denial."

Her voice had dipped and her eyes had a bright shine. She turned her face and took a breath. "It killed my sisters, too. I don't know why it never touched me. Or you, Sabelle. All I know is that when it was over, all that was left was the two of us."

"Why did you hide their deaths from me?" Sabelle asked. "Why did you make me think they were all still alive?"

"At first, you were quarantined. After that . . . well, you were also so emotional. When your feelings were hurt, you wouldn't see. I needed you to see more than I cared for your feelings. It wouldn't have benefited either one of us for you to know."

The eyes were hard and cold again. No pain. No feeling at all.

"I thought I sucked as a seer."

"Desperate means."

Sabelle hadn't thought it possible to hurt more, to feel more betrayed. Now she saw how wrong she'd been.

Joel fairly vibrated with anger. Sabelle had grown numb from it.

"None of this matters now," Aisa said. "It's over. Had we known, we might have done things differently."

Might. A critical word choice.

"Like not being so bloodthirsty with your male spawn?" Joel said with a dry laugh.

"Yes. Like that."

Sabelle found her voice and her courage in the same instant. "So what was the point of all this? Do you want to punish us?"

Aisa laughed again. "That would be counterproductive. I've learned from my mistakes."

"I doubt it." Joel, ever defiant.

"You, too, would do well to learn, spawn. Elijah isn't the only human who can be hurt."

"You've made that clear, but you made a deal. Our consent for their lives."

"At that moment," Aisa qualified. "Not forever."

Sabelle shut her eyes. Ryan had known—he'd begged Sabelle to take it back. To stay, because he'd known that going with Aisa would only give her all the power. As long as Aisa lived, Sabelle's and Joel's loved ones would be threatened.

"We need to bring life back into the palace," Aisa said, suddenly smiling again. "New life. *Rejuvenating* life."

"How are you going to manage that?" Joel said.

She beamed at him. "You are going to help us."

Joel looked Aisa, then at Sabelle, and back again. Aisa raised her brows expectantly, letting him work out the logistics without her prompting. Sadly, Sabelle had connected the twisted dots already. Either Joel refused to see or he refused to admit it. Either way, Joel remained stubbornly silent.

"Do the math, Joel. There are two lovely females here, both capable of breeding. And you, our handsome stud, will reap the benefits. My mistake the first time was mating with humans, but both of you are half-breeds. You have my blood in your veins already. Our offspring will be strong enough to endure."

"Are you out of your mind?" Sabelle exclaimed at the same time Joel let loose a hoot of laughter, exclaiming, "You're a fucking lunatic."

"He's your son. My brother," Sabelle said.

"Yes," Aisa said enthusiastically. "It's perfect."

"It's incest," Joel said.

"Gods and goddesses have been mating within their family for millennia."

"Well, that explains why everything they do is so fucked-up."

"I'm not asking for your permission," Aisa said. "You will do as I say."

"You seem to have missed one big detail in your little plan, Mommy," Joel said. "I'm not wired that way."

"Oh," she said, "I'm sure you can find a way to rise to the occasion. If you don't, Sabelle will be punished. I can be very creative, as you might imagine. If that doesn't work, there's always Elijah. Hospitals can be very dangerous places."

She turned and glided to the door, light in her sneakers. "Eat. Talk amongst yourselves. I'll be back soon. No need to put things off. Best to rip the bandage off the wound all at once."

With that, she left the room, leaving the door open. No need to lock when her seers wore collars. Her shoes squeaked against the marble and echoed in the quiet. Sabelle spun around and marched to the table. Aisa was too smart to have left knives. She hadn't even left forks. A spoon would have to do.

27

Ryan expected something more dramatic. A secret chamber. A hidden door. But the reaper didn't even need open space for what he had planned. He took two chairs from the table and set them in the middle of the room, facing one another.

"Sit," he said.

"Why?" Ryan asked.

Santo seemed amused by the question. "So you don't fall down," he replied, shooting Roxanne an enigmatic look over his shoulder.

Roxanne didn't seem to like the response any more than Ryan did. "How are you going to pull this off, Santo? Ryan can't just walk into the Beyond," she said.

Ryan was pretty interested in the answer, not that it would make a bit of difference. Sabelle was in the Beyond. He was going to bring her back. End of story.

"Ryan will have to let his soul do the walking, Roxanne. You know as well as I that the Beyond is not a corporeal place."

Ryan frowned, hoping he'd misunderstood what that meant. Roxanne stopped pacing and stared at Santo with a look of shock and dismay.

"What does that mean? I won't have a body?" Ryan asked, trying to ignore the clenching feeling in his chest. When they'd talked about this before, in the bright morning light, logistics hadn't even come up. There'd been so much debate and revelation that details had seemed the least of their worries.

Now his perspective had changed quite a bit. If the look on his sister's face was anything to go by, he'd just signed up for hell.

Maybe he'd see Reece on the way.

Sabelle had screamed when she came to this world. She'd screamed when Aisa tore her from it today. He had no reason to believe it would be any less unpleasant for him.

Roxanne had Santo locked in a glare. The man practically radiated danger, but she wagged a finger at him like he was a puppy who'd just peed on the floor. Santo looked down at the scolding finger with indulgent eyes.

"I don't know what you're—"

"How is this going to work?" Ryan interrupted, raising his voice. "If I don't have a body, how's it going to work?"

Roxanne spun to face him and her expression held so much fear that Ryan had to fight a closed throat to swallow. Warily, he cut his eyes between Santo and his sister.

"You're going to have to die, Ryan," Santo said gently.

Roxanne made a choking sound and turned her back. Ryan stared at the reaper numbly.

"I'm what?"

"How did you imagine you would make this journey?" Santo asked curiously. "A bus?"

"You're going to kill me? That's the big plan? I'm not like Roxanne . . . You kill me and it's over."

"Maybe not. You said it yourself—the same blood flows in your veins."

Ryan's mouth fell open but he couldn't manage to get any words out.

"Have you ever died before?"

He'd been asked that question before. He'd always had a snappy comeback for it. Now he only whispered, "No."

"Well, then," the reaper said, as if that solved everything.

"Ryan, please don't do this," Roxanne said. "We'll find another way."

Santo looked at her with a placid expression. He didn't believe her. Ryan didn't either. If there was another way, Santo wouldn't be suggesting he kill the brother of the woman he supposedly loved.

"You'll need to be quick, Ryan," Santo went on as if she hadn't spoken. "You won't have a lot of time."

"Because I'll be dead," Ryan said, still filled with disbelief that they were even having this conversation.

"There's that," Santo agreed. "But the hope is you won't stay that way."

"That's a good hope."

"You'll have no more than ten minutes before lack of oxygen will start to damage your organs."

Just like the movies. Except this was real. If Ryan failed, the lights wouldn't be coming on with the credits at the end.

"How are you going to do it?" Ryan asked, when he probably didn't want to know.

"Suffocation. It's the safest way without damaging your body. You'll want it whole when you get back."

Good thinking.

"There'll be two stages to this," the reaper went on. "I'll lead you into the darkness. When you find Sabelle and Joel, you call me. I'll come and take them."

"Call you with what?"

"Your mind. Call me with your thoughts. I'll be listening."

"After you take them, you'll come back for me?"

For the first time, Santo looked uncomfortable. He glanced at Roxanne from the corner of his eye. Her head came up, her face white. Stark realization pulled her features.

"No," he answered. "I can't bring you home."

"Why not?"

His voice wanted to break with the dread pooling in his gut but somehow he kept it steady. Just talking about dying. No big deal. Keeping it casual.

Santo shrugged, looking like he'd give anything not to answer.

"You're human. Your ticket only works one way."

Ryan forced a smile. "Was that a joke?" he said, looking at Roxanne. "Is he being funny?"

"He has his moments," Roxanne answered, pacing anxiously behind them. "This isn't one of them. This is the worst idea I've ever heard."

The pit of Ryan's stomach had fallen out of his body. He felt numb. Surreal. And scared. There was no denying that. His heart rate had accelerated and he couldn't seem to catch his breath.

"Do you understand what he's saying, Ryan?" Roxanne demanded.

Yeah. It couldn't be much clearer. "He's going to kill me and leave me in the Beyond to save Sabelle and Joel in ten minutes or less."

"And destroy Aisa," Santo corrected.

"How could I forget? Any suggestions on how to do the deed?" Ryan muttered, not expecting any.

The reaper gave him a thoughtful look. "Aisa is forbidden to leave the Beyond, except in illusion. She *can't* leave." Santo paused. "You need to throw her out."

Throw her out? Ryan could hardly grasp how *he* was going to get *in*. "If you're not taking me out with you," he said, "how am I supposed to find my way back, let alone with an evil bitch on my hands?"

Both of them looked at Roxanne. She gave a disheartened shrug. "For me, the light of life was always brighter than the one of the afterlife. That's the one I followed."

Well, that cleared everything up.

"Sounds easy enough," he said, like it really helped.

"She brings up another subject," Santo said. "Lights. You'll be dead and the Beyond will be waiting for you. Your instincts will pull you to the light. Most find it irresistible. You're going to have to fight it. Following the light . . ."

Ryan held up his hand. "I get it. End of the road."

"Ryan . . ." Roxanne said.

Ryan looked into Roxanne's worried face and took her hand. "If it wasn't for Sabelle, I'd be dead already, Roxy. It's her turn to be rescued. I can't leave her and Joel there. You know that."

Roxanne's tears spilled down her cheeks, but she nodded and embraced him. For a long moment they held each other in silence that spoke for them. At last she pulled back.

"No good-byes," Ryan warned.

"No," she agreed. "No good-byes."

She stepped away, but didn't go far. Ryan swallowed, looked at Santo, and nodded. "I'm ready."

"Keep your thoughts on your goal," Santo said.

Sabelle. She was in his heart. He'd have no problem holding her in his thoughts.

"And then what?"

"Find them."

"That's it? Find them?"

"Call me when you do." At Ryan's nonplussed look, he said, "Do you have something that belongs to Sabelle? That will help you. And you'll need something to bring you home."

Ryan pulled the penny from his pocket and held it tight in one hand. Next he crossed to the rug where Brandy lay watching them. He scratched the dog's belly and slipped a tag from her collar. "Be back soon, girl."

Brandy gave him an uncertain *woof.*

The steps back to the chair felt epic. The plan didn't just suck, it was fucked-up beyond belief. The odds of succeeding were less than zero. Getting in would be hard enough. Escaping the pull of *the light*, a challenge. Finding—*saving*—Sabelle and Joel? Getting out? With Aisa? *When he was dead?*

A disbelieving laugh burst from his lips.

"Why are you laughing?" Roxanne demanded.

"I'm going to a place I can't even imagine, with a reaper I only half believe in, to save a grouchy seer I hardly know and my not-quite-human girlfriend from a fate she had a hand in creating. But first I'm going to let your boyfriend kill me." He laughed harder. "I'm fucking insane."

The reaper gave him a dry look. "That runs in your family, too," he said.

The laughter felt good, and once he started, he couldn't seem to stop. Roxanne shook her head, but his laughter was contagious and she finally joined in. Even the reaper smiled, revealing a dimple that made Ryan double over with mirth.

"You sure you want to do this?" Santo asked.

"Not even a little bit," Ryan answered, and that was even funnier.

His laughter ended in bits and burst and then abruptly all at once. Yet Ryan felt better for it. Stronger. Bonded with this man his sister loved. Santo was taking a big risk going into the Beyond in order to help Ryan. Gratitude for what he was willing to do welled up inside.

"Thank you," Ryan said.

"What I do, I do for your sister," Santo replied simply.

Ryan nodded in understanding. His sister's reaper might not like to admit to human emotions, but they were there, beneath the surface. When it came to Roxanne, Santo would face anything.

Roxanne gave Ryan another hug. Then she took Santo in her arms and whispered something in his ear and that made him smile again. Ryan decided he was good not knowing what she'd said.

Santo gave Roxanne a gentle push toward the kitchen. "Don't watch, *angelita*," he said.

"Don't tell me what to do," she chided with a sad smile, but she did as he asked and turned away, her arms crossed. "Take care of my brother. I want you both back."

"I will do my best," Santo told her before facing Ryan. "Ready?"

"As I'll ever—"

Santo had neglected to tell him he planned to put out Ryan's lights before he smothered him. Ryan never saw the punch coming.

28

The darkness felt thick. Cool. Vast.

The impressions hit Ryan in waves. He was weightless. Blinded by the pervasive pitch of the layered black. But he wasn't alone. He felt the pull of the reaper, like a current tugging him along, just shy of the dangerous riptide lapping hungrily at his heels.

When she was younger, Roxanne had talked about the darkness that waited for her when she died. She'd said it was warm and inviting. Reece, on the other hand, had screaming nightmares about it for weeks afterward.

For Ryan, it was a little of both.

He was awake. Aware that he'd died. But alert and so scared that he didn't dare let himself think about what he'd just done. He held the key chain in his hand, palm tight around its flattened edges. It still felt warm. He'd quit asking how or why. He shoved his other hand into his pocket and curled his fingers over Brandy's dog tag, knowing he didn't really have a hand or a pocket, but in this dark place it felt like he did. *Go with it, Ryan.*

The darkness seemed to grow thicker, deeper, and bigger as Ryan moved through the gloom, searching for a flicker of light; even the dreaded one would be welcome now. Anything to relieve the pitch-black texture.

The pull from Santo eased before stopping altogether, leaving Ryan suspended in limbo and so fucking afraid. The feeling was immense and aggressive, filling him so quickly he had no hope of staunching it. He searched for the reaper, felt his presence, but understood that this was where the train stopped. From here on, Ryan was on his own.

Ryan nodded, though he didn't know if the reaper could see. White light cracked the inky atmosphere and he felt the pull of it on a visceral level. It called him by name, coaxed him closer.

Light. Warmth. Love. Acceptance. He squeezed his eyes tight and fought. His fingers gripped the penny tighter, and he thought of Sabelle. Pictured her pretty face, her wide smile and guileless eyes. Her small wrists and elegant hands. Her mouth . . .

He was moving before he knew it, fast, hurtling away. His whole being felt that light, begging him to return. He wanted to follow it so badly that it hurt to deny it.

He clenched the penny, remembered the feel of her against him. He imagined her scent and the way she looked at him. The wonder when he introduced a new taste or sensation. He pushed on, resisting the light and hugging the shadows that followed like a sentry. He sensed things within them. Things without names, without shape or form. Entities of the Beyond that might mean him harm and might yet dole it out.

And then suddenly he burst through the darkness and into a world of shadowed light where a pearly castle poked up to the sky and evil sorceresses enslaved innocents for their own purposes. It looked nothing like what he'd imagined and at the same time it was exactly what he'd expected. Sabelle had called it a palace, but it lacked any grace or grandeur. More like a prison where the guard towers wore camouflage. It was a cold, unyielding place, from stone walls to sharp corners.

Ryan sailed over the gated wall and came down fast and hard with wind whistling in his ears and burning his skin. He hit the ground with enough force to bounce and skid. It took some grit to bite back a shout of pain when it felt like every bone inside him had been broken and the skin flayed from his limbs. No wonder Sabelle had screamed when she'd traveled through. Nothing up to that point had prepared him for the agony of it.

He lay motionless for a time, aware of rough stonework beneath him and cool twilight above. Silence came from everywhere, a snake that slithered with deadly stealth. He caught his breath, braced his hands, and stood. Two massive doors gaped open just ahead. Cautiously, he went through them.

A great hall stretched out before him, bathed in lavender hues from the dusky sky that peeked in through open arches in the painted ceiling. From pillars and platforms, sculptured gods and goddesses looked down with serene expressions, but Ryan knew that menace lurked behind their masks. Vestal marble couldn't hide the sickness that seeped from the marble. This place was a tomb as much as a temple.

He stood looking down his naked body at cuts and bruises that had come with the transition. He still held the penny in his palm, but Brandy's dog tag, the thing that was supposed to get him home . . . well, who knew where that was.

His bare feet were quiet on the cold tiles, but his awareness of his nudity and vulnerability made every sound seem to echo. He eyed the statues as he passed, recognizing a few unmistakable iconic figures among the many goddesses with their nubile figures and come-hither smiles. Poseidon and Zeus gave him mocking glances. This was no place for a human.

At the end of the hall, two figures dressed in armor stood at attention. Ryan approached warily, but the helmets were empty. He peeked inside, hoping they wore clothes as well as steel, but their stick-figure frames didn't care about the family jewels getting caught in a hinge. Not even a loincloth inside.

To his right, another hall was flanked by two knights on stuffed black steeds. More empty armor, but both of the dutiful squires looked so real that he had to touch them to be sure they weren't. Relieved when the figure didn't move, he stripped the one closest to his size and put on its draped tunic. The garment hit Ryan mid-thigh but hid his parts well enough. The squire had also worn a vest of chain mail, which Ryan hefted up and over his head. It fell across his chest and back with a rattle. There were weird tights with strange fastenings as well, but he slipped on the leather boots without bothering to figure them out. Last he lifted the heavy sword that hung at the hips. The blade was dull, but it could still do some serious damage.

Trying not to stab himself, he slipped the sword into the scabbard he fastened at his waist. The entire getup weighed about a hundred pounds, but it was worth it. Ryan was armed and felt dangerous and fierce as he moved down the hall, listening for sounds, terrified he'd wander for days without locating Sabelle.

He wanted to call for her, but he forced himself to stay quiet, turning corners until he came to a narrow corridor that was one of three arms spiking from a common center. He counted the doors on the left: five. Six on the right, eleven in each hall. One for each of the seers who'd lived there. Died there. All except for Sabelle.

Carefully, he opened the nearest door and peered inside. The room was richly decorated with a canopy bed, a small sitting area around a cold fireplace, a bookshelf. A veranda door with sheer curtains was straight ahead. He stepped inside, closed the door behind him, and carefully moved to it. Outside, the view he saw was just as Sabelle had described it. Perpetual twilight, dim stars. Tranquil, except for its aberrancy.

He heard the sound of shoes squeaking and hurried to peer out of the room in time to see Aisa, dressed in workout clothes and attitude, stroll by. She walked alone, looking very pleased with herself. Her hair gleamed like silk, not a hint of gray. Even her face looked smoother, softer. Illusion? If so, for whose benefit?

She turned, heading down the corridor he'd just come from. Ryan let out a breath of relief and rested his forehead on the door frame. A minute either way and they'd have met each other in the hall. He planned to come face-to-face with her eventually, but only after Sabelle and Joel were safe.

He lifted his head. She'd be passing right by the statues. If she saw the stripped squire, she'd know someone had broken in. She'd know it was him. He needed to move fast.

He was hell and gone from a knight in shining armor, but do or die, he was here to rescue the princess from the dragon.

29

Sabelle reached for Joel's collar, wedging the spoon's handle inside a link and using it as a lever to pry the link open. Joel looked older, beaten.

"She means to torture the ones we love," she said, giving him a shake.

"I know."

"That negates our consent."

"I'm with you."

"These things she has around our necks will help her track us. Nona, the youngest sister, used them on her seers. She was very suspicious. In the days when we were allowed to run free, she would collar them so she'd know everything they did. Blood, crystal, copper. It's powerful."

"Beyond's version of GPS?"

"Something like that."

The links didn't give. Fighting the feeling of futility,

she jammed the spoon handle through a different spot and tried again. "Am I hurting you?"

"Nope."

The spoon bent. The collar stayed intact.

"Let me try." Joel took a fresh spoon and worked on hers, bent that spoon, and grabbed another.

They took turns trying to break the links on each other's collars, then on their own, but nothing gave. Finally, in frustration, Sabelle threw the bent spoon across the room, where it clattered into the corner. She stared at the misshapen thing and froze.

Joel was cussing creatively when he noticed. "What? You see something?"

Sabelle turned her wide eyes on him. "He could bend spoons with his mind."

"Who?"

"Ryan said it."

"Ryan can bend spoons? Bully for him. How's that going to help us?"

"No, no. He said a guy had come into the bar who could do it. Bend spoons with his mind."

"Why does that matter?"

"These chains—in the human world they were necklaces. Delicate, breakable."

Joel nodded, but he didn't understand.

"I knew she wouldn't put such a flimsy thing around my neck unless it became something *more* when we got here."

Joel was still nodding, still not understanding. "Looks like you were right."

"It's what she wanted me to think. She could have put steel around our necks in your world and I wouldn't have been as afraid of them as I was of this small thing she expected to have such power. She did that because she knew *we'd* make them strong. With our minds, Joel. She knew our fear would give them all the power we didn't see."

He stopped nodding. "You think?"

"I do. We are bound to her by blood because of our birth. That means we might be just as powerful as she. Right now she's weak—that's why she looks old—but she's drawing from us already. I watched her hair turn dark right before our eyes."

"Okay. So what do we do?"

"Take it back. Own our own power instead of letting her steal it. Bend the spoons, Joel."

With that, she gently reached up and lifted the collar. Its weight had become overwhelming, but as she cleared her mind and pictured what it had looked like when Aisa settled it around her neck, it began to feel lighter. Thinner. Breakable. She smiled triumphantly as she began to pull the weakest links apart with her fingers.

30

Sabelle wasn't behind any of the doors in the first hall or second. Ryan came up empty in the third and panic set in. He skidded down another hall and saw a door that was cracked open a few inches. Cautiously, he approached it. Standing to the side, he used his fingertips to swing it back enough that he could look in. On the other side was a dining hall loaded with dishes and food. A roasted pig, complete with apple in its mouth, lay on a gold platter next to loaves of crusty bread, soufflés, puddings, cakes, and candies. A feast fit for gods.

His stomach rolled. He turned to see the rest of the room and someone tackled him from behind. Even though he was dressed in mail, his attacker had the element of surprise and knocked Ryan off balance. He came down hard and skidded across the slick floor. A man flipped him over and drew back with a clenched fist. In the same instant, they recognized each other.

Joel jumped off him. "What the fuck are you doing here?" he demanded, helping Ryan up.

Before he could answer, Ryan's searching gaze found Sabelle. She stood to the right of the table, dressed in a simple gown that couldn't hide all of her curves. She had shadows under her eyes and scratches and scrapes on her arms, chest, and throat.

She stared at him with those baby blues that glistened with tears. Then she clenched her eyes tight and shook her head.

He approached like he had that first night, murmuring soft hushing noises as he drew close. Gently he cupped her faced and kissed her.

Sabelle's sob tore his heart. He gathered her in his arms and made his body the anchor she needed.

"It's really you," she cried, pressing her face into the hollow of his throat and breathing in his scent. "It's really you."

He did the same, his nose at her temple, her scent filling him. Calming him. It took more than one try to speak but at last he managed. "I'm here to take you home, snowflake."

Suddenly a shriek echoed from deep in the castle, rolling down the corridor like thunder. An alarm, pealing stridently. Aisa had found the naked squire.

Ryan turned to Joel, keeping Sabelle tucked against his body. "Your ride is coming, Joel. When it gets here, you get on and get out. You and Sabelle both. Understand?"

Joel narrowed his eyes, reading the message on Ryan's face. The determined look in his eye.

"You and Sabelle both," Ryan repeated. "Don't look back."

"What about you? Shouldn't we go together?" Sabelle asked. "Stick together? I'm not afraid of Aisa anymore. I can bend spoons."

Ryan looked at her in surprise. "That's good. You'll have to show me how, when I get home."

He kissed her again while in his head he called for the reaper. Santo answered in seconds. Ryan hadn't been sure he would.

Ryan saw Santo coming this time, seeping through the door and onto the floor. It was all happening so fast. It needed to happen fast, but now that the time had come, he felt the pain of it. Ryan pressed his mouth to Sabelle's, then held her away. He met Joel's eyes over her head. Joel nodded reluctantly.

"You sure about this?" he asked.

Ryan nodded. "Every bit of me."

In the next moment, Aisa rushed into the room, followed by what seemed a world of swirling black. *Her* reapers. But Santo was quicker. He pooled at Joel's and Sabelle's feet and covered them in an instant. Ryan's last sight was of Sabelle as realization came over her. "No," she cried, reaching out to him.

Then she was gone, leaving Ryan alone with Aisa.

He faced the fury that had once been a goddess. Her appearance decomposed as he stared, becoming light, dark, then a swirling mass that resembled nightmares and smoke. Her reapers glommed on to her, hungry and desperate but too well trained to attack without her signal.

"Looks like we've got a problem," he said.

He held the penny tight in his hand, and as he watched the horror show in front of him, thoughts played through his mind. Bits and pieces of conversations with significance he'd somehow missed. The room seemed to be getting brighter.

A death in the Beyond is always noticed.

He looked over his shoulder and saw the powerful light he'd seen in the beginning gleaming through the French doors that opened onto a balcony. Everything inside him turned like a flower to the sun, seeking its warmth. The light called to him and he wanted to answer.

The light of life was always brighter than the one of the afterlife. That's the one I followed.

Penny in one hand, he drew the sword from its sheath with the other.

In our world, she's only an illusion.

But in this one, she could be hurt.

Her reapers recoiled from the brightness, fighting with each other in their ravenous hunger. His soul was still fresh, and as much as they feared it, they wanted it. They distracted Aisa.

Ryan moved fast, before she realized that he was armed. He swung at her and she managed to dodge, sucking items into her whirlwind of rage as she spun. She churned the banquet on the table into missiles, hurling plates and spoons and heavy goblets at him. One struck his head like a hammer and he staggered back, the unwieldy sword falling from his hand before he'd even found a target.

She'll die if she comes to the human world.

Blood gushed from the wound at his temple. He fell to his knees among the scattered debris on the floor. An apple rolled from beneath the table and banged against his leg. He stared at it as Aisa moved in for the kill.

Roxanne whispered in his head, her voice clear. *Does she have poisoned apples?*

Aisa's shape was slowly coming back into focus now that she had him on his knees, but her terrible visage had lost all relation to humanity. She looked like a two-legged monster in gym shorts.

Copper is a blood metal. Your blood is special.

Santo this time, with that amused note in his voice that couldn't hide how much he cared. A thick drop of blood rolled down Ryan's face and onto the red skin of the apple.

Copper. Blood. Power.

He scooped up the apple, jammed the penny into its meat, and rammed his body into Aisa's. He hit her hard and low, shoulder to her belly. Monster or no, it knocked the breath out of her. She doubled over, mouth open as she fought to draw in air. Ryan didn't hesitate. He shoved the apple in, wedging it between her pointy teeth at the same time he brought a left hook hard and up to her chin.

From a speedy blur to a painful drag, time warped, then stopped altogether. The writhing creature Aisa had become staggered away from him. The apple was still jammed in her open mouth just like it had been in the pig's. Poetic justice he hoped he'd one day have a chance to appreciate.

She reached for the apple and tried to pull it out, but it was lodged tight.

Ryan smiled. “Good luck with that.”

Panic flashed across her face as she struggled, muffled screams making the black cloud of reapers recoil.

Shocked that he’d stopped her—or at least slowed her down—Ryan scrambled to his feet and darted through the open doors of the veranda. He glanced back as she bit off the hunk of apple wedged in her mouth and threw the rest away. Furious, she tried to spit the rest out, but the bite was lodged behind her teeth and she began to choke on it. Fury and fear filled her eyes, but she was too stubborn to let either win—and she’d yet to realize the significance of what he’d put in her mouth. Glaring at Ryan with demented triumph, she swallowed hard.

Ryan could almost see the fruit’s flesh sliding down her throat, copper penny embedded in its flesh, his own blood part of the sweet mix. With a cry of rage, Aisa came after him.

Exactly as he’d hoped.

He jumped over the balcony to the ground floor and raced away.

The mail was heavy, his steps labored, and his head light, but he ran for all he was worth, making sure she kept pace with him. He tore through the palace gates, out of the perpetual twilight and into the gloom, with Aisa gaining on him at every turn. Good. He kept going, blind in the dark, until a bright light shone above. Ryan felt it calling to him and he stopped, turning to catch Aisa in his arms.

He held her tight, owning her through blood and strength as she screeched and scratched, trying to get free. The light above called him, but that was not the light he wanted. Like a tow beam, it pulled him and dragged him toward the end he couldn't avoid, though. He fought for as long as he could, looking away, down, up—everywhere. Searching. Seeking the light that Roxanne had always seen.

The only thing he found was more darkness clustered around that one blinding beacon.

Unlike his remarkable sister, there was no other light to bring Ryan home. He closed his eyes, accepting his fate. At least it would be the last that Aisa would ever control.

He pictured Sabelle, safe with his sister and Joel. They would take care of her. In time, she'd move on. Fate may have brought them together, but in the end, destiny had forced them apart.

The light felt warm on his face. Aisa's struggles weakened as they moved closer. He didn't know if it calmed her, too, or if she understood that he'd meant to expel her from the Beyond and failed. The will to care drained as the light inexorably drew him closer.

He was almost there when something winked in the corner of his vision. Before he could turn, Aisa gave a bloodcurdling scream and began to fight anew.

31

Sabelle noticed the quiet first, the pain second. Coming back hurt just as bad as it had when she'd escaped. The shrill agony, the feeling of being flayed. Then she was through, her body trembling as she hit the floor hard. She opened her eyes with a gasp and sat up. She was in a small room with a couch, a lamp pooling soft light from the corner, and Brandy. The dog watched her with pricked ears and lolling tongue. Her fur was covered in dried mud. For a moment, Sabelle simply stared at her, trying to remember why.

It came back to her in a rush. Being pulled from this world like an orange from its skin. Aisa. Joel. Ryan, coming to the rescue.

To bring her home.

She turned, looking for him, and found Santo kneeling nearby with a blanket in his hands. He spoke softly, as if to a wild animal, as he draped it over her shoulders. Sabelle knew he spoke to her, but his words fell away as she searched the room for Ryan. She spotted Joel first, a few feet away, just as he sat up, his eyes wild, hair sticking out in all directions. Santo crossed to his side and handed him another blanket.

Behind her was a couch. A lump lodged in her throat as she turned and her gaze settled on Ryan's inert figure stretched on top of it. Roxanne was on her knees beside him, putting pressure on his chest, holding his nose and breathing into his lungs. She was sobbing as she did it, calling his name.

"It's been too long, *angelita*," Santo said and pulled her away.

Sabelle scrambled on hands and knees to Ryan's side. He was so still. So pale.

"The ambulance should be here," Roxanne said. "What's taking them so long? They'll help." She nodded, as if this would make it so. "They'll save him."

Sabelle took Ryan's hand in hers. It felt like ice. Tears swelled over her lashes and streamed down her face. She'd come here to save this man. In doing so, she'd forced him to give his life to save hers. The bitter irony of it made her sob. She crossed her arms over his thighs and cried for a heart so broken that she would never survive it.

"Why isn't he coming back?" Roxanne asked in a broken voice.

Santo pulled her into his arms. "For some the light of the Beyond is irresistible, *angelita*."

"But he took something to bring him back," she whispered. "Why isn't it working?"

Roxanne turned her face into Santo's chest. Sabelle turned her attention to Ryan. As if from a distance, she heard Joel asking about Elijah, Roxanne telling him that the hospital had called. He'd be okay. That was good. Now she needed to help Ryan be okay, too.

What had he taken to bring him back? She ignored everyone else and climbed on top of Ryan, straddling his hips. She felt the pockets of his shirt, moving down to his jeans. The dog tag was in his pocket, warm from its place against his body. She pulled it out and let it dangle on her finger. It caught the lamplight and glittered.

With a deep breath, Sabelle blocked everything else out. All that mattered was Ryan. She took his hand in hers, palm to palm, tag centered between them. Her other hand cupped his beloved face. "Don't leave me here on my own. Not without you."

Loving Ryan had been like a fairy tale. He'd been her knight, her prince, her only love. She refused to let death be the ending of their story.

"That is not how it's meant to be, my love."

Wiping her tears, Sabelle tore his shirt away so his chest was bare, wrapped them both in the blanket, and pressed her body close to his, stretching out on top of him. He was still warm, but not the furnace she'd known him to be. She closed her eyes, focused on her own heartbeat, and then she kissed him.

She kissed him like he was the air and the sea, the wind and the field, the rain upon parched earth. She kissed him like she was the sun and he the moon, pulling each other across the sky. She kissed him with love and hope, as he'd done to her so many times, focusing completely on the feel of his lips, the shape of his mouth. She gave him her heart. She gave him her breath.

"Come back to me."

Quiet settled over the room, sucking away the sound of voices, the shifting of feet, the anxious fidgeting. Sabelle felt it deep inside her, a sinkhole that widened and deepened until nothing existed.

Eyes closed, she let her consciousness seep into it, using the sound of her breath to ground her as she slipped through. She kept Ryan in her mind, picturing Brandy's dog tag spinning in the light, catching, reflecting, illuminating the way.

The dark of her thoughts began to glow like a tiny flame to kindling. She blew softly against it and the flame jumped and spread. She called his name and from somewhere deep in the great unknown she heard a sound.

She focused harder, keeping Ryan's face in her mind, using her thoughts to turn the flames to an inferno that would light the way. She thought she heard her name, but a long, ragged scream shrieked through the dark and tried to snuff out her light. Sabelle clenched the dog tag and Ryan's motionless hand tighter.

Rage filled the shouts now, but Ryan's fingers twitched. She was sure of it.

"Come back to me, come back to me, come back . . ."

A ragged gasp raised his chest and rattled through his lungs, lifting Sabelle as air rushed in. Another breath followed the first. The screams from the Beyond echoed in the room, bouncing off the walls. The light in the kitchen shattered and the one on the table beside Ryan began to pulse.

"Ryan, come back to me."

For an instant, the room lit up like a spotlight had been aimed at the windows. In it, she saw the shadow image of Ryan's silhouette clutching a fighting, snarling Aisa. The light flared, making her wince, forcing her to look away. She heard Roxanne cry her brother's name as Sabelle clenched her eyes against the blinding brightness. The shrieks made her head ring and then suddenly . . .

Silence.

She opened her eyes, looking down at Ryan. His chest rose and fell. She pressed her hands to his face, feeling the warmth against her fingers. Brandy seemed to understand and laid her nose on his legs.

His eyes moved beneath the lids and then . . .

They opened.

Sabelle stared into his beautiful green eyes and felt tears, hot on her face. His arms came up around her and he pulled her against him as she sobbed. At last she lifted her face and stared at him with all the love she felt.

"You did it, Ryan," she murmured. "She's gone."

The barest hint of a smile curled his lips. He laid a hand against her wet cheek. "And I'm still here, snowflake," he said. "Thanks for turning on the lights."

And then he kissed her again, sealing their fate with his love.

Don't miss Erin Quinn's next book in her Beyond series,

The Seven Sins of Ruby Love

Coming spring 2016 from Pocket Books!